YA Coplin
Copling, Steve,
Sage Alexander and the blood of
Seth /
$18.99   on1037181501

WITHDRAWN

3 4028 09471 1299
HARRIS COUNTY PUBLIC LIBRARY

D0463673

GREAT
GRANITE
GATE

Nephilim Terri

Rephaim Territory

Emim Territory

Acheron River

Wastelands

SETH

STYX
MARSH

Belphegor's

HUMAN EXPERIMENTATION AREA

SWITCHING
STATION

Cocytus River

SHAFT
FROM TOPSIDE

SAGE ALEXANDER

AND THE

BLOOD OF SETH

SAGE ALEXANDER

AND THE
BLOOD OF SETH

STEVE COPLING

BROWN BOOKS
PUBLISHING GROUP

© 2018 Steve Copling

All rights reserved. No part of this book may be used or reproduced in any manner without written permission except in the case of brief quotations embodied in critical articles or reviews.

This is a work of fiction. Any similarity to real persons, living or dead, is coincidental and not intended by the author.

Sage Alexander and the Blood of Seth

Brown Books Publishing Group
16250 Knoll Trail Drive, Suite 205
Dallas, Texas 75248
www.BrownBooks.com
(972) 381-0009

A New Era in Publishing®

Publisher's Cataloging-In-Publication Data

Names: Copling, Steve.
Title: Sage Alexander and the blood of Seth / Steve Copling.
Other Titles: Blood of Seth

Description: Dallas, Texas : Brown Books Publishing Group, [2018] | Series: [Sage Alexander series] ; [2] | Interest age level: 012-018. | Summary: "Sage Alexander's life was irreparably changed when he learned that the strange manifestations he-- and only he--had seen his whole life were real. After learning of and harnessing his otherworldly powers, Sage saves his father from Greed, one of the Seven Princes of Hell, and has only just brought things back to normal, or so he thinks, when the Prince of Sloth grasps Sage's little brother, Nick. Will Sage defeat Sloth, or will his journey meet its end?"--Provided by publisher.

Identifiers: ISBN 9781612549903
Subjects: LCSH: Teenage boys--Juvenile fiction. | Good and evil--Juvenile fiction. | Rescues--Juvenile fiction. | Angels--Juvenile fiction. | CYAC: Teenage boys--Fiction. | Good and evil--Fiction. | Rescues--Fiction. | Angels--Fiction. | LCGFT: Fantasy fiction.
Classification: LCC PZ7.1.C66 Sb 2018 | DDC [Fic]--dc23

ISBN 978-1-61254-990-3
LCCN 2017962928

Printed in the United States
10 9 8 7 6 5 4 3 2 1

For more information or to contact the author, please go to www.SageAlexander.net.

This book is dedicated to Nikhil Steven Copling, Sage's younger brother in real life and the template for the Nick Alexander character in this series. Like the real-life Sage, Nikhil is an inspiration to me. He's a loving, creative, imaginative boy who makes friends easily. He's an avid reader, loves to write stories, and is a huge superhero fan of both the Marvel and DC Comics franchises. Nikhil adores his family and friends and is loved dearly by Myla, currently the only girl in the Copling clan. Nikhil made many suggestions about the content of this book, as well as of future stories in the series. May God bless Nikhil in all ways for the life that lies ahead.

ACKNOWLEDGMENTS

Book two in a series is a trickier proposition than the first. *The Blood of Seth* is a story that explores the mythology of the series, allowing the reader to see the origins of the Angelic Response Council and the world of the Elioudians. The staff at Brown Books Publishing Group—especially Katlin Stewart, the project coordinator for this book—was exceptionally insightful in ensuring the correct balance existed between Sage's family relationships and the adventure that takes place while trying to escape the underworld. While the staff at Brown were all their usual professional selves, including Thomas Reale, Milli Brown, and Cathy Williams from The Agency at Brown Books, a special shout-out goes to Katlin and to the line editor, Alex Charest. They made the book better and more readable and kept me on task with all the small things.

My family continues to motivate me to press forward with this series. Sage and Nikhil Copling, the two biggest heroes, and their parents, Jason and Payal, provide inspiration on a daily basis. They are a family of avid readers and worked hard to spread the word about the first book. Justin Copling, my middle son, his wife, Kari, and their children—Elliot, Myla, Oliver, and the soon-to-come Hadley—provide me with contentment and joy. They are raising godly children who will serve as templates for angelic-human characters in future books. Joel Copling, my youngest son, a movie enthusiast, must often sit through sessions with me reading short passages to ensure the flow and mood are spot on. And then there is Sonora: my wife, my rock, my reason for being. She encourages me daily and willingly line edited the manuscript before I sent it out to anyone else for a test read. Without her, I'd probably be a drifting beach bum, wandering the country in search of life's direction. Carolyn Johnston, CEO of Innersight Entertainment, is a constant presence and works harder than anyone I've ever met. If the Sage Alexander franchise takes off, she will have served as the engine that made it go.

PROLOGUE

T he boy did this," Lucifer growled. "Sage Alexander." The
Prince of Pride turned his fiery eyes upon the rest of the
group. "Mortality speaks its ugly truth. Observe, Sloth, the future
that awaits you."

Sloth. How Belphegor hated the way Lucifer habitually turned
that title into an insult. He stood away from the other five Princes,
repulsed by the scene before him. Mammon's collection site stood
quiet and dark, guarded by lieutenants from each of the remaining six armies. The smell of rotting flesh hung thick and heavy.
Mammon, the Prince of Greed, and nine of his offspring littered
the great hall amid piles of decay and filth. Greed had deserved
his fate and now lay slaughtered, propped against the broken remains of his own graven image. The other six Princes had warned
him not to assault and capture members of the Angelic Response
Council, but Mammon's ravenous quest for power blinded him
to the possible consequences of his actions. Ripped apart by a boy

with unimaginable powers, the other Princes stood in quiet dread of their own possible fate.

Sloth and the others were in their natural state—Rephaim—not the weak human forms each used in the mortal world. Lucifer towered above the rest, his magnificent wings expanded in full splendor. His breathing grew heavy as he further surveyed the scene. "For six thousand years we thought ourselves invincible, linked as one entity, untouched by the feeble efforts of the Angelic Response Council. Yet we now stand weakened amidst a ruin of chaos and destruction, and expressions of confusion are heavy upon your faces." He again made eye contact with the other Princes but waited until last to glare at Belphegor. "I blame Sloth, the Prince of apathy and idleness."

It was why Sloth stood apart from the rest; they each held him culpable for this catastrophe, and Belphegor knew what Pride would demand as a result. "You believed that Rupert, the weakest of my many sons, could have simultaneously defeated the boy of prophecy *and* the girl with Persuasion?" Belphegor attempted to protest further, but the fury in Lucifer's eyes silenced him.

"Rupert's failure in capturing the girl led to this," Lucifer said. "You deny this truth?"

Belphegor watched the others—Asmodeus, Sathanus, Beelzebub, and Aamon—as they moved behind Lucifer in a show of servitude. So, it had come to this: shunned and cast out. The other Princes had disrespected Belphegor since their escape from the underworld but never with such open disdain. He stood at his full height and faced them squarely. He would not be cowed.

"You defend your offspring's ineptitude?" Lucifer asked. "Or was your slothful nature to blame for your failure to oversee the operation?"

"*Mammon's* operation," Belphegor shot back. "Not a single time in a thousand years did he give us warning about which Council member he would seize. Rupert was overtaken only because Mammon's crustacean abomination breached into the human realm with complete disregard for caution." He saw two of the other Princes nod in agreement—Asmodeus and Beelzebub—and knew he had spoken what the others believed. Their affirmation emboldened him. "Rupert discovered the Council spies and would have killed the girl had Mammon not interfered at that precise moment." He pointed to the Prince of Greed's decapitated head. "His thirst for power led to his slaughter. Do not blame me *or* my offspring."

The other Princes had mocked Sloth's control over his section of humans far too long. Little did they understand the depths of his influence. He granted humans discovery, seduced them with ingenious inventions, and then tempted fabulous riches to sow discord. He drove them to believe their riches were enough to sustain them. They became selfish hoarders, suspicious of others, arrogant in their successes, and too lazy to share their good fortune for fear of losing it all. He influenced entire governments to give handouts to undeserving citizens, creating a world of dependency and need, while crippling the urge to provide for oneself. He harvested off the greed Mammon had sown and convinced millions they could survive with little effort of their own. Yes, his influence took longer to germinate, but the results were undeniable. He would *not* stand here as an outcast among peers and take blame for Mammon's failure.

"Do not look to me as an outlet for your rage, Lucifer. I will not have it." Belphegor placed a hand on his sword and stepped forward. "I will defend my place within our world. Do not assume otherwise."

The four Princes behind Pride moved away to create space. There had been few fights between the Princes since their escape from the Territories, but those that did occur often lasted for days at a time. Sloth was prepared, should it come to that. He took another pace forward and drew his sword. "Unlike Mammon, I have no interest in displacing you from your seat of leadership. However, I *will* defend against any accusation of disloyalty. Your suspicion is baseless and insulting."

Lucifer folded his wings and tucked them against his body, then opened his arms wide, clearly unconcerned about exposing himself against an attack. "I wish not to battle you, Belphegor. I simply state the obvious. Your offspring failed in his attempt to kill the girl, and we see signs throughout this hall where her scorching light of Persuasion helped slaughter our people. You must be held accountable for the incompetency of your progeny."

Sloth sheathed his sword and stepped back. It was what he feared. His own survival would hinge upon his ability to find and kill the boy of prophecy. There had been many attempts to discover his location, but the Council had hidden him well. Until now.

"Mammon's blood was mixed with the boy's," Sloth said. "We all smelled it as we entered. My hellhounds will soon track him to his lair."

Lucifer turned and again studied the destruction of Mammon's body. The other Princes followed his lead. Belphegor looked elsewhere and noticed for the first time the remnants of an angelic chain. Some of Mammon's offspring had been crushed with blows only possible by a Council member gifted with Might. Others had been slain by a swordsman of a style found only among Council warriors. Along with the girl's Persuasion, that meant a team of at least five.

So, the boy hadn't been alone. Maybe he wasn't as all-powerful as Belphegor had first believed. "I will find him," he told the others.

"A direct attack will fail," Lucifer said. "You must force him into a Dark realm."

"You now direct my plan?" Sloth asked. "Must I clear all actions through your superior intelligence? Must I prostrate myself before you to soothe your wounded pride?"

In the next instant, Lucifer's wings shot open and his sword was in his hand. "Taunt me, Sloth, if it eases your bruised self-worth. Just know that if I am forced to hunt the boy myself, I will have no need for you."

Belphegor turned his back to the Prince of Pride, but not before he noticed the looks of hatred from the other Princes. He had no concerns about developing a plan to capture the boy, but he would not share it with them. Sleight of hand was how he had lured millions of humans into his influence, and though it would take some time to maneuver the boy into the proper position, already a germ of an idea had taken root.

Success came to those with the patience to execute a complicated operation. The fact that his own patience had been miscast as slothfulness for six thousand years didn't deter him. The other Princes would soon understand just how fully they had underestimated him, and after he killed the boy, they would never ridicule him again.

1

Sage sat quietly and stared at the lampshade on the corner of his desk. It was an ugly thing: ratty and torn, stained from an exploded mustard packet two summers before. Splashes of Coke he'd spewed through his nose in a fit of laugher dappled the shade like an errant shotgun blast. It was rather egg shaped now, the result of a wild swing with his practice sword. It stood in stark contrast to the rest of his neat and tidy bedroom. His mom had tried to throw it out, but Sage wouldn't allow it, especially over the last month.

"That was Leah's seat," Sage told Elsbeth. "Right there, on top of that lamp." He sniffed away a sudden bout of emotion and looked away.

"I can't believe she's gone," Elsbeth said. "Just like that."

His Guardian had left nearly a month ago, and Sage was only now starting to adjust. The first few summer nights without her had been some of the hardest of his life.

"What did she say?" Elsbeth asked. "You told me a little of it; tell me the rest."

Sage looked at Elsbeth—with those big brown eyes, a scattering of freckles across her nose, her hair tied back into a French braid—and knew she'd simply stare at him until he told her. He glanced at his open bedroom door and wished he could swing it shut before telling her but knew his mom and dad would use their bat sense and open it again within seconds.

The house was full of activity, everyone preparing to leave on separate trips: Mom and Dad on a three-week cruise to celebrate their twenty-year wedding anniversary, Nick grudgingly packing for his trip into the jungle with Sage, Grandpa, and Ronan. Sage's duffel bag was packed and ready, sitting next to his bed.

Despite the rumble of noise drifting into his room, Sage knew he needed to speak softly so the rest of his family didn't hear their discussion about Leah. His family had largely forgotten about him speaking to or about someone none of them had ever believed existed, and now that Leah was gone, he wouldn't risk dredging it all back up. So, he shifted, then continued, keeping his voice low.

"Leah said her time with me was finished." Sage thought for a moment. "Her precise words were, 'My time is completed; my task is fulfilled.' She said she had another assignment, somewhere in China."

Elsbeth frowned. "Another angelic-human?"

"She didn't say." He grabbed one of his pillows, crunched it against his stomach, and folded his arms across it. "I asked if I'd ever see her again."

"What'd she say?"

He shrugged. "Said she didn't know, that her future is determined by others, that it wasn't her job to question assignments. Grandpa and Ronan suspected it was coming. Her leaving. They were surprised she hung around as long as she did." He thought for a moment and shook his head. "Do you know how many times over the years I begged her to leave me alone? To get out of my life? She must have thought I hated her."

"She didn't think that," Elsbeth whispered. "Do you really believe you're the first one to ever resist? How many thousands of years has she been a Guardian?"

Sage could picture Leah now, perched on top of the lampshade, dressed in her Roman gladiator outfit with her sparkling, jewel-studded scabbard reflecting a multicolored light show on the ceiling.

"Do you know when I really started appreciating her? The very moment my entire attitude changed?"

"When?"

"Last summer, when all of us stepped out of the Dark realm after our battle in Mammon's prison. I was *so happy* to see her waiting for me. At that moment, I knew how much I loved her, and I realized how her constant—well, nagging, for lack of a better term—was exactly what I had needed to survive Mammon."

"Growth," Elsbeth said quietly. "Maturity. Your battle with the Prince of Greed set you on the path Leah trained you for. Maybe she needed to hang around for nine months to make sure all of it stuck. To make sure your attitude really *had* changed. You think?"

"I thought of that," Sage said. "We didn't train a whole lot once I returned from the Dark realm. Well, I trained, but she didn't do much instructing. We talked, mostly. About what I'd faced in Mammon's prison, my feelings and fears, whether I'd had nightmares, how I rationalized killing other living beings. She got more out of me than any five shrinks put together. I started calling her Dr. Leah." He laughed out loud. "She joked once. Leah *actually* told a joke. I did a double take because Leah never joked. Ever. About anything. I couldn't believe it."

Elsbeth smiled. "What was it?"

"The first time I called her Dr. Leah, she called herself Leah Freud. She struck a pose with an ink pen in her hand, stood exactly like that famous picture of Sigmund Freud: right hand with the pen, left hand on her hip, all serious like a learned professor. I laughed for ten minutes." Sage climbed off the bed and stood. "I really miss her, Elsbeth, but I think I'm gonna be OK."

Elsbeth stood and walked over, glanced at the open door, and gave him a warm hug. "You're going to be more than OK," she whispered warmly.

"Hey," Nick said from the doorway.

Sage looked at his brother as Elsbeth released him and stepped back, pink rising into her cheeks. Nick's lanky frame was tightly muscled and heavily tanned. His dark hair fell nearly to his eyes, which gleamed with delight. He appeared thrilled at having caught Sage and Elsbeth in a private moment.

"Shouldn't you be packing?" Sage asked. "How long are you going to put it off? Grandpa and Ronan will be here soon."

"I'm mainly packed," Nick said. "I'm still hoping Mom and Dad will relent and let me go on the cruise. Beats stomping around in the jungle, getting carried away by bat-sized mosquitoes and having my blood sucked by leeches the size of catfish." He looked at Elsbeth. "Would you pick a cruise to the Greek Isles or a hot and sweaty jungle full of life-draining bugs?"

Elsbeth started to answer, then looked at Sage. "Well . . . I'd pick—"

"Wherever Sage was at," Nick said. "Right? Why'd I bother asking?"

"Just drop it," Sage said. "Mom and Dad don't want you hanging around on their anniversary trip. You're the main reason they're gonna be gone for three weeks. They need a break."

Nick snorted. "Whatever." He looked down at Sage's bag, nudged it with his foot, and shook his head. "That thing must weigh eighty pounds. We're only gonna be gone for two weeks. Got the kitchen sink in there?"

"Best to be prepared," Sage said. "Just pack the things on the checklist Grandpa gave you, then anything else you think you need. Now get out of my room. Grandpa wants to get going as soon as he gets here."

Nick rolled his eyes and disappeared into his room across the hall. Sage knew Nick didn't want to go on Grandpa's trip, but it was summertime, and Mom and Dad were leaving in a few days—long before Grandpa, Ronan, and Sage would return from their trip to the Mexican jungle—so Nick had to go. He wasn't staying at home alone, not at thirteen, and although he was too old for a babysitter, per se, Nick had complained that he didn't need Grandpa to mind him for two weeks.

"He's not taking it any better?" Elsbeth asked.

"Oh, maybe a little bit. He's missing a gaming tourney in Oklahoma City, missing three soccer games, and I think he just started getting interested in a girl he met at the County Fair last week." Sage picked up his duffel. Nick was right: it did weigh a lot. "He's bringing three portable game systems and extra battery packs, so he'll be fine. Besides, Grandpa wants to expose him to some ancient ruins, assuming he can find them."

"Nobody mentioned that I didn't arrive in a car," Elsbeth said. "Did you tell everybody what we discussed?"

"Yeah, that you walked over. Very generic, no details." He couldn't tell his family that she'd teleported in thirty-mile bursts all the way from New Orleans. They assumed Elsbeth lived in town. Fortunately, they'd never come straight out and asked Sage where. They didn't know anything about the world of the Angelic Response Council. Sage suspected they'd possibly know one of these days, but until then, Grandpa insisted that their being kept in the dark was crucial to their survival.

"Well, I did walk about a block. I teleported just inside the tree line on the path leading to your grandpa's house."

They both hated the deception and went out of their way to remain as truthful as possible. Mostly, they avoided answering questions that would force them to lie outright. Since this was only Elsbeth's third trip to Sage's house in the past ten months, they'd been successful in keeping everything neat and organized.

Sage heard Grandpa's truck pull up outside. "Hey, they're here. Let's go." He led Elsbeth out to the living room, where his mom and dad were taking inventory of all the things they were bringing with them. It covered the entire dining room table.

Mom wore classic gray sweats, still a little sweaty after her run. Sage had always been impressed with her constant effort at staying fit. She didn't have a single gray hair; it was still the same auburn color it had always been. She and Elsbeth were the same size, although his mom seemed leaner and more athletic. Despite her college point-guard days being long behind her, Sage figured she could still run the court and dribble just as well now. She regularly beat her boys in one-on-one games, much to Sage's irritation. Mom smiled at Sage and Elsbeth as they came in.

"Elsbeth, opinion." Mom said. "We have three formal nights on our cruise, one each week. So, should I bring three dresses or wear one three times? Kevin thinks I should bring one. What do you say?"

"I only say that, Jenna," Sage's dad said, "because of how beautiful you look in all of them. One is all you need. People don't remember clothes from one week to the next."

"The people who sit at our table will remember," Mom said. "We have assigned seats. Same table. Same people."

Sage's dad had lost weight over the past ten months. After his release from the Prince of Greed's influence, he'd totally shifted his life's focus. Before, as he slowly turned into a monster too hideous for Sage to look upon, he'd cared only about making money, growing his business, and destroying anyone who got in his way. Now, he gave loads of money to their church and multiple charities, worked out regularly, spent time with his family—especially his wife—and had scaled back all the hours at the office. Sage couldn't remember him happier. His dark hair was longer, his shoulders and arms more developed, and his smile more infectious. He was smiling now as Elsbeth struggled to give an answer that wouldn't offend either of them.

"I think Mr. Alexander is right in one aspect but incorrect in another," Elsbeth said. "You probably look beautiful in all three dresses, but if so, that will make you *more* memorable. Therefore, bring all three."

Mom and Dad nodded approvingly at Elsbeth's comment. "We really wish you'd call us by our names, Elsbeth," Dad said. "We wouldn't be offended."

Elsbeth smiled and glanced at Sage. "I guess I could."

Sage heard Grandpa's voice on the front porch just before he pounded once on the door and opened it. "Hello, anyone home?" Grandpa smiled as he leaned in. He'd let his silver hair grow out over the past several months and had a matching Van Dyke. He wore his jungle clothes—Nick's term for them, because the pants and shirt had pockets everywhere—along with a floppy hat to keep the sun at bay. He was nearly seven hundred and fifty years old, in excellent condition, and far stronger than any "mortal" grandpa Sage knew. He played his role of being old and weak so well that he surely deserved an Academy Award. When Sage found out last summer that he was angelic-human, Grandpa explained how he'd been forced to become a master of disguise to protect his children that never developed angelic-human gifts. At some point in the future, Grandpa would be forced to sever ties with his son and daughter-in-law to avoid having to explain the Angelic Response Council universe. He'd faked his death twice before, both times centuries ago. Only his angelic-human children, three boys from two other marriages, knew he was still alive. Kevin was his only regular human child still living.

"Come on in, Dad," Sage's dad said.

"How's all the packing coming along?" Grandpa asked. He looked at Sage. "You ready? Nick?"

Sage pointed to his duffel. "I'm good. You might have to go encourage Nick."

Ronan came in the door behind Grandpa. Six foot five, his upper body shaped like a V, hair nearly to his waist, Grandpa's assistant and bodyguard wore a smile and clothes identical to Grandpa's. Gifted with Might, he'd been Grandpa's protector and friend for a long time. He winked at Sage, nodded to Elsbeth, and searched for Nick. "Where's Mr. Resistant?" Ronan asked. "Where's Mr. I'd-Rather-Sit-At-The-Pool-On-A-Cruise-Ship-Than-Sweat-In-The-Jungle?"

"Go easy on him, Ronan," Grandpa said. "Can't say I really blame him." Grandpa walked over and gave Mom a hug. "I assume you haven't given in to Nick's demands about going with you and Kevin?"

"Ha," Dad said. "Not a chance. He's not coming with us. This is our anniversary trip, not a family vacation. He's yours until we get back. I'll buy him a shirt, a pair of funny boxer shorts, and take a picture of the ship's pool. It'll have to do."

"I heard that," Nick said, as he dragged his bag into the living room. "Keep the shirt and boxers, and bring me a pair of authentic European soccer shoes. Size nine. Black, to go with my uniform." He dropped his bag and gave Grandpa a hug. Then he turned toward Ronan. "So, let me clear something up. I don't mind sweating.

I sweat gallons at soccer and track practice, and I sweat when I'm killing beasts on my gaming system. So there."

"Got bug spray?" Ronan asked. "Cause they're going to carry you off if you sweat that much." He pulled Nick into a hug and rubbed his hair. "You're my favorite punching bag, so just ignore my barbs, OK?"

Nick laughed. "It's all good. I thought maybe I could charm my way onto the cruise ship, or whine my way on. Neither method worked."

"So, what are you hunting for this time?" Dad asked Grandpa. "I'm still a little confused."

"Incans in Mexico," Mom said. "He explained it last week."

"Right, got that," Dad said. "That's the confusing part. Incans. Wrong country, wrong continent."

The real reason they were heading to a jungle northeast of Guadalajara was because Grandpa believed that an entrance to the Dark spiritual realm was somewhere down there. Although it hadn't happened yet, in theory, Grandpa's gift of Pathfinding gave him the ability to see entrances into the Dark realm.

"I'm working on the belief that a rogue sect of Incan warriors fled Peru years before disease wiped out their civilization in the early 1600s," Grandpa said. "I discovered letters written by a Spanish captain, one of the conquistadors who conquered the Incans, describing the band of warriors who fled to a specific area of Mexico. Should be a great trip. Steeped in history. The boys will learn a lot."

"I'm sure we will," Nick said. "I'm fired up!"

Sage saw Nick hold back a laugh just before reaching down and grabbing his duffel bag. Elsbeth must have seen it, too, because she leaned over and whispered something to him that Sage couldn't hear. Nick smiled at her and shook his head.

"Really, Grandpa," Nick said. "I'm kinda pumped about going. I'm over the fact that Mom and Dad have cast me aside like so much refuse."

Mom grabbed one of Dad's T-shirts off the table, rolled it up, and threw it at Nick. "Little brat."

"Just teasing," Nick said. "Mom, I'm dragging this thing out to the truck. I'll be back in for goodbyes in a second."

Ronan grabbed Nick and Sage's bags and hefted them onto his shoulders. "I'll pack them. I've got a system." He led Nick outside.

Sage gave his mom and dad long hugs goodbye. So did Elsbeth, who told them she was heading home. Sage followed her outside as Grandpa was reminding Mom and Dad that they'd be home from the jungle before they returned from their cruise, since it didn't leave for another week.

"Do you have helmet cameras?" Elsbeth asked. "You promised to make a video for me in case you find the ruins."

"Got 'em," Sage said. "Nick and I both. Don't think we'll have cell phone service, so Grandpa got some satellite phones. He gave me a lesson on them last night. Pretty cool. I'll keep in touch."

"You'd better." Elsbeth glanced around. Nick and Ronan were busy in the front of the truck, not watching. She grabbed Sage into a quick hug. "I'm heading home. See you in two weeks. Be safe. Don't get eaten by a wild animal."

"This trip will be a breeze," Sage said quietly. "Probably pretty boring, but don't tell Grandpa I said that."

"Well, you and Nick can be bored together. Just take plenty of video. I've never seen a jungle before."

"I wish you'd come. You sure you can't?"

"Impossible," she said. "My dad has barely let me out of his sight since we got back from Mammon's prison. I would if I could; you know that."

"Yeah, I know. See you in two weeks. Teleport up once I get back, OK?"

"You know I will." She walked over to Nick and Ronan, said her goodbyes, and headed off around the corner of the house.

Sage walked to the same corner a few seconds later, but she was gone. Thirty miles away by now. Maybe sixty. In another few minutes it would be hundreds. She'd be home in New Orleans before Grandpa's exploration team got five miles out of town.

Nick stormed into the house to say his goodbyes just as Grandpa came out. "You guys ready?" Grandpa asked. "We've got a long haul ahead."

Ready? Yeah, Sage was ready. Three long days on the road, a one-day hike to the campsite, four days in the jungle, and then the return trip. Then a couple of weeks to rest up before school started. Easy. Nothing like last summer.

"Let's hit the road, Grandpa," Sage said. "I'm kind of looking forward to an adventure where the scariest thing I'll see is Ronan's ugly mug."

"Keep talking, Sage," Ronan said, "and I'll strap you down on the top of the truck."

By the time Grandpa got the engine started, Nick had joined them and already cranked up one of his portable gaming systems, killing monsters faster than Sage could keep track. Nick could handle the monsters on this trip. Sage was just glad those were the only kind he would see this summer. A lazy trip to the jungle. Yep, he could handle that.

2

The four of them stared at the entrance to the cave just as the sun broke over the horizon. Sage looked at his grandpa and smiled. "Changed your mind yet? Last day before we head home?"

"Do it, Grandpa." Nick slapped him on the back. "Gonna be great in there."

"Old men have limits," Ronan said, after chomping a bite of apple. "And your grandpa is old, Nick. Old."

"Old is a mind-set," Grandpa said, "but that cave has worn me out this week."

Their tents were behind them, in a clearing underneath a canopy of trees thick enough that only dappled sunlight broke through. A light mist swirled around them, and it felt great on Sage's skin. Anything to combat the oppressive heat, even this early, was a good thing.

"I've been crawling around in there for three days," Grandpa said. He held up a steaming mug of coffee. "And today, the only time I plan on bending over is to refill this."

"You can do it, Grandpa," Nick said. "Just one tunnel left to explore."

Sage looked up at the clear sky. It was odd not to see a squad of Archangels hovering fifty feet above his head, keeping at bay the Darks that had followed him, up until a month ago, his entire life. Even odder was Leah's absence. More than a few times this week, he'd turned to ask her a question or comment on something he'd seen in the jungle. It might be a while before he stopped doing that.

"Well, Nick, it'll be a great bonding time for you boys." Grandpa sipped his coffee and looked at the sky. "Since it's gonna be a scorcher out here again today, the best place for both of you will be in there."

Nick and Sage already had their spelunking gear on: knee and elbow pads, helmets, headlamps, steel-toed boots, and long-sleeved shirts and gloves. They'd charged their headlamp batteries overnight and wore an extra battery pack. Each had GoPro cameras mounted to the side of his helmet, with the long-life batteries fully charged. Sage also had a short mountaineering rope attached to a carabiner, as well as a pocketknife in a leather pouch.

"Do you remember how to get to the passage?" Grandpa asked Sage.

"Yep. The main chamber until it forks. Hang a right until it forks again. Then left. Go to the flat rock that looks like a Frisbee and squirm underneath."

"Ronan wouldn't fit under the flat rock, anyway." Nick laughed and winked at the big man. "And it's too far back to tie a rope around his shoulders and yank him out."

Ronan nodded. "Good point, Nick. So, if y'all get stuck, we'll just leave you in there."

"Nick's too skinny to get stuck," Sage said. And he was. Although tall for a thirteen-year-old, nearly five feet nine, he probably didn't weigh 120 pounds soaking wet.

"He'll fill out like you did," Grandpa told Sage.

That might be true, Sage thought, but since Sage had been swinging a sword for most of his fifteen years, his chest and shoulders were overdeveloped compared to guys his age. Nick had a lot of catching up to do in that department.

"Well, you ready?" Nick asked Sage.

"Yep." Sage turned toward his grandpa. "Final search for those ruins?"

"I'm starting to think those ruins might be a rumor," Grandpa said. "Anyway, I'm thinking that direction." He pointed south with his coffee cup.

Sage's gift of Pathfinding was even more powerful than Grandpa's. He'd searched some with Grandpa while Ronan took Nick off to explore other things, but they'd found nothing. Since the group had hiked in from the north, and they'd searched east and west, south was Grandpa's last shot, and they both knew it. The main reason for exploring the cave three days straight was the possibility that the Incans had built their ruins underground. That hadn't panned out, either.

"Maybe your information was wrong, Grandpa," Nick said.

They were there due to parchments found at an archeological dig in Belize about the Incan tribe that had disappeared over the course of a few days. The documents described creatures with wings that appeared out of nowhere. It gave the location. Here, or somewhere close.

"Maybe it was, Nick. Guess we'll know by the end of the day, huh?" Grandpa peered skyward again. "We'd best get moving before it gets too hot. Ronan, you ready?"

"Just lead the way, Old Wise One." Ronan winked at Nick.

"We're ready, too." Nick said. "Might find something good under that rock." He stepped toward the cave opening and glanced back. "See ya, Grandpa. Don't let Ronan get you lost!" Then he laughed and walked toward the mouth of the cave. "Cameras on, Sage. Don't forget."

Grandpa glanced at the cave. "Don't let Nick get too far ahead. I'm not a big fan of that place."

Sage understood. There was an odor—a weird combination of smells that shouldn't be coming from a cave in the middle of a jungle. All four of them had noticed it the first day, but it seemed to worry Grandpa the most.

"Taking your phone with you?" Sage asked.

Grandpa patted his pants pocket. "Got it. But once you get fifty feet inside the cave, yours will be useless."

"I know," Sage said. "But I'm thinking we'll be finished a lot sooner than you. I'll give you a call when we come out."

"Sounds like a plan." Grandpa gave him a fist bump, and Sage hurried after Nick. He turned on his camera as he went, then hit record. It didn't take long to catch Nick, who'd stopped at the edge of the fading light. The beam from his headlamp bounced off the walls.

"Let's roll," Nick said. "I'm going first. You guard my backside."

"OK," Sage said. "Let me hook up the rope." He clicked the loop he'd tied at one end of the rope into Nick's carabiner, hanging on his belt near his lower back. The other end was clipped to Sage's in front.

Nick led the way with confidence born of the previous trips down this same passage. They'd followed every vein except for the one they would hit this morning. Besides their cave-exploring gear, each wore a fanny pack in the small of their backs. Nick's held snacks; Sage's, water. The headlamps illuminated nearly every inch in front of them. Sage could see their footprints from previous trips.

Despite Nick's initial reluctance to come on this trip, he'd had a blast this week. He was funny, eager to explore, full of barbs toward Ronan and Grandpa, teased Sage relentlessly about Elsbeth, and hadn't complained about bugs or snakes or the oppressing humidity. He'd even mentioned last night that he wished they could stay another couple of days, but there was no point to that. Grandpa's quest was a bust, and all of them knew it. With Mom and Dad's cruise now barely underway, they'd be home in plenty of time to rest before school started in a few weeks and for Sage to see Elsbeth for as long as she was allowed to stay.

"Think Grandpa will find the ruins?" Nick asked. "He sure takes that stuff seriously."

"If anyone can find them, he can," Sage said. "I don't think there are ruins here, though. Grandpa probably doesn't, either. And, yeah, he's pretty determined."

"I really don't get it. So, he finds the place, then what?" Nick glanced back and nearly blinded Sage with his light.

"Hey, light forward!"

"Sorry," Nick said. He turned back around. "But really, so what? He wants to prove some Incas came as far north as Mexico. Who cares? They're all dead now, anyway."

Sage laughed. "History means nothing?"

Nick walked for a bit before answering. "To some people it does, I guess. Don't think I'd break my back proving some obscure little point, though."

"Well, it makes him happy, so why not?" Sage couldn't tell Nick what Grandpa was really doing, so he changed the subject. "You notice the smell isn't as strong today?"

"Yeah, nice. Just thought about that." Nick ducked under a low-hanging stalactite. "I noticed you didn't bring your sword this time. I feel soooo scared now." He laughed and looked back again, but swung his head forward as soon as Sage squinted from the light.

"Well, I've scratched the handle against a rock wall every day this week," Sage said. "We're about to crawl on our bellies, and I don't wanna bang it up any more than I already have." *Because it's a thousand-year-old sword used by Beowulf to slay a Grendel so a little girl could be born, which allowed our family line to continue.* Nope, couldn't tell Nick *that* was why he didn't want to damage it any further.

Nick took a right at the first fork, and the ceiling was noticeably lower. Sage bent over, put his hands on his knees, and pushed on.

"Taking a left," Nick announced at the next fork several minutes later. "Getting low now." Sage had to duckwalk, while Nick squatted. In another few minutes they were there. "Flat rock. Here we go."

"Still want to go first?" Sage asked.

"Yep. You promised, remember? Gonna name it 'Nick Alexander's Cave of Treasures,'" he said. "Just kidding. I think the only treasure we're gonna find here is a thousand years of petrified bat poop." Sniffing the air, he bent over and put his face in the opening underneath the rock. "That weird smell is stronger here. Bat poop overload."

They flattened themselves on the ground and scooted forward. There was about eighteen inches of space, just enough for Nick's helmet lamp to clear the rock and light his way. Sage waited until Nick's feet disappeared. There was almost twenty feet of rope between them, so Sage wasn't in a hurry.

"Getting tighter," Nick narrated. "Can't see anything but rock. No moisture."

Sage edged forward; the bottoms of Nick's shoes were several feet ahead of him. Sage held the rope between his hands and kept enough pressure on it to know that Nick was crawling faster than him.

"Seeing a bigger chamber," Nick said. "But it's up a ways."

"OK." Sage's light bumped the rock above his head, and it tilted downward. Nick's feet disappeared in the darkness. More rope slid through Sage's hands. Nick was really moving.

"Just a little farther," Nick said. "Can see a pretty big room up there. Cool. Definitely gonna name it after me. We're probably the first people who ever came back here."

Sage tried readjusting his light several times, but he kept bumping his head and knocking it back down. His circle of light reached only a short distance ahead of him.

"I'm out," Nick called. "A pretty big . . . whoa . . . hey . . . something's got me!" The rope jerked in Sage's hand. "Help, Sage! Let go! Help!" The rope tightened so hard and so fast it began dragging Sage forward. "Noooo! Let me go!"

Sage scrambled on his knees and elbows, trying to keep up as the rope pulled him forward.

"Sage!" The rope went slack.

"Sage!" Nick's voice echoed through the cave. He screamed again, but his voice wasn't as loud. "Sage!" It faded suddenly, as though being driven away in a high-speed car.

Sage cleared the flat rock and exploded onto his feet. There. Ahead. Movement. He adjusted his light and sprinted forward as Nick's voice faded into nothingness.

The chamber was large, but not overwhelming. Frantic, Sage spun around and searched, but his light wasn't strong enough to reach all the walls. He saw Nick's helmet lying on the ground, the lamp smashed. He ran over and picked it up. No blood. Just a broken chin strap. His camera looked undamaged.

Sage set it aside and adjusted his helmet lamp again, then moved his head around, searching the chamber more thoroughly. He was gone. Nick was gone. His voice had faded so fast it was like he'd stepped into a bottomless pit. Sage looked at the floor, hoping to see where Nick had been dragged, but the hard, unforgiving rock revealed no clues. He set off to his right to look closely for hidden passageways. He'd only gone a few yards when he heard breathing coming from somewhere ahead. An alcove. Maybe a full tunnel. He veered sideways, a sharp angle, turned his head as he moved, and kept his light focused where the heavy breathing had suddenly gone silent.

"You will never get him back, angel boy," a voice growled. "He's gone. No way out."

Sage froze. Held his breath. Made no sound at all.

"Gone forever," the voice said with a guttural belch that sounded full of mucus. "Revenge so sweet."

Sage needed his sword. His only weapons were the short piece of rope dangling from his belt and a nearly useless pocketknife.

"Who are you?" Sage asked, showing no hint of fear. "Where have you taken him?" He'd faced some scary creatures last summer. Could this be worse? He finally angled himself enough to see into the alcove.

A Rephaim offspring. In full, natural state. Seven feet tall, slick head, golf-ball-sized eyes, demon face, bulging muscles, and wings fully expanded.

A bolt of fear caused Sage to take a half-step back. He recognized the blue-skinned beast immediately. "You descend from Belphegor, Prince of Sloth," he said. The Princes of Hell produced offspring identical to their respective fathers. Sage was the only Council member who could recognize them in their natural form.

"So, my Prince told no tales about the boy of prophecy knowing us," the beast said, his black eyes narrowing. He held a sword in his right hand. At his feet was the fanny pack of food Nick had worn around his waist. Nick's extra battery pack for his headlamp lay crushed underneath his left foot.

Sage felt vibrations deep within his bones, his body now ready to teleport with the faintest of thought. He glanced around the chamber but couldn't see an exit. The Dark spiritual realm? Was the entrance in this chamber? No. He would see its blue-green glow and the out-of-focus hue that his Pathfinding gift allowed. How had the Rephaim gotten here? Might this entrance into the Dark realm be hidden even from him? He knew from last summer that entrances had never been found. Legend held that each Prince had an area of his own, but nothing about that sounded right. This beast had been lying in wait. It knew Nick was his brother, and it knew they were coming. Or maybe not. He thought about the missing Incans from centuries ago and wondered if this was how they'd disappeared.

"Tell me why I shouldn't kill you now," Sage said.

The laugh that burst from the beast sent a wave of stench rolling over Sage. "You? Kill me?" Then he charged and swung his sword with speed not found in the human world.

Sage teleported to the far side of the chamber before the sword came fully around. He unclipped the rope from his carabiner and pulled it tightly between his hands. The monster spun around, saw Sage, and charged again. Its speed was no match for teleportation, and Sage appeared inside the alcove, hoping it was the entrance to the Dark realm. It wasn't.

Before the creature even got his feet set, it twirled and charged a third time. Sage disappeared and landed against the far wall opposite the alcove. "We can do this for the next hundred years," Sage mocked, "and you will get no closer to me."

"And you will get no closer to your brother." The Rephaim walked slowly over to the flat rock as though intending to prevent Sage's escape, but that wasn't it. The beast transformed into a lean and athletic human in his midtwenties and scampered out of the chamber so fast Sage hardly believed his eyes.

"Nick!" Sage shouted as loudly as he could, now that he was alone in the chamber. "Nick!" His own echoing voice was the only reply.

Sage searched every fissure and crack in the room but found no other entrances. *How had Nick's voice just faded away?* He shined his light to the ceiling and saw nothing but rock. That left only the floor. Inch by inch he searched—then he saw the scratch marks. A large rock in front of the alcove had been dragged a couple of feet toward the rear of the chamber. Sage shoved on it, but it didn't budge. He tried again, but it was too heavy.

Nick's under there, he thought. *Nick's under there!*

Sage focused his mind on the front of the cave and teleported there. He stormed into the sunlight and pulled out the satellite phone. It took a moment to connect, and Sage was in his tent before Grandpa answered. "Wow, out already?"

"Nick's gone," Sage shouted into the phone. "Get back here. I need help!" He punched the phone off.

They'd brought two folding shovels, a medium-sized crowbar, and an assortment of small brooms. Grandpa thought they might do some excavation if they found the ruins. Sage grabbed his sword first and strapped it on, then took both shovels and the crowbar. He teleported back inside the flat-rock chamber, positioned the shovels on the ground next to the boulder, wedged the crowbar underneath it, and pushed down. It moved a couple of inches. He repositioned the shovels and did it again. More movement.

It took him a while, but he finally moved it enough to uncover part of a hole. The opening dropped straight into the earth. "Nick! Nick!" Nothing. He disconnected his headlamp and pushed it as far down as he could. Just a bottomless well of darkness. He grabbed Nick's helmet, teleported back outside, and found Grandpa pacing back and forth. Ronan stood with his arms crossed, worry evident on his face.

"He's in a hole," Sage said. "Too deep to see the bottom. I'm going down to get him."

Grandpa put both hands on Sage's shoulders. "Just breathe, OK? Relax. Tell me what happened."

He did. Grandpa forced him to slow down and repeat some of it. "I don't know where the Rephaim went. There must be another entrance we don't know about."

"Steven," Ronan said. "Do you know what this means? Sage, do you?"

Grandpa glanced at Sage, who had no idea what Ronan was talking about. "Nick's gone," Sage said. "What else would it mean?"

Ronan took a step forward and lowered his voice. "It means the Princes know who you are. They know how to find you."

The three of them stood silently for several beats. It took that long for the reality of Ronan's words to seep through Sage's panic. They knew for a fact that up until last summer, before Sage's battle with Mammon, none of the Seven Princes of Hell knew Sage's identity or that he was the boy of prophecy who might one day slay them all. The Princes knew a boy would arrive at some point, but until last summer, they would've had no way to discover it was Sage.

"It'll mean full protection going forward," Ronan said. "Or we move you."

Sage and Grandpa had discussed this a few months ago. The Council always knew that if one of the Princes found him within the human realm, discovered his identity, he would need to go into hiding and hunt the Princes from a secured location.

"Well, we'll worry about that later," Sage said. "After we get Nick back." He handed Nick's helmet to Grandpa and disconnected the camera from his own. "I don't know if Nick recorded the beast, but I'm sure I did." He handed over his camera. "I *know* I did. Download everything. Study it. But right now, I've gotta get Nick out. I'm going in."

"We need to wait for help," Ronan said.

"No! That'll take forever! We're way out in the middle of nowhere. He could be hurt." Sage ran to the tents and grabbed the first aid kit. Then he shoved more water into his fanny pack and crammed what snacks he could fit inside too. He slung their only long rope over his head and shoulder. "I'm going down to get him. You call for help. Whoever you think is best. But whoever you get, make sure they're Council members. Cause that hole, Grandpa, might be the entrance into the Dark realm we've been searching for. You know as well as I do that we'll need Council members if it is."

Grandpa nodded, a grim expression. "Does it look like an entrance?"

"No. But what if it's below the surface? Beyond what I can see? If it is, Nick doesn't have much time." Humans inside a Dark realm had twenty-four hours before their minds started going, forty-eight before death.

Grandpa looked at Ronan. "What do you think?"

"I should go with Sage. We can't send him alone." Ronan looked hard at Sage, and Sage felt a wave of relief wash over him.

Being accompanied by a man with Might certainly wasn't anything to complain about.

Sage looked at Grandpa, who nodded. "Go. Both of you. But understand something: help will be several days behind you. Maybe more."

"We'll survive," Ronan said.

"For Nick's sake, we have to," Sage added.

"I'll grab my gear," Ronan said.

Sage said a silent prayer. Grandpa grabbed one of his hands. "Listen to me. This is important. I'll be coming with a rescue team. Know that. But if you get a chance to get Nick out of there, take it!" He held up a finger for emphasis. "You got that? If you get *one* chance, take it. Don't wait for us. We'll be OK. Do you understand?"

Sage nodded.

"Say it."

"Get Nick out if I get the chance." Sage started to pull away again, but his grandpa gripped his hand even tighter.

"Say it again. Promise me. You take the chance if you have it."

"I promise, Grandpa. If we get the chance, we'll take it."

Ronan jogged up. He wore a shoulder harness that held his signature weapon—a hardened steel club that weighed two hundred pounds. He strapped on dual hip packs that held enough food and water for several days. A heavy-duty flashlight hung from his belt. "I'm ready."

Grandpa pulled Sage into a hard hug. "I love you," he whispered. "And I *will* be seeing you again, either down there or back on the surface. Now go."

3

Nick hadn't clearly seen the monster that grabbed him. It came from behind, and the light from his helmet only caught flashes, but he'd seen a black wing, a claw, and a sword.

The hole wasn't a straight drop. It was more a steep slope, like a huge, swirling slide at a water park. He screamed Sage's name as he descended, his cries lifting and fading away. His body slammed against sides of the earth and filled his pant legs with dirt. He clawed at the soil surrounding him, dug his heels in, arched his back, pushed against the walls of the shaft with everything he had, and fought a losing battle with gravity.

Down and down he went, faster and faster, the dirt loose and soft, pushing against him, crawling into his shirt, shoes, mouth, and nose. He gagged and spit, put his hands over his face to cover his eyes. Screaming wasn't possible now; it was all he could do to breathe. He tried to relax as he plummeted ever downward.

Faster still, steeper, almost a straight drop, Nick rocketed down the earthen tube. He finally tucked his knees to his chest, curled his head forward, and rode down on his back, his body vibrating and shimmering.

Hundreds of feet. At least. Thousands. *Did this hole lead to the very center of the earth?*

After several minutes, Nick slowed as the slope flattened, and he thought he might stop—just before dropping off the edge of a low cliff and landing on his back. The impact knocked the wind out of him, and panic rose in his throat. He brought his knees to his chest, tried to breathe, then rolled onto his side. Finally, the air came.

It took him a long time to move, but he eventually took stock of his injuries and knew he was OK. Sore back and neck, cuts and scrapes, dirt in his nose and mouth and every inch of his clothes, but nothing major.

The tunnel on the way down was complete blackness, but here there was dim light. *Where is "here"?* He sat up. The air was different somehow—thicker and purer, but with a stronger scent of the same odor they'd smelled all week inside the cave.

"What is this place?" he whispered. *What is this place?*

Mars. Or Venus. Maybe the surface of Jupiter. A desolate cavern stretched as far as he could see. Jagged cliffs, small streams of bubbling water, a harsh, red landscape without a hint of life, and a smell of rotten eggs and spoiled meat. A light mist swirled high in the air, pushing outward from somewhere deep in the cavern. Despite the bleakness, the air seemed different—tinted with a hue of blue-green—faint but there, almost like a computer-generated effect. Either that or he had dust in his eyes and he wasn't seeing clearly.

And bones. Thousands of bones. They littered the ground, protruded from the dirt, clogged the nasty streams, and hung draped over jagged boulders as far as he could see. Nick hugged himself as he slowly turned in a circle. Sudden tears blurred everything, but he bit his lower lip to keep from crying out. Except for the bubbling of the rancid water, he heard nothing at all. He sat heavily on the ground and, with trembling hands, pulled off his shoes and dumped the dirt out. Above his head, well out of reach, he saw the edge of the cliff he'd fallen from and the black hole leading to the surface.

Climbing out would be impossible. Even if he climbed up the cliff, the hole was too long and much too steep. The dirt was loose and slippery. Nobody would hear him scream if he yelled for a hundred years, so he wouldn't waste his breath.

He stood, and his foot caught on something buried in the dirt. Metal. He yanked it free. An old Spanish helmet—one a conquistador would wear. One of Grandpa's lost Spaniards had found the hole. High up, protruding below a ceiling he couldn't see, the light was leaking from flickering bulbs barely able to penetrate the mist swirling around them. Lightbulbs? A mile underground? How could there *be* a lighting system?

I need to stay right here, he realized suddenly. Sage *had* to have heard him shout; he would know that something, or someone, had pushed him down here. Sage would tell Grandpa and Ronan, and they'd send a search party. He wouldn't die down here. He wouldn't.

Then he heard something. A hiss. Or a whisper. Two things, maybe. Different tones, as if people were talking but not wanting to be heard.

Nick folded his hands under his armpits so they wouldn't shake. All around, the desolation was so vast and complete it was as though a living thing didn't exist anywhere else in the world. He'd heard a preacher say once that Hell would be like this—each soul totally alone, the despair from isolation so real and terrifying that they would plead for forgiveness and salvation for all eternity, with only the silence of the dead to hear their pleas.

There. Again. The hissing sound seemed everywhere; and an odor—faint but getting stronger—a sweaty, putrid smell thick enough to stick to his clothes. He looked for a place to hide and saw a large rock near one of the bubbling streams. He scrambled over and flattened himself on the ground. The sound was so faint he could have mistaken it for the nervous inhalation of his own breath. A minute passed. Maybe two. Scuffling. A grunt. Close. *Really* close. He clamped a hand over his mouth and waited, tears blurring his vision. When a shadow blotted out the light from above, he cried out as creatures from his most unimaginable nightmare fell upon him.

Ronan lifted the huge stone, tossed it aside, and uncovered the entire circumference of the hole. It was between two and three feet across, Sage believed, and large enough for Ronan's shoulders to fit through.

Sage tied one end of his rope around the stone and the other around his legs and waist. He slid his feet into the hole, fastened the headlamp to his belt, and aimed it downward. He looked at Ronan. "Nick's got twenty-four hours before his mind starts going, but he'll start hallucinating well before then. We've gotta get him out of there. And fast."

"*If* it's the Dark realm," Ronan said. "You don't know that. Don't panic without all the facts. OK?" He reached over, snapped the knot Sage had tied near his waist, and tossed the rope away. "That's a waste of time. Not nearly long enough. Just need to slide down."

Sage took a deep breath and forced himself to focus. *Nick is OK. He's OK. We'll find him.* He stared at the hole then looked at Ronan. "Nick was right after all."

"About what?"

"Going on the cruise."

Ronan's face went hard and he leaned toward Sage. "Don't *ever* say that to your grandfather. *Ever.*"

Sage had never heard Ronan sound like that. He tried to lean back to put some distance between them, but the big man's expression seemed to swallow the space between them and freeze him in place. "I didn't mean—"

"Blame the Prince of Sloth," Ronan said. "Not your parents or grandfather. Or yourself. Focus on things that matter, and you just might survive this. Get your head in the game. Clear?"

A Leah lesson, but with a decidedly harder edge. "Yes. Clear." He took a cleansing breath and wondered if his face looked as hot as it felt.

"I'll wait one minute and follow you down." Ronan gripped Sage's shoulder. "Use your training."

Sage dropped into the hole. He didn't open his eyes, didn't scream, didn't fight it. He just plunged down the tube at warp speed, confident that he would survive the journey.

He didn't know how deep he slid, but it was thousands of feet. Endless, it seemed, until the tube flattened out, and he dropped off a low cliff and landed ten feet below the edge, sword in hand. He stepped to the side, moving far enough away that Ronan wouldn't flatten him. Since he'd stuffed his pant legs into his boots and tucked in his shirt before dropping, there wasn't much dirt to shake out.

The entire area looked as if the bottom had fallen out of the world's largest cemetery. Except these weren't human bones. He saw horns six feet long, ribcages large enough to drive a car through, and huge, odd-shaped skulls with pieces of hair still attached. The smell was awful: rotten eggs, spoiled meat, and a fresh smell of some wet animal. A troll, maybe, or a hellhound. The landscape reminded him a little of the Dark realm outside Prince Mammon's collection site last summer. The only things missing were the hundreds of thousands of Darks hovering over the Prince of Greed's prison.

Sage heard Ronan coming before the big man dropped onto the ground in front of him. He raised his steel bar, ready for battle, and glanced at Sage. "Anything?"

"Nothing," Sage said. "Not a sound, not a sighting."

Ronan took several moments to study the area. He turned in a complete circle, his face a mixture of surprise and fear. Sage saw him grip his bar a little tighter, then come to a decision. "Fan out," he said. "Look for footprints." The dirt was loose enough to see fresh disturbances, and twenty seconds hadn't passed before Ronan shouted. "Here."

Sage met him near a large rock, where Ronan had squatted. "Blood," Ronan said. "Not much, but enough to worry me."

Heart racing, Sage knelt and looked. A glistening spot the size of a softball was splattered against the side of the rock.

"Footprints," Ronan said. He stood and stepped back, pointed to the ground around them. "At least two beasts. Cloven hooves. Nothing human, which means Nick was carried off." He inspected the tracks and moved several paces away. "Wouldn't mind having Kato Hunter with us."

Kato, gifted with Fighting Arts, was a master tracker, a skill neither Sage nor Ronan possessed. Sage had rescued Kato last summer from Mammon's prison, and he'd personally witnessed the great warrior's tracking abilities.

Sage fought to keep his imagination from running wild. Nick was alive. There wasn't enough blood to really worry about, and if this were revenge from last summer, the Prince of Sloth would use him as bait to lure Sage to a specific place.

"Is this the Dark realm?" Ronan asked. Despite his four and a half centuries of fighting monsters, Sage knew Ronan had never entered the place where they dwelt. "You notice the blue-green hue?" Ronan asked. "It's like how you described the area outside Mammon's prison."

"Yeah," Sage said. "This is the Dark realm." Which meant the clock was ticking for Nick.

"There's a difference in the air," Ronan said. "Even with the smell, it feels thicker."

"The air wasn't like this in Mammon's Dark realm." The temperature was cave cool and probably held the stench in check. Sage glanced around and wondered about the lights at the top of the cavern. How was that possible?

"Wonder where that mist is coming from?" Ronan asked. "And what it is?"

Sage was curious about that himself, but they didn't have time to dwell on it. "Can we track the prints?" They led away from the nearest stream and toward a wider part of the cavern, in the direction the mist was coming from.

"We can track them," Ronan said. He pulled a flashlight out of a pocket and illuminated the ground ahead of him.

They hiked for several minutes toward a narrow tunnel set high in the middle of a granite wall, picking their way through the bones. They were different shapes and sizes, most white, but some dark gray or black. Sage wondered if the creatures of the underworld came here to die.

"Looks like an extinction event," Sage said quietly. "A massive die-off."

"You can't even tell what there were," Ronan said. "Old, though. Some barely recognizable as skeletons." He stopped at the base of the wall and looked up. Steps carved into the rock crisscrossed against the face and disappeared into the passage. "They went up. The ground is undisturbed in all other directions." He was about to climb when a roar sounded behind them.

Sage spun around. A twelve-foot man with four horns, wings, and white fur staggered out from behind a boulder, a spiked club in each hand. His emaciated body appeared barely strong enough to wield the clubs, yet he moved with an athleticism Sage wished he possessed. The giant glanced briefly at Ronan, then chose the much smaller Sage, crashing through a pile of skeletons toward him.

"Separate!" Ronan shouted. "Left. Go left!"

Sage sprinted left and tripped over a piece of ribcage. His chest slammed against a protruding skullcap, and his left knee whacked a small boulder. He raised his sword high and hung onto it as he rolled onto his back.

"Sage, get up!"

He climbed to his feet and saw Ronan charging, bar raised, but he'd never intercept the creature in time. Sage teleported away just as one of the spiked clubs slapped the ground where his head would have been. Ronan took two huge steps forward and swung his bar flat and low. The sound of breaking leg bones echoed through the canyon, and the beast roared and staggered back. Ronan pivoted on his planted foot and spun in a complete circle, allowing the momentum of the swing to come around again but at twice the speed. The bar crushed one arm and drove several inches into the beast's left ribcage. A scream died in its throat when Ronan stepped back and flattened its head with a third blow.

Sage stood there and watched as the beast fell silent. This was the first time he'd ever seen Ronan in battle. He was so light on his feet he resembled a ballet dancer. His facial expression hadn't changed, his breathing was normal, and except for his shouted order for Sage to separate and move left, he hadn't shown a morsel of emotion.

Ronan slid the bar into its holster and turned toward Sage. "We only lost a minute or so. Should be good." He pointed to the tunnel at the top of the cliff. "Let's roll."

Sage looked up and teleported. The shaft—a ten-foot circle—was pitch black just a few feet from the entrance. He saw a smear of fresh blood on the right side, eye level, and his anger rose again. Nick was still bleeding.

The silence of the cavern was again absolute, save the water bubbling in the distance and Ronan's slight breathing as he climbed the steps. The floor of the passageway was rock and showed no evidence of the cloven hoofprints.

Ronan finally made it and gave Sage a scolding look. "Don't do that!" he whispered. "I'll lead the way!"

It was all Sage could do not to snap about how slowly they were going, so he gritted his teeth and motioned for Ronan to proceed. The big man glared as he passed.

After a few yards, Sage noticed something odd. Unlike the loose dirt of the tube leading from the surface, this tunnel was perfectly round, with millions of scrape marks that could only have been left by tools.

He wanted to teleport ahead in short bursts but knew he couldn't. What if the beasts carrying Nick ventured off into some side tunnel that Sage didn't see because he had teleported past it? No. They would keep Ronan's plodding pace and hope to see some evidence that Nick was still alive.

———⊦———

Teleporting into an unknown area was exceedingly dangerous. Elsbeth knew that. When she got the call from Sage's grandfather about what happened, she immediately got on Google Earth and plotted her trip using a series of longitude and latitude readings, looking at each spot using satellite view, and choosing remote areas so she wouldn't be seen as she skipped in thirty-mile bursts across two thousand miles.

She arrived at the camp three hours after receiving the call, sweaty and exhausted. The sun was high in the sky, and heat waves radiated off the hard ground in front of the cave. She wore multi-pocketed tactical pants, a small backpack with food, water, and a couple changes of clothes, and boots suitable for rough terrain. She had no weapons, because her weapons came from the heavens.

"Elsbeth!" Sage's grandfather waved as he got up from a canvas chair in front of three tents. She gave him a long hug and felt tears welling in her eyes. "I'm sorry about Nick," she whispered. "We'll get him back."

He smiled as tears slid down his cheeks. "I know we will. Sage and Ronan are down there now, and we've got good people coming. Thank you for getting here so fast." He walked her over to the tents and offered her a chair and a bottle of cold water from his portable fridge. "How's Calvin? Did he have a problem with your coming?"

Elsbeth drank a long swallow before answering. "Dad's OK. And no. He insisted I come. Can I see the video?"

"All set up in my tent." Steven unzipped the first tent on the right and held open the flap. There was a cot with a sleeping bag and a large duffel bag in the corner. Two camping stools were open next to the cot. A tablet computer was hooked to a GoPro camera on top of the sleeping bag. "I've downloaded the video from both of their cameras." He wiped his forehead and paused for several moments. "Hard to watch Nick's footage." He hit play and turned his head while Elsbeth watched.

A lump formed in Elsbeth's throat during the part when Nick blinded Sage with his light. The look on Sage's face—his squinting, the way he shielded his eyes, the grin that accompanied his mock anger—was classic him. She missed him already, and she'd seen him just last week. The last part of the video, Nick's screams, caused goose bumps on her arms. The video was so jerky and frantic she couldn't see much of Nick's attacker. Pieces of a wing, a black head, a snippet of a claw. She'd never have known it was Rephaim based on the video.

"You can't see what happens to him," she said. "Just his voice fading away."

"Right," Steven said. "Sage's video has everything." He punched up the next one, leaned back, and allowed Elsbeth full access.

It began with him entering the cave and talking with Nick about their grandpa finding the Incan ruins. When they got to the flat rock and Elsbeth heard Nick say he was going to name the chamber "Nick Alexander's Cave of Treasures," she fought back tears at the joy Nick had experienced just before he began screaming for his life.

Steven reached over and turned the volume all the way up. "I want you to hear it speak," he said to Elsbeth. "Listen to what it says."

She let it play up to the point where the Rephaim turned into a young man and escaped under the rock. *You will never get him back, angel boy. He's gone. No way out. Gone forever. Revenge so sweet. So, my Prince told no tales about the boy of prophecy knowing us.* Elsbeth played the video again, this time closing her eyes and listening only to the words the beast spoke.

"What do you think?" Steven asked after she played it a third time.

Elsbeth reversed the video to the point that Sage first saw the Rephaim standing in the alcove. The light from his helmet illuminated the beast perfectly. She hit pause and turned the tablet toward Steven. "You heard Sage identify which Prince spawned this monster."

"Yes. Belphegor."

"Do you know the significance of that?" Elsbeth knew Steven had written the official report to the Council about Sage's mission in Mammon's prison the previous summer, but she didn't know how deeply he'd drilled into the details.

Steven shook his head. "I don't."

"We killed Rupert," Elsbeth said. "Sage and me. While preventing my capture. Rupert was from the Belphegor line. The Prince of Sloth." She tapped the tablet screen. "This beast said, 'Revenge so sweet.' This is no coincidence." She clenched her fists.

Steven sat in silence while he thought about it. "So, they weren't sure they could attack Sage directly but knew he would rescue his brother."

"Rescue him from where?" Elsbeth asked. "Where does it lead?"

Sage's grandfather sighed heavily. "Maybe to the Dark realm, and possibly the three evil Territories."

"They really exist? The Territories surrounding Tartarus and the Elioudians? I thought all of that was just legend. Or ancient history and gone for eons." Elsbeth had studied Council ancestry for a solid year and read every book she could find on the subject at the Tomb of Ancient Documents, the Council's repository of historical information. "So, if all of it's real, can they make it to Tartarus for safekeeping?"

"Seems logical to me that if the hole drops into one of the Territories, then making it to Tartarus is technically possible." Steven stared off for a moment. "But logic often doesn't follow reality."

"I thought access to Tartarus was guarded by Archangels?" Elsbeth said. "I thought all entrance was forbidden? No one could survive in one of the Territories for long. Not even Sage."

"I called Council headquarters and spoke to Abigail Vaughn," Steven said. "She couldn't add anything."

A bead of sweat trickled down the side of Elsbeth's face. How could this happen? She started to ask something, then stopped.

"What?" Steven said. "You were going to say something."

"How is any of this possible? How did all of you happen to be here? Right here, at a spot where a hole drops into the Territories? How could they have been waiting for him?"

Sage's grandfather sat silently for several beats. "I've thought of little else in the last few hours. We were led here. Or I was. Documents were found inside an old relic on an archeological expedition about nine months ago. It claimed the presence of winged creatures appearing out of nowhere near the site of a lost Incan tribe that had relocated to Mexico before the rest of the civilization died off. I researched for months and narrowed it down to here."

"You were tricked?" Elsbeth could hardly believe that.

"Apparently. A lie filled with enough truth to make it appear genuine." Steven stared at his feet. "The Princes know we hunt for entrances into their realm, and Sloth used it against us. Against me."

The look of guilt on Steven's face caused Elsbeth to reach over and grab one of his hands. "This isn't your fault, if that's what you're thinking."

"I should have left Sage and Nick at home. They shouldn't have been here." Steven sighed. "Kevin and Jenna told me they had no problem leaving both boys at home while they were on their cruise, but they wouldn't leave Nick by himself. Why didn't I do that?"

She couldn't dispute that, so she said nothing. Steven would have to work through his guilt on his own. For now, they had bigger things to worry about. "Did you call Theo?" she asked. Theophylaktos Alastair, the Council member with the most enhanced gift of Sight, should have seen this coming, especially since it dealt with Sage.

"It was the first call I made," Steven said. "He received no visions about this. He contacted the others gifted with Sight and called me back a few minutes ago. None of them saw this."

"How's that possible?" Elsbeth asked. "What's it mean?"

Steven sat quietly as he thought about how to answer. Elsbeth couldn't read his expression exactly, but she knew it wasn't good. "It means that somehow, those gifted with Sight are blocked out of the Territories, assuming that's where they ended up."

Elsbeth rubbed the cold plastic bottle across her sweaty forehead. She didn't have a full understanding how Sight worked or whether it was unusual that Theo was blind to this event. Regardless, the information sat like a cold stone in her stomach.

"It means," Steven continued, "that anything could happen, and we're not going to know about it until we get down there." He looked hard at Elsbeth. "They're on their own. Truly on their own. At least for a while."

4

*F*ather.

Finally, Sloth thought as he waited quietly inside his contemplation room. *My most trusted progeny reports. Yes, Zagan, I await your account.*

As you predicted, they found the chamber.

Belphegor leaned his head back and exhaled slowly. Then he smiled. He almost wished Lucifer and his five arrogant worshipers could witness his genius unfolding. Too soon, however, to relish an accomplishment yet fully realized. *Tell me of your actions, Zagan, and how the angel boy responded.*

They entered the chamber on the fourth day, Father. I watched from the darkness while the youngest of the brothers spoke of being the first to enter. I sent him to the Depths, then mocked the boy of prophecy before fleeing. The angel boy and the one with Strength entered the Depths soon after.

Step one completed. Though brilliant in its execution, there were many steps left to accomplish. *And what of the old man? What of the entrance to the Depths?*

The old man weeps, makes telephone calls, and pleads for help. The entrance remains unguarded. The girl with Light has arrived to help him. I remain hidden and await your next command. Should I kill them?

You cannot kill the girl by yourself, Zagan. She is exceedingly dangerous. Besides, an opportunity awaits us, and killing the old man and the girl before they have summoned enough Council members to impact their war against us would be folly. Patience, young Zagan, you must learn patience. Cunning and misdirection will rule the day, not direct attacks like that of the foolish Mammon.

Sloth's telepathic connection with his son was solid. As was the connection with Gadrell, his twin, yet trapped within the hell of the Rephaim territory. Gadrell deserved his freedom from the pits; if not for Lucifer's treachery and betrayal, he would have escaped during the Battle at the Gate. For six thousand years Belphegor had remained in contact with his brother, plotting a way to release him. For the first time, it was a real possibility that his release could happen soon. Gadrell had a dozen disciples prepared to join Belphegor within the human realm to overthrow Lucifer.

Descend to the Depths, Zagan. Track the boy and the man with Strength, but do not interfere. I caution you, remain hidden always, for your discovery would jeopardize everything. Sloth hadn't told Zagan of Gadrell's upcoming role, nor would he. For now, Zagan needed to focus fully on observing, from afar, the actions of the angel boy.

If I descend to the Depths, Father, I might be unable to return.

Sloth heard and felt Zagan's desperation, yet it mattered not. *A hero is recognized not only by the battles he wins but by the sacrifices he makes. You will ascend, Zagan, both from the Depths and within the new world order created when my plan has fully matured. Report back soon, for much is at stake.*

Yes, Father.

Sloth stood and glanced at his watch, cleansed his mind, and prepared for his human duties. His contemplation room was little more than a glorified closet, yet it served his purposes. It was barren, secure, and free from any electronic distractions. He was the first in a long line of chief executives to use the room in this manner, yet he did not care. His privacy was critical to his success.

A light knock on the door coincided with the meeting he was already late for. Belphegor opened the door and smiled at the secretary tasked with keeping him on time. "The general is waiting, sir."

"Thank you, Susan. Grab me a glass of sweet tea and bring the general a cup of strong black coffee. He's going to need it." He smiled again and headed for his office. The human world was such a complicated place. And after six thousand years, he was finally ready to begin molding it into his *own* image.

Sage and Ronan came out of the tunnel passage and into another giant cavern. The number of bones seemed half of that in the other cavern, but they still littered the ground like a desecrated cemetery. The mist hovered near the ceiling, highlighted by bulbs powerful enough to light the chamber throughout.

It took Ronan just a few seconds to spot the beasts carrying Nick. "There, along the wall to the right." They were too far away for Sage to see details but not too far to know how many. Two. "We'll never catch them," Ronan said. "They're a quarter mile away."

Movement to the left caught Sage's eyes. "What's that?"

A cloud of fast-moving dust trailed a pack of beasts running upright like men. They were small but muscular, lean, and fast. They raced across the canyon toward the beasts carrying Nick and began spreading out in attack formation once they got within a hundred yards.

"How many are there?" Ronan asked.

Sage couldn't tell. "Maybe a dozen."

Ronan grabbed hold of Sage's arm and held tight. "Don't go anywhere. This needs to play out. There's nothing we can do. Yet."

Howls and cries echoed through the canyon as the hunting pack raised clubs in the air and circled their prey. The beast carrying Nick over one shoulder placed him on the ground, drew a club from a holster on his back, and turned toward the approaching herd. The second beast protected Nick's limp form from the other direction. They crouched back to back, their weapons low and ready.

"I've gotta save Nick," Sage said. He tried pulling away, but Ronan held fast.

"And get yourself killed trying?" Ronan said. He reached around and grabbed Sage in a hard bear hug. "Don't even think of teleporting over there."

Sage knew he could teleport out of Ronan's grip, but he also knew it would be a suicide mission. The attackers had completely encircled the two larger beasts and had worked themselves into a preattack frenzy. Nick appeared so small from this distance, so helpless.

The war cries died as a single voice echoed a command in a language Sage didn't understand. The attacking hoard split into two groups, evenly divided against Nick's kidnappers. The leader of the group stood apart, shouting commands and pointing with his club. He screamed and jabbed and stomped a foot, motioned and rushed forward, then stopped and swung his club as though demonstrating what he wanted them to do. It did no good. The two groups shuffled their feet, switched their clubs from one hand to another, and looked at each other, but mainly they just stared at the much larger beasts guarding Nick.

"He's having trouble convincing his people to attack," Ronan whispered. "Their prey haven't moved at all and don't appear that worried about what might happen."

"They're three times taller and ten times heavier," Sage said. "With their long clubs, their reach is a huge advantage."

The leader finally stopped yelling and led the attack himself. He sprinted forward and leapt high in the air, his club positioned to crash down on the head of the creature on the left. He never made it. The one on the right swung his club like Babe Ruth and crushed the little attacker in midflight. As soon the limp body hit the ground, another shout sounded, and the entire group fled.

"Gotta love their instinct for survival," Ronan said. "Despite their numbers, their chances didn't look good."

By the time Nick was again slung over a shoulder, the fleeing herd was nearly out of sight. The two beasts then resumed their journey. Sage shrugged out of Ronan's grip. "Run fast," Sage told him. "See you in a few minutes. I'm going." He teleported just as Ronan shouted a protest and tried to grab him.

He appeared directly in front of the beast carrying Nick over one shoulder, sword ready, and shoved it into the center of its belly, missing one of Nick's arms by inches. Sage fell onto his back as he twisted the sword and ripped it sideways. One entire side of the monster's midsection burst open and spilled its contents. The beast grunted and fell forward in a mess of grossness. Nick tumbled, hit the ground hard, and rolled several feet away.

Sage teleported again, landed on top of the second beast, and shoved his sword down into its chest. It shouted and tried to respond but simply stumbled several steps before finally collapsing. Sage rode it all the way and hopped off just as it slammed against the ground.

Minotaurs. Huge—nearly eight feet tall—with bull heads two feet wide. Their muscular bodies, covered in short brown hair, stank so badly Sage nearly gagged. The one carrying Nick was dead; the other lay gasping, its chest wound jagged and deep. Sage separated its head from its body.

"For Nick," he whispered.

Nick was out. Sage rolled him over and saw an ugly wound on his head. Bleeding, but not too badly. He also saw a large puncture wound at the base of his throat with green pus oozing out. A putrid stench wafted into his nose, but he couldn't tell if it was the pus or the smell of the minotaurs.

Sage was about to sheath his sword when it suddenly sizzled itself clean of the minotaur blood. He wasn't sure how that happened, but it had also cleaned itself during his battles with Dark beasts last summer. He slid it into its scabbard, then took a minute to get Nick hoisted over his left shoulder. Ronan was running hard toward them, panting, but making good time. Sage headed his way.

"Again, you defy my order," Ronan said. He stopped in front of Sage, bent over, and put his hands on his knees to catch his breath. "Is this how this mission's gonna go?"

"Take him, Man of Might." Sage transferred Nick to Ronan's left shoulder. "We could have run for an hour and never caught them. You know it, and so do I. Stop acting so surprised."

Ronan started to say something, but Sage cut him off. "You told me to focus on the important stuff and I might survive this. That's what I'm doing. I'm not a kid anymore. I've fought my battles, even though you weren't there to witness them. Now . . . let's concentrate on getting out of here. I don't want Nick seeing those dead minotaurs."

With a grunt and shake of his head, Ronan headed back toward the tunnel passage. They stopped and looked at the short beast the minotaurs had killed. Four feet tall, hairless, pure white skin, pointed ears, teeth like some deformed werewolf's, and feet big enough for a man twice his size. "Any idea what it is?" Sage asked.

"Never seen anything like it," Ronan said, after staring for several moments. "Maybe some kind of goblin?"

The minotaur's club had crushed the goblin's entire left side, broken its left arm, and snapped its neck. It was splayed out on the ground in a position only achievable by the dead.

Ronan took off at a brisk pace. "Let's go."

Sage drew his sword again and walked behind him, keeping an eye out in case the other goblins decided they were easier prey than the minotaurs. From his position behind Ronan, he could see Nick's head injury. It didn't look too serious. In fact, it looked a little better than just a few minutes ago. The pus seeping from his neck punctures was Sage's biggest concern. He thought about Mom and Dad on their cruise, how he wished Nick were with them. He couldn't imagine what they'd do if they knew about all of this. If Nick died down here . . .

They made good time getting back to their starting point. Ronan had just placed Nick on the ground near the bloodstained rock when Sage saw movement on the far side of the cavern. "Ronan," he whispered. "Don't look, but we've got a watcher at ten o'clock. Behind a boulder. Just one."

"OK," Ronan said quietly. "How far?"

"Five hundred yards. Maybe six. White. Just caught a glimpse."

"Roger that. Another goblin?"

"Too far to tell," Sage said. "Seemed taller."

Nick moaned, and his eyes fluttered, then he went quiet again. Ronan put a finger against his neck. "His pulse is strong. Bleeding's stopped. Breathing good."

Sage watched the white spot across the cavern. "Any idea about where we are? This place?"

"Oh, yeah. I got an idea, but you ain't gonna like it."

"One of the three Territories?" Sage glanced at him. "That's what you're thinking?"

"Where else could we be?"

"Thought all that was just legend." Sage moved behind the rock and sat down. The white spot hadn't moved. "We sit here until the team comes? Is that the best plan?"

Ronan looked around, didn't say anything for a bit. Finally, "Beats wandering around and getting lost." He looked at Sage. "You could teleport up to the surface, tell them what we've got."

"No," Sage said immediately. "This was a planned attack. They took Nick to get me down here. When the minotaurs don't show up to wherever they were taking him, Sloth is going to send a lot bigger group to find out what went wrong. Besides, we were attacked by a twelve-foot, furry man with horns, have seen a herd of goblins, and have something else watching us right now. I'm not leaving you alone." He looked hard at Ronan. "Don't mention it again."

The big man smiled. "You are turning into quite the confident young man. OK. Dead topic."

"Got more movement," Sage said. The white figure moved from behind the boulder, then stopped. A moment later a second figure appeared. "Two of them," he whispered. "Heading this way."

Ronan and Sage moved in front of Nick. "My eyes aren't what they used to be," Ronan said after a minute, "but I've never seen the likes of them."

Once the subjects were within a hundred yards, Sage saw them more clearly. They were lean and narrow, completely bald, and wore swords in sparkling scabbards that reached their knees. With each step, they became more visible: smooth heads, pointed ears like Spock's from *Star Trek*, large, narrow noses, and no eyebrows above green eyes that were at least ten times the size of a regular human's. Their chins were pointed, their cheeks sunken, with skin as white as a July Texas sun.

"What do we have here?" Ronan whispered. "Evolved goblins?"

"They look peaceful," Sage said quietly.

They wore one-piece bodysuits—white—that clung tightly against their bodies. Their hands were large, with big knuckles and wide fingers. Muscles rippled through their arms and shoulders. They were lean and narrow and of average height. Sage was at least a head taller than either of them.

Ronan held up his left hand like a traffic cop and held his metal bar in his right. "Do not come any closer."

They stopped several yards away and held their hands in front of them, clearly signaling peaceful intentions. One appeared much older than the other, and it was he who spoke. "You are Topsiders," he said in a gentle voice. "Voice of the English. We will converse in your tongue. Do not be afraid."

"We will not harm you," the younger one said. "We are your friends."

Sage glanced at Ronan and motioned for him to take the lead. "Who are you?" Ronan asked. "What are you? What is this place?"

"This place is the Wastelands, on the outskirts of Tartarus," said the older one. "Belphegor's region. We are Elioud. I am Aquila. This is Ephraim. Our blood is redeemed and not of the same strain as the abominable angelic races you have thus encountered."

Belphegor's region? So, it *was* the Prince of Sloth that planned all this. Sage felt heat rising in his face. Belphegor would kill Nick just to get to him? *Of course, he's a Prince of Hell.* Sage felt like an idiot even wondering about it.

Aquila pointed at Nick. "Does your young companion yet live? I see the mark of the Double Horn on his throat. The poison can kill."

"What?" Sage asked. "Poison?"

Aquila took a small step forward. "The Double Horns stab prey in the neck to disable them. The green substance covering the wound is the blood being attacked. Should he survive, he will be in much pain."

Sage dropped to his knees and rolled Nick over to inspect the wound. A golf-ball-sized knot had formed under the puncture marks. The pus now covered several inches of his chest as it continued to leak out. "Will it kill him?" Sage asked. He tried keeping the anxiety out of his voice, but he had little success. "Can you help him?"

"We have an antidote," Aquila said. "We must treat the wound soon, for most do not survive long without it."

"How far?" Ronan asked. "I can carry him."

"Many leagues from here," Aquila said. "We should leave immediately."

Ronan scooped Nick into his arms, then introduced himself and Sage. "And this is Nick. Thank you for your help."

Aquila pointed back the way they had come and began navigating through the graveyard of skeletons. "Follow us." Ronan fell in behind Aquila, Sage followed Ronan, and Ephraim brought up the rear.

"Have you studied the Elioud?" Aquila asked. "Tartarus?"

"We have," Ronan said.

Sage hadn't but didn't say anything. He'd heard of the Wastelands and the Elioudians, but his total knowledge wouldn't fill a sixty-second conversation.

"Then you know the danger of the Wastelands," Aquila said. "Already more beasts approach. We must hurry to avoid the risk of being overwhelmed." He picked up his pace.

Sage looked all around but didn't see any beasts approaching. He didn't hear anything, either.

"Help is on its way," Ronan said. "They'll come down the hole. I'm worried that they'll arrive in the middle of a mess if we're not there to keep the area clear."

"It has been many decades since that passage was used to provide human test subjects for Belphegor," Aquila said.

"Has Belphegor begun experimenting again, Aquila?" Ephraim asked. "Our scouts haven't mentioned activity for many years."

"What experiments?" Sage asked.

"Human to demonic transfiguration," Aquila said. "He dragged humans into this part of the Wastelands for many centuries. We believed his experiments had concluded."

"Like a furry man with four horns on his head?" Sage asked. "Or goblin-looking creatures?"

"Precisely," Ephraim said. "The horned giant you reference is the youst, evolved from a larger creature called the hourder, which is now nearly extinct. The novence, the small goblins you mentioned, are also Belphegor's experiments. They hunt in packs but are skittish and cowardly."

Aquila held up his hand and stopped the group. He cocked his head as though listening to a distant sound. "They come. Many beasts. They will track us to our gate once they know they have failed."

"You hear anything?" Sage asked Ronan quietly. "I don't."

"I think we should take their word for it," Ronan said.

They followed the Elioudians over a small stream and around a large group of boulders before trekking across a wide, open area. Sage didn't fully trust Aquila and Ephraim, so he hadn't sheathed his sword. Nor would he, at least not yet. He caught snatches of Nick's face as Ronan stepped around rocks and crevices. Nick moaned, and his eyes fluttered, but he still hadn't woken up. It was starting to scare Sage.

When they approached a fifteen-foot-tall wall of jagged rocks, Aquila motioned for them to stop. They were close to the spot where Sage had first seen the Elioudians from across the clearing.

"Observe," Aquila said.

Between a small space in the rocks, Ronan looked back where they'd been standing a few minutes before.

"What are they?" he asked. "What in the name of mercy *are* they?"

The slight screech in Ronan's voice caught Sage's attention. Fear. Raw fear. In Ronan's voice? "Let me see," he said.

Ronan stepped aside, careful not to hit Nick's head against the boulders. "Those monsters aren't in any books at the Tomb."

Sage peered through the crack, and his breath caught. There were at least thirty identical humanoid creatures: eight feet tall, with broad shoulders, short wings, claws, bald heads, tall, pointy ears, and multicolored skin that appeared as thick as elephant hide. Some held clubs, others swords. A few were inspecting the ground. "They're trying to pick up a trail," Sage said.

"If they're any good, it won't take them long." Ronan shifted Nick in his arms and spoke to Aquila. "Traveling with him will be slow. How far?"

"Many leagues. The Belphei look fiercer than they are. Somewhat like the novence, they are intellectually inferior beings with no imagination. They roam in packs to protect one another. Best, however, to avoid bloodshed whenever possible. Even an inferior opponent can occasionally inflict a mortal wound." Aquila turned to his partner. "Lead the way. Make haste."

The young Elioudian took off at a brisk pace deeper into the stand of rocks.

Ronan made eye contact with Sage. "We'll be fine." He whispered the encouragement despite the expression on his face not matching his words. "I've been in tighter spots."

Maybe true, Sage thought, *but not with an injured thirteen-year-old to babysit.* "I'll take rear guard. You just make sure Nick is safe. OK?"

"No worries. Just watch my back."

Ronan had only taken a few steps when Nick woke up and began to scream. A few seconds later, Sage heard a roar that would shame a pride of lions. Ronan clamped a hand over Nick's mouth. "Nick, quiet. You're safe." He took off in a sprint.

Sage followed him. Nick's eyes, solid black and streaming a putrid pus, went wide as he tried screaming through Ronan's strong grip. "Nick, I'm here," Sage said. "We've got you. OK? We've got you, but you've gotta be quiet." His brother nodded. Frantic.

Ronan took his hand away. "Monsters," Nick said immediately. "There were monsters!"

"We got them," Ronan said. "We'll explain it later."

They ran at Ronan's plodding pace, and Sage saw them losing ground to the Elioudians. He wished desperately that he could grab Nick and teleport him away, but it didn't work that way. Sage couldn't teleport anyone else. He wasn't some magical horse that could whisk people from one place to another. Had that been the case, he would've come down here alone and gotten Nick back to the surface immediately.

They ran for a long time. Not an hour, but it seemed that long. The roar of the beasts eventually fell silent. "We need to go faster, Ronan," Sage said.

The big man grunted but picked up his speed. Ephraim, the young Elioudian, who was now almost two hundred yards ahead, stopped at the entrance to a cave and waited. Shadows hung heavy there, and Sage watched Aquila disappear into darkness as he passed Ephraim. Ronan arrived and ducked inside a few seconds later.

"Can you run, Nick?" Ronan asked. "Are you too hurt to run?"

"I can run," Nick said, his words vibrating. "But I can't see."

Sage knew how terrified Nick was, but he'd seen his brother step up in tough situations before. Nothing like this, obviously, but Nick had a grit that ran deeper than most boys his age. "Just hang on to Ronan's belt," Sage told him.

"There is another passageway up ahead," Aquila said. "Ephraim will guide the way. I will follow."

They plunged into a darkness so complete it was as if light didn't exist at all. Then Ronan turned on his flashlight, and Sage could see Ephraim making good time ahead of them. Nick was behind Ronan and had a firm grip on his belt. The smell of rotting flesh was stronger here and overpowered the sulfur-laced atmosphere. The beasts behind them had fallen completely silent. Like assassins.

"Here," Ephraim said. He was somewhere ahead in the darkness, totally hidden until Ronan's light reflected off his eyes. He darted down the tunnel just before Ronan got there. Sage glanced back just before following Ronan and Nick around the turn.

"We must hurry," Aquila said. "The beasts come."

Sage heard a sword being drawn behind him. Ahead, through the flashes from Ronan's flashlight, he saw that Ephraim had also drawn his sword. Things were about to get serious.

The tunnel curved, then straightened, then curved again. They weren't running hard enough to get completely exhausted, but Sage could hear Nick breathing hard. The passageway narrowed enough to force them to stop and squeeze through one by one. Ronan had a tough time.

It was only after Aquila made it through that Ronan shined his light around. They were in a chamber about thirty yards deep and fifty yards wide. A small opening on the far side would require them to exit on their hands and knees if they were forced to leave that way. The ceiling was low, but high enough to stand upright. Only a few scattered bones littered the floor.

"Place Nick inside the small tunnel," Aquila said. "He will be safe there while we make our stand. Can each of you fight?"

"Don't worry about us," Ronan said. "Why fight here?"

"The Belphei travel at greater speeds than you," Aquila said. "They would eventually overtake us if we continued on open ground. If we can substantially reduce the size of their pack, they will retreat."

"They only engage when they are sure of their own survival," Ephraim added. "They are swarm fighters and do not like enclosed spaces. We can drive them away from within this chamber."

Sage led Nick over to the small opening on the far wall. Nick wobbled and leaned on him, then grabbed Sage's arm and held on. His grip was weak. "I'm blind, Sage," he whispered. "I can't see anything. Where are we? Who are these people? Who's chasing us?" The beam from Ronan's flashlight showed the terror in Nick's face. The pus streaming from his unnatural black eyes was the same color as that oozing from the wound in his neck.

"We're in a place nobody thought existed," Sage said quietly. "I've got a lot of stuff to tell you. OK? But first we've gotta get out of here. Our friends have some medicine to make you better, but we can't get the medicine if we don't win this little skirmish. Now crawl in there and go about ten or twelve feet. Totally out of sight. OK? Put your hands over your ears. Conserve your strength."

Ronan walked up and put a hand on Nick's shoulder. "Do what Sage says. Get way back in there, and cover your ears. You'll be fine."

"What's chasing us?" Nick pleaded, tears streaming. "What are they?"

"We're not sure exactly what they are," Ronan said. "But they have no idea what they're about to wade into. Just get into that tunnel and wait."

"They come," Aquila said softly. "Prepare yourselves."

Nick dropped to his hands and knees, and Sage guided him inside the escape passage. After he disappeared, Sage turned and faced the primary opening.

"We can see in total darkness," Aquila said. "As can the Belphei. We do not need your light."

"We need it," Ronan said. "If we're going to be any help at all, it stays on." He crammed the flashlight into a crack high off the ground. "Let's get to work."

Aquila and Ephraim stood forty-five degrees on opposite sides of the opening, about twelve feet in. Sage and Ronan took up positions directly in front but farther back. "I need room to swing my bar," Ronan told Sage. "Move a couple of feet to the right."

A low-volume clattering grew loud enough to cover the scuffling of dozens of approaching feet. Then the first Belphei exploded into the chamber with otherworldly speed. It thrust a short sword directly at Ephraim's throat, but the Elioudian sidestepped and drove his own sword underneath its armpit. Then, in one fluid motion, he spun and engaged the next beast through. It stumbled as Ephraim's sword hit it just below its left knee. His backswing caught the side of its neck and nearly decapitated it.

"Let them in," Aquila said. He motioned Sage and Ronan toward the back of the chamber as Ephraim stepped away from the first dead monsters. "They must understand the futility of the attack."

Ephraim again moved opposite Aquila, and then both backed way up. The four of them now stood in a line, seven yards separating them. The two dead Belphei cluttered the space in front of the entrance. The insect-like clattering suddenly fell silent.

"They hesitate," Aquila whispered.

"Did you see the third beast start to enter and back out?" Ephraim asked. "They smell human scent, and it confuses them."

They smell humans? Sage almost laughed out loud. The Belphei smelled like spoiled cabbage and rotten eggs poured over a plate of decayed skunk. How could they *possibly* smell a human? He gripped his sword and felt the tingling of Teleportation vibrate through his bones. He heard Nick cough and hoped he'd crawled far enough into the small tunnel to truly isolate himself from danger.

"Prepare," Aquila said softly.

Not five seconds later, the full assault began. Belphei stormed into the chamber as fast as they could maneuver through the tight opening. Instead of attacking immediately, they peeled away from the entrance and began lining up along the walls in both directions. They looked different up close than they had from the distance Sage had first seen them. Although most were taller than eight feet, with broad shoulders and long arms, they were surprisingly lean and thin chested. Their bald heads were shaped aerodynamically—like bicycle helmets—and sported ears pointing several inches above their crowns. Their skin glimmered in the beam of Ronan's flashlight. Most had protruding jaws with canine teeth visible over their bottom lips, and some wore bone necklaces. None of their short wings seemed capable of giving them flight, and Sage was grateful for that.

Sage knew that a group of at least thirty was hunting them, but only half that number had filed into the chamber. Most held swords, but a few wielded spiked clubs. The beasts appeared ready to attack but didn't. A moment later, Sage understood why. A taller and huskier creature squeezed through the cavern doorway, grunted an unintelligible command to his troops, and showed empty hands to Aquila.

"I am Nearatook," he said. "Commander of the east wing of the Belphei expedition group." He wore swords on each hip and had long, curved blades strapped to each thigh.

His gravelly voice sounded friendly, Sage thought, not unlike some grandfatherly figure speaking to a group of fellow geriatrics at a VFW meeting.

"You are Aquila," Nearatook continued, "former scout and master tracker of the Elioudian Ancients. I come under the direction of Prince Belphegor to collect the humans that rightfully fell into his jurisdiction. They belong to him. We have no dispute with the Elioudian Ancients but are prepared to take the humans by force."

One of the Belphei barked a word in an unknown language and pointed at the small tunnel Nick was hiding in. *So, they really can smell us*, Sage thought. He took a small step to the side and placed himself more directly in front of Nick's hiding place. *They'll have to kill me to get to him.* Aquila said nothing, nor did he give any indication that Nearatook had even spoken.

"The claim of tenure over humans falling into Belphegor's territorial domain was established epochs ago. It is an undisputed decree." Nearatook rested each hand on the hilt of a sword. He inspected Ronan, then looked at Sage for several moments before again addressing Aquila. "I offer you and your fellow Elioudian Ancient life and safety. You will not be harmed. We do not seek another war with you. Instruct the humans to cast their weapons aside. They will be led peacefully to the Prince's throne. I do not know upon which task the humans will be set."

The sound of retching floated out of Nick's hiding place. Then Nick coughed and moaned and threw up again. "Help me, Sage," he cried weakly.

Sage fought against a panic of hopelessness rising into his chest. All this talking was a giant waste of time. Ronan probably thought the same thing, because he shifted his weight a little as he adjusted his feet. Aquila must have sensed something, because he held up a hand to quiet Sage and Ronan's nerves.

"Your medicine man awaits outside?" Aquila asked Nearatook.

"As protocol demands," Nearatook said.

"Then we will begin negotiations with a show of good faith," Aquila said. "As your law requires. Agreed?"

"We do not negotiate for that which is lawfully ours," Nearatook said.

"To the contrary. There are many humans safely within the walls of Tartarus to which Belphegor laid claim. To speak otherwise discredits both you and the Belphei." Aquila spoke softly yet kept his sword positioned for immediate use.

Other humans? In Tartarus? Aquila hadn't spoken in past tense. He said many humans *are* safely within the walls of Tartarus. Sage caught Ronan's glance and knew he'd picked up on the same point.

"*These* humans are not for negotiation," Nearatook said. He looked at Sage and pointed. "This one must be brought to the Prince. Dead or alive."

A dozen jumbled thoughts raced through Sage's mind, but one fact stood out: Prince Belphegor wanted revenge and would not be denied.

Nearatook cocked his head as though listening to a voice in his head, then offered a hand toward Sage and spoke directly to him. "The Prince offers you a chance to save the other two humans: come with us and the others, and live. Refuse, and all of you die."

Before Sage could offer a response, Aquila spoke. "You communicate with Belphegor now? Does he hear and see through you? You are his conduit?"

"His messenger," Nearatook said. "He is all-knowing."

"Should you fall in battle, will he connect with another of your tribe?" Aquila still hadn't spoken with any emotion. He was as flat as roadkill, and it made Sage kind of envious. The old Elioudian demonstrated textbook battlefield self-control.

"I have survived battles against far greater odds," Nearatook said.

The Belphei leader still hadn't drawn a sword. Though he stood straight and tall and slightly behind the beasts lined along the wall and probably felt safe, Sage saw an opening and took it. He teleported directly in front of Nearatook and jammed his sword up through the bottom of his chin. His sword traveled through the beast's jaw and behind his eyes and exploded out of the top of his head. Sage yanked his sword free and teleported back to his place before Nearatook's body collapsed. "I needed to turn off Belphegor's transmitter," Sage told Ronan. "I'm thinking you need to start using that bar."

Pandemonium broke out. Ronan rushed forward and took out two Belphei with his first blow. He crushed them with a swing from downtown and blasted the beasts into the next county. Sage appeared out of thin air in front of a beast heading for Ronan and drove his sword through the center of its chest. As he pulled it free, he caught movement near the entrance and saw Aquila and Ephraim battling with such speed and skill, it was all Sage could do not to stand and gape.

Sage killed one more Belphei, and then it was over. Eighteen Belphei lay strewn around the front half of the chamber. None had escaped.

Aquila stepped away from the wreckage and stopped in front of Sage. "Are you the Sage from prophecy? The boy our ancients spoke of? The Prophecy of Seth?"

"Yes." Sage sheathed his sword, which had already sizzled itself clean. The silence of the chamber echoed Nick's moaning. "But I'm not talking about that right now. Tell me more about the Belphei medicine man."

"He carries an antidote to combat the poison of a Double Horn, among other things." Aquila turned toward Ronan. "Please get young Nick out of the passage. The expulsion of stomach contents is the beginning of a period that includes violent seizures. We must secure him to prevent injuries during the throes."

Ronan hurried off as Aquila turned back to Sage. "The rest of the Belphei have fled. It is their nature. The moment you killed Nearatook, you snapped the unseen joining of the group. They will secure themselves inside their lair until Belphegor appoints another leader."

"Give me a hand, Sage," Ronan said. He had Nick underneath the shoulders, trying not to hurt him as he dragged him out.

Sage grabbed one of Nick's arms and slid a hand underneath his lower back. They lifted him out and placed him on the ground in front of the passage. Nick's face was turning black from his eyes out. Angry red streaks pulsed out from the puncture wound and snaked across the front of his neck and down his chest. The tips of his fingers were blue. Vomit coated his mouth and nose and had splattered down his shirt. He trembled all over and was barely conscious. He appeared close to death.

"Do we have time to get to your antidote?" Ronan asked Aquila. "Is he too far gone?"

Sage held his breath as Aquila took several moments to answer. "I cannot be certain." He looked at Sage. "I am sorry. I cannot assure you that he will survive the trip to our closest gate station. It is still many leagues from here."

It only took Sage a moment to decide what to do. He stood and pulled his sword. "What will the Belphei medicine man look like? Will he have a supply pack? Does he wear any type of special clothing?"

Ronan stood and put a hand on Sage's chest. "No. Forget it."

"Remove your hand, Ronan," Sage snapped. "We're not having this conversation again." He looked at Aquila. "How can I tell the medicine man from the others?"

"He wears a sling looped around his neck and left shoulder. The pouch with medicines hangs near his lower back. It is protected by a wide leather belt. He is the most heavily armed and the fiercest of the group. He travels in the center of the pack. Always in the center."

"Which way is the lair? When I get out of the tunnel, will I go back toward where we came from?" Ronan grabbed Sage's arm, but Sage jerked it away. "I'm not letting Nick die! And unless you plan on knocking me unconscious, there's no physical way to stop me. You know it, and so do I." He took several steps away and turned to Aquila one last time. "Which direction will they go? How would you attack the group? How would you get the medicine pouch?"

Aquila stood quietly for a moment. Ephraim answered for him. "Their direction of travel from here is unknowable. None know the precise location of their home." Ephraim glanced at Aquila as though seeking permission to continue. Aquila nodded for him to proceed. "To get the medicine pouch," Ephraim said, "you will have to kill them all."

Dread spread from the center of Sage's gut. His mouth suddenly went dry.

"They will protect their medicine man to the last living warrior," Aquila said. "He is their last hope against attacks from other beasts. The pouches of healing ointments and salves are in high demand throughout the Wastelands."

"You will never overtake them now," Ephraim said. "Their speed is great, and much time has passed since you killed Nearatook."

"I'm not worried about that," Sage said. "Catching them will be the least of my problems." He thought for a moment about how to attack a group of fifteen beasts and knew only one thing would work. He turned toward Ronan. "Stay here so I'll know where to bring the medicine. And don't let Nick out of your sight!" He saw Ronan start to protest just as he teleported away.

5

Elsbeth yawned and lit the Coleman lantern sitting on the table between her and Sage's grandfather. Night was close, and she was ready to crash. She would use Sage and Nick's tent, which was already set up with air mattresses, pillows, and blankets. Teleporting used a lot of energy, and she'd never come close to traveling the distance she had today. Then with all the worrying, phone calls between her and her father, and constant pacing back and forth, she felt dead on her feet.

She stewed for hours over the thought of Sage and Nick having to travel through the Territories of the Nephilim, Emim, and Rephaim. What little she knew made her shudder with worry. Ancient writings chronicling the journey of the original two hundred Council members as they traveled through the Territories six thousand years ago described them as killing grounds, filled with creatures and monsters unseen since before the Great Flood. The original Council's survival would have been impossible without a band of Archangels providing escort.

Because many early Council documents had been destroyed when a village in southern Italy was burned to extinguish the Black Plague, eyewitness accounts recorded by the original Council members were lost forever. That left half-truths, exaggerations, and guesswork as the only sources of information available to those who wished to study the Territories. Although Elsbeth had spent a great deal of time researching the topic, she was far from an expert. She'd spent most of this afternoon allowing her active imagination to fill in the gaps missing from her historical knowledge.

Steven Alexander had worked his Council satellite phone to the point of exhaustion—making notes, leaving messages, returning calls, pleading, complaining, begging, and consoling. Every time Elsbeth tried engaging him in conversation about who was coming to help, his phone would ring, and he'd either scratch someone off the list or add someone to it.

Council members didn't just sit around an office and shuffle paperwork. They actively fought evil, being dispatched all over the globe. Getting them to jump up and converge on a central Mexican jungle was no easy task, but after hours of work, he pushed the end button for the final time, seemingly satisfied with his efforts.

"Well?" she asked him. "Who's on the team?"

"Kato Hunter was at Council headquarters in Istanbul. He's already on a plane headed this way," Steven said. "The Council is sending a historian with him. They'll parachute in sometime in the middle of the night."

She smiled. "Kato Hunter." Elsbeth knew Kato from last summer. Like her, Kato had been trapped in Mammon's prison and freed by Sage. He was the most accomplished sword fighter in the Council, and Sage still raved about him. He was rough-and-tumble with the heart of a servant.

She'd spoken to him a few months after his release from the prison, after he'd traveled back to Africa to check on his family. Because he had spent nearly two hundred years trapped within the Dark realm, he found his tiny village long gone, his family dead for at least a century. He lived in a tent for weeks as he hiked the area and searched for remnants of his old life. He visited nearby villages and spoke to hundreds of people before finally coming to grips with a hard truth: he was alone in the world. He told Elsbeth that he would rebuild his life, that the Angelic Response Council would keep him plenty busy, and that the survivors of Mammon's prison would always hold a special place in his heart. No, Elsbeth wasn't surprised Kato was already on a plane heading their way; she would have been shocked had he not been.

"Who's the historian?" Elsbeth asked. "What's his specialty?"

"His name is Horace Brahms. His specialty is Tartarus and the three Territories." Steven looked at a notepad he'd been scribbling in all afternoon.

Elsbeth took a deep breath and said a prayer of thanks. "I didn't know they had anyone who studied that specifically."

"He owns a private collection of papers that describe the journey of the original two hundred. He's old but wants to help. He'll piggyback on Kato during the drop." Steven smiled. "Brave soul."

"Sounds young at heart." Elsbeth just hoped he could survive the trip. The rescue team needed his knowledge. "Who else is coming?"

"Malcolm and Gavin Alexander, the sons from my first marriage."

"Malcolm and Gavin," Elsbeth said. "The millionaire fashion kings?"

Steven laughed. "Sage's pet name for them. Yes, they've saved more money over the past two centuries than anyone else in the Council. And, I must admit, they keep up with all the latest fashions and look good enough to have careers as models. Fortunately, they took after their mother. Nick calls them Elvis One and Elvis Two after the Dr. Seuss book *The Cat in the Hat*, where Thing One and Thing Two create havoc. Nick's humor makes me laugh. Malcolm and Gavin love the names."

Elsbeth smiled. That sounded like Nick. "Do Sage and Nick know they're really their uncles, or do they just call them that?" Steven's seven-century tightrope walk through life, having sons hundreds of years old while Sage's parents were normal humans, would be difficult to manage. She wondered if Kevin, Sage's dad, knew Malcolm and Gavin's true relationship with Steven.

"Sage knows," Steven said. "If Nick eventually develops an angelic gift, he'll be told as well. Kevin has called them his uncles since he was a boy. All of us in the Council with regular human children are forced to become master makeup artists. It's a constant juggling act. Malcolm and Gavin don't visit often when Kevin and Jenna are present and keep the visits short when they do. I've only heard one comment from Kevin about how Malcolm and Gavin are aging well. They do a good job keeping everything as normal looking as possible."

"When were you first married?" Elsbeth asked.

"In the 1500s. Malcolm is the oldest, gifted with Absorption. Gavin is five years younger and his teammate. Fighting Arts."

Absorption was the ability to absorb and deplete another's powers or skills, rendering them absent of everything. Afterward, the Council member would be spent and unable to defend himself. Those with Absorption couldn't use any of the powers they'd just taken, but the gift was still extremely valuable. A Fighting Arts master to protect Malcolm would be critical to his survival. "Well, I'm certain Sage and Nick will love seeing them. Who else is coming?"

Steven glanced at his notepad. "Endora Morgan. I believe you've met her."

"Sage and I met her last summer at Council headquarters. Sage didn't care for her. She's pretty intense."

"That's an understatement," Steven said. "She called and insisted on coming. And you're right about her. Intensity rolls out of her ears in little red waves."

"Is Jarvis coming?" Elsbeth asked. Jarvis was Endora's partner, personally as well as professionally.

"No. He's on another mission and can't break free." Steven looked at his list again. "David Brock."

The boy with Might. The biggest braggart Elsbeth knew. A legend in his own mind. Despite all that, he was the most fearless warrior she had ever met and had every ounce of respect Sage could muster. Sage would be glad to see him. David Brock had also been one of Mammon's prisoners. This mission was turning into a regular reunion. "David is willing to break away from his tanning bed and hair stylist?" Elsbeth gave Steven a little smile.

"He also called me," Steven said. "Word spread fast about what happened. I've actually turned people down who want to help." He took a sip of water. "David said he recently mastered some new attack katas from his martial arts instructor, and there'd never be a better time to use them in the real world."

"Gee, I'm *really shocked* he'd volunteer to kill things with his steel bar." She knew she'd sounded sarcastic, but she just couldn't help it. David Brock wore on her very last nerve. Then she felt embarrassed by her response. "I'm sorry. That was unfair. I can't think of a better guy to go with us."

"And Theo is coming here to run things from the top." Steven sighed heavily and looked at Elsbeth. "We have to get them back."

She reached over and took one of his hands. "We will, Mr. Alexander. We will." She tried blinking away her own tears. No luck. She smiled and squeezed his hand. "He wasn't prophesized as Sage the Warrior for nothing. He'll be OK until we catch up to him. I just know it."

But she didn't know it. From the sketchy history she knew, beasts still existed down there. Escaping the underworld was deemed impossible by the writings of the ancients. Elsbeth shivered at the thought of going down there herself, and she'd have six battle-tested warriors with her. She couldn't imagine what Sage was going through. Nor could she imagine life without him if he didn't make it.

"You know what I thought of about an hour ago?" she asked Steven.

"What?"

"What a stroke of genius it was for the Prince of Sloth to drag Nick into the underworld. Such a lazy way for him to kill Sage. Talk about fitting his name perfectly."

"What do you mean?"

"I mean Sloth, the Prince of laziness, has one of his sons push Nick into a place that might be impossible to escape from, knowing Sage will follow. Sloth won't need to lift another finger, because the beasts roaming the Territories will kill Sage while Sloth takes all the credit." Elsbeth's voice had risen, and she dialed it back.

Steven sat quietly for several moments. "Well," he said finally, "regardless of how genius it might appear, Sage is no easy target."

Elsbeth knew that to be true. She'd seen evidence of it last summer. But the underworld? The Territories? She shuddered at the horrid visions running through her head.

Sage appeared outside the mouth of the cave, sword in hand, inside the shadow of a boulder. If the Belphei went back the way they came, and if they eventually passed the spot Sage had dropped in from the surface, he could simply teleport there now and wait for them. He couldn't be sure that's what they'd do, however. Nick didn't have enough time for Sage to guess wrong.

The rocky ground offered few clues about their direction of travel, at least to his inexperienced eyes. He saw scuff marks and pieces of tracks but couldn't tell if they were coming or going. From his hiding place, he saw nothing but bleak landscape. The rocks and crevasses cast shadows he couldn't see into, but he doubted the Belphei had separated and hidden themselves.

He decided to skip ahead in large chunks. He chose a spot a hundred yards ahead and teleported there. It was in the direction they'd come from, and the disturbances on the ground confirmed that. The Belphei wore sandals with stiff leather soles that left spiked marks on the dusty trail. He noticed several that appeared to lead away from the cave.

Ahead another eighty yards, Sage saw more evidence that he might be behind the group. Most importantly, he thought he could smell them now. The odor was slight, but there, just strong enough to overcome the ever-present stench of sulfur. He teleported underneath a crag of red rocks another two hundred yards ahead and caught a glimpse of movement to his left. The shadows were deep, and the hanging dust made it difficult to determine exactly what it was, but something was moving away from him at high speed across a bowl of flat landscape more than a quarter mile away.

Sage could teleport more than sixty miles at a time, twice the distance Elsbeth could go. Getting ahead of this group would be child's play. Blindly doing so, however, wouldn't be wise. He would have one shot of engaging and getting the medicine pouch, and he couldn't risk screwing it up. The cloud of dust was drifting away from the area where Sage had dropped in from the surface. It was a good thing he hadn't just gone there and waited. The bowl of open area was bordered on one side by a row of jagged rocks. Sage picked a spot a hundred yards ahead of the dust and teleported.

He appeared in front of a large boulder and hid himself. A few seconds later, the Belphei came into full view. He counted thirteen beasts, all roughly the same size, all armed but not carrying their weapons. They ran in formation, footsteps in sync, at an impressive speed: four on the front row, four on the back row, and two flanking each side of the medicine man in the center. Their movements were precise and efficient; they kept their vision forward, but they weren't as tightly grouped as they could be. There was plenty of space between the front line and the medicine man in the middle; however, because of their speed, if Sage just teleported into the center, he'd get trampled.

Looking ahead of them in the distance, he didn't see much difference in the landscape, although it did appear darker. The lighting source seemed to diminish in the immediate horizon. The mist still clung to the ceiling, dipping low in some places and obscuring the lights above.

Last summer, he'd fought gargoyles by teleporting onto their backs and cutting them down. But gargoyles didn't have hands to grab him or swords to swing. If he killed the medicine man first but was unable to cut the pouch off his body quickly enough, would he get a second chance?

The group ran past Sage's hiding spot, and he was reminded again of just how large and scary they looked. The medicine man was the fiercest fighter, Aquila said, and the most heavily armed. That made him target number one, in Sage's view. It was time to stop thinking about it. Nick was almost out of time.

He teleported ahead again, this time onto higher ground. Now almost two hundred yards ahead of them, he closely studied their speed by picking out a spot and noting how much time elapsed from the time the line of lead runners passed a certain point until the medicine man arrived. Less than two seconds. Fifteen yards separated each of the groups. Sage wasn't as skilled at teleporting as Elsbeth—not by a long shot—but he could get in and out of a spot faster today than he'd been able to last summer. He would have one shot to create mass confusion. One.

Sage crouched into a leveraged battle position, right leg planted firmly, left leg bent, ready to absorb the collision about to occur. He gripped his sword in a locked and cocked position. He picked the exact spot he would appear and waited.

Now!

He appeared two yards in front of the medicine man and drove his sword into the center of his chest. Sage held on with every ounce of strength, spun, and pulled his sword out as the large Belphei grunted, stumbled, and fell forward. He teleported away just as the line of four Belphei behind him were about to trample him. The medicine man's falling body caused three of the Belphei running behind him to stumble and fall. Shouts rose in unison as the lead runners stopped and turned back. As the blood on Sage's sword sizzled itself away, he crouched lower behind a rock to avoid being seen.

The fallen beasts scrambled to their feet. All of them pulled their swords and began talking at once. Sage couldn't understand the words, but when one of them began talking louder than the others, mimicking Sage's actions, Sage knew what was being said. The rest began searching the area and focused heavily on the rock formation Sage had hidden himself within.

The medicine man was dead. Sage knew that for sure. He'd driven his sword straight through his heart, assuming the heart of the beast was where he guessed it would be. One of the Belphei dropped to his knees to look at him, and it only took a few seconds to confirm what Sage knew.

"Come on," Sage whispered. "Cut the pouch off. Come on."

As if receiving mental commands, one of the Belphei rolled the medicine man over, sliced through the strap holding the medicine pouch in place, and cut away the thick leather belt that secured it to his waist. As soon as the Belphei stood and turned toward one of the other beasts, Sage teleported next to him, grabbed the pouch with his free hand, and teleported back into the chamber where Nick lay dying.

"Here," Sage told Aquila. "Make Nick better."

Father.

The meeting raged around Belphegor, yet his thoughts were a mile underground. When he heard Zagan's voice, he raised his hand to quiet those around him. It took a moment for the five men and seven women to fall silent, but when they did, Sloth rose from his chair and pointed to his smartphone. "Something's come up. Please carry on without me." Several faces frowned, but they said nothing. Nor would they dare.

One moment, Zagan. I am isolating myself. He entered his office moments later and spoke to the guard before closing the door. "I am not to be disturbed." Once seated, he gazed out at the plush lawn and the roving armed patrols that secured the grounds. He couldn't ignore the irony that his biggest threat came not from men with guns who would assault this place but from a boy not yet old enough to drive. *I am ready for your accounting, Zagan.*

There is much to report, Father. I had just arrived within the Depths when I saw the angel boy and the man with Strength approaching from a distance. I hid myself. The man with Strength carried the younger brother. The boy is sick, stabbed by the Double Horn who found him after his descent. Soon, two Pure Ones arrived and led them away.

The Elioudians. Sloth sighed and leaned back in his chair. Could he have scripted his plan to run any smoother? He thought not. *Where did they go?*

The Pure Ones led them toward their nearest gate but were soon set upon by Nearatook's band of Belphei you sent to retrieve the boy.

Nearatook had been late in arriving. Sloth had known that as soon as he connected with the Belphei leader's mind. Not of real consequence, especially given the presence of the two Elioudians. Sloth had hoped the Pure Ones would intervene like they did, but had they not, Nearatook would have carried out Sloth's orders and eventually delivered the prisoners to them. *Continue.*

The Pure Ones led them to a cave. Half of Nearatook's band remained outside. Soon, the group waiting outside fled, and later, the angel boy appeared in front of the cave, found tracks to follow, and disappeared. He seeks the medicine man to heal his sick brother. I will wait here until the Pure Ones leave the cave and lead them through their gate.

Sloth knew of Nearatook's death; he'd seen the event through Nearatook's eyes. The speed of the boy's teleportation and the decisiveness of his sword strike had caused Sloth to flinch and nearly fall from his chair during the meeting. Several in the room had looked his way as sweat broke out along his hairline and dampened the collar of his shirt. This boy . . . this boy terrified him. His total lack of fear, the eagerness in his eyes, his hatred toward those who threatened the life of his brother. Even now, Sloth's hands trembled at the thought of what awaited him should the boy defeat his plan.

Should I follow the Pure Ones from here, Father, or await the arrival within the Depths of the old man, the girl with Light, and the others they bring?

Mammon's death had weakened the other six. Lucifer had mentioned it when they stood amidst the destruction inside Mammon's collection site. The purifying light from the girl was the cause. Is that why he trembled and flinched when the boy so easily slew Nearatook? He closed his eyes and took several cleansing breaths. He needed to relax. Yes, the boy was dangerous, as were other members of the Council, but Sloth's plan was about *more* than just defeating the boy. It was about building an empire. His plan was working better than he ever expected, but . . . the determination in the boy's eyes . . .

Father?

Follow the boy until he is secured behind the gate of the Pure Place.

Yes, Father.

Belphegor turned again toward the window overlooking the lawn. The bullet-resistant glass gave the scene a tinted look, as though the sun had drifted behind the clouds. Soon, he hoped, it would be time to contact Gadrell and instruct him to make final preparations for his release. The world, sunny and bright today, would look decidedly different should Gadrell and his disciples join him in the human realm. Darkness was coming. Finally.

Elsbeth heard men's voices and looked at her phone to see the time. Two a.m. She sat up and saw light glowing through the canvas of the tent. Sage's grandfather had said he would set up a circle of portable halogens as a landing zone for Kato Hunter and the historian.

She climbed to her feet, unzipped the tent, and stuck her head out. Steven stood halfway between the campsite and the mouth of the cave, watching two men unbuckle themselves from their parachute harnesses. She recognized Kato immediately—tall and lean; a slick, bald head; and a hatchet face that seemed to scowl even when he was happy. The other man, Horace Brahms, she'd never seen before. His frail body hunched against a harness that appeared bulky and uncomfortable. Like Kato, he was bald, but not by choice. He wore thick glasses and braces on both knees. He was having difficulty unbuckling himself.

"Let me help you," Steven said.

Elsbeth reached back inside her tent and pulled her boots on. She'd slept in her clothes, and her hair felt like a rat's nest. She found a ball cap in her backpack. After stretching and wiping the sleep from her eyes, she stepped out of the tent. "Hello there," she said.

Steven looked over. "Sorry to wake you, Elsbeth."

Kato dropped his harness to the ground and looked over. "Hello, young lady. It's so good to see you again, although I wish it were under different circumstances." He walked over and gave her a hug.

The three large scars that once ran down the middle of Kato's face were gone, fixed by plastic surgery in the year since she'd seen him last. He seemed more muscular, too. She'd always considered him the most intimidating black man she'd ever met. Removing his scars helped soften him up some, in her eyes, but danger and death still oozed from his every pore.

"You look good," she said, touching where his scars once dominated his face. "But Sage won't be nearly as frightened of you."

"If you could have seen us sword fight the day I met him, you would know he has no cause to fear me." Kato leaned forward and lowered his voice, his eyes bright with excitement. "I've found someone, Elsbeth."

She frowned for a moment, then realized what he meant. "A woman?"

He smiled and gave her a hug. "Yes, the most beautiful creature in all creation! The past three months have been a whirlwind. We're getting married as soon as I get back!"

Elsbeth laughed and hugged him back. "Congratulations! Who is she? What's her name? Where'd you meet her?"

"Her name is Savannah. I can't wait to tell you about her, but right at this moment, I'm being rude." Kato turned and held a hand out. "Meet Horace Brahms, Council historian. A man crazy enough to jump from a perfectly fine airplane in the middle of the night."

Horace, now free of his harness, hobbled over and stuck out a hand. "Crazy indeed. Pleased to meet you, Elsbeth. I've heard many wonderful things about you. It's nice to finally make your acquaintance. Kato did all the hard work tonight. He even provided a soft landing."

"I'll unhook the crate," Kato said. He smiled at Elsbeth as he walked off, mouthing the name Savannah.

"I'll help," Steven said.

Elsbeth was so happy for him. If anyone deserved someone special, it was Kato. She looked at the landing spot and saw a four-foot-square wooden crate just outside the circle of light and a collapsed parachute beside it. A long rope ran from the crate to the harness Kato had worn. Impressive. He'd not only descended with Horace attached to him but guided the crate along the way.

"Join me," Horace said. He pointed toward the chairs by the tents. "The younger men will attend to the gear. This old man needs to take a load off." He moved like the old man he was, placing each foot carefully before planting the next. He slumped down into a chair with a huge sigh and wiped his forehead. "My first field assignment in more than two hundred years. I must admit to a certain level of excitement when we jumped from the plane. Brought back memories of death and destruction. Good old days." He smiled at her.

"Tell me about your gift," Elsbeth said.

"Ha! I've served as a decoy, mostly. Played tricks with Animation. Distracted the beasts long enough for the real warriors to finish the job. History is my real passion, and I'm thankful for the opportunity to help with that."

Animation was the ability to bring certain inanimate objects to life for brief periods of time. A line-of-sight gift, one had to be in close physical proximity to the object and have total focus on the task. Elsbeth knew that Horace spoke the truth. Council members with Animation were part of a team, never sent into battle alone. They did very little killing and were rarely the tip of the spear against Dark creatures.

"You might be the most important part of our team," Elsbeth said. "We need information. Intelligence about what we'll face."

"My information is six thousand years old, Elsbeth. You do understand that, correct?"

"I know. But Steven says you have a map of the Territories."

"Indeed. I do. A copy." Horace leaned forward, his eyes on fire. "The original map was given to me as a boy by my great-grandfather. It was bundled with dozens of other handwritten accounts from the original two hundred. Great-Grandfather got it from his grandfather, who drew it from memory the moment he stepped foot on Topside."

This was a goldmine. Elsbeth felt a flame of hope growing within her. "That's wonderful news."

"Do you know how many times I studied that map as a child?" Horace asked. "Wishing I could explore the Territories?" He laughed and shook his head sadly. "The hours I wasted. And now that the Territories will be explored, I'm too old to fulfill my fantasy."

Elsbeth smiled politely but didn't feel bad for him. This mission might kill people, and she wished no one had to go at all. Was the professor really that clueless?

"But this is adventure enough." Horace waved his arms around. "In the middle of the jungle, near an undiscovered entrance. I never thought I would live long enough to see such a thing."

The expression on Horace's face made Elsbeth's stomach turn. How *dare* he take all of this so lightly? Did he even *care* that Sage and Nick and Ronan were down there?

"I suspect," Horace continued, "that Tartarus and the Territories look quite different now than they did six thousand years ago. Tartarus, better; the Territories, much worse. Can you imagine what the three evil races have done to the Elioudians' original homestead?" He laughed. "It must be in shambles by now."

Elsbeth looked over at Kato and Steven, too furious to respond. They had the crate disassembled and were hauling stuff out. She felt tempted to grab one of Kato's swords and hit Horace with it.

"Kato is going to pitch three more tents," Horace said. "That way the full camp will be ready when the others arrive. I brought a special air mattress and cot. A man my age needs his beauty rest." He leaned forward again and lowered his voice. "Tell me, Elsbeth, how it feels when you use Persuasion. Would you mind?"

She almost flinched. She wasn't about to share that with a stranger, especially this clown. She'd only told Sage how it felt a few months ago when he asked, but Sage was special to her.

Persuasion was the ability to channel purifying light from heaven through her body and project it into the body of a person or creature possessing angel blood. The Dark creatures feared it more than any other gift because of its ability to flip them from Dark to Light. She hadn't seen any creatures flip from Dark to Light yet, because every creature she'd ever used it on was so far gone to the side of evil that they'd simply died. What it felt like physically when the light pulsed through her body was nearly indescribable and so personal that she found it difficult to talk about.

"How does it feel to be the only one with such a powerful gift?" Horace asked.

"I feel inadequate next to Sage," she said after a beat. "He has six gifts that are stronger now than when I met him. If you had ever seen him in action, you'd know what I mean."

"Oh, I've heard the stories," Horace said. "I read the report Steven wrote about Sage's trip into Mammon's prison. It's quite remarkable."

"My gift is simply part of a bigger picture," she said. "And quite frankly, I doubt I'll even be able to use it so deep underground. I guess we'll find out." She stood and again smiled politely. "If you'll excuse me, I need to get more sleep. I'm exhausted."

"By all means," Horace said. "Thank you for your hospitality."

She zipped herself into Sage and Nick's tent feeling better about the team they were assembling. With Malcolm and Gavin Alexander due to arrive about twelve hours from now, she was hopeful the rescue team would get started much sooner than originally projected. And despite Horace's tone-deaf attitude and much-too-personal inquiry, his historical information just might be the key to their survival.

6

The battery from Ronan's flashlight was nearly dead. The long shadows in the chamber reminded Sage of just how deep under the surface they were. They'd sat for hours watching as Aquila worked Nick over with a variety of substances from the medicine pouch. He pushed ointment into the wound, then waited and watched as huge pockets of pus gathered under the skin. He squeezed the infection out, then repeated the process. Aquila told Sage that eventually all the poison would be drawn from the bloodstream, that it was simply a process of repeating the procedure many times.

Sage explained in detail how he'd snatched the bag without killing all the beasts, and both Elioudians seemed impressed by his ingenuity. Ronan slept on and off, Sage dozed some, and Ephraim guarded the entrance. After Ronan's light completely died, he dug a second one out of his bag and turned it on.

Nick was sleeping now, breathing easy, and his color was nearly back to normal. His eyes weren't clear yet, but Sage saw the white returning and his pupils shrinking to normal size. Aquila told them that he wanted Nick to sleep awhile before they resumed their journey to Tartarus. Ephraim asked Sage quietly, "How many decade celebration days have been recorded in your Book of Ages?"

Book of Ages? "I'm fifteen years old," Sage said. For the last hour, he'd been thinking about finally asking the one question he'd had since dropping through the hole. He might as well ask it now. "How do we get out of here? Back to the surface?"

Both Elioudians were quiet for several moments. Then Aquila answered. "No Topsider has ever returned to the surface. Not since my name was added to the Book of Ages."

Sage was about to speak when Ephraim did. "That is not quite true. They can be led to the Great Granite Gate through the Territories."

Aquila faced the younger Elioudian. "Your proposal would defy the primary law of Samyaza. Interference in the fate of humans is strictly forbidden."

"Samyaza's sin lives no more, Aquila." Ephraim glanced at Sage and Ronan before again addressing Aquila. "The law was enacted in ancient times, before the flood, once the Elioudians realized that Samyaza's sin led to the destruction of humanity. His interference created all the beasts that have terrorized humans since." He again turned to Aquila. "Surely we would not abide by it and prevent humans from traveling back to the surface."

"Travel through the Territories would be the death of them and their Elioudian escorts," Aquila said. "You are too young to understand. You do not know the history."

"I am *not* too young," Ephraim said. "I have recorded eighty-six decade celebration days in the Book of Ages. I have heard the stories."

Eighty-six decade celebration days? Ephraim was 860 years old? Had Sage heard that right?

"Ephraim, you are too young," Aquila said again. "The stories hide reality. Yes, we Elioud will cause no harm to a Topsider, but to try and pass them through the villages of the Emim is certain death. And what of the Rephaim? And the Nephilim? Would they not also kill them? I tell you, it cannot be done. It has never been done. We would be interfering with their lives. Their fate."

Aquila's voice was almost musical; it radiated a peace that put Sage at ease. Despite that peace, he didn't like what he'd just heard. Ephraim was trying to get them out of here, but Aquila wasn't buying it.

"But Aquila," Ephraim said. "The stories of old tell of safe passage for the Topsiders. Have my elders filled my head with nonsense?"

"We have rescued those Topsiders that have dropped from the surface, Ephraim. We agreed to allow them safe passage, because we knew their arrival would not be of their choosing. None, however, made it back to the surface. Your childhood stories served to shield you from the atrocities of the Nephilim and their ilk."

"What of Spartacus?" asked Ephraim. "*You* are the elder who told me that tale. Were you merely protecting my sensibilities, or was he not allowed safe passage?"

"Spartacus?" Sage asked. "Do you mean the gladiator who led an uprising against the Roman Republic?" Sage had seen a movie about him.

"It wasn't so long ago," Aquila said. "Only two hundred decade celebration days. I myself warned him of the dangers outside the walls of our villages. He took no heed."

Sage did the math in his head, too stunned to speak. Aquila was over two thousand years old.

Aquila addressed Ephraim. "Yes, Spartacus did fall into Tartarus, which is why the Topsiders never found his body after the Third Servile War. And yes, he insisted to be allowed passage. He was a great warrior on Topside. He believed he could wield his sword effectively enough to make it back. I warned him that he would be killed. I pleaded with him to stay, for I did not want God's wrath to fall upon me. He took no heed. A scout shadowed him as he began his journey. He was ripped apart outside the very first Emim village. There was nothing the scout could do for him. Had he attempted to save him, he also would have been killed. No Elioud agreed to accompany him, for they feared certain death." Aquila's voice had softened to the point of being hard to hear. "I chose to withhold that from you, yes, Ephraim, because you were young, but I did not say he made it to the surface."

Ephraim said nothing for a moment. "What of John Cabot, the explorer?"

"We allowed him passage, but no Elioud agreed to guide him. So, he changed course. He yet lives in the village of Seth."

"And Henry Hudson?" Ephraim asked, exasperated. "Was he also refused escort by the Elioud and allowed to perish?" His voice had risen to double its volume. "Are we so heartless that we allow God's chosen creatures to be slaughtered? Are we ruled by our cowardice? We follow the primary law of Samyaza, yet what good is it if our heartlessness also results in their deaths?"

"You must lower your voice," Aquila whispered. "Henry Hudson yet lives in the village of Seth, as do all of the Topsiders who have stumbled from the surface and yet live."

"Is that why the village of Seth is so heavily restricted?" Ephraim asked. "The tale of Nephilim attacks upon the village of Seth is a deception to protect Topsiders? Not one has yet again reached the surface?"

Aquila was about to answer when Nick shouted Sage's name. Sage jumped to his feet and rushed over. He put a hand on Nick's shoulder. "I'm here."

Nick's eyes popped open and stared, confused, for several moments. Then he reached up and grabbed Sage and hugged him tightly for a long time. He finally pulled away and looked at him in a full panic. "Something grabbed me, Sage. I don't know what it was." He swallowed hard. "It . . . it had claws. A slick, black head and big eyes. I know it sounds crazy, but it had wings, Sage. Big wings. I mean . . . it looked like . . . it looked like a demon." Tears flooded his eyes. "I'm not joking. It was huge. Like, seven feet tall or something. Did you see it? You were right behind me. Did you see it?"

Sage didn't say anything for several beats. He finally answered. "Yeah, Nick, I saw it."

"Oh, man! I'm not crazy?" Relief washed over his face. "What happened? What was it? Where did it go? Did it shove you down the hole, too?"

"It ran off," Sage said. "It slipped under the flat rock and ran off." He started to say something else but didn't.

"What?" Nick asked. "What else were you gonna say? Do you know what it was?"

Again, Sage hesitated. "I told Grandpa. He's calling people to come help us, but it's going to take them a while to get here. Ronan's here. With us."

Ronan stepped up and leaned over Nick. "I'm here, big guy, and we've got this under control."

"What was it? That thing? Do you know?" Nick's eyes were wild; his breathing shot out in little spurts.

"I don't know its precise name," Sage said, "but you know what? You're safe. Right?" He glanced at Ronan, then looked at Nick and gripped his shoulder. "Listen, we're thousands of feet below the surface, so it's going to be really hard to get out of here. Can you see OK?"

"Things are a little blurry, but I can see fine." Nick attempted to sit up but struggled.

"He needs to rest for another hour or so," Aquila said. "His strength will return quickly, but he is not yet ready to travel."

Nick jerked his head around at the unfamiliar voice. He flinched and started to scream when he saw the two Elioudians standing side by side. Sage maneuvered himself in front of Nick's vision. "They're friends, Nick. They saved your life."

"What . . . what are they?" Tears burst from his eyes as he tried to hold himself together. "Where are we? I don't understand." He tried saying more, but he couldn't get his mouth to work.

"Do not be afraid," Aquila said. "We are here to help you."

Then Nick saw the dead Belphei and screamed again. He scooted as far away as he could, all the way to the edge of the wall.

"They can't hurt us anymore," Sage said. "We're safe. OK? We're gonna be fine. These two guys are Aquila and Ephraim. Elioudians. Good guys. Friends. A race of ancient beings I never thought I'd get to meet."

Without taking his eyes off the dead Belphei, Nick frowned. "You've *heard* of them?"

"They've lived down here for a long time," Sage said. "They fled the surface to save their race from the waters of the Great Flood."

"They were one of the evil races, but they repented," Ronan said.

Nick leaned over and looked around Sage. He swallowed hard, glanced at Ronan, looked at Sage, studied the Elioudians again, and then stared at the dead beasts. With a quivering bottom lip, he said, "What evil races?"

Sage took a deep breath. Before he could answer, Ronan took over. "There's a world within your world, Nick, that we need to tell you about. There's a war being waged that you're now a part of. Since we can't move you for a while, now's the best time to clue you in." Ronan paused, then sat down next to Nick. "I'm about to give Nick a history lesson, so I'd suggest everyone get comfortable."

Sage sat next to Nick, which allowed his brother to stare at Aquila and Ephraim as Ronan spoke. "In the beginning," Ronan began, "God sent Watchers to earth to protect mankind. The Watchers were purely angelic but able to interact physically with humans. They had supernatural powers and turned evil when they began seeing themselves as gods.

"They committed an abomination in God's eyes when they mated with human women, producing four races of angelic-human offspring: Nephilim, Emim, Rephaim, and Elioud. The crossbreeding with human women—the corruption of flesh with the birds of the air and the beasts of the field—ran rampant throughout the earth. Wickedness reigned. Blasphemy spewed from the mouths of corrupted humans. The purity of man dwindled to a point that the only cure was to begin again."

Sage watched Nick as Ronan spoke. His brother was fixated on the two Elioudians, who didn't look that far removed from their angelic ancestors. Their bleached-white skin, huge eyes, rippling muscles, and reverent demeanor made it hard for Sage to comprehend their existence, and he'd lived his entire life knowing of them. He couldn't imagine what emotions were swirling around inside Nick.

"Through Noah," Ronan said, "God warned those who polluted the earth that unless they turned from their sinful ways, they would be destroyed. For 120 years, while Noah built the ark, he cautioned others of their coming destruction.

"Only the repentant Elioudians believed Noah. They prepared for their own survival by traveling to the deepest caverns to dig an underground world. Every male and female Elioudian dedicated their lives to saving their race. For more than a century they dug into the earth until they established a hiding place large enough to house all their people. They created a massive tunnel and built the Great Granite Gate, the only entrance into the underworld and easily strong enough to stop the floodwaters from destroying them."

Ronan paused and looked at Aquila. "I'm speaking your history as I learned it during my training at the Tomb of Ancient Documents. Have I gotten it right?"

"Yes," Aquila said. "You omitted how the Elioudians battled the evil races while digging their new homeland, but all you have said is accurate. Please continue."

"Like Noah did before boarding the ark," Ronan told Nick, "the Elioudians gathered animals of all types and took them into their great underground chambers. Their survival depended upon their ability to adapt to a life without sunlight. Despite being a new world, it was rich in natural resources. Elioudian scientists, gifted with intelligence reflective of the purity of their angelic blood, discovered electricity before the Great Flood. They erected a lighting system and growing lights, great generators to power their world. They perfected advanced building techniques, indoor plumbing, and sewer systems. They understood crop rotation and farming, the most effective way to raise livestock. They built libraries and learning centers for their children. In short, by the time the floodwaters destroyed everything on the surface, their new home was nearly complete. Like Noah, they were being guided by angels and directed by God. Their intent was to never live on the surface again."

Sage sat spellbound at Ronan's words. Because he had not yet studied at the Tomb, his own knowledge of the Elioudians and Tartarus was almost nonexistent. He leaned close to Nick and whispered, "Can you believe this?"

"Amazing," Nick whispered back.

"Unknown to the Elioudians at that time," Ronan continued, "the Nephilim, Emim, and Rephaim noted what the Elioudians were accomplishing. With barely enough time to save themselves, they banded together and created their own underground chamber. They secured themselves into great caverns not far from the entrance to the Elioudians' new world, but unlike the Elioudians, they had no intention of living underground forever. They simply created a haven in case Noah's warning of floodwaters came true. They brought enough supplies to last a few dozen years but knew they would eventually go back to the surface.

"When the rains began, and when the fountains of the great deep erupted and spewed water on the surface of earth, the Elioudians were safe, but the evil races were caught unaware. A few from each species survived behind their own granite gate, but most were lost in the flood. Those that did live found themselves trapped underground when great earthquakes forever sealed their entrance back to the surface."

Nick and Sage had grown up listening to Ronan tell stories. He had an easy cadence, emphasized all the right words, and really put feelings into what he was saying. This history lesson had Nick hanging on every syllable. A look of wonder replaced fear, and he was mostly watching Ronan now, not Aquila and Ephraim.

Ronan took a sip of water from one of his water bottles. "After the flood, dozens of empty caverns of enormous size—each hundreds of miles across and much deeper than the hand-dug areas the Elioudians prepared before the flood—presented an opportunity for them to expand their underground world. Over the course of five hundred years, they occupied and developed the caverns into their new home, abandoning the areas they had constructed prior to the flood. They called this new home Tartarus.

"Just before the Elioudians were ready to abandon their hand-dug caverns and seal themselves inside their new homeland, the survivors of the evil races finally succeeded in digging a passageway into the Elioudian chambers from the caves they had been trapped in for five centuries. A great battle ensued, but the Elioudians fought them off and barricaded themselves inside Tartarus. That left their original home to their evil cousins, and it became known as the Territories. They opened the Great Granite Gate, which allowed passage to and from earth's surface, but their numbers were so few they did not stray far from their underground homeland.

"Like the Elioudians, the evil ones dragged thousands of animals into their temporary caverns, and when the Elioudians moved into Tartarus, they moved everything over to the Territories. They captured and imprisoned one species the Elioudians did not: humans."

Sage knew Ronan was approaching the most important part of the history. He'd emphasized the word *humans* just before pausing and staring intently at Nick. This was it. This would be where everything would start to make sense to Nick, if, of course, he could link the history to the monster that had shoved him down the hole.

"Just before the flood," Ronan said, "the evil races had captured only a few dozen human men and women. But by the time they moved into the Territories five centuries later, there were several hundred, all held prisoner. For a full century after moving into the Territories, the Great Granite Gate remained open, and those several hundred grew into the thousands. While the three races increased the numbers of their own people, they experimented on the humans, bred them, and mixed their DNA with animals of all kinds. As the population on the surface expanded, the evil races continued dragging more humans in, building bigger pens and dedicating pockets of the Territories as slave labor camps. They dug caves and pits and secluded chambers for the experiments. They ate those that died and used their bones for medicine and weapons and jewelry."

Nick's face paled even more. Sage had never seen anyone so terrified, but he said nothing. He knew Nick needed to hear this. Ronan's words echoed in the small chamber, which gave the story an even creepier feel.

"The evil races sought immortality," Ronan said. "And superhuman strength. They sought to craft legions of beasts that would obey them to their dying breath. And they sought to breed into them a hatred for humans unmatched in all creation.

"It was during the unveiling of a new Emim human-animal abomination, an event treated as a grand celebration by all in the Territories, that the Great Granite Gate was closed and locked by the Magog, the largest of the Nephilim giants, who had struck a deal with the Archangels. Every Emim, every Rephaim, every Nephilim, and every offspring they had created or manufactured was trapped, never to be freed again. Rumors of the Territories grew widely on the surface of the earth. They came to be known as Hell."

They sat in silence as Ronan took another sip of water. The Elioudians stood quietly and offered no comment nor showed any expressions. Sage had heard most of this history from Leah, but hearing it again, in this setting and after having just killed several angelic-human abominations, which lay dead around them, gave all of it new meaning.

"A century passed," Ronan continued, "and the evil races increased in number. Their rage grew as the Magog refused to relent and allow passage to the surface. Finally, other sects of the Nephilim race banded with the Emim and Rephaim and attacked the gate. Many were slaughtered at the hands of the Magog, but the evil races prevailed for a brief time and succeeded in momentarily opening the Gate. Seven Rephaim escaped, along with dozens of Emim beasts and some of every other Nephilim sect. The Magog rallied in the battle and secured the Gate once more, driving the beasts back into the Territories. The seven Rephaim now rule the evil beasts prowling the surface to this day. Those seven are the Princes of Hell."

Ronan stood and stretched. He looked at everyone, then knelt and put a hand on Nick's shoulder. "The monster you saw, the beast that shoved you down the hole, was a descendent of one of the Seven Princes. These monsters lying dead around us? More abominations that exist in the shadows of our world. I will tell you more history later, but understand this: we are in a war, these Elioudians, your brother, and I, and you have been drawn into it now."

Sage couldn't read the emotions running across Nick's face, but he knew his brother hadn't heard any of the important stuff yet. The history of the Elioudians, the Angelic Response Council, the supernatural powers gifted to the Council members, or the battles Sage had been in. He didn't know why Ronan had stopped the history lesson there, but he trusted the big man to do what was best.

"I think we could all use some quiet time before we head out," Ronan said. "Aquila, what do you think?"

"I think that is wise counsel," Aquila said.

Ronan walked to the far side of the chamber, stuck his head into the opening leading out, and listened for a moment. Sage joined him there. "You left out the most important stuff," Sage whispered.

"Yes," Ronan said. "Didn't want to overwhelm him. Let him digest that for a bit. He'll be OK. He's a strong kid."

Sage glanced back at his brother. His thousand-yard stare was focused on a blank wall in front of him. Yeah, he was digesting. Big time. "OK," Sage said. "We'll go with that. Best to feed him only a few impossibilities at a time."

"Exactly so." Ronan slapped Sage on the shoulder before making his way back to Nick and sitting down beside him.

Sage moved away from the dead bodies of the Belphei. Between the two Elioudians standing guard and the dead monsters littering the floor, it wouldn't take much for Nick to believe the wild history lesson he'd just heard. What Nick probably didn't realize yet was that he would soon be part of a group about to make its own history.

Elsbeth watched the two parachutes descend from the sky as quietly as feathers. She blocked the morning sun with a hand as they floated toward them. Steven stood beside her, Kato next to him. Horace was asleep in his tent, a portable fan blowing on his cot.

"How long since you've seen them?" Elsbeth asked Steven.

"About a year," Steven said. "After Sage's mission last summer, after you and Sage went to Council headquarters, I arranged to meet Malcolm and Gavin in London for a weekend. They were fresh off a trip to southern Spain and were in London for some R&R. I gave them a blow-by-blow of your adventures in Mammon's prison."

"Families are like that," Kato said. "Always in each other's business." He smiled when he said it, and Steven nodded knowingly.

"They're both excited to meet you, Elsbeth," Steven added. "Malcolm once said that you and Sage would become the ultimate power couple."

Elsbeth's face heated up, but she didn't say anything. She cared for Sage, certainly, more than anyone except her father, but she wasn't about to go *that* far.

"If we can get the rest of the team to parachute in, we can get this show on the road." Kato looked at Steven. "Any chance of that happening?"

"Endora agreed to it," Steven said. "And David Brock. Endora will drop in early tomorrow morning, David tomorrow afternoon. Theo will chopper in tomorrow evening."

"So, that's everyone," Elsbeth said. "We make our descent the day after tomorrow?"

"Thirty-six hours," Steven said. "Four days sooner than I thought possible."

"Well, then," Kato said. "That's what I'm talking about."

Elsbeth sighed contently. Perfect. She'd seen Steven on the phone just a few minutes before and knew he'd been talking to

David and Theo. And though he looked pleased when he hung up, she'd had no idea the news was that good. The rescue team would only be three days behind Sage, Ronan, and Nick.

"Watch out," Steven said, backing up. "Looks like Gavin's going to miss his spot."

Malcolm dropped nearly straight down, landing dead center in the drop zone Steven had set up for Kato the night before. But Gavin yelled as he pulled his left toggle and leaned his body as far away from Horace's tent as he could. It didn't work. He crashed into the side of the tent, and the whole thing collapsed. Kato and Steven ran over just as Horace began shouting.

"Brilliant, Gavin," Malcolm yelled. He laughed as he pulled his parachute toward him.

Gavin picked himself off the ground and ran toward Malcolm, dragging everything off Horace's tent.

"What's that?" Horace's muffled voice sounded more irritated than scared. "What happened?" The historian punched and kicked the tent as Steven and Kato, both laughing, pulled around on the canvas until Steven found the door and unzipped it.

"Can a man not get a decent nap?" Horace said, as he crawled out on his hands and knees. Once free, he stood and looked around, his face a deep shade of red. "I really don't think anything is that funny."

"Sorry, Horace," Gavin said, as he crumpled his parachute into a tight ball. "A gust of wind caught me at the last moment."

Malcolm rolled his eyes and snorted. Gavin shot him a nasty look.

"I haven't felt even one puff of breeze since arriving in this forsaken tub of humidity, so I'd really like to know what wind you're referring to," Horace said. "Did you fail skydiving?"

"Now, now, Horace," Kato said. "Don't underestimate the difficulty of hitting a drop zone, especially one as small as that. You yearned for adventure. Don't complain when it drops in on your head." He laughed again and slapped Horace on the back.

Malcolm and Gavin Alexander could have been twins, Elsbeth thought as they peeled off their harnesses and helmets. Elvis One and Elvis Two. Nick had tagged them perfectly. Both were strapping, muscular men with jet-black hair that fell to their shoulders. Malcolm had a goatee where Gavin was clean shaven, but they had the same dark, penetrating brown eyes and square jaw. Elsbeth approached both and introduced herself.

"Ah, yes, the girl with two gifts," Gavin said.

"The girl with Persuasion," Malcolm said. "The talk of Council members everywhere. One half of the ultimate power couple."

"Don't make stuff up," Elsbeth said. "Just friends with Sage."

The brothers looked at each other and laughed. "Yeah," Gavin said. "Just friends with Sage. The team that killed one of the Seven Princes of Hell. Yep, just a couple of ordinary teenagers."

Elsbeth was somewhat aware of her growing fame among the Council, and, of course, Sage's name was already the most well known of all. This was her first real opportunity to spend time around multiple Council members, and she really hadn't prepared herself for the attention given to her, first by Horace and now by these two. Praise wasn't something she'd been exposed to growing up.

"We've looked forward to this trip," Malcolm said. He looked at his brother. "Haven't we?"

"It's all we've talked about for the last twenty-four hours." Gavin glanced at his father, who was helping Kato erect Horace's tent, and lowered his voice. "There isn't a Council member worth their salt who wouldn't give their left arm to travel into Tartarus and explore the Territories."

"Target-rich environment," Malcolm chimed in. "You want my opinion? Now that we've discovered a way in, we should send every Council member we have down there and clean it out for good."

The Alexander brothers stared at Elsbeth with an intensity that made her nervous. She worked up a nod, but not much else. Were they serious?

"Scare you, did we?" Gavin asked. "We're not crazy." He pointed to Steven. "We told him that on the phone when he called yesterday. Think about it. What's to stop more creatures down there from escaping? Huh? It took the Council six thousand years to find the first Rephaim Prince. What's to say there aren't a hundred more down there just like them? We want them up here?"

"I think not," Malcolm said.

"I think the only reason we haven't gone down there before now is because we didn't know how," Gavin said. "But that problem is solved. Let's take advantage of it."

Elsbeth was about to respond, but Horace didn't give her a chance. "The two of you have lost your collective minds," he said. "Foolishness." The historian hobbled over and faced Gavin directly. "Risk the entire Council on one mission? That's your plan? Two hundred of us came out of Tartarus, and two hundred of us remain. Does that tell you nothing?" Gavin looked at Malcolm and shrugged. "It explains why angelic gifts skip generations," Horace said. "God struck a bargain with our ancestors—two hundred of us would be granted gifts. As Council members die, more are born. It's the order of things. Yet you would risk the entirety of our people for one suicide mission?" The old man laughed. "Youth. Invincibility. Really, gentlemen, you should think things through." He walked away shaking his head, wiping sweat off his brow, and mumbling under his breath.

"Well," Elsbeth said. "This has already been an educational trip." She laughed nervously and glanced at Steven and Kato, who had stopped working to watch the show.

"I'm afraid my boys are more like me than I realized," Steven said.

"I like their attitude," Kato said. "Take the fight to them."

"In theory, the idea has merit," Steven told Horace, who'd planted himself in a chair outside Steven's tent. "I admit that sending the entire Council down there would be reckless, especially for the older members, at least until we know what we'd be facing. But to rid the earth of potential threats isn't, on the surface, out of bounds."

"I suspect we'd see some foes down there that are now extinct up here," Kato said.

"Like what?" Elsbeth asked. "What creatures are for certain extinct up here?" She asked the question because she'd learned in the Tomb that such thinking would only get you killed. She was surprised to hear Kato harbor that opinion.

"Well, we've not seen an ahool in nearly seventy-five years," Kato said.

"Ah, vampire delicacy," Horace said. "Feasting on one of the ingredients that created them."

It was true. Ahools, giant, blood-sucking bats, had been used by Emim alchemists to create vampires, among other things. Vampires had then hunted ahools until few, if any, still existed.

"Easy on the talk of vampires around Malcolm," Gavin said. "I've nearly lost him dozens of times battling those beasts. He breaks out in a cold sweat at the mere mention of them."

The Alexander brothers walked over and sat on the ground next to Horace's chair. "Try absorbing the powers of a vampire," Malcolm said, "and see how you like it."

"I'll stick to lopping off their heads after you've done the hard work," Gavin joked.

"What else is extinct?" Elsbeth asked, getting the conversation back on track.

Kato straightened the final pole on Horace's tent and tied it off. "Well, the girtablilu, for sure."

Elsbeth frowned. "What's that?"

"Scorpion man," Horace said. "The head, torso, and arms of a man and the body of a scorpion. Nasty beast. Not seen since Kato was a boy."

"The last one I saw," Kato said, "was mounted on a pole in a village not far from my childhood home."

"Not sure they're extinct, though," Steven said, looking at Malcolm and Gavin. "Remember Rome?"

"Not sure that's what it was, though," Malcolm said. He looked at Elsbeth. "Gavin and I were in Rome helping Dad find some ancient relic or something—don't remember for sure—which required us to break into a crypt belonging to a reputed wizard from Casape, a mountain town east of the city. The cemetery was dark and foggy, scary movie stuff, and we saw what looked like a girtablilu. But it ran off before we knew for sure."

"That's what it was," Gavin said. "We found venom."

"What we *think* was venom," Steven said. "Anyway, we've hijacked Elsbeth's question. I suspect Kato is correct. We'll find creatures in the Territories that we haven't seen up here for many moons. I guess none of us know for sure what's extinct and what's not."

"Like I said before," Malcolm said. "Target-rich environment."

"Likewise, for them," Horace said. "Do not underestimate what changes the beasts might have undergone in six thousand years." He looked at each of them and didn't flinch when Gavin chuckled.

"We're bringing a strong team," Gavin said. "Your words of confidence overwhelm me."

Horace shrugged. "And I will overwhelm you further once I brief all of you tomorrow. It's why I'm here: to give you an accurate accounting, despite how horrid the information."

The serious expression on the historian's face worried Elsbeth. She'd tried engaging Horace in conversation at breakfast about what he would be briefing them about once the full team was assembled, but he wasn't having any of that. He told her he was too old to repeat everything multiple times. Right now, Horace looked scared. Despite his status as a clinically cool scholar, he wore an expression of anxious dread.

The group just looked at each other until Malcolm broke the silence. "Kato, let's see what kind of toys you brought."

"In my tent," Kato said.

After the others left, Elsbeth looked at Horace. "It's bad, isn't it? The information about the Territories."

Horace dabbed his brow with a handkerchief. "For all that you may discover, when I think of what you may face down there—it is unimaginable, Ms. Brown."

7

Aquila led them out of the caves, and soon they were hiking over a terrain as rough as some spots in the Rocky Mountains. Not as tall, Sage knew, but the jagged rocks and steep cliffs were similar. The skeletons were fewer but still numerous enough to make him wonder just how many beasts must have occupied the Wastelands at some point.

They traveled for a long time, and Nick seemed to get stronger by the minute. Aquila told them to keep their talking to a minimum. They were still within the Dark spiritual realm; Sage could tell by the slightly offset color that gave everything a greenish-blue hint. They hadn't been there long enough for Nick to begin hallucinating, assuming the history of such things was accurate.

When the landscape flattened, Aquila pointed ahead to an area much brighter than the rest of the Wastelands. Their approach marked a stark increase of bones. Hundreds of skeletons, maybe thousands, littered the ground. A path had been cleared at some point, and piles of bones lined each side. Ahead, near an opening in a cliff face, were three Elioudians with spears, standing at attention. Aquila walked ahead, and the rest of them stopped several yards back. They spoke in a language Sage didn't recognize. The guards looked at Nick and Sage for several seconds and then inspected Ronan even longer. Finally, they stood aside, and Aquila motioned them forward. Sage noticed thousands of gouge marks in the rocks surrounding the opening and wondered how often this place had suffered attacks. They crossed over a large groove in the floor, walked several more feet, then stopped. Aquila barked an order, and the three sentries moved to a large wheel a few yards to the right and began cranking it around and around.

"Wait!" Ronan shouted, turning to Aquila. "We've got help coming." Aquila shouted an order, and the guards stopped. Ronan pointed to the gate. "We don't know how soon they'll get here. Several days. A week. Maybe longer. And we don't know how many there'll be, but they're our friends. Our family. They'll come to rescue us."

"Who?" Nick asked. "Who besides Grandpa?"

"Friends of Ronan's. And Grandpa's." Sage said. He turned to Aquila. "Tell these guards that more of us will show up. Can you do that? Can they open the gate and let them in?"

Aquila turned and spoke quietly to the guards. After an apparent agreement, the wheel began turning again. A two-foot-thick piece of round granite rolled out of the wall and closed the opening everyone had just passed through.

"They will allow passage," Aquila said. "Now come, we have far to travel." Without waiting for a response, he spun around and headed off, deeper into the world of Tartarus. They were alone, just the five of them, their footsteps echoing slightly off the granite floor. The tunnel they were in had structure now: granite floors and stone walls, with perfectly split logs as the ceiling. It was wide—large enough to drive a big truck through—and as straight as a ruler. It was so long that Sage couldn't see the end. Electric bulbs hung from the ceiling every fifty yards or so, creating pockets of light as far as he could see.

The greenish-blue hue was gone. Sage hadn't realized it until that moment. He glanced at Ronan and whispered, "We're out of the Dark realm. Did you notice?"

Ronan frowned and looked around. "No. But yeah, I can see it now." He motioned toward Nick. "He'll be OK now."

Sage smiled. "One hurdle gone."

"How large is Tartarus?" Nick asked the Elioudians.

"Infinite," Aquila said. "We have not yet explored it all."

Nick frowned. "But your people have been here for thousands of years. How can there still be unexplored areas?"

"We use what we need," Ephraim said. "We have little desire or need for any more space."

"So, you really can't say for sure that the only way out is through the Territories, can you?" Sage said. "You can't know *for certain* if you haven't explored it all."

"As I mentioned before, we call the unexplored areas the Wastelands," Aquila said. "You saw just a glimpse, and certainly the most tamed area. There are caverns of death, bottomless pits, dead-end trails, and passages that spew enough heat to roast you in seconds. There are poisonous streams, toxic rivers, and beds of lava that appear solid enough to walk on but will instantly suck you beneath the surface. There are packs of wild beasts that prowl the darkness, always seeking their next meal. If your thought, young Sage, is to seek another way to Topside by venturing into the Wastelands, you will be dinner for a predator Topside hasn't seen for thousands of years."

They walked. And walked. Sage noticed burn marks on the walls and floor. Gouges and cut marks, and what appeared to be dozens of dried bloodstains. There had been battles in this passage at some point. "The beasts have breached this tunnel, haven't they?" he asked.

"Yes," Aquila said. "Too many times to count. We have repelled them in each instance. They are persistent. The war is never ending."

After what seemed twenty miles but was probably only three or four, they came to a large iron gate with a single sentry standing at attention just on the other side. The guard looked the same as the others but was much taller—well over six feet—and had shoulders and arms like a bodybuilder. The signs of attack were heaviest here. The gate was thick and heavy but scarred and dented. The floors, walls, and ceiling all showed evidence of intense battles. Sage heard a humming sound that made his skin prickle.

Aquila spoke in his strange language, and the guard nodded and stepped away from the gate, disappearing behind a slab of granite to the right. After a few seconds, the humming sound died, and the guard reappeared and opened the gate.

"This is electrified, isn't it?" Sage asked. "Like the fence in *Jurassic Park*? To keep the T. rex inside his cage?"

Aquila looked at Ephraim, who said nothing. "The gate is charged with electric current, yes," Aquila said. "I do not understand your reference, however."

"Never mind. Look," Sage said to Nick. He pointed straight ahead. "A railroad track." The tunnel continued straight as far as he could see, but in the center of the floor were two metal rails. Sitting on those rails were several open-topped cars, each with enough room for all of them to sit.

"We will ride the balance of the distance," Aquila said.

The cars had three bench seats that faced the same direction. They climbed into the lead car, the Elioudians in the front seat, Nick and Sage behind them, and Ronan in the rear. Ephraim pressed a pedal with his foot to get them moving. Within seconds they were traveling at a nice speed. The overhead lights that before seemed spaced so far apart now flew by at a steady stream. The farther they traveled, the more amazed Sage became. The tunnel was wide and tall and clean, and the car was quiet as it purred down the track. The smell of smoke and ashes hadn't changed—just a faint whiff in the air. The thought that a place like this could exist in the center of the earth was mind warping.

Sage didn't talk as they rode, content to simply look around in amazement. He couldn't figure out how they were moving. There was no engine on the car, no electric motor that he could hear, no cables or ropes pulling them. They were really moving now—thirty miles per hour? Forty? It probably seemed faster in the opened-topped car, but they were flying.

"What's making us move?" Sage asked.

Ephraim looked back at him. "The earth is a huge magnet. We have used God's creation for our benefit. We have electrified the rails to create a magnetic field on which we propel the cart."

Nick looked at Sage, who shrugged. "I don't understand that," Nick said. "How can the car move so fast? It doesn't make any noise."

Ephraim turned all the way around in his seat and looked at Nick. "Magnetic lines of force originate from the North Pole of the earth and end at its South Pole. We are following the path of the magnetic line of force. We are being pulled toward the North Pole by the magnets embedded in the front of the cart. When we want to go the other direction, we disengage the front magnets and use those in the rear. It is really very simple. Do they not teach you about magnets on Topside?"

"Yes," Sage said. "I just didn't know you could do something like this with them."

The car had padded leather seats made from a material Sage had never seen before. It felt soft, yet strong and rugged. It also looked odd—brown with spots of green and black and gold—with little nubs like his dad's alligator boots. "What kind of animal is this leather from?"

Ephraim looked at Aquila and said something in their strange language. Aquila answered him, which led to a conversation that lasted almost a minute. Finally, Ephraim turned around and looked at Nick. "We call the animal Angry Lizard."

Before Sage could say anything, Nick blurted, "Is it a T. rex?"

"I do not know the names used on Topside," Ephraim said, "but we have been unable to domesticate the Angry Lizard. So, we harvest his hide, use his meat to feed some of our livestock, and boil his fat to use as lotion for certain illnesses. Unlike the Nephilim, Emim, and Rephaim, we Elioudians *do not eat* the Angry Lizard."

On and on they rode, and Sage wondered how it was possible for any of this to exist. How far had they traveled? They'd walked for miles, always in a straight line, and now they'd been riding for well over an hour. Aquila said Tartarus was infinitely large. Sage hadn't really understood what that meant, but he was getting a pretty good idea the farther they went.

Sage took that time to tell Nick of the conversation Aquila and Ephraim had had just before he regained consciousness in the cave: that humans were alive in a village named Seth. John Cabot and Henry Hudson, both famous humans that had disappeared and were presumed long dead. Ronan offered very little, seemingly content to sit and watch Nick slowly come to grips with what was happening around him. The idea of a village with humans nearly took Sage's breath away. Especially if many of them were still alive. Henry Hudson and John Cabot should have been dead more than a century ago. Nick hadn't seemed to grasp that point, but Sage knew him well enough to know that he'd eventually get there.

"Why were the two of you in the Wastelands?" Sage asked Aquila. "How is it possible that you just happened to be there when we came down the hole?"

"We venture out weekly during the venting periods," Aquila said. "There are more than one hundred teams such as ours that patrol the Wastelands nearest our six gates. We open the gates for one month every year to vent Tartarus. There are six flues such as the one you came down. During the thirty days of venting, we patrol the Wastelands and occasionally discover Topsiders who have fallen. We don't get many. The vent holes are well hidden and in areas where few Topsiders are prone to visit. Nonetheless, we must do our due diligence and check the areas around the shafts."

"Do you find dead people?" Nick asked.

"Occasionally. Maybe one every five centuries." Aquila paused and then continued. "Over the epochs, less than a hundred Topsiders have fallen or been dragged into the Wastelands that we have been able to save. During the period of Belphegor's experiments, hundreds more perished that were pushed through your hole. Most of the Topsiders we have found are in the village of Seth. Some dead, but most alive."

Father.

Belphegor awoke and sat up in bed. *Yes, Zagan.*

The angel boy and the man of Strength have entered the Pure Place. The sick boy has recovered. They are out of my reach. I await instruction. Should I ascend back to the surface?

Sloth lay back down. Light from a digital clock was all that illuminated the room, though he needed no light to see. He glanced at his sleeping wife beside him and was thankful of her inability to intercept his private communications.

Return to the entrance to the Depths and await the arrival of the girl with Light and her team. Report once you have determined their strengths.

Yes, Father.

It was nearly time for Sloth to contact Gadrell, but he would wait until Zagan reported back about the rescue team. Sloth's brother wasn't certain if the beasts in the Territories could defeat a team of strong Council members. One couldn't speculate until they knew what mixture of angelic gifts was involved. Yet, Gadrell had also warned Sloth that the beasts in the underworld were unpredictably savage and that the chances of the Council members surviving the journey to the Great Granite Gate were remote. Sloth had once shared Gadrell's pessimism about their survival, until he had taken stock of the angel boy's grit while facing down Nearatook and his band of warriors.

Sloth stared at the ceiling as his wife slept beside him, unable to shake the image of the boy's bloodthirsty eyes as he plunged his sword up through Nearatook's face. Maybe it would be best if the boy never made it to the Great Granite Gate, even if it meant that Gadrell would spend the rest of his life within the hell of his underworld prison.

It was another hour of riding before Nick finally saw the first indication of civilization. The tunnel began widening—twenty yards, then fifty, then the passage was no longer a tunnel at all but a vast expanse that stretched as far as he could see in each direction. The same thing happened to the ceiling; higher and higher it climbed until lights appeared as distant specks. Nick couldn't see the walls of the huge cavern at all. Multiple tracks now ran alongside the one they were on.

He felt the increased temperature before he noticed the glow of bright lights ahead. It wasn't until Sage nudged his arm and pointed straight in front of him that Nick noticed the crops. Grow lights hung from steel cables stretching over fields thousands of feet wide. Under the lights hung irrigation lines, some of which were watering the plants right then. As far as he could see in each direction were crops of amazing heights. Corn plants fifteen feet tall with ears of corn nearly two feet long. He saw tomatoes as big as soccer balls, potato plants taller than him, broccoli and cauliflower plants four feet tall and five feet across, and heads of lettuce bigger than basketballs. Hundreds of Elioudians were scattered throughout the fields, hoeing or harvesting or doing whatever farmers do. Dozens of other train cars were parked along the outside tracks.

Nick didn't even have time to comment before Sage pounded on his shoulder again. "Nick, look up there! Orchards."

He saw apple trees first, but not the little trees that grew at home. These were as big as oak trees with trunks five feet around, towering a hundred feet in the air, with fruit twice as big as cantaloupes. Cherry trees, peach trees, lemon trees, each three times as big as back home, with fruit so large only one would be needed to bake an entire pie.

"How do you grow things so big?" Nick asked Ephraim. "That's amazing!"

He saw Ephraim smile just a little. "That is always the first question Topsiders ask when they see our crops. We have higher oxygen levels, purer water, a perfect light source, and the right type of insects. We have perfected the arts of plant production and crop rotation. There are many hundreds of fields and orchards such as these throughout Tartarus. And many thousands of farmers. The wheat fields are so vast and the wheat stalks so tall that a herd of elephants can move within them without notice. It is nearly harvest time now. Like all the other Topsiders who see it for the first time, you will marvel at the process."

Nick turned around in his seat and looked at Ronan. Even he appeared amazed. Ronan glanced at Nick and mouthed, "Wow," before pointing toward the front. Nick turned. Up ahead was a junction, a switching area where multiple railroad tracks came in from several directions. Hundreds of cars like the one they were in sat parked, ready to use, outside a beautiful black granite building. Other Elioudians milled about, glancing at the three humans as their car slowed to a stop. If they were surprised to see Topsiders, they didn't show it.

The light was soft, like dusk on a cloudy day. Lights hung from poles a hundred feet off the ground and threw shadows everywhere.

"What is this place?" Sage asked.

"One of our switching stations," Ephraim said. "The tracks here connect to other parts of Tartarus. We must take another track to reach Seth, but first you need to eat. Follow me." He headed toward the big building without another word, Aquila following silently.

"We get to eat," Nick said to Sage. "I'm starving."

"That makes two of us," Ronan said.

Nick hadn't realized the size of the place from the outside. One main room stretched at least three hundred feet in front of them. At the very front, near where they entered, were tables and a food bar. Beyond the eating area and near the back sat counters and desks, bulletin boards and cubbyhole mailboxes, and a map that took up a large section of one wall.

The tables were capable of seating thirty people or more. Nick counted fifteen tables; at least two hundred people were eating now. The rumble of conversation slowly died until complete silence fell upon the room. Even those Elioudians in the very back stopped what they were doing to notice the three humans. Nick grabbed one of Sage's hands and held it tightly. Ronan put hands on both boys' shoulders.

Aquila spoke, his gentle voice carrying through the room like a rolling ocean wave. Nick couldn't understand him, but Aquila gestured toward the humans often, waving his hands, punctuating his words with jabs of a finger, and smiling often. Slowly heads began nodding, Elioudians glanced at each other with pleasant expressions, and some even smiled at him. Nick liked people smiling at him.

Finally, everyone went back to what they'd been doing, and Aquila looked at Ronan. "We must eat," he said. "Come, there is an empty table near the banquet rack."

"They all look the same," Sage whispered to Nick. "The Elioudians. I can't tell them apart."

Nick nodded. He'd been thinking the same thing. Some were bigger than others, taller and thicker, but their faces, the shape of their heads, their pointy ears, muscular frames, and clothes—all the same.

Aquila led them to the open table and then turned toward them. "We will sit here. The banquet rack has everything you could want. Ephraim will assist you in gathering your bounty. Eat as much as you desire. I must arrange for your passage to the village of Seth. I will return shortly." He was gone before Nick could even offer him thanks.

"Come along," Ephraim said.

Nick followed, with Sage and Ronan right behind him. The banquet rack was at least twenty feet long. Multiple types of fruits and vegetables, several selections of bread, and various meats and poultries and fruit pies were all laid out in abundance. Ephraim handed them each a metal platter and fork and motioned for them to help themselves.

Nick filled his platter to overflowing with at least one of everything. Sage was much pickier, choosing mostly meat and a couple of small potatoes, and, of course, four slices of pie. Ronan piled so much food on his plate it must have weighed ten pounds.

Nick dug in as soon as he sat down. He was too hungry to talk. But they hadn't been eating for even sixty seconds when Sage began bombarding Ephraim with questions. "What did Aquila say to everybody?"

"He spoke of your plight," Ephraim said. "Of your desire to return to the Topside. He asked if any man here would volunteer to escort you through the villages of our evil cousins so that you might be rejoined with your families. But, of course, no one stepped forward. So, we will bring you to the village of Seth, where the other humans reside. It is best that you dwell among your own kind. Everyone agreed."

"How far away is the village of Seth?" Sage asked, while chewing a mouthful of chicken leg.

"Many leagues," Ephraim said. "It lies on the outskirts of the Elioudian territory."

"You asked Aquila why Seth was so heavily guarded," Sage said. "Back in the cave before Nick woke up. Is it because of creatures attacking the village?"

"Much has been spoken of Nephilim attacks upon Seth," Ephraim said. "I have witnessed several. They attack not because of the humans but because of the assembly of written knowledge within the library. We put humans there because it is heavily fortified and the safest place in all of the Elioudian territory."

Sage asked, "What's in the library that's so important?"

"Information," Ephraim said. "Knowledge. Much power resides within the knowledge stored there. Now, you must finish eating and use the necessary closet. We will depart soon."

"What's a necessary closet?" Nick asked.

Ronan leaned over and whispered, "It's a bathroom."

Ephraim led them to the bathroom after lunch and stood outside while they used it. It looked a lot like a normal bathroom except the toilets were made from hollowed-out granite and the flush tanks sat high in the air. The sinks were also granite, and the faucets were stone with pump handles. There was no hot water.

Aquila was standing next to Ephraim and Ronan when Nick and Sage came out. "We are ready to proceed," Aquila said. "We will travel east to the very edge of Elioudian territory, through our livestock farms, across the Acheron River, and along the Styx Marsh. The village of Seth sits in a triangle between the rivers Acheron and Cocytus and the marsh. It is a long journey." Aquila held up a cloth bag. "I have packed food and three skins of water. Follow me." He turned away and headed off before Sage had a chance to ask another question.

They walked deeper into the building, toward the large map covering the wall on the right. Sage pointed to it. "Look," he whispered to Ronan, "it's a map of Tartarus and the Territories."

The map was thirty feet wide and twenty feet tall, hand drawn and color coded. The Elioudian area sat directly in the center and was clearly the largest of the four Territories. The other three, Emim, Rephaim and Nephilim, sat stacked upon one another directly north. It was as Aquila said: to get to Topside through the outer gate controlled by the Nephilim, one had to cross through the other Territories.

The Wastelands surrounded everything. Much of it was mapped; some of it was not. Bordering the eastern edge of Elioud, stuck in a triangle between two rivers and a marsh just as Aquila had said, was Seth. Nick noticed that a tiny slice of the border of the Nephilim Territory wrapped around the Emim and Rephaim territories and touched the Styx Marsh.

"Do the Nephilim attack Seth through the Styx Marsh?" Sage asked Aquila. "It appears the most obvious route."

Aquila looked at Ephraim for several moments. "You spoke of the Nephilim attacks?"

"They are inquisitive," Ephraim said.

"We're old enough to know," Sage said. "Don't shield information because we're young."

Aquila looked at Sage. "You are but a speck in the life of an Elioudian. A wisp of time so brief I have often forgotten whole segments lasting longer than your total years. Humans have overvalued their own worth since the dawn of time." He paused, then continued. "Yes, the Nephilim stage their attacks through the Styx Marsh, though it has been many years. Some assaults were thwarted by predators roaming the marsh. They lose many warriors even before encountering our defenses. You need not worry. No human has been lost to a Nephilim attack."

They stopped outside a train car three times as large as the one they'd ridden in before. Aquila directed Nick and Sage into the rear compartment; he and Ephraim took the front, Ronan the middle. Unlike the last one, this car had a roof, although there were no windows. But why would they need windows, Nick wondered? That was clearly a Topside thing. Nor were there dividers between the seats, meaning Sage could pepper them with more questions during their trip.

"We've been gone a long time," Nick told Sage. "Grandpa is really going to be worried. I wonder how Mom and Dad are doing on their cruise?" Nick felt his emotions welling up, and suddenly, with no warning at all, he burst into tears, shaking and jerking with violent sobs. He put his face in his hands and put his head against Sage's shoulder.

Sage wrapped him in his arms and whispered, "God is with us, Nick. We are specially made to withstand this. All is not lost." Despite his words, Nick cried even harder, releasing all the pent-up emotion of the last twelve hours. "Something tells me we'll be OK," Sage whispered. "We have the same blood running through us. Our angels hover close. Don't worry, little brother. You're just tired. Get some sleep."

8

Endora Morgan hit the drop zone dead center. Everyone was sitting around in a circle in front of the tents when she came in. By the time Elsbeth climbed to her feet, the athletic Endora had already dropped her harness and had her parachute halfway gathered. She was the only living Council member gifted with Voice. Elsbeth had learned that just an hour before when Horace mentioned it.

Endora's reputation was less than complimentary. Sage and Elsbeth had met her at Council headquarters last summer, but the entirety of the conversation between them had been, "Hello, nice to meet you," and "Likewise." Known as a fierce fighter, Endora lacked even the most rudimentary social skills. Malcolm and Gavin were the first to walk over and greet her. After brief hugs, Kato stepped up and gave her a long, crushing hug that clearly pleased Endora. Steven shook her hand and thanked her profusely for coming. Horace waved and shouted a greeting from his chair.

Finally, Endora saw Elsbeth and walked over. She was just a few inches taller than Elsbeth, no more than five feet eight, and she'd cut her jet-black hair to just below her ears. She wore a green jumping suit that hugged her muscular frame. Like every other Council member in the prime of their life, Endora stayed in excellent physical condition.

"It is good to see you again, Elsbeth," Endora said, her German accent strong. She pulled her helmet off and stuck it under her left armpit. "I am aware of your friendship with Sage, and I am sorry that this has happened. We will prevail."

"Thank you, Endora," Elsbeth said. *Wow. Friendly.* "And thank you for volunteering to help. Malcolm and Gavin have told me stories of your many battles. You might be our most important weapon."

Endora waved her off. "Nonsense. We are a team." She leaned in closer and lowered her voice. "I have heard rumors of Sage in battle. You have seen it, yes? He sounds plenty capable of protecting himself. Do not fret. Huh?" She patted Elsbeth on the arm and turned toward Steven. "Who is yet to arrive?"

"David Brock and Theo are an hour out by helicopter," Steven said. "Malcolm and Gavin are about to head to the landing zone and meet them."

Endora nodded. "Very good. Then they will arrive by nightfall. Excellent." She looked at Horace. "So, you will be the bearer of bad news?"

Horace chuckled. "I will keep it as positive as I possibly can."

"Do not dare," Endora said sharply. "If you wish to keep us alive, you should strive to frighten us to death."

The historian gestured acknowledgment. "I will give it to you straight."

"You have a weapon for me, Kato?" Endora asked him.

"As you wished," Kato said.

"Again, excellent." Endora inspected the campsite and nodded approvingly. "Which tent is uncluttered enough for me to take a nap until the last two arrive?"

"Use mine," Steven said. He stepped over and unzipped the flap. "We'll keep the noise down out here."

Endora smiled. "I do not wish to be rude, but I have been traveling for nearly twenty hours. I must sleep." She disappeared into Steven's tent and zipped herself in.

"Can I look at Sage's video again?" Elsbeth whispered to Steven.

"Sure. In Kato's tent." Steven looked at Horace. "You said you wanted to see it again?"

Horace climbed from his chair. "Yes," he said softly.

Once inside the tent, Elsbeth pulled up the GoPro file, chose Sage's video, and pressed play. She and Horace watched in silence up to the point where the Rephaim transformed into a young human male. Elsbeth paused it and studied the man's face.

"Steven sent this image to Council headquarters several hours ago," Horace said.

"What can they do with it?" Elsbeth asked.

Horace chuckled. "You have no idea. The Council has operatives in all the major intelligence and investigative agencies, and I'm not just talking about American ones. I can assure you, that young man's face has been run through every relevant database in existence by now. We'll find him."

Elsbeth wasn't convinced the Council was all that. She hadn't been impressed with the results of the information Sage had given the Council last summer, but because Horace worked at headquarters, she needed to choose her words carefully. "An artist did a drawing of Sage's description of the Prince of Greed's human face almost a year ago. The drawing was so good it looked like a photograph. We both expected the Council to have identified him by now, but they haven't. They can't find a billionaire, and I'm supposed to believe they're going to identify this nobody?" Elsbeth hid her disappointment in herself. That had come out all wrong. So much for choosing her words carefully. Her tone hadn't been very friendly either.

Horace's slight smile evaporated. "Do you have any idea the effort the Council has put into finding Mammon's human face?"

Elsbeth crossed her arms and shook her head. "Enlighten me."

Horace hobbled over to a chair and sat down. "They've used every known investigative tactic and piece of electronic equipment in existence. They've run that image against all known facial recognition programs in the world. Intelligence agencies across the globe have helped us. It has been a colossal undertaking, yet they've found nothing."

She took a deep breath and sat down on Kato's cot. "How's that possible?"

"If we knew that, we'd fix the problem." Horace said. "If they were easy to identify, we'd have won this war centuries ago. We will win, Elsbeth. When the time is right. The momentum is shifting."

The passage east toward the village of Seth was even more unbelievable than what they'd seen before. A couple of miles outside the train-switching area, on the left side, stood a forest of oak trees so thick that Sage couldn't see much of the forest floor. What he could see resembled an encyclopedia of rainforest vegetation. The towering trees reached at least two hundred feet and had trunks five feet across, totally hiding the growing lamps and irrigation system that hung somewhere along the ceiling of the cavern. Wildlife flourished to such an extent he felt like he was on a train viewing a zoo exhibit. Animals large and small milled about, carefree, unafraid of being hunted. The entire left side of the track—the whole of the forest—was fenced so the wildlife didn't escape.

Across the road was an expansive dairy farm. There were miles of green pastures with fields so deep the barns appeared as specks on the horizon. In addition to hundreds of black and white Holsteins, there were thousands of brown and white Hereford beef cattle. The cavern ceiling seemed to slope on that side of the road, and the growing lights and irrigation system hung much lower. He saw dozens of Elioudians on horseback, herding some of the cattle toward distant barns.

Then Sage saw something that made him sit straight up in his seat. He leaned forward and tapped Ronan on the shoulder. "A triceratops!" It appeared ten feet tall at the shoulder and thirty-feet long. It had large ropes tied around its shoulders and a bridle around its head. Three strong Elioudians rode on the front of the wagon, each gripping a rope. Mounds of cow dung dotted the massive fields, waiting to be hauled away. As their train car whizzed by, Sage saw another triceratops wagon team, then another still. He figured that with so many thousands of cows, picking up their poop was probably a full-time venture.

They passed a pig farm, more crops, another orchard, still more crops, and another forest, all before coming to a river. He hadn't really been paying attention when Aquila told them the name of the river, but something now tickled his brain about it. "Mr. Aquila, what river are we approaching?" he asked quietly, trying not to disturb Nick's peaceful sleep.

"The Acheron."

"I know about that from Greek mythology," Sage said. "River of Woe. When someone dies, their souls board a ferry, which is run by Charon, who takes the souls across the river Acheron. Did you know that?"

"We know of the Greeks," Aquila said. "We ignore their myths, however."

Sage thought about that. "How can stuff named in Greek mythology also be here? The Styx. The Cocytus River. Could some of these myths be truth instead? What's going on?"

"You are well read for someone so young," Aquila said. "Of all the humans residing in Seth, only you have inquired of such things."

"Oh, Sage is a smart one," Ronan said. "Just ask him, and he'll tell you so."

"It's basic stuff, Ronan," Sage said. "The greedy god Hades never allowed anyone entering his kingdom to leave. Kind of like what Aquila has been telling us. We've entered Tartarus and can't leave." Sage kept his tone respectful. He wasn't accusing them of anything, but he did want to verbalize the comparisons. There were other parallels as well, but for now he kept those things to himself. "So Greek mythology isn't actually myth?"

"Greek mythology," Aquila said, "is merely inaccurate reporting of the Nephilim and the wild tales they told the early Greeks. After the great deluge, but before the Great Granite Gate could be permanently sealed, multitudes of Nephilim climbed back to Topside and took up their evil ways. The Greeks then recorded gross exaggerations and created hundreds of fairy tales."

As their train car flew past miles of underworld, only Aquila's words held Sage's attention now. "You're saying that Zeus is modeled from a Nephilim?"

"From Anak," Aquila said. "The giant Nephilim and father to all that climbed back to the surface. Like Zeus was father to all Greek gods, Anak was father to all Nephilim giants after the deluge. Anak ruled from atop Mount Nebo so he could oversee the land of Canaan. Zeus ruled from atop Mount Olympus. Anak had many children, all giants possessing great power. Zeus had many children, all godly or heroic. The early Greeks were spellbound by the stories of Anak and his kind. They crafted fantasies that have endured throughout the ages. Pay no heed."

Sage sat in stunned silence.

"There is much for you to learn, young Sage, if you desire to spend the time doing so," Aquila said. "For now, it is late, and you must join your brother in slumber. We have a long journey yet, and you must maintain your strength for what lies ahead."

Sage lay down in his seat and curled up, his mind racing about the ancient knowledge that must exist down here. He had yet to ask about the village of Seth, about what awaited them, but he wouldn't do that now. Aquila was right; it was late, and he needed to rest. He closed his eyes, but it was a long time before sleep took him.

———⊢———

"So, Savannah," Elsbeth said. "Tell me all about her!" She sat with Kato in chairs near the tents but away from the others so they could talk privately.

"Well," Kato said. "She is beautiful, funny, smart, loves adventure, determined, and, let's see . . . in love with me. What's more important than that?" He laughed. "Seriously, she's a nurse. Lives in Copenhagen. I met her while rock climbing in Belgium, of all places. She's not angelic-human, so that will be a challenge, but I can make that work."

"I'm so happy for you," Elsbeth said. "Sage is going to want to meet her. I know I do."

"At our wedding," Kato said. "I've already told her that I'll have some American friends coming. Well, not just Americans. I called Rabbi Klauss Cohen last week and David the day before yesterday. I told Savannah we all met on a mission trip while doing God's work." He grinned.

"Very creative. I can't wait to meet her. And speaking of David . . ." They could hear David's group approach. Malcolm and Gavin had left an hour ago to a makeshift helicopter-landing zone to meet Theo and David. It was David's booming voice that everyone heard, carrying through the jungle like a roll of distant thunder.

"Who could forget that voice?" Kato asked. He stood and strolled over to the landing spot. Elsbeth followed him. "Is there a bigger braggart in the Council?"

"In the world?" she asked.

"Ha, good point." Kato laughed. "Remember our fight with the demonic scout last summer with Rabbi Cohen? When the beast threw David through the wall of that barn, he stormed back out with a face so red I thought his ears might bleed. David couldn't believe that something could toss him around like that."

Elsbeth laughed and shook her head. "And how about when he went all Tasmanian devil on Mammon's head?"

"David Brock, too cool to lose a fight." Kato lowered his voice. "Listen, I'm sorry about Sage. Just remember that if it weren't for him, we wouldn't be standing here right now. He might be tougher than any of us." He wrapped an arm around her shoulder and squeezed. "If you ever want to chat, just pull me aside, OK?"

"Thank you, Kato, I will."

Elsbeth glanced back toward the tents. Everyone except Endora was sitting in a circle outside of Steven's tent, passing the time until the final members of the team arrived. They'd been speaking quietly, allowing Endora the rest she needed after her long trip.

David blasted a huge laugh from somewhere through the trees. "I'm a little surprised Theo made the trip," Kato said quietly. "Given his age. He takes his role as Sage's mentor quite seriously."

"He does." Theo, the Council member with the most developed gift of Sight, should have been secured safely away at Council headquarters. But the old man had refused to sit idly by while other Council members did all the fieldwork. Instead, he had opened a curio shop in Sage's hometown with the express intent of be-friending him and serving as his mentor once Sage began his life's mission. "He's a nice man," Elsbeth said. "He's been a real friend to Sage."

"And to Nick," Steven said, walking up. "He loves both of those boys."

"He's the most stubborn man walking the face of the earth," Horace added, stopping beside Steven. "Although I admit that being born in the year 1000 gives a man a certain perspective about life."

Theo wasn't the oldest Council member, Elsbeth knew, but he was close. The fact that he had demanded to respond to the crisis in the middle of a Mexican jungle spoke volumes about how he felt about Sage and Nick.

"Are you sure putting two old men up here to guard the camp while we're gone is a good idea?" Kato asked Steven, winking at Horace.

"Don't be surprised at the ingenuity of two old men," Horace said. "Theo and I will manage fine."

"I'm just curious about which one of you thinks he knows the most," Kato said.

"It's not about who knows the most," Horace said. "It's about who is right about what he knows, and since Theo has seen the manner of all our deaths, I willingly submit to his unique and gifted point of view."

Elsbeth did a double take at Horace. *Theo has seen the manner of all our deaths?* "He knows how each of us dies?" she blurted.

Horace looked at her as though surprised at such a silly question. "Were you not aware of that?"

Elsbeth stammered. "Well . . . no . . . I . . . I had no idea. He knows when each of us dies?"

"Ah, I did not say that," Horace said. "He knows the manner of our deaths. He's seen them. He has recorded those visions within the Council archives. Make no mistake, that information is seen by no one."

"But why? Wouldn't it help prevent deaths?" Elsbeth didn't understand. "What a gift that would be!"

Horace looked hard at Elsbeth before turning to Steven and Kato. "It sounds as though they are getting close. Should I get into this now?"

Steven shook his head. "Malcolm and Gavin have argued the Council's take on this subject for the past two hundred years. I don't think we should be discussing it when they get here. Especially with Theo present, since he's the one who insisted on the Council's position." Steven looked at Elsbeth. "We'll talk about it later in private. It's more complicated than you understand."

"OK." She didn't want to make a scene. Just thinking about it for a moment, she could understand how strongly some would want to know the manner of their death and how much it could terrify others. Personally, she was not sure she would want to know.

The four of them waited quietly while David's voice grew louder. Birds flew from trees above their heads.

"What's all the racket?" Endora said, as she stepped out of Steven's tent. "Does that blasted child not understand the advantages of stealth movement?" She walked over, sleep heavy on her face.

"David often has one volume, Endora," Kato said. "You know him well enough to understand that."

Endora mumbled something in German under her breath. A few seconds later, Elsbeth saw Malcolm leading the three others through a stand of bushes. He'd promised Steven that he'd carry Theo's luggage on the trip back, and it appeared he'd kept that promise. He had a large backpack slung over one shoulder and a black canvas bag in his left hand.

Theo followed behind Malcolm, dressed in jungle fatigues and a safari hat. He appeared to be a man in his nineties and had lost weight since Elsbeth last saw him. He wore a pair of sunglasses that wrapped around the upper part of his face, nodding at David's endless tales of mystery and adventure.

David, behind Theo, was boasting about some troll he'd slain in the mountains of Austria when he was fifteen, just before getting involved in World War I, where he specialized in busting up German tanks for the British army. The Boy with Might was only slightly taller than the other three but was built like a tank himself. His shoulders and chest had grown considerably since Elsbeth had seen him last summer, yet his small waist hadn't expanded at all. His arms looked as big as Elsbeth's legs, with pencil-sized veins rippling through his forearms. Elsbeth wondered if his body fat was even close to 5 percent. He wore fashionable wraparound sunglasses, a shirt at least three sizes too small, and cargo pants that accented his powerful legs. Elsbeth had to admit that David Brock was a sight to behold. Eye candy for females everywhere, and Elsbeth knew he relished the attention. Like last summer, his blond hair reached to the middle of his back, although he'd since dyed the bottom three inches an obscene shade of purple. His backpack was small, considering how long their journey might last, and he had a five-foot steel bar propped over one shoulder, with leather straps fashioned on one end that would allow him to secure the bar to a forearm.

"Hello, good people," David belted as soon as they stepped into the clearing. He made eye contact with everyone and slapped all the men on their backs. He nodded at Endora but stayed at arm's length. "How is Jarvis?" he asked her. "Fine, I trust?"

"Jarvis is well," Endora said. "He wishes he could have been here." She smiled tightly. "I last heard you were chasing girls in the French Riviera? Was that just wild rumor?"

David laughed. "Just so. Chasing the theory of disembodied spirits of the Nephilim is more like it. I spend most days in class at the Tomb, but nothing would prevent me from rescuing Sage. First chance to return the favor from last summer. Helping that bloke will always be my one exception, no matter how busy I am." David turned to Elsbeth and bowed politely. "And how are you, Ms. Persuasion? Pleasure to see the little lass again." He gave her a grin, knowing how she felt about him calling her *little lass*. "Are you holding up with your beau in such a fix?"

Elsbeth didn't know how she felt about people assuming she and Sage were closer than they really were. Nearly everyone here had spoken to her as though she and Sage were practically married. "I'm fine, David. It's nice to see you. Thanks for coming."

"David, you and Gavin set tent now, yes?" Theo asked. The old man's Greek accent was as thick as ever. His voice, a rich baritone, projected warmth and friendliness. Elsbeth could listen to him talk all day.

"Splendid idea, Theo." David turned to Gavin. "Ready?"

The two of them wandered off, and Elsbeth walked over to give Theo a hug. "Thanks for coming," she said. "I never imagined you would make the trip."

"Because I am old?" He chuckled. "At my age, all fieldwork is excellent. Yes, Horace?"

The old professor nodded. "My thought exactly."

"Now, if not offensive to group," Theo said, "I rest weary bones."

"Over here," Steven said. He led the group to the circle of chairs.

"I'm resuming my nap," Endora said. "Please try to keep the noise down. Steven, I assume your tent will be free for the next couple of hours?"

"No worries," Steven said. "We'll talk quietly."

"Briefing later tonight, Endora," Horace said. "We'll wake you."

"Certainly," she said, before disappearing into the tent.

"I've got some prep work to do," Malcolm said, excusing himself.

"And you have yet to choose your sword, Steven," Kato said. "Let's get that settled before the briefing."

That left Elsbeth, Horace, and Theo. Elsbeth wished it were different circumstances that had brought them together. There was so much Council history and experience between these two men that she could spend a solid year with both and not scratch the surface of their knowledge.

"So, what you have in store for us, Horace?" Theo asked. "How bad down in Territories?"

Horace didn't answer until they were all seated. "The information is dated, as we know, but if it remains anywhere close to what my ancestor recorded, they will need God's guidance."

Elsbeth sank back in her chair, trying to make them forget she was there. She wanted information, and the best way to get it was by listening.

"Steven said none of those gifted with Sight saw this coming," Horace said. "What do you make of that?"

Theo cocked his head in thought. He'd removed his bulky sunglasses and replaced them with ordinary lenses. "It is true," he said finally. "None saw this." He looked at Horace and shrugged. "What can I say?"

"You can say what you make of it," Horace said. "Seems to me that at least *one* of you would have had something, if only a snippet."

Theo nodded and glanced at Elsbeth before turning his full attention to Horace. "I see point you make. Most not gifted with Sight would assume same. But most not gifted with Sight often wrong."

Elsbeth cut her eyes toward Horace and tried making herself even smaller in her chair. She wondered how long it had been since the professor suffered a rebuke in front of a witness. He didn't look happy about it. In the fading light, Elsbeth couldn't tell just how red Horace's face was, but if his expression was any indication, it probably resembled a bad sunburn.

The historian didn't snap back; he simply swallowed and gave Theo a tight smile. "Well, illuminate me, Theo. What's your analysis of why this slipped by everyone?"

"I think two reasons. First, not every moment of danger sent as vision. And visions received not come with date and time stamps. Besides, many versions of same future often provided. Many possibilities. Never certain which version true result. Second, maybe visions from Tartarus and Territories intentionally blocked from us. My whole life, none with Sight receive vision from underworld."

Horace frowned. "I don't understand the 'many versions of the future' comment. What does that mean?"

"Those without Sight rarely understand." Theo smiled at Horace and waved a buzzing fly away from his face. "All about faith, free will, and endless possibilities." He took a deep breath and eased it out slowly. "God provides images of possibilities. Sight takes long to master because vast information oftentimes conflicts."

Horace had said that Theo had seen the manner of death of all Council members. Now Elsbeth wondered if what Theo had seen was accurate. *Were the visions wrong? Is that why the manner of our death is kept secret?* She made eye contact with Theo, and he seemed to smile at her using only his eyes.

"So, these visions of possibilities," Horace said, "means that most of what you see is wrong? Isn't that what you're saying? That most of what you see doesn't come to pass?"

"Complicated," Theo said. "On surface, maybe appear so. However, I assure you information is accurate, only outcome might differ."

Horace blew out a frustrated sigh. "What are you saying? I'm not certain how that even makes sense."

Theo looked at Elsbeth. "Last summer, Sage's trip to Mammon's prison, how many beasts threaten his life?"

It didn't take Elsbeth any time to spout them out. "Well, a werewolf, a cave full of gargoyles, a troll, a hellhound, and dullahan. And then there was Rupert, Belphegor's offspring. And Mammon, of course."

"How many beasts kill him?"

Elsbeth flinched. "What? None, of course. Although a couple of them came close."

Theo's eyes looked large behind his glasses. He blinked slowly and looked off into the near distance. "I have seen very few versions of Sage's future. Some possibilities. Nothing set in stone. It is about faith, free will, and intervention of things I cannot see that impact future."

She frowned at him. He'd completely lost her, and Horace, by the expression he wore.

"I explain," Theo said. "On Sage's eleventh birthday, three years before prison trip, I see Sage die three ways battling beasts you mentioned."

"What did you see?" she asked.

"Throat opened by werewolf. Troll kill him with club. Defeated by Mammon. I was convinced he would die. His distant future very sketchy. Even after return from prison. Very vague." Theo smiled, but it was weak and full of hesitation. "In each case in prison, small event or trivial action change present and impact future. He survive each battle."

It took a few beats for Elsbeth to respond, but she finally did. "So, knowing he might be killed, you and his grandpa let him go anyway?"

"Well, he go without permission. Last minute escape into Godspace. But, you here today because of his disobedience." He smiled. "It is about faith. Different possibilities exist. Above all, must have faith."

She looked at Horace. The professor hadn't said anything for a while, and she wondered if he had somehow arranged this entire conversation just for her. Theo's words had been exactly what she needed.

Horace didn't stay silent much longer. "And you've seen nothing of his battles yet to come in the Territories?"

"Nothing," Theo said. "None have seen images from underworld. Whole place like black hole."

"So, if he dies," Horace said, "all of the visions you've seen of his future will have been wrong."

Theo sat quietly before answering. "Yes. As mentioned, Sage distant future sketchy. Almost vacant. Not much to see. But oldest with Sight, me, often wrong. Sage might not return from Territories. That is simple truth. Faith very important now."

Elsbeth squeezed her hands together to keep them from shaking and blinked hard to keep the tears at bay. Theo wasn't as much help as she'd thought he'd be.

Nick awoke when the train car jerked to a stop. He rubbed his eyes and saw Sage asleep in the seat opposite him. Ronan turned and smiled at him, then reached over and gave him a pat on the shoulder. Nick sat up and looked around. Their train car was one of dozens parked on multiple tracks all ending against a granite barrier. Towering behind the barrier was a wall rising hundreds of feet in the air. An entire platoon of Elioudians, each armed with swords, stood at attention in front of an open gate in the center.

Nick shook Sage awake. It took his brother a few moments to gather his wits, but once he took in the scene, he voiced the same concern Nick had.

"What are they guarding against?" Sage asked Aquila.

Ephraim answered. "You were asleep when we crossed the river. Beasts have been known to slip from the Wastelands into the Styx Marsh and make their way into the river. The Nephilim have also attacked in that manner, although as I said before, it has been ages. Nonetheless, the sentries are there primarily as an early warning for the residents of Seth. They are armed only in case they are unable to retreat back inside the gate before the enemy is upon them."

Nick looked back from the way they'd come. He saw the edge of the river—and the bridge that crossed over it—a full quarter mile behind them. He didn't see any way someone or something could sneak up on the gate. The overhead lights were brighter here, much more so than everywhere else they'd been, so the visibility was excellent. Except for the dozens of train cars, which weren't very tall, the line of sight was clear.

"Come," Aquila said.

Nick and Sage gawked at the size of the vast, impenetrable fortress in front of them. Behind Sage followed Ronan, who also wore a look of astonishment.

"How thick is the wall?" Sage asked Ephraim.

"Three cubits and a handbreadth," Ephraim said.

Sage looked at Nick and shrugged. "How much is that?" Nick asked.

"You must use their measurement standards," Aquila told Ephraim. He turned toward Nick. "It is approximately sixty-five of your inches. Just more than five of your feet."

As they approached the gate, Nick looked straight up and saw no gap between the top of the wall and the ceiling. The floor was also granite, as smooth as glass, harder than concrete. There would be no digging underneath to make entry. Nothing would get into the village of Seth unless it went through the gate. Aquila said some words to the sentries closest to the gate and then waved for everyone to follow.

"Look at the size of the guards," Sage whispered.

Nick hadn't really noticed the guards because he'd been so fixated on the wall. Sage was right; all the sentries stood at least seven feet tall. The swords they carried probably weighed fifty pounds.

Sage went through the gate first, right behind Ephraim and Aquila. As soon as he stepped through, Nick heard him gasp. Then Nick stepped through and understood why. Spread out before them was a cavern at least ten times the size of a football stadium. They'd entered near the top and could see the village at the bottom. Three waterfalls fell into streams that fed a lake in the middle, but the falls were on the far edges of the canyon, spread hundreds of yards apart. Dwellings were built along the walls between the waterfalls, built from white stones with masonry work that appeared majestic and angelic, and were accessible by thousands of stairs crisscrossing everywhere.

Nick couldn't take his eyes off the scene below him. Hundreds of Elioudians milled around, each doing whatever they did during a normal day. He saw small buildings around the lake, with benches and sidewalks and small trees. Looking up, he saw so many lights it appeared stars had dropped through the earth. On the far side of the lake was a magnificent building that reminded Nick of the Supreme Court building.

All three of them stood quietly for several moments. Nick glanced at Ronan. The big man had tears in his eyes. He swiped them away and put a hand on Nick's shoulder. "You're witnessing something no current Council member has ever seen. An event no other human on earth will live to tell about."

"Not counting the humans that live here," Sage said. "How many are there?" he asked Aquila.

"There are two thousand Elioudians living in Seth," Aquila said. "And seventy-seven humans." He pointed to the far right. "The group of housing on the far edge is the human colony."

Nick looked over and saw a group of cliff dwellings well separated from all the others. They were also much higher from the floor of the cavern. In fact, from where they stood, he noticed a path along the top rim of the bowl that led directly to them.

"Why are they way over there?" Sage asked.

"Humans are weaker than us," Ephraim said. "They age at a rate many times our own and lack the stamina to consistently climb the number of stairs required of those that live at the bottom. From their colony, they simply walk along the upper rim to pass through the gate. They are also more concerned about privacy, so seclusion is their desire. You will be placed among your kind. Come, follow me."

"I don't see any humans walking around," Sage whispered to Nick. "Do you?"

"No."

"Only a few of the humans arise this early," Aquila said. "They have democratically elected one to serve as their spokesperson. We are headed there now."

They walked along the edge, Nick peering down as they went. The drop would kill him if he fell, so he hugged the side of the path. Ephraim led the way, followed by Aquila. Sage walked behind Nick, pointing and gasping, trying to get Nick to look, but he wasn't about to take his eyes off the path. Ronan brought up the rear and didn't say anything at all.

The smell was wonderful—like baked bread or cake—and mist from the waterfalls gave the air a fresh, clean feel. Nick wished his mom and dad could see everything. Then tears welled in his eyes at the thought of possibly never seeing them again.

"Hey, Nick, look! Down on the other side, opposite from us. A tunnel."

But Nick didn't look. He'd have to completely turn around to see it, and he was afraid of falling.

"Where does that tunnel lead?" Sage asked the Elioudians.

"It leads to the edge of the river, near the swamp," Aquila said. "We have devised an irrigation system, and the tunnel allows us to service the pipes. It does not lead to anywhere."

"It also covers the pipes of the sewage system," Ephraim said. "Access is restricted."

They walked a while longer before Ephraim came to a short stairway. He climbed, then switched to another set of stairs, then to a third. He finally stopped in front of a wooden door and waited. Aquila joined him and glanced back at Nick and Sage before knocking.

A few moments later a woman's voice spoke through the door. "Who is it?"

"It is Aquila of Abel. I have three humans to turn over to your care."

The door opened, and a slim woman with brown hair and dark brown eyes smiled at them. "Hello, Aquila," she said. "Ephraim." She looked at Nick and Sage and smiled even wider, then studied Ronan for a moment and frowned. "How did three of you fall into the same hole?"

"I didn't fall," Nick said. "I was pushed. I'm Nick. My brother, Sage, came down to save me. Ronan came with him."

"We will leave them to your temporary care," Aquila said. "I will inform the High Council immediately. They will want to visit the circumstances of their arrival. They will also have great interest in their identities. In the meantime, please let the liaison officer know if we can assist you." The old Elioudian turned to Nick and bowed slightly. "It was my pleasure making your acquaintance, Master Nick. You have shown great courage for one so young. And in you, Sage, I see a young man with great love for his brother." He shook Ronan's hand. "We have plenty of space here. You are free to use it as long as you need."

"Thank you," Ronan said. "Let us know the moment your scouts hear about our friends."

"Certainly," Aquila said.

The four of them stood in silence for several moments. "I know what you're going through," said the woman. "My name is Amelia. Come in, please. I know you have a thousand questions."

Her dwelling was small, just three rooms that Nick could see. She had decorated it with wooden furniture, rugs woven in bright colors, pottery and paintings, and statues made from plaster. The kitchen on the left was nothing more than a small fireplace with big pots. In the other two rooms—a living room and bedroom— sat shelves filled with wooden carvings of airplanes.

"Do you have a bathroom?" Sage asked.

Amelia smiled. "A community bathroom. Down four flights of stairs on the north end. There are showers and toilets and bathtubs. One for men, one for women. There's a community kitchen on the same level, but down on the south end."

Nick looked at all the carvings of airplanes, amazed that some- one could make them in such detail. One said *The Spirit of St. Louis* on the side. Now that he thought about it, all of them were old propeller planes. "How do you know so much about planes?" he asked Amelia. "They all have model numbers on the tails."

"I used to be a pilot," she said, smiling.

"Were you named after Amelia Earhart?" Sage asked. "Is that why you like planes so much?"

She smiled even wider. "I *am* Amelia Earhart."

9

Sage's mouth had already dropped open when Nick looked at him in amazement. Nick didn't know much about the famous pilot except what little he'd learned in third grade.

"That's impossible," Sage said.

Nick looked at Ronan, who also appeared skeptical. "Amelia Earhart's plane went missing sometime in the 1930s," Ronan said. "She was in her forties. That was eighty years ago."

"It was 1937, and I was forty," Amelia said. "Yes, I know it sounds crazy, but it's true. I crashed my plane near a deserted island in the South Pacific, swam to shore, fell down a hole, and ended up here."

"The ventilation shafts Aquila mentioned?" Sage asked.

"Yes. There are six of them," Amelia said. "The Elioudians keep a close eye on them. I wandered around for just a few minutes before they found me."

"How can you look so young?" Nick asked. "The real Amelia Earhart would be over one hundred years old."

"I'm almost 120 years old." Amelia sat down on a chair and crossed her legs. She frowned before she answered, as though trying to figure out exactly how to explain her lack of aging. "The air is different down here. Thicker. Purer."

"I noticed that," Nick said. "I can see things better. I can hear better."

"Yes, all of that is true," she said. "So, we have a higher percentage of oxygen, I think, and we don't have any UV rays from the sun."

"What's that got to do with it?" Nick asked.

"Ultraviolet rays from the sun damage us," Ronan said. "I understand her point. They break us down; they age our skin, make us vulnerable to disease."

"And maybe the water. The big lake at the bottom of the village. I think the water has something in it. A kind of Fountain of Youth. Maybe. Possibly. At least that's what I think, though I'm no scientist." Amelia looked closely at them. "But honestly, I'm not sure why I haven't aged. None of us have."

"What happened to Fred Noonan, your navigator?" Ronan asked.

"He didn't survive the crash," she said softly. "He went down with the Electra when it sank. I still miss him, even after all these years."

"Aquila said there are seventy-seven humans down here," Sage said.

"Yes," Amelia said. "Eighty now, with the three of you. We can meet them later. Are you hungry?"

Nick was, and he told her that. Sage pulled him aside as Amelia began gathering some food in her little kitchen. Ronan positioned his body where Amelia couldn't see the conversation. "We aren't staying down here," Sage whispered to Nick. "We have a team coming. We'll give them a few days to arrive, but in the meantime, I want everybody down here to understand that we're going back home."

"But Aquila said there isn't a way out." Nick could feel the tears coming on and fought to keep his voice steady. "He said we'd get killed if we tried to leave."

"We can't live underground for the rest of our lives," Sage said. "Especially if we stop aging. Do you want to spend four or five hundred years down here?"

Nick blinked. "Four or five hundred years? A hundred and twenty is one thing, but there's no way we could live that long. We're humans!"

"We aren't normal humans, Nick," Ronan said, putting a hand on his shoulder. "How do you think your brother and I knew about the Elioudians and the creatures down here? I hadn't gotten around to explaining it to you yet, but the team we have coming, along with Sage and I, will get us back to the surface."

Hot tears leaked out of Nick's eyes. He hated crying in front of Sage, but this was just too much. "I don't wanna spend five hundred years down here, but I don't wanna get killed, either." He rubbed his cheeks dry.

Sage looked away, thinking, and then looked squarely into his eyes. "Ronan told you some stuff about our angelic gifts, but it's probably time you saw some of it." He had a look in his eyes Nick had never seen before. A spooky look. Almost a different person. Sage walked over to Amelia. "So, you've been here eighty years?"

"Eighty-two." She was laying out breads and fruits and a dried meat. She'd already filled three glasses with water. "I can predict what you're about to ask."

"Yeah, what's that?" Sage crossed his arms and glared at her.

Amelia folded her hands in front of her and leaned back against a table. "You want to leave," she said gently. "You can't imagine spending the rest of your life down here. You miss your family. Your friends. At the rate humans age here, you could live for centuries. You'd go just a little bit crazier each year, especially if you didn't at least *try* to escape. Am I right?"

Sage didn't say anything for a moment, so Nick did. "Yeah, you're right."

"I felt the same way," Amelia said softly. "It took me twenty years to get over it." She shrugged. "I'm probably still not over it completely. But you know what?"

"What?" Nick asked.

"It's better to be alive down here than dead." She smiled at them.

Nick glanced at Sage, who didn't look like he'd bought any of what she'd said. At all. "How many have tried to escape? That you know about?" Sage asked.

Amelia's smile faded. "Three."

"And what happened to them?"

"They were killed in the Emim territory." She'd almost whispered her answer.

"How do you know that?" Sage asked. "Did you see their bodies? Did someone witness their deaths?"

"It's known, Sage," Amelia said. "It's unquestioned."

"How is it known? Answer my questions. Did you see their bodies? Were there witnesses?" Sage's voice had risen, and Nick knew he was gearing up for a fight. "Aquila said you are the elected representative of the humans down here. You would know what I'm asking."

"Dial it back a little, Sage," Ronan warned. "Don't kill the messenger."

Amelia sighed and pushed away from the table. She walked past them into the living room and sat down. She waved her hand at the couch. "Everyone. Sit down."

Nick and Ronan did, but Sage didn't. He stood next to Nick with his arms crossed, defiance written all over his face.

"Two of the escape attempts occurred long before I arrived," Amelia said. "The first was the great warrior, Spartacus, who fell into the underworld with his sword. The Elioudians warned him to stay in Tartarus, but he refused. A young Elioudian scout shadowed him into the Emim territory and watched him battle one of the many creatures that live there. Spartacus was killed less than an hour after he entered their territory. The scout reported his death immediately." Amelia spoke quietly but without hesitation, almost as if she'd had this exact conversation many times before.

"Almost a hundred years before I arrived, there was a man named Yu Fang, a great samurai warrior, who lasted almost five years in Tartarus. The entire time he practiced his sword fighting skills in preparation for his attempt to return to Topside. The same Elioudian scout shadowed him into the Emim territory. Fang did much better than Spartacus; he lasted a full two days before he was slaughtered by a pack of creatures that spewed acid into his eyes and blinded him." Amelia paused her story and looked sadly at Sage. "I'd been here almost twenty years when a good friend of mine finally demanded to be shown the exit. I begged him not to go. Begged him. But he couldn't take it any longer."

Amelia wiped her eyes and looked away. Nick saw her bottom lip quivering. He glanced at Sage. His brother's face had softened, but he still looked determined to have his way. Ronan sat quietly, hands folded on his lap, with no expression whatsoever.

"My friend, Geoff, took no weapons with him," Amelia said. "He knew he couldn't defeat the creatures of the Territories, but he fancied himself a great tracker and thought he could sneak his way through." She wiped her eyes again and looked straight at Sage. "The Elioudian scout came back three days later and refused to tell me what the creatures did to him." Nick looked at the huge goose bumps that suddenly broke out on his arms. He rubbed them away. "So," Amelia continued, "even if you *think* you could make it through the Emim Territory, which no one has ever done, you would then have to make it through the Territories of the Rephaim and the Nephilim. It's impossible." Though her eyes were red, they were hard. It was clear to Nick that she didn't want any of them to be killed.

"What do you know of Elioudian history?" Sage asked her. "Of the Great Flood, of the Watchers, all of the mixing of angels and humans?"

"I know quite a lot. I know that all of them are offspring of the Watchers, that the Elioudians repented their wicked ways and sealed themselves away." Amelia cocked her head at Sage and raised an eyebrow. "Do you know more than that?"

"Do you know of the Angelic Response Council?" Sage glanced at Nick.

"No," Amelia said. "What's that?"

"After the Great Flood, some of the Nephilim, Emim, and Rephaim escaped their Territories to take control of humanity again. They wanted things like they were before the flood: all humans serving them." Sage paused and glanced at Nick a second time. Then he looked at Amelia and continued. "After the creatures escaped, a special group of Elioudian children were born, two hundred of them—children who looked human. A hundred years later, those human lookalikes were sent to the surface as the Angelic Response Council."

Nick frowned. To hear Sage expand upon the stuff Ronan had told him earlier somehow put a different spin on it. He'd never known Sage to exaggerate, and his brother certainly wasn't a liar.

"Each member of the special group of two hundred Elioudians possessed an angelic gift," Sage said. "A supernatural power, if you will." He paused and leaned forward just a little to emphasize his point. "I am angelic-human. So is Ronan. That's what Aquila meant when he told you that the High Council down here will be interested in our identities. We can survive the trip back to the surface. We only need a guide."

Amelia studied Sage for several moments before speaking. "You are angelic-human? You are Elioudian?"

"Our ancestors are Elioudian, yes. There's a team coming to rescue us. All of them Angelic Response Council members. I don't know who yet; my grandfather is arranging that. We're going to give them a few days to get here, but if they don't show, we're taking Nick back to the surface."

Nick didn't trust his emotions enough to say anything. Ronan seemed content to let Sage do the talking. The big man wore a slight grin below eyes that seemed to sparkle with glee. He was loving this. Whatever was going on in his mind, he appeared happier than Nick had seen him in a long time.

"So . . . you have a special gift? A power? Is that what I'm understanding?" Amelia asked.

"I have more than one," Sage said. "Ronan only has one, but it's a good one. Might. The strength of two hundred men."

Disbelief? Sympathy for Sage because of his mental illness? Nick couldn't tell exactly what Amelia was thinking by the expression she wore, but it was clear she wasn't buying any of it. "What gifts do you have?" she asked.

"Sword fighting. Well, technically, it's called Fighting Arts. Superhuman speed for me and seeing my opponent's moves in slow motion. And Teleportation. Sensing is coming along, but it's not reliable yet. And Memory Share, but that would only help *me* get out, and it would put me sometime in the past, which makes no sense in this case. I also have Clarity, which doesn't really help me right now. And Pathfinding—useless here, but it might be helpful during our journey. Not sure yet. Anyway. Yes. Six gifts." Sage looked at Ronan. "Anything to add about that?"

"You're doing great."

Nick looked at Amelia, who shifted in her seat, clearly irritated that this delusional teenager would minimize the dangers of the Territories with such foolishness. She stood. "Enough of this nonsense. You cannot return to the surface. You're stuck here. Just like me and everyone else. Get over it." Her voice shook just a little, and Nick thought she might be on the verge of tears. "I'll finish lunch," she said, and walked back into her little kitchen.

"Nick, watch," Sage whispered. "It's time to make a believer out of you, too." He disappeared. Amelia screamed when Sage blocked her path, having appeared directly in front of her.

"How did . . . where . . ." Amelia stepped back. "How did you do that?"

Sage wore a slight smile, almost smug but not quite. "Teleportation. The ability to move from one place to another without occupying the space in between. Here's another one." He pulled his sword, gripped it with both hands as he stepped back, and started swinging it in a circle so fast that his arms, hands, and sword became a fuzzy blur. A lawnmower blade. An airplane propeller. He grinned and moved. The air turbulence blew Amelia's clothes and hair. Amelia, white faced, didn't move. Then she threw her hands to her mouth, but no sound came out.

Sage stopped and sheathed his sword. "Ronan swings a steel bar that weighs over two hundred pounds. He hits beasts with such power that few survive more than one blow. We can get Nick out of here. I've defeated Emim beasts before." He looked at Nick. "I'll tell you about last summer in more detail later." Back to Amelia. "Regardless if our rescue team shows up, I'll need an Elioudian guide that can lead us out. I will ask the High Council about that when they get here."

It took a moment for Amelia to recover. "What are you?"

"I told you. I'm angelic-human. Descended from Elioudians. My birth was prophesized by an ancient Elioudian named Seth."

"The same Seth this village is named after?" Amelia shook her head. "I've heard nothing about this."

"Why would they tell you?" Sage asked her. "What purpose would it have served?"

She started to say something but didn't. Instead, she just stood there looking at him.

"We can lead others out," Sage said. "How many would want to come? The humans trapped down here?"

"Hold up, Sage," Ronan said. "We might need to talk about that first."

Sage shrugged. "OK. Just thinking out loud."

"I can't believe anyone would go with you," Amelia said. "It's too dangerous. You have no idea what kind of creatures are out there."

"I have some idea," Sage said. "If you knew what I went through last summer, you'd understand. If you'd seen the creatures we've faced and killed in the last twenty-four hours, you'd understand. You need to call a meeting. Of the people down here. The humans."

"I can send word that you want to meet with them, but they will never agree to follow you out." She leaned forward, her eyes blazing. "It's too dangerous! You don't understand." She looked at Nick, almost pleading with him. "He will get you killed."

Nick didn't say anything. He couldn't.

"Stop scaring him," Sage shouted. "You don't know what you don't know. So just stop it. We're going back to the surface. With our rescue team, I hope. But if not with them, then by ourselves."

Amelia stared at Sage for several moments, then turned toward Ronan with a look of pleading, but he offered her no support. After a few moments, she seemed to give up. "OK, let me finish making you something to eat. Then I'll send word that you want to meet with the humans. I'm not promising anything."

"Agreed," Sage said.

She sighed deeply, apparently defeated. "Fine. I'll arrange it." She looked at Nick, sorrow on her face.

10

"Every single day of my life," Sage told Nick. "Every day."

They were sitting on the steps outside Amelia's front door. They'd eaten breakfast and, true to her word, Amelia had left to pass along Sage's request for a meeting with the humans.

"Every day?" Nick asked. "You're not making it up? About that, I mean? You actually saw her?" His eyes shone; his face almost glowed.

Sage had just spent more than an hour telling Nick about his trip into Mammon's prison the year before. He hadn't gotten too detailed, because there was just so much information to share, but he'd told him the basics. That led to Leah. It would take Sage months to get him fully up to speed, but because Leah had been such a major part of Sage's life, it was important that his brother understand her. Ronan had sat quietly, affirming Sage's story when Nick looked at him for confirmation during parts of it. Sage knew that Ronan wouldn't interject; this was Sage's story to tell, a story that both knew had been coming for years. Nick's reaction had gone from near disbelief to reluctant acceptance before finally settling on amazement. Sage tried to understand the range of emotions he would have experienced had all of it been dumped on him, but he just couldn't get his head around it. The information they'd piled on Nick was colossal in scope and size.

"Nick," Sage said, as he looked out over the city of Seth, "I know it's hard for you to understand, but yes, I saw Leah, my Guardian, except during my time in Mammon's prison, every single day of my life. More than that. Nearly every *minute,* until she left a month ago." He swallowed, feeling the emptiness where she used to stand beside him, and turned his head to watch Elioudians mill about in the bottom of the bowl where the busiest part of the village was located. He saw a few other humans walking down the steps toward the lake. They glanced back at Sage, Nick, and Ronan but didn't come over and introduce themselves. *Has word about the freaky boy with superpowers spread that quickly?*

More humans came out of their houses and headed down the steps toward the village, but again, none came over to meet them. Sage suspected that Amelia had somehow spread the word for everyone to stay clear. Which suited Sage just fine. He wanted time with Nick, anyway.

"Can you explain Grandpa's gift again?" Nick asked. "I know we've been talking about this stuff for the last hour, but I'm still confused about it. Pathfinding."

Ronan smiled. "You ask him anything you want, Nick. He'll be happy to answer."

"For sure," Sage said. "Grandpa can track stuff into the spiritual realm. He's like a supernatural detective. He can make leaps in logic that ordinary humans can't. He sees threads of truth based on history, ancient writings, symbols, and obscure signs. Kind of a sixth sense, like he sees visions based on the vibrations he gets when he touches things."

"Visions? Like seeing the future?"

"The past. Not full, complete stories or anything. Just short snippets of information."

"Sage has Pathfinding, too," Ronan said. "But can't do what your grandpa can with that part of the gift."

"True," Sage said. "About a month ago. I went to Theo's shop with him. Theo got an ancient book from overseas and then called Grandpa on the phone and asked him to come over and look at it. I rode over there with him, and Theo led us to the back room. The book was wrapped in bubble plastic. Grandpa unwrapped it and opened the front cover, saw some writing—faded ink, jagged script like it came from a shaky hand. Grandpa looked at Theo and asked if it was legit. Theo said yes. Grandpa closed his eyes and ran his fingertips over the writing." Sage stopped talking and raised his eyebrows.

"Then what happened?" Nick asked.

"I watched Grandpa's face. It twitched. He frowned, sucked in a sudden breath. Tears filled his eyes."

"You think he had a vision?"

"I'm pretty sure," Sage said. "I asked him about it later, but he wouldn't answer me. I didn't push it. He would have told me if he thought I needed to know." Sage grinned at Nick. "So, then I tried doing it, since I have Pathfinding, and nothing happened. Grandpa's got some serious chops with his gift. Kinda weird, huh?"

"Spooky. Creepy." Nick gazed off, slowly inspecting the world around him. "You know," he said after a few moments. "It's kind of funny how I could have freaked out, but I didn't."

"Why?"

"Well, a monster grabs me and crams me into a hole that leads to an underground world that nobody on earth knows exists. I meet two people that look like space aliens, one of whom is more than 2000 years old. They take me to a city where Amelia Earhart is still alive. She's 120 years old and barely looks 40." He waved his arms around him. "Look at this place. There's a building that looks like the Supreme Court, next to the most beautiful lake I've ever seen, and it's inside a giant cavern that used to hold water that helped flood the earth." He shook his head and laughed. "And I'm freaking out that you can do what you do? Really? This time two days ago, *none* of this would have existed in my wildest dreams. That's what's funny."

"Well, when you put it like that, yeah, I guess that's funny." Down at the bottom of the bowl, near the foot of the steps of the big white building, Sage saw at least forty humans standing in a group, most of them looking up at them. "Know what else is funny?"

"What?"

"That not a single other human has come over to meet us. I'm wondering if Amelia sabotaged our meeting." Sage gestured toward the crowd. "Look. I almost feel like a carnival exhibit."

Nick looked that way, laughed, and slapped Sage on the shoulder. "You *are* a carnival exhibit."

Sage smiled. "Good point."

"I've seen such reactions before," Ronan said. "Nick, you may not realize it, but you are one of the few regular humans on earth that knows about all of this. The Council does everything in its power to fight this war in the shadows, but sometimes we're forced to reveal our gifts to save people. Fear. It drives people to do strange things. Even faced with certain death from a creature of unimaginable ruthlessness, people will view us—after we have saved their lives—as simply a different kind of monster. Sage, you haven't yet experienced that, but you will."

Sage sat quietly. He hadn't thought a lot about that, but it was a good point. He would need to consider that going forward. As he looked at the humans walking away from them, he wondered how many would risk their lives for a chance to rejoin humanity on the surface.

Nick touched Sage on the shoulder to get his attention. "I have one more question. Well, more than one, way more, but only one right now. What about me? Will I get a gift?"

"I don't know." Nick opened his mouth to respond, but Sage continued before he could. "Gifts skip people. I don't know how or why, but Mom and Dad both have angelic-humans in their family line, but neither have gifts."

"My guess would be yes," Ronan said. "Eventually. We've seen it before, brothers from the same parents. You're still young. Some gifts don't manifest until our early twenties, others much sooner than that. You're thirteen, so it could happen today or ten years from now. Don't give up hope." He slapped Nick on the back. "If it happens, I suspect it'll be awesome."

Nick didn't say anything, but he beamed at Ronan's words, clearly hopeful they would end up being true. It amazed Sage how quickly he'd accepted everything he'd been told over the past twenty-four hours. Then again, maybe he was still delirious from the poison.

"Let's explore around some," Sage said. "I'm tired of sitting. You game?"

"Yeah." Nick stood and gave Sage a sudden hug. He squeezed him tightly, then released him and turned away. "Yeah. Let's explore this joint. We might see more stuff nobody else in the world knows about." He laughed and took off down the stairs.

Ronan stepped close to Sage. "He'll be fine. He's strong. Rational. And has your grandpa's blood running through his veins."

———

They descended the steps from Amelia's front door to the bottom of the village. By the time they got there, the group of humans had disappeared. Nick approached the huge building in a state of awe. He kept glancing at Sage and Ronan, who seemed equally impressed. The architecture was ancient Roman or Italian, Nick thought, although he was hardly an expert. It was the centerpiece of the entire village of Seth, a structure that must have taken decades to build, given that they wouldn't have had heavy construction equipment. Elioudians walked in and out, each with at least one book in their hands and all of them closely inspecting the new humans as they passed.

"It must be the library Aquila mentioned," Sage said.

From where they stood, Nick saw the huge canyon from the other side. The giant gate looked small, and the lake in the middle, with water so clear he could see dozens of feet down, made the air a little cooler.

"Look," Sage said. He pointed to the far side of the lake.

Nick saw Amelia coming, two Elioudians with her. One was shorter than the other, but both looked about the same age as Ephraim. Like all the others here, they wore solid white clothes that clung tightly to their bodies.

"They look like they've been bodybuilders since the day they were born," Nick said.

Sage shrugged. "Probably natural. Remember, they are more angel than human."

They stood quietly as Amelia stopped in front of them. "Sage, Nick, Ronan, please meet Elah and Issur." She turned to Elah. "The older boy is Sage."

Nick studied Amelia's face and thought she looked kind of embarrassed, like it was beneath her having to serve as an errand girl. Elah and Issur weren't as old as Aquila but were certainly older than Ephraim. Nick wasn't about to guess their ages, given that Ephraim was more than 860 and looked 25.

The shorter and stockier of the two spoke. "You are Sage the Warrior? Of the prophecy of Seth?"

Sage stood to his full height. "I am. My Guardian was Leah. I possess six total gifts: Teleportation, Clarity, Pathfinding, Fighting Arts, and Memory Share have fully manifested, and Sensing is getting there."

The same one spoke. "I am Elah, the senior academic fellow of this village. I hold a seat on the Assembly of Histories. Prophecy says nothing of your visit to Tartarus." He bowed slightly. "I am most honored to meet you but must ask for proof of bequeath. It is an ancient command but required of all returning Council members, should one ever return. You are the first."

Nick had no idea what he was talking about, and apparently neither did Amelia, whose face looked as confused as Nick felt. He glanced at Ronan, who also wore a blank expression.

"What's that mean?" Sage asked. "Proof of bequeath."

The other one answered. "I am Issur, senior brother of the Convention of Exploration. We welcome your presence among us. If you are truly the Sage of prophecy, you must offer evidence that gifts have been bequeathed to you."

"Oh, I get it," Sage said. "You want a demonstration."

Nick felt his heart quicken. He'd already seen Sage disappear from one place and appear at another. What else could he do?

"How well trained are your Elioudian guards?" Sage asked Elah. "In sword fighting?"

"Our best have spent centuries perfecting their craft," Elah said. "All Elioudian males are required to train weekly, for the benefit of their rotations in the Wastelands." He pointed at Issur. "My friend spent fifty decade celebration days leading scout teams into the Wastelands before becoming senior brethren on the Convention of Exploration. His swordsman skills have measured superior for five centuries."

"Then we should spar," Sage said to Issur. "Do you have a sword handy?"

"You can't be serious," Amelia said. "Young man, I have seen these men practice against each other. You have no idea of the skills they possess."

Her voice had risen, and Nick was suddenly afraid for Sage. Yeah, he was a muscular fifteen-year-old, but these Elioudians looked twenty times stronger, and they'd been fighting for centuries. Yet Sage didn't look worried at all. He just stood there so relaxed and calm you might have thought somebody had just challenged him to a game of checkers.

"Show them something else," Amelia said. "That disappearing thing."

"That'd be easier," Ronan said. "No reason to risk an injury."

"That's fine," Sage said. "The gift of Teleportation. Observe." He vanished.

Nick looked everywhere, and so did everyone else. He stepped to the side and searched around the lake, the gate they'd come through, and up in the cliffs near Amelia's house. Nothing. He was gone. Finally, Issur pointed to the very top of the white building.

"Hey down there!" Sage shouted from the top of the pitched roof.

Nick laughed. "You have *got* to be kidding me!" He laughed again and looked at Amelia. She looked so shocked Nick thought she might faint. Ronan wore a huge smile and watched the reactions of the Elioudians.

Sage appeared before them, beaming like a little kid. "That's Teleportation. Is that proof of bequeath?"

Elah, in a state of awe, stepped forward and bowed. "The prophecy lives. We will send messengers to Abel and assemble the leaders of Tartarus."

"I've requested a scout to lead us through the three Territories," Sage said.

"I am aware of your request, Sage the Warrior, but such decisions do not rest with me. It will take the full assemblage of Elioudian leadership to make such a determination."

This guy was just a filter, Nick thought—somebody to confirm whether the kid claiming to be angelic-human was just some nut. He looked at Amelia, and her expression had totally changed. She now seemed shell shocked that someone of great importance to the Elioudian race had shown up on her doorstep.

Nick didn't understand why she should be so surprised. He was the one that should be shell shocked. He'd known Sage all his life and had no idea he possessed such amazing powers. Amelia, on the other hand, had been living in this hidden world for eighty years. Plenty of time to absorb the fact that a lot of stuff existed that ordinary people didn't know anything about.

Sage shook Nick's arm. "Hey, earth to Nick. Did you hear me?"

"What?" Nick hadn't realized that Amelia and the others had walked away.

"They said we could wait in the library." Sage motioned toward the big white building.

"Wait for what?"

"They're sending some messengers out to the capitol of Tartarus. A place called Abel. It'll take them a few hours to get back." Sage pulled on Nick's arm, and they headed to the entrance of the building. "Ronan, we're leaving Tartarus, scout or no scout. No question about that. I just hope they'll give us some supplies if they refuse the scout."

"Don't get all worked up about it," Ronan said. "Just keep the faith. We'll be all right."

Nick didn't say anything. He didn't like the idea of leaving without a scout. He'd never seen Sage's Angelic Fighting Arts in action—and they were probably stout—but how could he fight off hordes of creatures all at once? Yeah, there'd be Ronan, too, and his steel bar looked wicked and dangerous, but two people against dozens of creatures? Going through a territory they were unfamiliar with? He wouldn't want to know their odds of survival.

The library had doors large enough to drive a concrete truck through. Thick columns stood sixty feet apart and towered at least a hundred feet high. "Wow," Sage mumbled under his breath as they stepped inside the building.

He'd taken the word right out of Nick's mouth. An expansive room opened in front of them, with dozens of tables in neat rows in the center. On the ceiling, five stories up, was a mural of angels in battle with horrific beasts. Staircases on each side of the room led to different floors, all of which they could see from where they stood. Thousands of books lined hundreds of shelves ringing the chamber on the first two levels. The top three levels held shelves loaded with scrolls.

"Where did they get all of this?" Sage asked. "Look at all the scrolls. Can you imagine how old they are?"

"Hello, guys." Amelia walked up behind them. "The look on your faces reminds me of the first time I saw this." She smiled like a proud parent. "Have you heard of the Lost Library of Alexandria?"

"What! That's here?" Sage asked before Nick had a chance to say anything. "Are you saying . . ."

"I'm saying the contents rival those of the Lost Library. Exceed, probably. The history recorded within this place chronicles events long forgotten to humanity."

Nick had studied the Library of Alexandria in school. They had attempted to collect all the world's knowledge and put it in one place. Caesar's army destroyed it in a fire.

Amelia wore a look of frustration and stood quietly for a moment before speaking again. "All of you will be killed if you try and go back. Can't you see that?"

She'd come back to talk them out of it, Nick realized. Again. She truly cared about their safety, and it suddenly made Nick question Sage's confidence. Maybe it *was* best they stay down here.

No, Nick suddenly comprehended; it wasn't best. He was only thirteen years old. Amelia had been here for more than eighty years and she still looked forty. As young as he was, he might live for eight hundred years. A thousand. Or more. No *way* he could do that. Simply not possible. He'd go crazy.

Sage glanced at Nick and Ronan before speaking. "I understand your doubt, Ms. Earhart, but like I said before, you don't know what you don't know. We'll be fine. Besides, it won't be just us. There are more Council members coming. Not sure when, but they'll get here soon. When they do, you'll better understand my confidence."

The meeting took place four hours later in a room at the back of the library. Aquila and Ephraim had returned, as had Elah and Issur.

Amelia was there, the only human besides Nick, Sage, and Ronan, and the only human they would see, at least for now. Amelia suggested they keep their distance from the others until the Elioudian leaders decided what to make of Sage's request to return to the surface. Ronan agreed, as did Sage. Nick didn't really care one way or the other.

"Who else is coming?" Ronan asked Aquila.

"The primary members of the High Council," Aquila said. He turned to Sage. "When you demonstrated the ability to teleport while in the Wastelands, I connected your name with the Prophecy of Seth. I said nothing to Ephraim at that time but did report our experience to a messenger upon our arrival at the switching station. He traveled to Abel immediately. Members of the council began their travels here even before we arrived at Seth."

"Is a scout coming?" Sage asked with a hint of impatience.

Nick could read his brother like a book. Sage was getting antsy, which would lead to irritation in short order.

"They will summon a scout," Aquila said, "for his opinion will be important in this matter. However, I do not know if the scout will arrive today. Or tomorrow, for that matter. There is only one that could possibly fulfill your request, and he is a man of many travels."

"Tell me of the Angelic Response Council," said Elah, the one who held a seat on the Assembly of Histories. "There has been much speculation about the success of the Council. Tell me, what is the status of the war that rages on the surface?"

"War?" Nick asked, and looked at Sage. "What war?"

"Spiritual war," Sage answered. He looked at Elah. "Are you asking about the Seven?"

"Yes!" Elah said. "They are defeated?"

Sage shook his head. "One is defeated. Mammon."

Amelia looked lost. "The seven what?" she asked Sage. "Who's Mammon?"

"Mammon, the Prince of Greed," Sage said. "From the Rephaim race. One of the Seven Princes of Hell."

Amelia's face drained of color. The four Elioudians looked impassive, as if they were sitting around discussing whether to put mustard or mayo on a hamburger. "Who destroyed Mammon?" she asked.

Sage looked at her for several moments. "I did. Last summer. Well, I had help from a girl named Elsbeth Brown and three other Council members, all of whom I hope will be on our rescue team."

"A girl?" Amelia asked. "With a gift?"

"Two," Sage said. "Teleportation and Persuasion."

"Persuasion," Elah said. "A powerful gift, much feared by the Seven." The Elioudian historian almost sounded giddy, Nick thought, sitting around talking about all this stuff.

"She's the only angelic-human other than me with more than one," Sage said. "She's very special."

"It has taken the Council six thousand years to destroy only one of the Seven?" Aquila asked. "That is most disappointing."

Elah turned to Aquila. "You misunderstand the histories, Aquila. Prophecy speaks of the Warrior's battle with all of them. It may yet take the boy several centuries to defeat them, but I am now confident it will happen."

Nick jumped to his feet. "Wait!" He looked at Sage but pointed at Elah. "He said prophecy says you will battle all seven. That means we will make it back to the surface alive!"

The four Elioudians looked at each other. "Sage could make it back to the surface now," Aquila said to Nick. "He could teleport out. It does not, however, mean that *you* will survive the trip."

A creeping coldness invaded Nick's scalp. Aquila was right. If Sage's sword-fighting skills were as good as Sage said they were, Sage would probably make it, but there were no guarantees he himself would.

"We're *all* going to make it," Ronan said. "So, I'd appreciate all of you stop being so negative about it."

"You destroyed one of the Seven Princes of Hell?" Amelia asked, her voice in a total state of awe. "For real?"

"Yeah, and you know what? Charitable giving throughout the world has risen to levels never seen before. Rich nations are helping poor nations. Rich people are chipping in to build schools in poor neighborhoods. Fewer people are starving." Sage looked at Nick. "You aren't aware of any of that, are you?"

"No." Nick couldn't believe how clueless he'd been. His world was soccer, reading, online gaming, and watching scary movies.

"The surface will never heal until the Seven are destroyed," Elah said. "Only when they are gone will the Elioudians consider revealing ourselves to Topside."

"What!" Amelia blurted. "You're saying you may travel to Topside?"

"He did not say that," Aquila said. "He said we may consider making ourselves known to humans on the surface. Since it has taken six thousand years to destroy the first of the Seven, I doubt if any of the humans presently in Tartarus will be alive when the last is destroyed."

"I hear the assembly coming," Issur said, standing. "I will escort them back."

All Nick could hear was the faint noise of dozens of Elioudians moving around in the library stacks. "I didn't hear anything," he whispered to Sage.

"Issur led expedition parties into the Wastelands for five hundred years," Elah said to Nick. "He doesn't actually hear noises like the rest of us. He feels the changes in atmospheric pressure. It is impossible to approach him without him knowing. His gift made him one of our top exploration leaders."

An angelic gift? Nick wondered. They sat in silence for a few moments, and then the entire library went quiet except for the sound of footsteps, which grew louder with each passing second.

"People are unaccustomed to seeing our leaders outside the city of Abel," Ephraim said quietly. "They are held in great esteem."

The seven of them sat there, waiting. Amelia looked relaxed, Sage and Ronan confident, and the three Elioudians a little anxious. Nick was simply curious.

When the footsteps sounded close, all three Elioudians stood and faced away, turning their backs toward the door. Issur entered first. He stepped into the room, bowed deeply to the group at the table, stepped to the side, and turned his back to those coming in behind him. "Presenting Hannah, director of historical studies," Issur belted in a powerful voice.

A woman entered, hobbling quietly, bent with age, using a cane that clicked heavily against the granite floor. Hannah's large eyes swept the room and focused on Sage and Nick with an intense concentration. Dressed in a flowing white garment that hung to her toes, she walked several steps into the room and turned her back toward the person entering next.

"Presenting Achim, keeper of prophetic writings," Issur announced.

A man even older than Hannah came in next. At least seven feet tall, his cane was twice the length of Hannah's, but it made no sound as he moved. Achim also wore a floor-length garment, but it looked like something a man might wear in India. He nodded at Amelia, gave her a little smile, and then studied Nick, Sage, and Ronan. He turned his back toward the door and waited.

"Presenting Maarav, overseer of exploration," Issur said.

The next Elioudian wasn't quite as old, but he used two canes, each clicking sharply. Maarav wore the same outfit as Achim but was barely half as tall. Like every other Elioudian, his muscular body had little body fat, and he moved with the grace of a great athlete. He positioned himself next to Hannah and turned his back to the door.

"Presenting Vale, angelic liaison," Issur pronounced loudly.

It was several moments before the next Elioudian entered, but when he did, Nick could hardly take his eyes off him or the man assisting him. Vale was frail and bent, hunched over in a chair on wheels and being pushed by a strapping young Elioudian nearly nine feet tall, larger even than the guards standing post outside the main gate of the village of Seth. The old man wore the same white outfit as all the others, but it hung on his emaciated frame like cheap curtains. His eyes looked even larger on such a shrunken and wrinkled face, but they were bright and alert and carefully studied both Nick and Sage. He glanced at Ronan and made a hand motion to his assistant, who then rolled the chair across the room and parked it directly across the table from Sage.

"Respect acknowledged," Vale said in a surprisingly strong voice.

Upon hearing the words, the other seven Elioudians in the room turned around and faced the group. They each grabbed a chair around the table and sat down. Nick studied their faces while he waited for one of them to speak.

Vale did. "Which of you is the boy of prophecy?" The man's voice sounded like a professional singer's, Nick thought, a rich baritone he'd once heard during a musical his mom took him to.

"I am," Sage said, puffing out his chest a little. He held Vale's stare without flinching. "I am Sage. This is my brother, Nick. This is Ronan, a Council member gifted with Might, whom I have known all my life."

The man in the wheelchair nodded and turned toward Achim, the keeper of prophetic writings. "The prophet Seth wrote of a boy with such a name. All Elioudians have studied the lessons. You have taken witness to the testimony of Elah and Issur, who observed the boy's Teleportation?"

"It is confirmed," Achim said.

"It is your belief that the prophetic writings have been fulfilled?" Vale's gaze was just as intense when aimed at the others of his race as it was when it was aimed at Sage.

"It would appear so, Master Vale," Achim said. "I can offer no other explanation for the boy's gifts."

"Is your memory so faded, Master Vale, that you fail to recall the very utterances of your own father?" Hannah asked, with a shaky voice. "Are you not the most versed among us to decipher what the prophet Seth saw in his visions?"

Nick glanced at Sage, whose eyes had gone a little wider. Vale was Seth's son? It was all Nick could do to hold his tongue. Aquila just mentioned that Seth made the prophecy six thousand years ago. Nick knew that Aquila was more than two thousand years old, and since Vale looked way older than him, could Vale be twice that?

"He hardly gave me a physical description of the boy," Vale told Hannah. "And it was many decade celebration days ago." He turned to Sage. "Tell me of the Seven."

"I destroyed Mammon a year ago," he said, his voice a little less confident than it had been just a minute before. "Assisted by a girl gifted with Teleportation and Persuasion, a boy with Might, a warrior with Fighting Arts, and a rabbi with Angelic Chains."

Vale considered this and turned back to Achim. "Can one *not* of the bloodline of Seth possess two gifts?"

The old man in the wheelchair looked skeptical, Nick thought. He also thought it was weird that Vale felt it necessary to question everything Sage said. And then Nick realized something. Vale had said *not* of the bloodline of Seth.

"We are direct descendants of Seth?" Nick blurted at Sage, not caring if he interrupted the proceeding.

Sage turned to him and grinned. "We are."

"And you knew it all along?" Nick's head was swimming. How much more did Sage know that he hadn't told him?

"We are directly descended from the prophet Seth," Sage said before turning back to Vale. "Which makes him our grandfather."

The old man sat quietly for several moments before speaking. "Indeed." He turned to Nick and spoke warmly. "Do you not possess a gift?"

"I didn't even know about angelic gifts until a few hours ago. I didn't know anything about this stuff." *And I didn't know an entire world existed below the surface of the earth, either. Or that monsters were real. Or that dinosaurs still existed. Or that Sage was practically a superhero!* But he said none of that. He didn't want to risk angering the people who could provide a scout to lead them back to the surface.

"Our blood runs pure," Vale said to Nick. "I am certain it will only be a matter of time." He then addressed Sage. "Tell me of your battle with Mammon."

Sage glanced at Ronan, who grinned slightly and motioned for him to proceed. Sage folded his hands in front of him and looked at all the Elioudians at the table. "It took place within the Dark spiritual realm, in a prison Mammon created to hold Angelic Response Council members captive. He had captured thirty-two over a span of a thousand years. Most were dead when I arrived. Five were still alive. I freed all but one, which greatly strengthened the Council. We battled him within the great hall of his prison." He paused for a moment and looked at Vale. "Without their help, I would never have defeated him."

"Was the beast hit with a blast of Persuasion?" Vale asked.

"More than one," Sage said. "It's not what killed him, but he took a couple of solid shots from Elsbeth."

"Then you have broken the chain that binds them," said Hannah in her cackling voice. The director of historical studies pointed a long finger at Sage. "It has begun. They cannot rest now until you are defeated."

"What do you mean?" Sage asked.

"Evidence within the ancient scrolls cites a bond between the Seven that will weaken and collapse if one of them is destroyed in a certain manner." Hannah turned toward Vale. "I suspect the angelic liaison knows of what I speak."

Nick couldn't tell if Vale nodded or if his advanced age simply caused involuntary movements, but the old man in the wheelchair confirmed Hannah's statement. "All of them were affected by the purifying light of Persuasion," Vale said. "All were weakened. They will begin to bicker, to distrust one another, each suspecting conspiracies and plots to overthrow the others. If you destroy a second in the same manner, using Persuasion as a weapon against them, they will weaken further. Tell me, young Sage, do you know the location of the other six?"

"We're working on it," Sage said. "They are very well hidden." He started to say something else, hesitated, but finally did. "Can I ask a question of you?"

"Certainly."

"The Elioudian race is cousin to the Emim, Rephaim, and Nephilim. Yet only the descendants of our people have angelic gifts." Sage glanced around the table. "I understand my gifts were bestowed upon me because the Elioudians repented from their evil ways prior to the Great Flood. But the other races have angelic blood, too. The Seven are Rephaim. If they do not have gifts, how can they do what they do? They've been alive for more than six thousand years. They take the form of humans and live among us. Yet they are part spiritual and command entire armies of beasts. They freely travel to and from the human and Dark spiritual realms. Are those not the most terrifying gifts of all?"

Goose bumps crawled up Nick's arms. Sage's face, as he spoke, had a haunted look, clearly recalling the battle he'd waged against Mammon. Nick rubbed his arms to warm himself.

"Gifts are bestowed by God," Vale said. "The most dangerous gift to them, as you witnessed during your battle with Greed, is the purifying light of Persuasion. The sorcery of the Rephaim cannot stand against it. While immortality and shape shifting may present themselves as gifts, they are nothing more than ancient spells that rely on the chain of unity bonding the Seven together."

"It took all seven to curse Leviathan, the great water beast," Hannah said. "The eyewitness account is heavily documented within our historical scrolls." Sage's expression turned suddenly pensive. The old woman regarded him for a moment; then she turned her gaze upon Nick and smiled at him. "I suspect your older brother knows the story of Leviathan. Have him tell you during your journey back to the surface."

Sage jumped up. "You're providing a scout?"

"It was never in doubt," Vale said. "Your value to your people, both in Tartarus and on Topside, is up there, fighting to destroy the rest of the Seven."

Sage offered a fist bump to Nick, then slapped a high five to Ronan. "I made a promise to my grandfather," Sage said. "A vow. That if I got an opportunity to get Nick out of here, even if it is before my rescue team arrives, that I should take it. I plan to keep that promise. Will you help me?"

"Yes," Vale said. "But we must warn you, the journey is long, and the Territories are rife with danger." He looked straight at Nick. "You must be brave, for the odds of survival are slim."

Nick's sudden joy disappeared just as fast as it had appeared. His odds of survival were slim.

11

They held the briefing around the campfire, although Elsbeth considered the pile of branches Gavin and Malcolm had gathered more of a bonfire. There weren't enough chairs to go around, so the oldest of the group got to sit, with Horace off by himself facing the rest. Theo got a chair, as did Steven, Kato, Endora, and Malcolm. Gavin, David, and Elsbeth sat on a big log off to the side, far enough from the fire to avoid most of the heat but close enough to keep the bugs away.

Horace had a tablet computer open on his lap and a list of things he wanted to cover. Elsbeth took a quick look at everyone's faces and didn't see any of the fear and anxiety that churned deep within her own stomach. David and Kato might have been deciding what kind of pizza they were about to order. Malcolm and Gavin were trading quiet jabs at one another, laughing about a hellhound they'd slain just last week. Endora was speaking quietly to Steven about something that made her smile.

Only Theo seemed distressed as he waited for Horace to call the meeting to order. Since he'd confessed to the real possibility that Sage might be killed in the Territories, the Council's most accomplished Sight practitioner had been staring into the mouth of the cave, alone. Elsbeth wondered if he might have been sorting through various visions of the demise of those about to plunge into the underworld.

Individually, each of them had prepared themselves for the journey. Packed, rested, mentally ready, the group reminded Elsbeth of a football team about to play for the championship. Too bad she didn't feel that way. She couldn't shake an incredible sense of dread. Was seven enough? The skill set of the team, in total, was formidable. If they could catch up to Sage and Ronan before they got the bright idea of traveling through the Territories without them, the group would be nearly unbeatable.

Horace held up a hand. "Let's get started."

The popping of the fire, the shadows pushing in from all directions, the noise of the jungle, and the sudden intensity on everyone's faces caused Elsbeth to close her eyes and take several deep breaths. This was her time to be strong. Though she was the youngest one here and knew the group had confidence in her, it wouldn't serve to reveal her building dread.

"When the original Council left Tartarus six thousand years ago," Horace said, "they were escorted through the Territories of the Emim, Rephaim, and Nephilim by a host of Archangels large enough to discourage any of the evil races from engaging them. They suffered no losses, engaged in no battles. One of the Council members, my fifth great-grandfather, Abraham, made sketches as they traveled, which he later turned into a map." Horace held up his tablet computer and showed it to them. "I've copied that map and loaded it on each of the tablets you will carry with you.

"After the Council made it to the surface, Grandfather Abraham wrote detailed notes of what he saw. He also recorded what the others told him they'd seen, carefully transcribing direct quotes about their impressions of the underworld." He waved the tablet at them again. "I've created a summarized list of the most salient points and included them on here."

Each of them would carry a tablet, Elsbeth knew, and because there would be no way to recharge them, they had already determined in which order they would be used. They would use Kato's tablet first. The next one wouldn't be powered up and used until Kato's battery died. They estimated they could make them last at least a month before all of them gave out. And only then would they break out the paper maps Horace had prepared for them.

The professor sat quietly for a bit as he organized his thoughts. "The area now known as the Territories was the first home of our Elioudian ancestors. They—"

"All here know the history," Endora interrupted. She smiled tightly. "Please, we are no longer students of yours. Just tell us of the danger. Is this not why you have traveled five thousand miles?"

"I'm with Endora," Kato said gently. "We expect Tartarus to be in much better shape than the Territories, and we know that your information is six thousand years old. We just want some clarity about what the original Council saw as they traveled to the surface."

"I intended to paint a picture for you," Horace said, his voice not quite as commanding as a minute before. "Fine, I will cut to the chase." He powered off his tablet and set it at his feet. "Like Noah and the Elioudians before them, the evils dragged thousands of beasts into their cavern. The one species the evils captured and imprisoned that our ancestors did not was humans." He looked at Endora and Kato. "So, what did the original Council see? They saw hundreds upon hundreds of monsters. They saw the pits, the mass graves, the torture chambers. They saw rivers of blood, entire villages filled with disease that rotted flesh yet did not kill. They saw slave camps where living, breathing human hybrids ruled over humans not yet transformed into nightmares we can only dream of." The professor paused. "Yet, they saw evidence of organization, of enough civilization to grow crops and livestock, to keep the infrastructure operating at the most basic level. They also saw that the evil races had divided themselves into their own kind. The Emim and their creations had segregated themselves into the territory closest to the Elioudians. Next, they traveled into the area occupied only by the Rephaim. And finally, through the land of the giants. The Nephilim."

Elsbeth glanced at Endora and noticed that her face had softened. Theo's gaze was somewhere distant, as though seeing a vision at that moment. Kato sat with his hands folded, patiently waiting for the rest of it. David held his steel bar across his lap and polished it with the tail of his shirt.

"Remember that the original Council made their trip a century after the Battle at the Gate," Horace said. "The Emim, as you know, is the race that has created most of the beasts we have spent our lives battling. That territory was the worst. But because of the sorcery of the Rephaim, the power of their wickedness, the fact they most closely resemble the Watchers, the group treaded carefully while passing through there. The giants were the most organized of the three and had been successful in keeping the others out of their territory. Yet the giants were the only ones that openly challenged the Archangels as they escorted the Elioudians out."

"So, what do you expect after six thousand years?" Steven asked Horace. "What might we find down there?"

The professor didn't answer right away. He started to speak several times but stopped himself, clearly troubled about how to answer. "I expect one of two things," he said finally. "Either everything devolved into total chaos eons ago and all of them destroyed themselves, or they somehow found a way to survive and perfect their experiments. If it is the latter, you might be facing beasts more powerful and deadly than anything you've experienced on the surface. If it's the former, you won't have anything to worry about at all."

"Theo," Gavin said, "Elsbeth told me a few minutes ago that those gifted with Sight have never seen a vision from there. Is that true?"

"Yes," Theo said.

"Could it be because nothing is there? That they destroyed each other thousands of years ago? Or starved themselves?"

Gavin's tone sounded as though he shared the same kernel of hope that had penetrated Elsbeth's every thought for the past two hours—that the three Territories were nothing now but a wasteland of long-forgotten nightmares.

"Yes, would explain," Theo said, nodding and smiling just a little.

"Do you think that's the most reasonable explanation?" Kato asked.

Theo thought for a while before answering. "Maybe everything dead. Not certain. But . . . Archangels make agreement with Magog to keep Granite Gate sealed. Agreement for one-time passage, to let original Council out. My fear simple. Even if team find Sage and get to Gate, maybe Gate not open."

As reality washed over Elsbeth, she suddenly understood why Theo had appeared so distressed throughout Horace's history lesson. There were no images from the underworld. Why? No one knew. Maybe they would all be killed. Or maybe they wouldn't and would have to spend the rest of their lives down there. "Yet we must have faith and go anyway," she said to Theo. "Isn't that the lesson you shared today?"

"Would go myself if physically able," Theo said.

"I have more details to share," Horace said. "Some specific things that might prove valuable."

"Take your time," Steven said. "Because even though I said we would leave tonight, I think all of us need a good night's sleep before we go. Another few hours won't make any difference. Any objections?" The group looked at each other, but no one disagreed. "It's settled, then. We'll leave in the morning. Horace, finish up so we can all hit the rack."

For the next hour Elsbeth listened to the old professor speak of horrors too awful to visualize. And no matter how hard she would try and sleep later, she figured it probably wouldn't happen.

The Elioudian High Council set Sage, Nick, and Ronan up in an empty house on the Elioudian side of the lake, at the bottom of the great bowl. It didn't look much different than the house Amelia lived in, Sage thought, except for the quality of furniture. Everything was handmade and oversized, built for people seven feet tall. He wondered if some of the gate guards routinely stayed there. Sage and Nick were alone now. Ronan had excused himself for a bit of exploration. At least that's what he'd told Nick. Sage knew the big man was talking privately to some of the Elioudians about what might await them in the Territories.

"When do you think our rescue team will come?" Nick asked.

They'd just eaten a meal of roasted meat and potatoes, steamed veggies, and a strange berry pie. They set their tray of dishes outside the door, as instructed, and now were lounging on sofas in the living room.

"Not sure," Sage said. "Soon, I'd think."

"Who do you think he might bring?"

"I've been thinking a lot about that," Sage said. "A variety of gifts, is what I'd bring. Fighting Arts, for sure. Maybe Angelic Bells. Voice. Chains. Gifts that stun, that slow the beasts down so they can be killed."

The look on Nick's face reminded Sage of what his brother always looked like before he got sick to his stomach. "Are the monsters indestructible?" he asked. "Can you lose?"

Sage needed to be careful here. He didn't really know what they'd face, and the last thing he wanted was to exaggerate anything. "I can lose," he said, remembering how he'd nearly been killed by a werewolf last summer when he tried to save Mordoc Nevingham in old London. "But none of what we'll face is indestructible. Anything can be beaten. That's why I think Grandpa will bring a team of varied gifts to make sure we're prepared for anything." He'd given Nick several short descriptions about what kind of evil they might face in the Territories, but since he didn't know what awaited them, he kept it generic.

Nick yawned and stretched, his eyes drooping with fatigue. They hadn't done much today, but they'd walked so far yesterday and slept so fitfully, they were both ready for a night on the comfortable feather beds waiting in the other room. The poison in Nick's system was gone now. The only remaining evidence was a slight bump in his neck from the initial stab wound. His eyes were totally clear.

"How long will we wait for the team?" Nick asked. "What are you thinking?"

"Until they get here," Sage said. "I can handle myself pretty well. So can Ronan. But we've gotta make sure you're OK during the trip, so there's no sense pushing our luck."

Nick was quiet for a moment. "Yeah, that sounds good. Do you think Grandpa will come?"

"I don't think there's anyone on earth who could stop him," Sage said. "Even though none of this is his fault, he probably blames himself."

Sage followed Nick into the bedroom, and they both collapsed into separate beds. A third bed was ready for Ronan once he returned. The rock walls were decorated with ancient masks and hand tools, as well as colorful, handwoven rugs. A single lamp burned in a corner, throwing odd-shaped shadows onto the ceiling.

"The Prince who had me pulled down here doesn't think we'll get out, does he?" Nick asked. "He thinks we're going to die down here."

"Yeah, he probably thinks we're toast," Sage said, "but I wouldn't worry about that so much."

"Why?"

"Because the Prince from last summer didn't think we'd rescue the Council members locked in his prison, but we did. They've been wrong before; they'll be wrong again."

"Can we keep the light on? All night?"

"Sure." Nick sounded younger than thirteen, Sage thought. Way younger.

They both got quiet, Sage's mind running full steam about what was going on with the rescue team. Elsbeth would come; he knew that. She would have been the first one Grandpa called. She probably got there first, skipping and hopping across the North American continent in her thirty-mile bursts, careful not to teleport into an area with people. Gavin and Malcolm, probably. David Brock, Sage hoped. Then maybe Kato . . .

"They're keeping the other humans away from us, aren't they?" Nick asked. "Afraid we might give them false hope about getting back to the surface."

Sage looked over, and Nick was on his side, facing away from him. "I think so."

"There aren't any kids down here. When we saw that group down in front of the big building earlier, there weren't any kids."

"I didn't notice." And he hadn't. He didn't think it was a big deal and really didn't understand why Nick had brought it up.

"Wouldn't you think that a bunch of humans over the decades would have gotten lonely and married each other?" Nick asked. "Maybe had a couple of kids?"

"Maybe they did," Sage said. "And they're all grown up." Nick didn't say anything. "Or maybe they just didn't want to bring a kid into this world. I wouldn't."

Nick sat up and faced him. "Maybe the Elioudians took them."

Sage propped himself up on an elbow. "Took them where?"

Nick shrugged. "To another part of Tartarus."

"Why would they do that?"

"To raise them as Elioudians."

"For what purpose?" The look on Nick's face worried Sage. His brother wasn't thinking rationally.

"To breed with them." Nick stared at Sage with an intensity he'd never seen before.

Sage sat all the way up in the bed. "Nick, what in the world are you talking about?"

Nick sat up, too, and then stood. "What if the Elioudians are mixing humans with their race to create kids with powers? Like you have. And Elsbeth. If it happened six thousand years ago, maybe they think it could happen again." Sage started to respond, but Nick cut him off. "Maybe they think the humans dropping into the Wastelands are sent by God. For them to use as they please." His voice was shaky, full of terror.

They looked at each other for a long time. Sage wasn't going to ridicule his brother, not in the emotional state he was in. "Do you think Amelia would put up with that?" Sage asked. "Did she look like she's had a baby?"

"She's been here for eighty years," Nick said. "She could have had twenty kids during that time. Or thirty. She might believe the Elioudians are building a race of superhumans that will eventually get her out of here. Maybe they all think that. Or hope. Maybe that's why they haven't let any of the other humans talk to us. Maybe they're scared they will accidentally leak something to us."

"That's a lot of maybes. I think—"

"Think about it," Nick said. "If there are thirty women down here, and some of them have been here longer than Amelia, the Elioudians could have hundreds of kids stashed away, each of them with superpowers. Maybe they're building an army so they can go into the Territories and clean house."

Wow. Sage didn't know what to say to all of that. "So, if that's true, you think they'd want us out of here quick so we won't discover it."

"Maybe."

"Wouldn't it make more sense for them to lock me up and make me have kids with some Elioudian women? They *know* I've got powers. Wouldn't I be a grand prize?"

"Maybe."

"Yet they're willing to provide a guide and let me go."

"Because they know they can't hold you," Nick said. "You'd teleport away from them. Or use your Fighting Arts to hurt them. Better to let you go than risk exposing the whole scheme."

Again, they just looked at each other. "OK, how about this?" Sage said. "Tomorrow we'll do a little scouting around on our own and see if we can figure out what's going on. They said it's gonna take the scout another full day to get here, anyway. Might as well do some investigating." He smiled at Nick, hoping his fears would be sated just little.

Nick nodded. "OK."

"Know what I really think, though?"

"What?"

"That all the online gaming you do has absolutely cracked your imagination wide open." Sage smiled. "I mean, I know you've always had a vivid imagination, but all the monsters you kill with your game controller have twisted you into a supernatural conspiracy theorist."

Nick grinned just a little. "Maybe." Then he pointed at Sage. "But if we meet an Elioudian kid with angelic gifts, don't say I didn't tell you."

They both plopped back down with smiles. "OK. I won't say it. Goodnight, Nick. I love you."

"I love you, too, Sage. And thanks for coming down to rescue me."

"You'd have done the same for me."

Sage heard heavy breathing less than two minutes later. He looked over and saw the most peaceful face he'd seen on his brother in years. He just wished it would stay that way. He had his doubts, but at least it could be his hope.

12

They stood around the hole, each lost in their own thoughts. *This is it*, Elsbeth thought. Horace's description of the Territories still echoed inside her head. Visions of doom danced in her imagination. It would all start here at this innocent little hole in the earth. No turning back. They were as ready as time would allow.

Each of them had a backpack crammed with gear: clothes, flashlights, food, and water. They had mountain-climbing equipment, like harnesses and ropes and anchors, ascenders, carabiners, hooks, and climbing hammers. They had cameras and extra batteries, tablet computers, and portable radios with headsets. They had the laminated map of the Territories Horace had provided, along with a list of beasts they might encounter. Each of them also had several copies of a small handbook about the history of the Council to give to the Elioudians as gifts. And, of course, they all had the weapons they felt most comfortable with. Their shoes were solid, their clothing the best money could buy, and all had GoPro cameras secured to their helmets. The Council insisted on them recording as much of this expedition as they could.

"Glad the hole is big enough," David said. "Course, that wanker Ronan fit, so I don't know why I had my knickers in a knot about it."

The boy with Might had the broadest shoulders of the group. He'd boasted to Elsbeth the previous night that he'd spent months in a remote castle near Council headquarters lifting and throwing boulders of all sizes to build strength and endurance. She couldn't even imagine what kind of power he possessed now. Ronan claimed that David Brock was half again as strong as any other Council member gifted with Might. David's problem was that his ego was just as big as his shoulders.

"Oh, I just realized I forgot something," Elsbeth said. She wanted to bring Sage's GoPro camera, and she'd left it in the tent she'd been using.

"Make it quick," Steven said. "We're ready to go."

She teleported into the tent, grabbed it, stuck it into her pack, and was about to head back when Horace stuck his head in the flap. "I thought I heard someone in here. Forget something? I thought half of you would be sliding to the center of the earth by now."

"About to head down now." She smiled, but it felt forced.

"Before you go, Elsbeth, I'd like to say something."

"Sure. What?"

The professor wiped a hand across his balding head and hobbled over to a chair. "It is fortunate we are able to visit before you descend."

She waited patiently while Horace mentally searched for the words. "I have sensed a fear in you that is uncharacteristic of your reputation. A great hesitation. Tremendous doubt. Am I mistaken?"

Elsbeth readjusted her backpack and looked away. "No."

"Does your doubt come from the fear that Persuasion won't work that far underground?"

"I don't see how it can."

"So, you're wondering what good you'll do while you're down there," Horace said. "You have Teleportation but are average with a sword and thus won't be much help in defeating the beasts you'll face. You think you'll be a burden. That the others will be forced to look after you when they should be doing everything they can to get back to the surface. How wrong am I?"

How could she admit all of that? It was true. Every word. But how could she admit such weakness to one of the legends of the Council? If she did and the mission failed because of her uselessness, the Council would never forgive her for not declining to go. And Sage's family? They'd hate her if something happened to either of their boys because of her. This was a mission for grownups, not scared little girls with doubts the size of Texas. So, she wasn't about to tell Horace the truth.

"I've gotta get back, Professor. Thanks for everything you've done for the team. Your information will be invaluable."

Horace smiled with a knowing expression. "It was my pleasure. And your refusal to respond to my queries demonstrates a determination I believe you'll need. Godspeed, Elsbeth. We will secure this location once all of you are gone. No human will ever again drop into the underworld from inside this cave. Be certain of that."

She teleported back into the chamber, hoping she didn't look as stricken as she felt. "Ready, now. Sorry."

"There's the little lass," David said. He hefted his steel bar and punched it on the floor of the cave. "Let's go meet and greet some special new mates. Maybe they'll have a welcome committee waiting for us." He grinned and looked at everyone. "Who's first?"

"Before we go," Steven said, "I'd like to know if Theo has any last words for us."

Everyone turned Theo's way. They'd tried talking him out of coming this far into the cave, but he'd insisted. Elsbeth couldn't believe it when he'd dropped onto his belly and crawled under the flat rock.

"Rare when future blind to me," Theo said. "Have faith. Believe in each other. Trust training. There is Master Plan, even if not all return." He wiped tears from his eyes and nodded. "That is all. Go before I bawl like three-year-old."

Elsbeth was the first of the group to walk over and give him a hug. "Thank you," she whispered. "I'll tell Sage you are with us in spirit." She stepped away and smiled at him.

One by one the rescue group gave Theo a hug or slap on the back, giving thanks to his many years of service to the Council. Elsbeth couldn't help but notice that many of the comments sounded like final farewells.

Kato went first. He dropped into the hole without a sound, backpack clung against his chest, his sword and scabbard clutched tightly in his right hand. Gavin, also gifted with Fighting Arts, waited one minute and dropped in next. Endora, shifting from foot to foot, impatiently watched the time and then disappeared without a word.

David sat down and scooted both feet into the hole. "Going be a riot, Elsbeth," he said, a broad smile on his face. "Another jolly adventure. We should make this a summer tradition." He pressed his steel bar tightly against his chest next to his backpack.

Elsbeth smiled weakly. She hoped not.

"Off we go, then," David said. He disappeared down the hole. "Long live the queen!" His voice faded as he plummeted into the darkness.

Malcolm stepped to the hole next. His backpack was a little smaller than the others, and he carried a short sword and scabbard. His eyes shone with excitement; Elsbeth wished she shared his enthusiasm. "You're next, Elsbeth," he said. "We'll be waiting." He glanced at his watch and dropped in.

With a quickening heart, Elsbeth adjusted the pack against her chest and held tightly to the small sword she'd chosen from Kato's collection. Like everyone else, she assumed she would end up sliding down on her back, and she didn't want to destroy anything on the trip down.

"Council will prevail," Theo told her softly. "Your team strong. Even with no Persuasion, Teleportation devastating. Evil in Territories not seen likes of you."

She swallowed hard. Fear had squeezed her throat, and she couldn't speak.

"See you at the bottom," Steven said.

At the one-minute mark, she closed her eyes, tightened her grip on everything, and dropped into a world she hoped wasn't as horrible as the one living within her imagination.

Sage pulled the ancient volume from the bookshelf and placed it carefully on the table in front of Nick. His hands trembled with excitement, but he handled the book as though it might crumble in his fingers.

"Are you sure that's it?" Nick asked. "Just looks like a bunch of scribbling to me."

"It's Adamic," Sage said. "I studied it with Leah for years."

"The language of angels?" Nick asked. "This isn't a joke?"

Sage looked at him. "No joke."

They'd spent the morning wandering around Seth, trying to engage Elioudians in conversation, but everyone had politely refused to talk to them. Then they'd tried finding a few humans, but none of them had come out of their houses all morning. They had knocked on Amelia's door, but she hadn't answered. Finally, desperate to try and figure out why none of the other humans would even acknowledge their presence, they'd knocked on some of their doors. Nothing.

Ronan had disappeared early with Aquila and told Sage that he'd be gone much of the day. Ronan wasn't much for reading books, and when Aquila volunteered to give him a personal tour of Seth, to include the underground generators, irrigation system, and natural aqueducts, he'd jumped at the chance.

So, Sage and Nick had ended up in the library. Sage had asked an Elioudian that appeared to know his way around the stacks if there were any books on the formation of the original Territories. It had taken a few minutes, but he'd found one that chronicled not only the days on the surface just before the Great Flood but also several decades afterwards.

"What's it called?" Nick asked. "The name of the book?"

"*Conception.*" Sage looked at Nick and smiled. "What do you think that means?"

"I don't know." Nick thought for a second. "A new nation? The birth of a new nation?"

"That's pretty good. Maybe the seed of a nation rising from the womb of earth." He smiled. "Could mean a lot of things, I guess." He opened the book and found the pages were different—vellum or papyrus—and had a thin strip of wood along the outer edges to allow someone to easily turn them. The book cover was a darkened piece of thick, hard leather.

"Some believe Adam and Eve spoke Adamic in the Garden of Eden," Sage said. "That Adam spoke with angels. Leah said the language is of divine origin and unchangeable." He pointed to a single sentence in the middle of the first page. "*Beauty in destruction, wickedness in rebirth.*"

"What's that mean?" Nick asked.

"I don't know." Sage turned the page and read a few lines. Then he looked at several other pages. "It's written like separate journal entries, but by the same hand. Almost like a scribe sat down and simply wrote down what people said."

"Read one," Nick said. "Read the first one."

"OK." Sage studied the strange words in front of him and was suddenly thankful that Leah had drilled him relentlessly on his studies. "*The world ends. Creatures run amok. The end of humanity is at hand. The water will come.*" Sage looked at Nick. "There's some words I don't understand. A bunch, in fact. That's all I recognize off this page."

"So, this was before the flood?" Nick asked.

"I guess so." Sage turned the page. "OK, here's some that I recognize. *Ursula's army attacked our compound, but Seth's visions allowed us to prepare. The Emim beasts—the wolf men with wings—broke our protection ring around the young. Three were carried off. The Great Granite Gate is near completion. Soon we will secure ourselves.*"

"Wolf men with wings?" Nick asked, wide eyed. "Are you sure that's what it says?"

"Yeah, I'm sure." Sage skimmed another page, then another. "OK, here's more. *Most of the nation is secured. Remnants remain, those still battling the beasts. Mankind is lost. Corrupted by the Fallen Hosts. No purity left except Noah and his people.*" He paused, unsure of the next couple of sentences. "*The Rephaim attacked as we attempted to close the gate. Some succeeded entry but were quickly slain. The earth erupted, the sky opened, the foundation of civilization is no more. All is lost. The ark rises and saves humanity.*"

Sage turned several pages and stopped when one caught his eye. "Listen to this. *Gehenna is completed. Home now to our people. Evil is destroyed. Soon, purity will again grace the surface of God's creation. We are depleted but alive, ready to serve the will of the All-Knowing. Here will we remain, forever mindful of our true nature.*"

"You read the language of the ancients?" a voice said from behind Sage.

Both he and Nick jumped at the sudden intrusion. Sage turned and saw Hannah, the director of historical studies, leaning on her cane. He'd been so absorbed with translating the Adamic into English that he hadn't heard her approach.

"Some," Sage answered her. "My Guardian taught me. I'm not super fluent, evidently, because there's a lot of words here I don't recognize."

Hannah pulled out a chair and sat down next to Nick. "Some words do not have an English equivalent. Some words mean entire sentences. Others speak of things no longer in existence." She smiled. "You have chosen a volume of the early times. This interests you?"

"The early Territories interest me," Sage said.

Hannah's oversized eyes were as green as a cat's. She wore a necklace made from a leather strap that held a ruby the size of a silver dollar. It sparkled and threw red dots all over the table.

"Our original homeland," Hannah said. She rested her cane against her chair and sat back in her seat. "I have never seen it. Except our scouts, none in Tartarus have. But my grandmother was one of the originals. She told me many stories."

"What was it like?" Nick asked.

"Much like this place, with homes and villages and crops and livestock. Our people were only there for five hundred years before fully moving into Tartarus, so it was not as developed as our world here. But when we abandoned it, there was enough infrastructure to survive until the end of times."

Sage turned a page in the book and a sentence grabbed his attention. *Leviathan sings praises within the watery depths, forever free of the wages of battle.* Leviathan! Battling the evil races even before the flood! Sage read it again, unable to resist the memory of being wrapped within its hide last summer.

"Is there a book in here that describes all the monsters that walked the earth before the flood?" Nick asked.

"There is," Hannah said. "I spent many months studying the volume as a youngster. It is terrifying to know what abominations my ancestors battled on the surface. God had no choice but to destroy the world."

"Can we see it?" Nick asked. "The book?"

Hannah sat quietly for several moments before answering. "I would advise against it."

"Why?" Sage asked.

"Because some of those beasts roam the Territories to this day. It would only serve to weaken your confidence of survival. Better you should begin your journey aware only that beasts exist. Better to begin your journey with your resolve unshaken by visions of such horror."

Hannah's words made a lot of sense. "I can't argue with that," Sage told Nick. He looked at the old woman. "How soon after the flood did the Elioudians discover the great caverns of Tartarus? How soon did they start to develop them?"

"Almost immediately. The earth shook with volcanic eruptions all over the globe. Our underground world shook and vibrated for a month straight. The releasing of the water raged just on the other side of a rock wall at the far edge of Gehenna. When the noise ceased, Elioudian diggers broke through the wall and found what later became our new homeland."

"Were there any normal humans left on the surface?" Sage asked. "This book said the end of humanity was at hand. It mentioned wolf men with wings."

Hannah leaned forward and looked solemnly at both boys. "Humanity was lost. The seed of destruction had impregnated every human bloodline except for Noah and his family. The fallen angels were many, the evil complete. None could be trusted. If not for Elioudian repentance, if not for our ancestors fighting side-by-side with the angels of light, all might have been lost." The director of historical studies sighed and interlocked her fingers. She stared off into the middle distance and sat quietly for several beats before speaking to Sage. "You see the spiritual realm, yes?"

He nodded.

"What do those on Topside call the evil spectral beings that can slide within the body of a human?"

"I call them Darks," Sage said. "Most on earth call them demons."

"Do you understand their origin?"

Sage thought about it and realized he didn't know. He'd never asked Leah about their origin. None of the books he'd read addressed it. How could he *not* know? Then he realized that this was the kind of stuff he would learn at the Tomb of Ancient Documents once he trained there. All Council members eventually spent a year at the Tomb. Elsbeth had, and she probably knew all of this. "Well . . . I assume they're fallen angels. Those cast from Heaven."

Hannah cocked her head. "You believe that God created angels that look like them? You believe He created light and dark angels to both occupy the same place? You believe your Darks looked that way prior to being cast from Heaven?"

Sage started to answer but realized he didn't have one. "I've never thought about it." He glanced at Nick, who sat spellbound at the conversation.

"It is our belief," Hannah said, "that your Darks are simply the souls of the slain beasts created when the Watchers procreated with human women. The Watchers themselves have been shackled by God, locked away for an eternity until the end times." She leaned forward slightly and lowered her voice. "During your journey through the Territories, you should, if possible, twice kill the abominations you face."

"What do you mean?" Sage asked. "Twice kill?"

"You must first kill the body, then the black soul that will escape after death. The souls must be slain either by angels of light or the only other angelic creature capable: an Elioudian. Otherwise, they will simply escape through the vent flues into the world above and join with the Seven." She reached over and took one of Sage's hands. "They cannot recognize you as Elioudian and so will not expect you to kill the soul."

"What? I had eight Archangels and Leah protecting me my entire life, and you're saying Darks didn't know I was Elioudian? I had hundreds attack me in my life."

The old woman smiled. "They were not attacking you, young Sage. They were attacking your Guardian. Like you, thousands of regular humans are protected by Guardians. Hundreds of thousands. Most Guardians have help from Archangels. In the eyes of the Darks, you are simply one of legions of humans that God has deemed important enough to shield for the future crafting of history. The Darks, as you call them, attempt to interrupt that future. If they can defeat the Guardians and expose these important humans to danger, they become valuable targets for the Princes. Some, not all, Council members had Guardian protection until their angelic gift fully manifested. None continued to have that protection once their gift had matured. Is your Leah still with you?"

"No, she's been gone for a month." He sat quietly. Grandpa hadn't told him any of this. Nor had Leah, which Sage found almost impossible to believe. Yeah, on a few occasions Sage had seen other Guardians hovering around humans—a couple in their small Oklahoma town and several more in Oklahoma City—but he hadn't thought much about it. He knew some humans were important enough to protect. He'd never asked about it, and Leah wasn't one to simply strike up a conversation about random topics. She couldn't read his mind and mainly just answered questions he asked. It made sense, in a way, that Darks didn't know he was Elioudian or the boy from prophecy, which explained why he or his family hadn't suffered a full-scale attack by the Princes. It also explained why the Council had never been worried about the Darks always hovering around. He *really* needed to train at the Tomb. There were lots of things he didn't know.

"So that's why the Princes were never able to find me," Sage said. "Until now, I mean. Before my trip into Mammon's prison, they didn't know who I was."

"Certainly not," Hannah said. "They cannot see the angelic gifts residing within you. When the two hundred special Elioudian children were born in Tartarus after the Battle at the Gate, the Archangels assured us that the Seven would never be able to discover their identity by mere observation. It remains true today and always will. It is only after Council members move against a Dark Beast that the Princes learn of their identity." She squeezed his hand and released it.

"How many are there?" Sage asked. "Creatures in the Territories?"

"No one knows for certain," she said.

"How can Sage kill the Darks?" Nick asked.

"He must use a blade tempered by the blood of the repented." She looked at Sage. "I see such a sword at your waist. I recognize the design from ancient drawings I have seen. It is the blade crafted to be used by Beowulf and hidden until presented to you?"

"Yes. I used it last summer against Mammon." Sage pulled it out and laid it on the table to allow Hannah to inspect it. "I'm told it was made here." The three-foot blade shimmered and reflected light in waves of faint colors. "Do you know how it can sizzle away the blood of Dark Beasts and clean itself?"

"The blood of the Fallen flees from the Light," she said. "Crafted by Elioudian priests with assistance of a Dominion angel, this sword is not unlike those used by the Archangels. No other such sword exists in the world."

He realized then that Hannah might be able to read the unknown script engraved within the fuller. He pointed to the groove in the center of the blade. "Do you know what that says?"

She leaned forward. *"Fear not the blood of the corrupt."* She turned the sword over and read another passage engraved within the fuller on the other side. *"Power flows from the blood of the redeemed."*

Sage stood quietly for a bit, then sheathed his sword, closed the leather-bound book, and sat down. "When will the scout arrive?" he asked Hannah.

"Soon," she said. "Now that we have spoken, I will send word that he is free to make contact." She grabbed the handle of her cane and pushed herself to her feet. "Heed the words of your grandfather, young Sage, and take the first opportunity to escape the underworld." She smiled at Nick and walked away, tapping her cane softly against the granite floor.

Sage looked at Nick and then grabbed him in a bear hug. "Gonna be OK, little bro. Kind of a scary conversation, but it's gonna be OK." He just wished the words had come out sounding more confident.

13

By the time Elsbeth dropped onto the ground, sword ready, dirt rolling off her back and shoulders, the others had spread out in a defensive formation.

"Over here, lass," David said from behind her. "Don't want Sage's grandfather landing on your head."

The landscape was completely foreign: red rock and dirt, bleak and grim. With the stink of sulfur in the air thick enough to gag her, Elsbeth thought the humans' name for this place—Hell—might not be too far off. A bubbling stream to her left seemed to boil; steam rose from the water in waves of gagging putridity. Thousands of skeletons gave the scene its final touch of creepiness. Elsbeth glanced at David Brock, who wore a crazy smile. His heavy steel bar lay propped lazily on one shoulder, although she could tell from how his eyes searched their surroundings that he was more alert than his air of nonchalance showed.

She heard Steven sliding down the hole and walked over next to David. Spots of lights glowing through a misty ceiling illuminated the cavern well enough for her to flip off her headlamp. Jagged rock formations seemed to stretch for miles in all directions.

"Is this the Territories, you think?" David whispered to her. "And how in the name of the queen are we going to find those blokes? They could have gone anywhere."

"We've got Kato," Elsbeth whispered back. "Have you forgotten his tracking skills?"

"Hardly," David said. "Don't see how even he can track someone through this cock-up. Then again, might not be too difficult to follow Ronan's giant feet."

Sage's grandpa dropped onto the ground, stumbled, and fell to his knees, then quickly jumped to his feet and looked around. "Anybody hurt?" he asked.

"Look at this place," Gavin said to everyone. "We dropped thousands of feet. And a lighting system? How is this possible?"

"How is this place even real?" Malcolm asked.

"The Elioudians are our ancestors," Endora said. "Nearly pure angelic beings. Do not doubt their capabilities. We must think beyond the boundaries of weak humans." She looked at Kato. "Can you find a trail? The rest of us need to stay alert." She raised her sword and turned away.

Elsbeth leaned over and whispered to David. "I'm really starting to like her. Tough leader traits. We could have used her against Mammon."

"I've heard about her," David whispered back. "She *is* tough. Tortured, though, from what I hear." He twirled a finger in small circles at the side of his head. "Maybe a *little* off her trolley. Wound tighter than the king's cummerbund. But hey, look at me: a perfect male specimen, prettier than any three men combined, nearly a god in every way, yet I'm a little barmy, too. Like the purple in my hair?" He flipped it at her.

Elsbeth couldn't help but laugh. "I actually think you've gotten *worse* since last year." She nearly thanked him for breaking the tension but knew it might be too soon, given that plenty of tension lay ahead for her.

The greenish-blue hue of the atmosphere reminded Elsbeth of the Dark spiritual realm outside of Mammon's prison last summer. She walked over to Sage's grandpa. "This is the Dark realm. Almost exactly like what we saw last summer."

"Hope Sage found Nick in time," Steven said. "Got him inside Tartarus."

Kato spent a long time inspecting the ground around them. Elsbeth couldn't imagine trying to make sense of all the scuff marks she saw in the loose dirt. The tracker walked in ever widening circles, often dropping to the ground to touch a footprint. Except for the bubbling stream, the only sound was Kato's occasional mumble as he tried figuring out which way Sage, Nick, and Ronan had gone.

After more than thirty minutes of searching, Kato finally rejoined the group. "I cannot know for certain which direction they went," he said, "though one theory dominates the other."

"Well, mate," David said. "Don't keep us in suspense."

"I suspect Nick was injured. Either during the fall or after. I found blood over near that rock, where I believe Nick hid for a time. His prints, the smallest of the three, do not lead away from the rock at all. I believe he was carried away by someone or something. The blood loss is small, not life threatening, and there are no blood drops anywhere."

"So, you think he's alive?" Steven asked, his voice tight.

"Cannot know for certain," Kato said, "but he didn't bleed enough to indicate death. Remember, Sage and Ronan arrived no more than fifteen minutes after Nick. I think it's possible that Ronan carried him away."

Steven released a slow breath, clearly relieved at the encouraging words. "What else do you see?" he asked. "Direction of travel?"

"That's what's confusing. Remember that I studied Sage's and Ronan's shoe treads from up top before sliding down here. If we assume they have the only modern hiking boots in this godforsaken place except for Nick's, it is easy to determine their tracks from the others. The problem is, they head out in two different directions. I followed them both for a distance. One set follows two sets of cloven hooves going that way." Kato pointed toward a high cliff on his left. "The other set go that way, toward that cluster of boulders in the opposite direction, along with a set of smoother prints made from shoes with a tough leather hide. I think that's the way to go."

"Why?" Elsbeth asked. "How can you be sure? I'd hate to waste time if you guess wrong."

"Understandable. Two reasons. First, I think Sage and Ronan were tracking the cloven hooves. Possibly because the beasts had injured Nick and carried him off. I think it's reasonable to believe they rescued Nick and brought him back here. Their tracks *do* return from that direction. Second, their tracks don't return from the other direction. Also, many other tracks followed them away from here toward the cluster of boulders. Those tracks are nearly twice as large, oddly shaped, with little spurs jutting from the heels. It appears Sage and Ronan ran from here; their strides were much farther apart than those heading off to follow the cloven hooves."

"They were being hunted," David said. "That's what you're saying? Chased?"

"It appears so," Kato said.

"Then we must proceed," Endora said. "Kato, you lead; I will follow."

They all looked at Steven, who motioned for Kato to head out. David followed Endora, then Gavin, Malcolm, Elsbeth, and Steven. They'd agreed beforehand to keep enough distance between themselves that a single beast couldn't take out more than one of them at a time. Elsbeth carried her short sword, but she doubted she would use it much. She just wasn't very good with it. They'd also agreed to walk in silence until they got a feel for what awaited them.

They stopped amid the collection of boulders to look back at where they'd dropped in from the surface. Kato inspected the ground constantly and seemed to get more confident the farther they went. Through the rocks, they hit a wide expanse and made good time. They saw no beasts, heard no strange noises, and smelled nothing other than sulfuric stench. The size of the caverns was breathtaking, as were the number of bones. Thousands of beasts, some human-type skeletons, had perished in this part of the underworld. They had truly entered a world unlike any other.

Elsbeth glanced at her watch. Almost two hours had passed already. By now up on the surface, Theo and Horace would have welcomed a helicopter full of young Council members, all students at the Tomb of Ancient Documents, bringing several crates of supplies. They would stay at the cave site until Theo got word from Council headquarters that Sage and the rescue team had gotten out. Then they would seal the area under the flat rock so no one else would ever again fall into the hole.

"Water break," Steven said from behind her.

Kato and Endora stopped and turned back. Elsbeth grabbed a protein bar from her pack and ate half of it in one bite. She studied each of the other six faces for signs of fear. Nothing. They seemed as relaxed as a Sunday stroll after church. Elsbeth wished she felt so calm.

"Horace said there are six flues to vent Tartarus," Malcolm said.

"We all heard him," Endora said. "He gave us many useless facts."

"I wouldn't call that a useless fact," Malcolm said.

"And why not? Does that bit of information help us survive this mission?" Endora's voice echoed just a little and magnified her irritation.

Malcolm chuckled. "Well, Endora, it gives us information we can use. Maybe the hole we dropped into is a kind of flue. If so, it allows air down here. That's a good thing."

"It is a useless fact. Just as useless as telling us that the blind prophet Seth was born the same day as Noah. Interesting, but worth nothing to us now." She mumbled something more in German under her breath.

Elsbeth wondered if David was right about Endora being just a little off her trolley. Maybe she just didn't like Horace very much.

Nobody said anything else. They just looked at each other and started off again. A short time later Kato stopped at the mouth of a cave. He inspected a large area of the ground for several minutes.

"They went into the cave," Kato said, "but came out again, heading that way." He pointed in the same direction they'd been traveling. "Steven, should we proceed or investigate the cave?"

"If the blokes came out of the cave, what good would it be for us to go in?" David asked.

"We've been following four sets of footprints," Gavin said. "Do all four enter and exit?"

"Four went in, and five came out." Kato pointed to the ground. "Nick's smaller boot treads didn't go in, but they did come out."

"So, they weren't carrying him any longer," Steven said. He leaned against the cave wall and closed his eyes. The relief on his face took ten years off his age.

"Dog's bollocks," David said. "I knew he'd be all right. Sage always told me Nick was a tough little mate. Don't see a reason to go cave exploring, then."

"I agree," Malcolm said. "Seems a waste of time."

"Let's just move on," Endora said.

"Theirs are the most recent tracks coming out," Kato said. "They're on top of the spur-heeled tracks, which go in but don't come out. They weren't followed coming out."

"So, they somehow lost their pursuers after they entered the cave?" Steven asked.

"Which means the creatures following them either haven't come out yet or left a different way," Gavin said. "If they're still in there, it makes no sense for us to risk going in."

Kato bent over and inspected the ground again. After several moments, he stood and faced the group. "I think the beasts that followed them inside are still there. Dead. There are blood traces in several of the boot prints: both Ronan's and Sage's. Spur-heeled prints lead away from the cave but did not come out of the cave."

"What does that mean?" Endora asked.

"A large group followed Sage's group here," Kato said. "Some went in, and some stood right over there. The inside group never came out, and the outside group left. I think Sage's team killed the inside group and chased the others off."

"You can tell all of that from footprints?" Gavin said. "Remind me to never give you reason to hunt me down."

"Is it worth investigating?" Malcolm asked Steven. "Do we care if they killed some beasts?"

"I don't see how it benefits us to know that," Steven said. "I'm not interested in getting caught inside a confined space for no reason. Let's push on."

An hour later it was Steven that stopped the group. "Hold up," he whispered. He drew his sword and squatted. "Down. Everybody!"

They all followed suit without hesitation. Steven's role as rear guard was probably the most important. Elsbeth had glanced back several times and noticed Sage's grandpa focusing most of his attention behind them. He faced that way now, hand held up for silence. Kato and Gavin moved to either side of him.

"What do you see?" Kato asked.

"Shadows. Multiple. On the ground and among the rocks."

They were in a kind of cone-shaped bowl, passing through a long stretch of towering rock formations that narrowed the farther forward they traveled. It wouldn't take much to block their way in the front, and their escape to the rear might already have been compromised.

"Perfect place for an ambush," Gavin whispered.

"If the wankers want to die this day, let them try," David said. "Elsbeth, did you know that I learned some new attack katas at the dojo I joined? Watch when I fight. You'll see some fancy pirouettes, some elegant swirls and cute little jumps, all while swinging my bar with a vicious and powerful grace. I'm quite the warrior."

"You're quite the nut," Elsbeth said.

"David, please," Kato said. "Enough. Steven, did you get a look at anything? Description?"

"No." Steven pointed high to his right. "The tallest jagged rock, the one shaped like a desert cactus. There's something there. Glowing eyes. Red. Set far apart. Either it's very large, or not something we've seen before."

"Movement ahead of us," Endora said. "At the narrowest spot. It was big, whatever it was."

Malcolm repositioned to his left and motioned for David to move next to Elsbeth. They turned their backs to one another and formed a circle facing outward. "Do we wait here for them to attack?" Elsbeth asked.

"Not much room to fight up ahead," Malcolm said.

"We could retreat," Endora said. "There was that wide-open area about a half-mile back."

"Going back isn't an option," Kato said. "Just puts us farther away. Sage's group went through here. Their tracks are clear. We have to move forward."

"Temporarily," Endora snapped. "To better fight this group of beasts."

"I knew what you meant," Kato said. "I still say no. An ambush works best when you catch your enemy unaware. Thanks to Steven, we are not unaware."

"Need a new lineup," David said. "Endora goes first. Me next. She sings her wicked song at the first sign of trouble, I knock them into next week. Need Fighting Arts at the rear. Everyone else in the center. Agreed?"

Elsbeth felt like the fifth person on a double date. Persuasion didn't work down here—she'd tried it several times—and her sword skills had barely been good enough to allow her to graduate after her year at the Tomb.

"Endora's Voice will draw every beast within three miles," Malcolm said. "These canyons are a huge echo chamber."

"And my Voice will stun those that hide close," Endora said, making no attempt to hide her irritation. "This is *precisely* why I am here."

"Just laying it all out there," Malcolm said. "Just not sure it's best to draw attention to ourselves."

"Well, clearly, we have already failed," Endora said. "They have us boxed in like Jewish prisoners heading to Auschwitz. It is time to engage them. Lingering further only allows them to more strategically position themselves."

"Endora's right," Gavin said. "We've stood around long enough."

"I agree," Steven said. "Endora, lead the way. David, be ready behind her. Kato and Gavin, bring up the rear. Malcolm, Elsbeth, and I will occupy the middle. Let's go."

They moved quietly, weapons ready, eyes searching, as the passage narrowed to a choke point no more than fifteen feet wide. The jagged rocks cast shadows too dark to see into, and that made Elsbeth realize that the lighting along this stretch of the passageway was poorer than anywhere else. They were walking into a darkness that took away any small advantage they might have.

"Headlamps?" Elsbeth whispered. "Yes or no?"

"Stop," Endora said. They were twenty-five yards from the entrance to the narrow pass. "Smell."

It reminded Elsbeth of skunk. On steroids. Mixed with decaying flesh and drifting over them in a sudden wave that almost drove her to her knees.

"More movement behind us," Gavin said. "They're jumping between boulders and staying out of direct view."

"And to the sides," Kato said. "Several dozen."

"I know that smell," Endora said. "I have encountered it before."

"Not a smell I would forget," David said.

"Yeren," Endora said. "In the jungles of China. Zhejiang province. Before the first Great War. One of the most brutal battles I have ever been involved in. Prepare yourselves."

Elsbeth knew what a yeren was. Eight to ten feet tall. An ape-like creature with deep red hair. A meat eater, cunning, that hunted in packs, with athletic ability off the charts and the strength of ten men.

"They will scream before attacking," Endora said. "They will spring from the shadows above us in one coordinated attack. I will wait to use Voice until after that scream. When I sing, move away quickly. Separate. Make sure the stunned beasts do not land on you."

Elsbeth still hadn't seen any evidence of beasts ahead. She thought she'd seen a shadow move but wasn't sure.

"Let's go, Endora," David said. "It's hard controlling my urge to smash something."

They all moved forward, heads up, eyes searching. Elsbeth glanced back. Kato and Gavin were focused behind them. Scattered pebbles bounced down the cliff walls ahead of them, and Elsbeth jerked her head forward. The stench nearly overwhelmed her ability to concentrate. The gloom of the trail ahead got even darker as they pressed deeper into the channel between the walls of rock.

"Prepare," Endora said. She'd spoken so softly that Elsbeth's quickened breathing nearly covered the warning.

One more glance back confirmed that Kato and Gavin had finally entered the ambush area. The kill zone. Elsbeth heard shuffling above her. Before she had a chance to look, a blood-freezing scream came from somewhere in front. For a split second the voice of a single monster rang out; then dozens joined the chorus from all around them.

Even before Elsbeth and the others had a chance to separate, Endora belted her gift of Angelic Voice. The sound rippled through the air, ricocheted off the stone walls, and sliced through the screeching of the beasts, killing it just as suddenly as it had begun. The first monster to fall bounced off a sharp rock above David's head and landed at his feet, an expression of agony on its face. David swung his steel bar and crushed its skull.

Endora kept singing, and more beasts tumbled from their hiding places. They fell like frozen birds, stiff and unresponsive, yet alive with the fear of death frozen on their faces. Elsbeth's team killed as they moved forward, with Kato and Gavin doing most of the work with the superhuman speed of their swords. Like Endora, David sang as he worked, although Elsbeth couldn't decipher the words of his song over Endora's Voice. Stunned yeren blocked the passageway. Kato and Gavin moved to the front and killed the beasts, which allowed the rest of the team to simply step over them. Elsbeth watched Dark spirits flee from the bodies of the beasts as they died, and it made her wonder if that was where all Darks came from. They disappeared into the gloom of the canyon almost instantly.

The echoing of the chamber worked in their favor. Endora's Voice stunned all creatures with the unrepentant blood of the Watchers running through their veins. The louder she sang, the more powerful the effect. This underground world echoed and magnified what was already a powerful weapon. Elsbeth glanced behind her and saw that the dozens of yeren that had flowed out of the shadows to block their escape now lay scattered on the ground, unable to move.

"I've got the leader," David shouted. He raced up a small group of boulders and drove the end of his steel bar through the chest of a huge beast that had toppled sideways onto a slanted rock. He raised his bar in victory and looked around. "I think that'll do it, Endora. You are truly the bee's knees."

Endora fell silent, bent over at the waist, and worked to catch her breath. Steven walked over and rubbed her back, then whispered something in her ear. She looked up and smiled before sheathing the sword she hadn't used.

"I count three dozen dead," Malcolm said. He looked at Endora. "How long will it take the others to recover? The ones behind us?"

"Three to five minutes," Endora said. "Kato. Lead the way. We need to put some distance in."

Kato wiped his sword across the leg of a dead yeren and set off at a light jog. "Ronan's boot prints are easy to see. Let's do double time."

Elsbeth hadn't used her sword. She put it up and took off behind David, whose steel bar had blood dripping off the end. The Brit still hummed his tune, his voice full of cheer.

After several minutes of jogging, Kato waved Elsbeth to the front next to him. "You doing OK?"

"I think so." She glanced behind them.

"The monsters won't follow," Kato said. "After their heads clear, they'll find all their dead friends and decide otherwise."

"Then why are we running?" Elsbeth asked.

Kato chuckled. "In case I'm wrong, I guess."

"You mean in case beasts from all over the underworld heard Endora's announcement of our arrival," Elsbeth asked.

"Yeah, that too. Hey, I told Savannah I was going rock climbing in the States. Maybe get in a few runs, do some hiking, visit with my American friends. Does this trip qualify for all of that?"

"Just don't show her the video," Elsbeth said, "and you should be fine."

Kato laughed. "Good point. I got some footage of Endora's Voice and beasts dropping from above like some B-rated horror flick. You're right—probably should give that to the Council before I head home. OK, time to focus on what I'm supposed to be doing."

Elsbeth had never seen the gift of Angelic Voice in action, and now she understood why Endora was on this mission. But Elsbeth had done little more than gawk while the rest of the team slaughtered the beasts. She suspected the rest of the team had noticed. Just standing around like some teenage girl was the last thing she needed to do. The fears she had about being useless without her Persuasion had just played out in front of everyone. This initial encounter with monsters of the underworld had been short lived and simple. They wouldn't all be that way. It would get harder than this, and she'd better figure out a way to contribute.

⚔

Two hours later they saw a faint glow of bright light in the distance. "Civilization?" Gavin asked.

"The trail leads directly there," Kato said. "I am hopeful."

It took another half hour to reach the light. Elsbeth saw an open area with a high archway and a round slab of granite set in grooves in the floor. The granite gate was set into a wall of jagged rocks and showed evidence of multiple attacks against it. Piles of bones littered the area well away from the gate.

"I assume this is one of the entrances to Tartarus," Kato said.

"How do we get in?" Elsbeth asked. She looked around for a doorbell or porthole. "Because we sure aren't breaking through that thing."

David approached and tapped the stone with his bar. "You're right on that account, lass."

"Endora, your gift of Voice might penetrate," Steven said.

"How about we simply tap a sword against it?" Malcolm said. "Or David's bar."

Elsbeth looked up at several light fixtures hanging from the ceiling twenty feet above their heads. She visually followed a tube from the light fixture and saw that it disappeared into the rock wall above the gate. "How thick do you think this granite is?"

"I'd say a couple of feet," Steven said. "Anything more would make it hard to maneuver. Malcolm, Gavin, what say you?"

"I'd say about that," Malcolm said. "Maybe three or four."

"Why do you ask?" Steven asked Elsbeth.

"Because I could teleport in and ask them to open up." Steven began shaking his head before she'd gotten all the words out. "I know it's not wise to teleport into areas I can't see," she said. "But it's clear they went in there. At worst, I would surprise somebody who might overreact. But I think Sage and Ronan would have told them somebody would be coming."

"At worst, you could teleport into the lair of beasts who would eat you for dinner," Gavin said.

"I really don't want to argue about it," Elsbeth said. She set her mind sixty feet beyond the granite wall and looked at Steven. "If it's dangerous, I'll be right back."

She appeared in the middle of a much different environment. It was a great tunnel: wide, straight as a ruler, longer than the horizon, with electric lights hanging from the ceiling about every fifty yards. She turned back to the gate, and three huge beings were coming out of a guardhouse. She held her breath, not quite believing what she was seeing. The men were nearly seven feet tall, dressed in all white, with completely bald heads and striking green eyes slightly bigger than golf balls. They each carried a sword longer than Elsbeth's body. They had muscles stacked upon muscles.

They approached slowly, fanning out in a diamond shape to prevent her escape.

She swallowed hard. "My name is Elsbeth," she said clearly, keeping the fear from her voice. "I am here to find my friends— two boys, Sage and Nick Alexander, and Ronan, an adult human who accompanied them. They came here four days ago."

The three guards stopped. The one in the middle glanced at the other two and nodded. All three put their swords away. Elsbeth sighed quietly.

"How did you get in here?" the leader in the middle asked with an accent that sounded alien.

"I am of Elioudian ancestry," Elsbeth said. "A descendant of one of the original Angelic Council Members. I am gifted with Teleportation." She pointed at the gate. "More descendants are waiting out there. We've come to rescue our friends. Will you please open the gate and let them in?"

The leader nodded and motioned at the other two. The rest of the team walked through a minute later. Steven shook a finger at Elsbeth but smiled.

Endora walked over and slapped her lightly on the shoulder. "I like someone who is unafraid to take charge. That is the

Elsbeth I hoped would join us." She walked off before Elsbeth could respond.

"Sure beats banging the thing down," David said. "Which I could have done with enough time, by the way. Nice work, girly. You've already earned your keep."

Elsbeth couldn't help but smile just a little, but David's comment did confirm that all of them had probably viewed her as more of a hindrance than a help. She would just have to prove them wrong.

While Steven spoke to the three Elioudians, the rest of the group stood in a circle several feet away. Endora smiled at Elsbeth again. She was clearly a woman who needed to see other Council members in action before forming her opinion of them.

"Well, this is nothing like I imagined it," Gavin said. "We could drive a truck through here."

"It's almost as big as your Tuscan house, Gavin," Malcolm said. "Or your Sydney mansion. Your Virginia horse ranch, and Texas cattle ranch."

Gavin smiled and wiped the sweat from his forehead. "Don't forget about my Alaskan cabin."

"The bloke is a regular jet setter," David said. "Maybe in about three hundred years I'll be able to afford all of that."

"Not if you keep spending all your money on hair products," Gavin said. He winked at Elsbeth as David laughed.

"Wonder how far this goes?" Malcolm asked. "Look at the stone walls. Must be millions of stones. Imagine the work involved."

"I still can't believe they have electricity," Gavin said. "And look how friendly the Elioudians are. This is shaping up to be a vacation spot."

"Yeah, just keep talking like that," Kato said. "Maybe you'll convince yourself by the time we take our first step into Hell."

Gavin grinned. "Well, there *is* that."

"OK, here's the deal," Steven said, approaching. "We've got a long way to walk, but at least we won't get lost. We go that way."

"Oh, look, Gav, our old man cracks a joke." Malcolm slapped Steven on the back.

"He used to be a lot funnier," Gavin said. "When we rode horses everywhere, he cracked a joke a minute."

"We rode donkeys most of the time," Steven said. "You *had* to joke, or you'd go crazy. Two hundred years from now we'll be riding on levitating boots. But right now, we do it the old-fashioned way."

They walked with no weapons drawn and with a much more relaxed demeanor. Elsbeth felt like she could breathe deeply for the first time in hours. They appeared safe, at least for now. David told stories of blasting tanks in WWI, Kato recounted the trip with Sage into the nest of gargoyles, and even Endora recounted an adventure through a haunted forest and the vampires she'd faced there. Yet with all those stories, there were still many minutes of shared silence as they traveled the long, barren tunnel leading them into the heart of Tartarus. She didn't know how long it took them to reach the metal gate, but she was ready for a break by the time they saw it ahead.

"It's electrified," Kato said, looking at the rest.

"Wait here," Steven said.

In another minute they were all through, and Elsbeth saw something that made her spirits soar: open-topped railcars. Not even a minute after that, they were hurling down a railroad track at thirty miles an hour.

Sage and Nick, here we come, Elsbeth thought, smiling with satisfaction.

14

Father.

Sloth, alone in his armored limo, ended his phone call and slid the partition up to isolate himself from his driver.

Yes, Zagan.

I have completed my scout of the rescue team. They are formidable. Seven members. A Singer—a woman. A boy with Strength. Two Swords. The girl with Light. The old man and another man whose gift I cannot discern. I tracked them through the Depths and watched them easily dispatch a large herd of yeren. The team was well coordinated and patient and did not rattle. The boy with Strength sang songs as he killed. I noted a thread of insanity in his demeanor. The Singer froze me in place with her song for several minutes, but because I was well hidden, I was not discovered. They have entered the Pure Place. I await your next instruction.

Ascend through the entrance to the surface, Zagan, but be aware that the chamber might now be watched. Exit through the rear of the cave, and make sure you are not seen. Return to our gathering place, and await further instruction.

Yes, Father.

Sloth considered the information about the angel boy's rescue team and didn't know for sure what to think. It was small, but it would be nimble and quick in battle. He had hoped they would send a larger group—for the more that died in the Territories, the fewer he and the other Princes would have to deal with on the surface. Counting the angel boy and the man with Strength, nine Council members might be slaughtered in one fell swoop. If so, Sloth would have engineered the largest rout in history—enough, clearly, to hoist him to hero status in the eyes of all except Lucifer.

Even so, such a defeat was only the second-best result of his plan. If the boy could get the Granite Gate open, the real prize would be won, and Lucifer's opinion would cease to matter at all.

The scout's name was Hieronymus. Sage and Nick followed Issur, the senior brother of the Convention of Exploration, to a vacant Elioudian residence on the far edge of the great lake. Ronan would arrive later, after his tour with Aquila was completed. Hieronymus had traveled from the village of Abel with the members of the High Council, but he had been instructed to wait in the vacant house until word from Hannah authorized the meeting.

Hieronymus looked like the others but more rugged. Scars crisscrossed his face, neck, and upper arms; his large hands were hard and calloused, with several fingers that appeared to have broken and healed wrong. He wore dark clothing that smelled like he'd just taken a bath in a sewer. He wasn't a large man, standing only a head taller than Sage.

"Hieronymus is one of two out-scouts in Tartarus," Issur said. "He is the most seasoned."

"What's an out-scout?" Nick asked.

"They focus on how to leave Tartarus," Issur said. "As you heard in the meeting, when the Seven have been vanquished, Elioudian leaders will decide whether to reveal our existence to the citizens of Topside. Out-scouts will lead a party to the top should that decision be made. We prepare for that eventuality by scouting a way through the three occupied Territories."

"It is not possible to exit through the Wastelands," Hieronymus said. "Therefore, I have concentrated my efforts on the Territories for the past two centuries. There is but one survivable path through the Territories, although that does not mean we will survive."

"How old are you?" Nick couldn't help but ask.

Hieronymus looked at him and smiled. "All of the humans in Tartarus ask the same question. Why is your race so fascinated with age?"

Nick shrugged. "Because in our world very few people make it to one hundred. And by the time they get there they don't have many things that still work right. Living ten or twenty times longer than that is just amazing, that's all."

"I have seen 165 decade celebration days," Hieronymus said. "I became an out-scout after my tenth. I have explored and lived within the Territories more than any other in the history of Tartarus.

I have the scars to prove it." He pointed at Sage. "It is confirmed, then? You are the boy of prophecy?"

"Yes." Sage said.

"Gifted with Fighting Arts combined with Teleportation, I am told," Hieronymus said. "I noticed your sword." He looked at Nick. "And for you?"

Nick flinched. "Uh . . . what? Do I want a sword?" He almost laughed. "No. I'll just stick close to you two and Ronan."

"Our companion, Ronan, is gifted with Might. He will arrive soon," Sage said. "He carries a metal bar he uses for a club."

"We were introduced a short time ago. I have already informed him much of what you and I will discuss." Hieronymus turned to Issur. "Their clothes are inadequate, as you know. Have you made arrangements?"

"Yes, Ephraim is gathering all the supplies now." Issur paused for a moment before continuing. "Have you decided on assistance?"

"I will take Kaja. She is ready." Hieronymus pulled a small scroll from a leather pouch he wore on his left hip and spread it across a nearby table. "Come, boys, and see what we face." He rolled a sheepskin parchment flat. Before addressing the map, he looked hard at them. "The only way to the Great Granite Gate is through the Territories. While I have made the journey hundreds of times, I was forced to turn back more than two thousand. It has been more than a decade since my last attempt. During each trip, I was forced to kill at least one beast. Most trips I killed too many beasts to count."

Nick tried to swallow but couldn't. He looked at Sage, who wore a grim expression.

Hieronymus pointed to a large gray area on the left edge of the parchment. "This is Tartarus. The first territory we will enter is Emim." He looked at Sage. "Do you know of the Emim?"

"I do."

"The next territory is the Rephaim," Hieronymus said. "They are sorcerers and magicians. Then the Nephilim, the most physically powerful beings on earth." He stood straight and began rolling the map. "Kaja will be here soon. Issur will prepare you for our journey. I will meet you here in one hour's time."

Sage held up a hand. "Hold on. I want to wait on my rescue team. All Council members. All great warriors gifted with powers that will help us."

Hieronymus shook his head. "I was told that you expect a team to arrive soon. If it were any other week of the year, I would grant your request, but we must leave immediately."

"Why?" Sage put his hands on his hips.

"In three days' time, the Ceremony of Godhood begins within the main Rephaim village. It draws many from all three Territories. It lasts for seven days. It is a period of peace for all three races. They do not battle during the festival. If we can reach the Rephaim territory before the time the festival ends, we will dramatically increase our chances to slip through without being noticed. Our journey will take us through one of the smaller Rephaim villages. It might be vacant if we time it right. Our timetable is short. We must leave now to allow ourselves some room for error."

"What is that?" Nick asked. "The Ceremony of Godhood?"

"The Rephaim consider themselves gods. They are convinced that those who escaped to Topside are worshiped as such. They also believe they will one day return to the surface and take their rightful place ruling over humans. Every year they hold a festival where many from the Territories come to worship them. They are quite delusional."

"But my team would be a big help," Sage said. "They've each killed beasts for centuries."

Hieronymus shook his head more forcefully. "We will not wait. The High Council insisted that *you* are the one that must survive. We leave soon. Prepare yourselves." The scout nodded once and left them standing there.

Nick and Sage watched him walk out. Sage looked at Issur. "There's no changing his mind?"

"No. His instructions are clear. If he were to delay, the best chance for your survival would be to wait until next year's festival."

"We can't wait a year," Nick said. He grabbed Sage's arm. "A year? No way. You said Grandpa told you to get me out if you had a chance."

"I know what he said. I'm just worried about the rescue team."

"Hieronymus will leave a trail for them to follow," Issur said. "If they are only a few days behind you, they might also make it through before the festival concludes."

The three of them looked at each other. "So, I've got no choice," Sage said.

"It is for the best," Issur said.

"Who's Kaja?" Sage asked. "Why did Hieronymus choose her to come?"

"Because she is like you, young Sage. A direct descendent of Seth. Her bloodline bears angelic gifts. She is the only such

Elioudian in Tartarus. Vale is her seventh great-grandfather. She is your cousin many times removed."

"What?" Nick said. "There's an Elioudian child with angelic gifts?" He glared at Sage. "What'd I say last night when you called me crazy?"

Sage stood quietly for several moments. "I didn't call you crazy."

"You thought I was." Nick turned toward Issur. "Is she half-Elioudian, half-human?"

Issur frowned. "I should say *not*. What are you implying?"

"He's implying nothing," Sage said. "He had a warped thought last night, and now he thinks he knows everything. I'm sure Kaja is pure Elioudian."

"Her bloodline is the most direct from Seth himself," Issur said with a hint of indignation. "If we had royalty in Tartarus, she would certainly qualify."

Nick didn't know what to say, so he didn't say anything. He knew Sage was right. Maybe there'd been so much thrown at him the past few days his brain was in hyperdrive.

"What gift does Kaja have?" Sage asked.

"I do not know," Issur said. "The nature of her ability is a national secret. Only the highest-ranking members of the Exploration team know of her status. Now come, we must get you prepared to travel."

———

During the hour of preparation, they changed into clothes impregnated with the same nasty smell that covered those Hieronymus wore; they smeared a gooey substance over their exposed skin, which darkened it enough to blend in with the environment of the journey. They were given heavy backpacks with enough food to last many days. Once ready, they sat quietly in the same room as before, waiting for their scout's arrival.

"What kind of creatures did you battle?" Nick asked Sage. "That you didn't tell me about before all this happened." He'd tried keeping the bitterness out of his voice, but he knew he hadn't. His feelings had been hurt before, but now it was making him angry.

Sage took in a deep breath and let it out slowly. "I know it'll take a while for you to get over being left in the dark, but that's the decision all of us made. Mom and Dad both have angelic blood, but neither have angelic gifts. Grandpa never told Dad anything about what he does—nothing about angels or Darks or gifts. The reason he didn't is because he didn't want to complicate his life if it turned out he didn't get gifts. So we did the same thing with you." His tone then got a little harsher. "But now you know and need to get over it."

Nick spread his arms wide. "I'm over it. I just wanna know what kind of creatures you've battled. That's it. Nothing more. I'm not making a protest statement. You told me some stuff, but I'd like to hear more."

"OK, fair enough." Sage rubbed his forehead. "A troll. Fought a werewolf, but that didn't work out too well. A hellhound. A dulla-han. I'll explain that one to you later. A gargoyle. A whole nest of them. And Mammon. I still have nightmares about—"

"You are the boy from prophecy?" asked a female voice from the doorway. "The boy with gifts?"

Nick turned toward the door and saw a short Elioudian girl that looked about Sage's age, which probably meant she was a couple hundred years old. She was taller than Nick but not as tall as Sage. She wore black clothes and had the same dark gunk smeared over her alabaster skin. Though her eyes were just as large as others in the Elioudian race, they seemed softer somehow, inquisitive, full of wonder. She *definitely* wasn't half human.

"I am Kaja, granddaughter of Vale, bloodline of Seth the prophet." She stepped into the room and did a little bow.

Her voice made Nick think of a bird chirping. She cut off each word with a distinctive squeak several octaves higher than a human voice.

"I am Sage." He stood up and bowed. "This is Nick. We are also grandsons of Vale. You are our distant cousin." Sage smiled widely, stepped forward, and held out a hand for a shake.

Kaja stared at his hand, uncertain about what to do. "You have angelic gifts?" she asked Sage.

"I do. And you?"

She stepped back out of the room and looked both ways, then hurried back over to them and lowered her voice. "Yes, but it is most secret. I work exclusively with Hieronymus. You have studied the angelic gifts as mentioned in prophecy?"

"I have," Sage whispered. "What do you have?"

"You know of Animation?" Kaja asked.

"Sure," Sage said, his eyes bright with excitement.

"I don't," Nick said. "What's that?"

"It's the ability to bring certain inanimate objects to life for brief periods of time," Sage said.

She lowered her voice even more. "I am *so* happy to speak of these things with someone who understands! Do you know of Projection?"

"What's that?" Nick asked.

"The ability to project overwhelming emotions—both good and bad—into your surrounding environment," Sage said. "I can't wait to get that one. Is that all?"

She put her hand on the hilt of her sword. "Fighting Arts."

"How many decade celebration days have you had?" Nick asked. "You look the same age as Sage." Nick didn't know why he wanted to know.

"I will soon celebrate my twenty-eighth decade day," Kaja said. "I began scouting with Hieronymus on my eighteenth day. But I have only traveled the Wastelands, never in the territories."

Kaja walked back to the door and grabbed a pack sitting just outside. She shrugged it on as though it weighed nothing at all. Nick knew just by looking at her that she was a very powerful person.

Ronan appeared at that moment, nasty clothes and black goo over most of his exposed skin. His backpack was slung over his shoulder, and he carried his metal bar in his right hand. "So, you've met Kaja," he said to Sage. "When Hieronymus mentioned he was bringing a scout with angelic gifts, I couldn't believe it. Every little bit helps."

Nick heard footsteps approaching. Kaja turned her back to the door and waited, just like Nick had seen the others do at the meeting yesterday.

Hieronymus walked through the door with purpose. "Respect acknowledged," he said as he passed Kaja. She turned without comment and waited quietly. Hieronymus had covered himself with the same camouflaging substance the rest of them had. He looked closely at Sage, Nick, and Ronan. "Let us proceed." He spun around and headed toward the door. "Kaja will bring up the rear," he said over his shoulder.

It took several minutes to climb the winding steps leading to the main gate. Nick was third in line, sandwiched between Sage and Ronan. As they climbed, Nick looked at the dozens of dwellings where the humans lived. Though they hadn't met any of them, dozens now stood outside their houses, watching their departure. He found Amelia's house and saw almost twenty humans standing around her.

The scene made Nick sad. He'd wanted to meet them, spend time with them, find out how they'd come to be down here. He wanted to ask them personally if they would have left with them. He knew, though, in his heart, that Hieronymus would never have allowed a huge group to travel with them. It would have endangered them all. It could very well have been a massive slaughter. Smaller was better. He knew that, but it didn't make it easier to see some of the sad faces watching them go.

When they got to the top, Hieronymus stopped and looked back over the village below. It was an amazing sight, Nick thought. Breathtaking. He knew he'd never see it again in his lifetime, and he really wished he had a camera.

"Let us proceed," Hieronymus said.

Outside the gate the entire group from the library meeting waited for them. Hieronymus and Kaja stopped and turned their backs to them.

"Respect acknowledged," Vale said from his wheelchair, his voice much louder and more powerful than what he'd exhibited the first time they met him. The two scouts turned and bowed before the group.

Vale pointed to Sage. "Approach, young man." Sage walked over and bowed deeper than the others had. "I now feel my life is complete," Vale said. "I often wondered why I lived longer than any other. I have my answer. Hold out your arms, and turn your palms up." Sage looked confused but did what he was told. The old man displayed a short dagger and stared at Sage. "You have great healing powers, do you not?"

"I do," Sage said, his voice carrying clear and strong.

"Then prepare," Vale said. He sliced a long cut down the length of his own forearm. Blood flowed. Without grimacing or flinching, he then sliced Sage's left arm in the same manner. "Place your wound against mine," he told Sage.

Sage stepped forward, carefully aligned his arm with Vale's, and pressed them together. "May the blood of the Elioudian people again run freely within your veins," Vale said loudly. "As a reminder of the repentance made to God, go forward, and do His will."

Vale moved his arm and pointed at Nick with the dagger. "Come forward."

Nick froze. *What? Me?* He started to protest but looked at Sage before saying anything. Sage gave him a small nod and stepped aside. Nick looked at the huge cut on Sage's arm and saw that it had already started to heal. After a glance at Ronan, and with steps as confident as he could take, he walked over and held out his left arm.

Vale grabbed it securely and ran the dagger from Nick's elbow to his wrist. There wasn't any pain at first, but then his brain kicked in, and Nick had to grit his teeth to avoid fainting. Blood ran from his arm like somebody had turned on a faucet.

"Place your wound against mine," Vale said.

Nick did. A sudden buzzing started along the wound as soon as the old man's blood mixed with his own.

"May the blood of the Elioudian people again run freely within your veins," Vale repeated. "As a reminder of the repentance made to God, go forward, and do His will."

Nick stepped back, his arm buzzing even stronger now. Vale's blood was a deeper red than his own. He watched as that blood literally crawled into his cut like metal shards attracted to a magnet. As soon as the old man's blood secured itself inside Nick's body, the pain began to fade, and the wound began to heal.

Holy mackerel! He looked at Sage, who stood grinning like he knew a huge something that Nick didn't. Nick stepped over and whispered. "What's happening to my arm?"

Sage shook his head and mouthed, "Later."

"The Elioudian people send you back to Topside with wishes of great peace and comfort," Vale said. "With our blood now running willingly within your veins, you will be recognized as one of us by the evil within the Territories. Godspeed, Hieronymus. Travel well."

The group of Elioudian leaders turned their backs to Hieronymus, who bowed deeply. "Follow me," he said to Kaja, Sage, Nick, and Ronan.

They headed toward the bridge that ran over the Cocytus River. Farther along the road was a second bridge crossing the

Acheron River. And sitting between them, like the bottom point of a triangle, was the edge of the Styx Marsh, which ran deep into the Emim territory and skirted a small ribbon of Nephilim territory. Nick remembered all of that from the huge map hanging at the switching station.

Though Nick followed Hieronymus with an awareness of where they were headed, he couldn't get over what was happening to his arm. The buzzing along the edges of his cut had spread throughout his body. The wound itself was almost totally healed. He licked his fingers, rubbed away some of the dried blood, and saw nothing but puffy pink flesh where just a couple of minutes before had been a slice in his skin a quarter-inch wide. He tapped Sage on the shoulder and leaned forward to whisper. "My arm is almost healed already. How did that happen?"

Sage slowed his pace just a little and allowed Nick to fall into step beside him. "Leah told me that the blood of the Elioudian race is 75 percent angelic. It's why they live so long. It's why they don't get sick or get fat. Their flesh heals almost immediately. Now, maybe yours will too."

Nick didn't say anything, content to watch the pink of his scar slowly fade away. Maybe he'd live a lot longer himself now. That wouldn't be too bad. Just needed to get out of here first.

15

Their train car came to a stop in front of a black building with dozens of other cars outside. Elsbeth hadn't said much since they left the station with the electrified fence, partly because of fatigue but mostly because she'd been left speechless by the underground world that no one on the surface knew about.

She, Sage's grandfather, and Gavin were in the lead car. Endora, Kato, Malcolm, and David rode behind them. She heard David shout and point and laugh dozens of times as they hurled through Tartarus. It made her smile, seeing the sheer joy he demonstrated each moment of his life. It was early evening, hours before her normal bedtime, but fatigue pulled at her, and she wished she could sleep. By the time she stepped from the railcar, the group from the rear car was out and pointing to the building.

"Think Sage and Nick came this way?" Elsbeth asked Steven.

Sage's grandfather looked around before answering. "They made it to this point, certainly. Where else could they have gone? But from here they could have gone in five different directions."

It was true. Elsbeth looked around and saw railroad tracks coming in from everywhere, like a switching station at a rail yard. The area was so expansive she knew they'd never find them unless somebody inside the building knew where they'd gone. "We need to ask inside," she said.

"The guard at the electric gate said they were with Aquila and Ephraim," Steven said. "He assumed they would be taken to Abel, the capital of Tartarus, but that was only his guess. You're right, Elsbeth, we need to ask."

"We should split up," Malcolm said. "Cover more ground."

"I think we should pair up," Endora said. "I do not yet trust them as much as the rest of you. We cannot afford any casualities this early in the mission." She made intense eye contact with everyone, and nobody argued.

"I'll go with Elsbeth and David," Steven said. "Since we have an odd number."

Once inside, they struck out in different directions. The first thing Elsbeth noticed was the food bar stocked with every kind of fruit and vegetable imaginable. It also had various meats and breads and desserts. Her mouth watered.

"Let's find an employee," Steven said. He made a face. "Well, not sure if 'employee' is accurate, but somebody whose duty is here, anyway."

"There," David said. He pointed to an older man sweeping the floor.

They weaved through several large, square tables and approached him. "Excuse me," Steven said. "Do you understand my tongue?"

He looked up and stopped sweeping. "The language of humans? Yes, most of us speak your tongue."

"We're looking for three humans that were here some days ago," Steven said. "They were with Aquila and Ephraim. Did you see them?"

"Word spread quickly about their arrival," the Elioudian said. "But no, I did not see them." He nodded and looked at Elsbeth. "I am Ureic. It is pleasant to make your acquaintance."

"You don't seem surprised to see us," Steven said. "Are you not surprised by our arrival?"

"I have seen many things in my long days," Ureic said.

"Where would Aquila and Ephraim have taken them?" Elsbeth asked.

"I am not certain. I would assume to the High Council in Abel, at least initially. It is our capital city. A few humans have joined us through the centuries. Those still alive reside in the village of Seth."

"Which way is Abel?" David asked Ureic.

"North. There are three major cities besides Abel. Seth, Adam, and Enoch." Ureic pointed over to the left. "Abel is closest, about fifty leagues. Seth is most distant, twice as far."

Elsbeth knew that a league was about 3 miles, which meant Abel was about 150 miles away. And Seth was 300 hundred miles. She glanced at both Steven and David and saw the looks of amazement on their faces. She felt the same way. *Just how big was Tartarus? And other humans were here?*

"Do you think anyone here would know for sure where they were taken?" Steven asked.

Ureic leaned on his broom handle as he thought about it. "Many of my people come here each day during their time of relaxation. It is possible that many saw the boys. However, it is also likely that few know of their destination. Aquila is well known as a man who needs little advice. I should ask around, if I were you. You might come upon someone with more knowledge than I." He smiled at all of them and then turned away and continued sweeping.

Elsbeth saw Malcolm and Gavin talking to a couple of people. She saw Kato and Endora doing the same. There were no more than fifty or sixty Elioudians in there. What amazed her was how much all of them looked alike. If not for the varying heights, she didn't know if she'd be able to tell them apart. She didn't see one female.

"Look at the map," David said, pointing to one of the walls.

They all walked over. Elsbeth didn't think the map was to scale because of the distances just given them by Ureic. Regardless, the parts listed as Tartarus were small compared to the area listed as the Wastelands.

"What's the Wastelands?" she asked Steven.

"Not sure, but we probably just came from there." He pointed to the top of the map. "There are the Territories."

"Look off to the side," David said, "in the middle of the Territories. The name 'Gehenna.'" He looked at Elsbeth. "Recognize that name?"

"Mentioned in the New Testament as the place also referred to as Hades," she said. Gehenna was small when compared to the vast expanse of Tartarus, Elsbeth thought, but smaller or not, the thought of stepping one foot in there went against everything she'd ever been taught.

"We're hearing different things," Malcolm said as he walked up, Gavin at his side. "They took the boys to the capital, Abel. Or they took them to Enoch, the village with all the industry, where all the technology stuff is made, like lightbulbs and metal and other things. Or they took them to Adam, the original city in Tartarus, or that they're in Seth, the most heavily guarded location. What did you find out?"

"Abel or Seth," Steven said. "Although we only asked one guy."

"Abel, is what we're hearing," Kato said as he walked up. "But there were other views, with the other most likely place being Seth."

They stood around looking at each other. "This Aquila character lives in Abel," Endora said. "We asked about him, thinking he might take the boys to familiar ground."

"Which is also the capital," Gavin said. "Where the High Council is located."

Elsbeth looked at Sage's grandfather. "Would Sage and Ronan have told them who Sage was? About the prophecy? I mean, with Nick there to hear it?"

Steven rubbed his temple. "I think so. Sage and I discussed just last week about when the appropriate time might be to include Nick in what was going on. Sage believed that, angelic or not, things were getting too difficult to keep Nick in the dark. With what's happened, I don't see how Sage would have any choice. Anybody have any thoughts about that?"

Nobody said anything until Elsbeth gave her opinion. "I think he'd have to tell them. The Prophecy of Seth is a big deal to the Elioudians. So is the original Council. He'd have to tell them. And they'd do everything they could to make sure he got back to the surface in one piece."

"I think you're right," Endora said. "I think Aquila would take the boys to the capital to meet with the High Council. According to this map, it is the closet city from here."

"Does anybody else think differently?" Steven asked. "Do we head to Abel?"

"Seth is closest to the Territories," Malcolm said. "If they're going to lead him to the surface, assuming they agree to do that, wouldn't they leave from there?"

They all looked at the map again. "Makes sense to me," Gavin said. "But wouldn't the High Council have to approve it? Didn't the original High Council approve the original Council to travel through the Territories?"

"Too bad Horace isn't here to ask," Endora said. She didn't hide her sarcasm.

"Who's to say there isn't another way into the Territories?" Kato said. "But I agree that if the map is correct, they would leave from Seth."

"We could split up," David said. "Three of us go to Seth, four go to Abel."

"No," Steven, Kato, and Endora said at the same time.

"We do *not* split up," Endora said. "We have strength in numbers. Our gifts complement one another's."

David held up his hands in surrender. "OK, got it. Don't bite your arm off. Just a thought."

"I think we should go to Abel," Elsbeth said. "I think they'd take him in front of the High Council and then they'd arrange his escort to the surface."

Steven nodded. "I agree. The Elioudian leadership would have to approve sending anyone into the Territories." No one argued.

"Then it's decided. We go to Abel." Steven looked at David. "Would you mind asking the gentleman we spoke to earlier to come outside and confirm which track leads to the capital? I didn't see any signs outside, and we can't afford any delays."

"Sure." David walked off as Elsbeth hoped they'd guessed correctly.

———◆———

Hieronymus stopped at the edge of the Styx Marsh and faced the group. "Deeper into the marsh, we will come upon a great fence, built by us to keep the beasts out of our territory. Beyond that is the edge of Emim." He looked at Kaja. "Once through that wall, our journey begins. All eyes forward and ears open." He pointed to Nick. "Let me know if you experience any changes."

Nick frowned. "What do you mean?"

"You will know what I mean if it happens." Hieronymus looked at Ronan and Sage. "All angelic gifts are in play from this point forward. Do not hesitate. Understood?"

"Yes, sir," Sage said. He placed his hand on the hilt of his sword. Ronan dipped his head and raised the bottom of his steel bar in acknowledgment.

"Then let us proceed." Hieronymus turned and headed out, his head constantly sweeping from side to side, scanning for threats.

They skirted the edge of the marsh in single file. Hieronymus led the way with Kaja several paces behind him. Nick watched the ground in front of him. He didn't want to veer off the path and step into quicksand or something. He could hear Sage moving closely behind him, and Ronan's heavy steps bringing up the rear.

The lighting system was not as well equipped near the swamp, but the Elioudians hadn't ignored the area, either. They could still see well enough to move without stumbling. The smell of sulfur was faint here, Nick thought, but it seemed to be getting stronger the farther they traveled. Kaja glanced back at him once and smiled, her large eyes glowing green in the gloomy, gray surroundings. She pointed over to her left and mouthed, "Bones," while drawing a finger across her throat.

Nick looked left and didn't see anything at first. But then, lying on a dry patch of land at the edge of the water, was the blackened skeleton of an animal he'd never seen before. Not that he would have recognized the skeletal remains of anything at all, but the fact that it had solid-black, six-foot spikes growing out of its spine made him confident that it came from a beast not found in his world.

The water of the swamp rippled and moved in the center but had greenish algae growing along the shorelines. There wasn't any vegetation, just jagged rocks and hard-packed dirt. The swamp appeared to be overflow from the Cocytus and Acheron Rivers and looked deep in the middle. There was no footpath on the far side, only sharp rocks jutting from the cavern floor.

They walked in silence for what seemed two miles. Nick's mind began to wander as he thought about getting home and how happy he would be to see the sunshine again. And then he bumped into the back of Kaja, who had stopped behind Hieronymus.

"Look at that fence," Sage whispered into Nick's ear.

It was a stone wall. A collection of rocks rising so high Nick couldn't see the top. It went left and right as far as they could see and rose out of the center of the swamp like the Hoover Dam.

"How does it not dam the swamp?" Nick ask Kaja.

"See?" She pointed. "There are many holes that allow the water to flow but that are too small to allow beasts to slither through to our side. But there are two areas about a half league apart, where the rivers drain into underground caverns and empty into the Territories, where beasts sometimes fight their way into Tartarus. We have many guards at those spots."

They stood in silence for at least a couple of minutes before Hieronymus said, "Follow me."

They took a right off the path. They'd been walking for only a minute, edging along the wall, when Sage stopped all of them. "Hieronymus, wait." The scout stopped and turned back, unable to hide the irritation on his face. "I'm getting some major vibes right now," Sage said. He pointed straight down the wall in the opposite direction.

"What is a vibe?" Hieronymus asked.

"Oh, sorry." Sage turned around to look behind them. "I'm sensing something really bad that way. In the other direction."

"As in the gift of Sensing?" Kaja asked. "You have Sensing?"

"Sometimes," Sage said. "My vision gets all weird, blurry around the edges but clear in the middle. As long as I don't turn my head away from the clear vision, I'll know where the beast is."

"Even if it is hiding?" Kaja asked.

"Yes." Sage looked at Hieronymus. "What's in that direction? At the other end of the wall?"

"The wall runs around the back side of the village of Seth for a great distance."

Ronan stepped up to Sage and put a hand on his shoulder. "Tell us what you've got." He looked at Hieronymus. "We need to pay attention when he tells us something like this."

Sage held his head between his hands, slowly turning it back and forth. "Something bad is that way," he said. "Really bad."

"What kind of something?" Nick asked. His heart started to pound.

"Dark angel beasts," Sage said.

"On this side of the wall?" Hieronymus said. "I do not believe that. Maybe your gift is seeing through the wall, sensing something lurking on the other side."

Sage continued moving his head back and forth, slowly, carefully. After a full minute, he turned and faced the scout. "No. Not on the other side. This side. Whatever is there, it's very powerful, very distant. From here, it's at about a fifteen-degree angle off the wall."

Hieronymus stepped toward Sage and looked beyond him, gazing into the far distance, well beyond the edges of the swamp. "Are you certain?"

"What's in that direction?" Sage asked. "What's behind the village of Seth?"

Hieronymus didn't answer right away. He just stood there and gazed into the distance. Nick glanced at Kaja. She looked worried. And she also looked ready to shout out the answer.

"The least explored section of the Wastelands," Hieronymus said finally. "That is what lies at the end of this wall many leagues behind the village of Seth."

"Aquila said a lot of beasts live in the Wastelands," Nick said, a tremor in his words. He cleared his throat and tried speaking without sounding like a scared little girl. "He said horrible things live there. We saw some, so we know that's true."

"That part of the Wastelands is walled off from Tartarus," Hieronymus said. "And though that section is the least explored and the most dangerous, there has never been a breach into Tartarus from there." He looked hard at Sage. "How far does your gift of Sensing work?"

"It's still developing," Sage said. "It's only worked a few times. The farthest I know of is about a mile."

"A third of a league?" Hieronymus asked. "The entrance to that part of the Wastelands is more than thirty of your Topside miles."

"Has a creature breached the barrier into Tartarus?" Kaja asked Hieronymus, her voice filled more with wonder than fear. "Is it possible?"

The scout looked at her and said nothing for several moments. Then he addressed Sage. "Is it your belief that a dark beast stalks us from the other side of the swamp?"

"I don't have a belief at all," Sage said. "I just know that every time I've had this weird vision thing, something demonic has been the cause of it. I can tell you one thing, though: I've never felt it this strong."

"What do you mean, felt it?" Nick asked.

"Not only does my vision fade around the edges, depending on how close I am, an overwhelming dread envelops me. A depression, almost. It's hard to describe." Sage took a deep breath and pointed toward where he'd been staring. "I've never felt anything like that before. I still feel it, radiating toward me in constant waves, an ocean of evil. A constant pulse of wickedness. Many times more powerful than what I felt facing Mammon." He looked at all three of them with an expression of fear Nick had never seen before. "Whatever it is, it's huge."

Ronan grabbed Sage's shoulder and squeezed. "Did you feel the dread before your vision altered?"

"Yeah. Just as we made the turn." Sage looked at all of them for a moment. "Whatever it is . . . well, it's just on a different level. Maybe the wall is somehow channeling it toward me. You know, like riding along the edges toward us."

Many times more powerful than one of the Princes of Hell? Nick shuddered and felt goose bumps break out up and down both arms. They hadn't even entered the Territories yet, and he wanted to go back. Nick saw Hieronymus and Kaja staring at each other, some kind of silent communication. *They know something. Something bad.*

"We must proceed," Hieronymus said suddenly. "We have much distance to cover." He walked off in the direction he'd been heading before, not waiting to see if anyone objected.

They skimmed along the stone wall for at least a mile before slowing, crossing a rocky patch, and circling around a giant boulder. Standing there were three of the biggest Elioudian guards Nick had seen yet. Bigger than those standing sentry outside the gate at the village of Seth. Bigger than Vale's bodyguard. They were nearly ten feet tall, with shoulders almost four feet across. They held swords that looked heavy enough to kill an elephant with a single blow.

"They guard entry from the Emim territory," Hieronymus said, as though reading Nick's mind. "We have similar guards at various spots guarding entrances into the Wasteland," he told Sage and Ronan. "Including the area we discussed a few minutes ago." The scout unlocked a thick steel door that opened into the wall. "Go through there, and wait for me," he said.

Kaja went first. She disappeared into a dark passageway barely wide and tall enough for a full-size Elioudian. Nick stuck his hands out, touched both sides of the wall, and entered. Sage was behind him. Then Ronan. After several steps, he heard the gate close behind him. Nick continued, feeling his way through the pitch black, amazed at how thick the wall was. He finally saw Kaja ahead of him as she unlocked, opened, and stepped through a second gate.

The landscape on the other side of the wall was no different, Nick thought, but then, why would he expect it to be? Until Sage tapped him on the shoulder and whispered into his ear. "Look at the boneyard."

It was hard to see it at first, but then he did. Dozens of animal skeletons littered the ground along the edge of the wall, some within a few feet of the gate. Some of the bones were almost dust now, others just broken pieces, scattered around as though ravaged by other animals.

Hieronymus stepped out of the wall and locked the gate with a chain and padlock. "It has been many centuries since the Emim beasts ventured this close to the wall on a regular basis," he said. "They long ago stopped trying to breach it, and few can fit through the passageway should they succeed in opening the first gate."

"How long did it take to build the wall?" Ronan asked.

"It was completed prior to my birth. I am told the early Elioudians labored for nearly a thousand years to complete it. It is six leagues long and is the only thing separating Tartarus from the three Territories." Hieronymus adjusted the pack on his back and pointed forward. "Come. We waste time."

"How far is a league again?" Nick asked Sage quietly.

"Three miles," his brother answered.

They walked in the same formation as before. Hieronymus explained that the Territories were once known as Gehenna and had belonged to the Elioudians. "The area we are in now is part of the vast caverns that once held water. Soon we will begin climbing a steep, narrow passage that will lead to the hand-dug homeland we used to occupy."

Then he fell silent, intent on making his way through the rugged landscape under the dim glow of the overhead lights. Nick saw more strange skeletons, black stains on some of the jagged rocks—dried blood, maybe—and remnants of several types of animal skin. They were moving away from the swampy area, heading slowly to the right as the ground gradually increased in grade. The smell of sulfur hung lightly in the air, but something else was present, too.

His arm was fully healed now, and he couldn't even see a scar. The buzzing caused by Vale's blood now vibrated throughout his body: behind his eyes, in his fingertips, and deep within his head. He wondered if Sage felt the same thing.

"Do the Emim have a village?" Sage asked Hieronymus. "Are the creatures organized enough to live together?"

"There are several Emim villages. In the beginning the Emim were not too different in appearance from us," Hieronymus said. "But their experiments with animals changed them. Now, although they still have great intelligence inherited from the Watchers, they are clannish and distrustful of one another." The scout stopped and looked at Sage. "They group together by type. There are small pockets spread out among their territory. Soon we will climb the shaft leading into our former homeland. I expect to find Emim there, guarding that entrance."

The upward grade increased dramatically in the next few minutes. Hieronymus explained quietly that the shaft they would soon enter was discovered after the Great Flood when a scout stumbled and fell, dislodging a rock that rolled into the earth. He had dug into the wall to follow the rock and found a crevice that he widened enough to crawl into and explore. After days of exploration using nothing more than a burning torch, he had returned to the High Council and reported his discovery.

Hieronymus's deep baritone voice mesmerized Nick and kept his mind off the dangers that surely awaited them. Then he finished his story and said nothing more for several minutes. When he finally stopped and gathered them around him, the scout pointed to the path ahead.

"The shaft is near," he whispered. "We will approach with great caution. When we reach the top, we will hold and survey the area. We will prepare for the worst but expect the best. Come."

Hieronymus stopped in front of a wall of rock, which stretched before them as far as Nick could see in either direction. From here it was up the shaft and into the thick of Emim territory. The lights hanging high in the ceiling, a single row of powerful bulbs like those in Tartarus, were spaced much farther apart than normal. The shadows were so great Nick couldn't see where the beginning of the shaft began. He soon found out. Hieronymus turned right, went about a hundred yards, and disappeared into the wall of rock.

The shaft was at least thirty feet wide. Nick used all his focus to climb. Rocks jutted out of the sides like stairs, and it went nearly straight up. He tried to see Kaja, but it was too dark. They stopped twice to rest. They didn't speak; they just stopped when they ran into each other. Finally, he saw a slight glow above him, ambient light from the old lighting system the Elioudians had installed prior to moving into their new home.

When they reached the top, Hieronymus motioned for them to lie on their bellies and peek over the edge. The remains of an ancient village sat off in the distance, built with stone but long destroyed. Dozens of dried carcasses, most dead for eons, were scattered about like the remains of a battlefield. Nick smelled a rancid odor, though it was faint, mixed with the ever-constant sulfur. They remained silent as they visually searched the area for signs of living creatures but saw nothing.

"It remains unchanged since I was here last," Hieronymus said. "Come, I think we are safe for now."

They spread out in a line and moved together, the two scouts to Nick's right and Sage and Ronan to his left. By the time they got to the dilapidated stone buildings, Nick had seen more bones than he could possibly count. A massacre had surely occurred in this place.

Nick imagined a huge four-headed monster rising from the rubble of the nearest building and breathing fire from each mouth. He shivered from the image.

"Look out!" Sage shouted, as he grabbed Nick by the arm and threw him to the ground. Ronan jumped in front of Nick and Sage and cocked his steel bar into a fighting stance.

"Separate," Hieronymus commanded. He pushed Kaja to one side while he sprinted in the other direction.

Nick slammed against the ground, the full weight of Sage's body against him. He covered his head and waited to be killed.

"Where'd it go?" Sage shouted again. "Hieronymus, Ronan, where did it go?"

"It just disappeared," Kaja said. "It was there, and then it wasn't."

"What was it?" Sage climbed to his feet, sword ready, searching frantically in all directions. "Hieronymus, what was that thing?"

Nick sat up, rubbing his ribs where he'd landed on a fist-sized rock. "What did you see?" Nick asked. "I didn't see anything. Where was it?"

"There," Hieronymus said, pointing his sword to the nearest collapsed building. He looked at Sage. "I do not know what it was."

"I didn't see anything," Nick said.

Kaja walked over, her face rigid with fright. "How could you not have seen it?" she asked. "It was right in front of us."

"What?" Nick asked. "What was? I was looking right at that building and didn't see anything."

The others looked at him strangely. "How is that possible, Nick?" Sage said. "It was at least thirty feet tall and had four heads. Fire shot out of all four mouths like some crazy dragon. How could you not see that?"

16

Brother.

Sloth waited quietly for Gadrell to answer. It was midnight—time to give his twin an update. His wife had retired an hour ago, and his armed guards knew not to disturb him. A single nightlight illuminated his contemplation room. Music played softly.

Yes, Belphegor. What news awaits me?

The plan, dear brother, has matured. It is as we hoped. Soon, you will begin to hear rumors of strangers within your midst. The angel boy and his younger brother must be allowed to reach the gate. The gate will not be opened except upon his insistence. A group follows the boy, Pure Ones disguised as humans. Kill them at your leisure.

I cannot control those in the other Territories, Belphegor. We have discussed this. The possibility remains that all will perish, including the angel boy.

Yes, Gadrell, an unfortunate reality. I advise only to control what you can. Prepare for freedom. Assemble your disciples. The aroma of freedom awaits. Soon, dear brother, we will rule together. I will await to embrace you outside the gate.

Soon, Belphegor, we will rule together. I will contact you once I am sure the boy is soon to approach the gate.

Sloth reclined in his chair, eyes closed, and absorbed the soft piano music. Sage Alexander, the greatest tool ever created to defeat the Princes, used by Sloth as the cause for the rise of a dozen more. He couldn't help but smile. Then the face of the sword-wielding boy, eyes on fire, jamming the sword up through Nearatook's face, intruded. His hands got clammy and he dried them on his pants. He might soon be required to confront that boy's sword, and he had to be ready. If he wanted to rule as his brilliance deserved, he *would* be ready.

The landscape changed from farmland to forestland. Elsbeth rode in the front railcar heading to Abel, with Gavin beside her and Malcolm and Steven in the back seat. Endora and Kato rode in the front seat in the second car, with David spread out behind them.

"Is it possible to have a higher level of oxygen down here?" Elsbeth asked Gavin. They'd seen nothing but hardwood forests on both sides of the road for at least thirty miles. The cavern they were passing through was the largest yet, with winding creeks snaking everywhere. "I feel different," she said. "Almost like I'm breathing oxygen out of a mask. I can see better, hear better, and my mind seems sharper. Is it possible?"

"With all these trees?" Gavin said. "I'd think it might be possible, given the closed environment. Dad, what say you?"

"I'm no scientist," Steven said. "But it makes sense from a logical point of view. And Elsbeth, I'm feeling the same differences you are."

They'd seen a few Elioudians walking among the trees, a few signs of wildlife, but nothing that appeared remotely dangerous. It was a perfect environment, Elsbeth thought. No crime, no stress of high-paying jobs or rude neighbors, no wars or border skirmishes, no guns or other weapons of death.

"If you could get used to not having malls or fancy restaurants or movie theaters, it wouldn't be a bad place to live," Malcolm said from the back seat, seemingly reading Elsbeth's thoughts.

"Or beaches," Gavin added. "Or mountains, television, NFL football, airplane rides, exotic and romantic weekend getaway spots. Or technology, sunshine, rain, snow, an occasional breeze, the feel of sand between your toes and ocean waves lapping at your ankles. Sure, if you don't mind giving all that up, and about a thousand other things I could name, this would be a great place to hang out for a thousand years." He glanced at Elsbeth, his crooked grin matching the sarcasm dripping from every word.

"Or Elvis records?" Elsbeth asked.

Gavin laughed out loud. "Nick and his games."

"Are you Elvis One or Two?" Elsbeth asked.

"Two, because I'm younger than Malcolm." Gavin laughed again. "I'm not even sure how Nick knows who Elvis is. Or was. Then again, what do I know? I ain't nothing but a hound dog."

Malcolm groaned. "That joke again?"

"Look, Elsbeth," Gavin said. "Don't be cruel. Just love me tender, in the ghetto, at my heartbreak hotel in some Kentucky rain. And if you have a suspicious mind, jump on my mystery train with your good luck charm. Just don't be a hardheaded woman, little sister." He started laughing as Malcolm slapped him on the side of the head.

"You just *had* to get him started, didn't you, Elsbeth? You're lucky he only gave you his short list of Elvis songs. I watched him try to woo a woman in a restaurant by stringing together a list of more than twenty. He had his hair all done up, had a sparkly shirt on, the sideburns, the swagger. She walked away before he got halfway through his ridiculous, song-titled, incoherent pickup line."

"I think it was my exposed chest hair that turned her off," Gavin said. "Or maybe my platform shoes."

"They were both big Elvis fans," Steven said from the back seat. "Even dressed like him for about a decade. I think Nick got the idea to call them that after a picture he saw. It was brilliant on his part."

"That boy has got *one* crazy imagination," Malcolm said.

They rode in silence for several moments, and Elsbeth decided to ask a question she'd been wondering about since meeting Endora. "Can someone tell me about Endora? David called her tortured. If you'd rather not tell me, that's fine. I just want to better understand her."

"I'll tell it, Dad," Gavin said. "If you're OK with that."

"OK," Steven said. "Just speak softly. Endora's railcar isn't that far behind us."

"She was born in Germany, as you probably know from her accent," Gavin said. "She was a childhood friend of Mozart, the composer, and was at his bedside with his wife and sister when he died at thirty-five. Mozart was like the brother she never had. She called him the most brilliant musician she'd ever met, including Beethoven, whom she also loved like a brother."

"Is she drawn to music because of Voice?" Elsbeth asked.

"Makes sense, doesn't it?" Gavin said. "Her parents were killed during some of the early Napoleonic battles, her first husband during the French Revolutionary War, her second during the Battle of the Nations when Napoleon was defeated. She was later than most becoming a Council member, almost sixty years old. By that time, she'd buried her entire family and two husbands. Her first contact with the Council was Rabbi Cohen, a fellow countryman. They fought together for more than two decades before she paired up with Jarvis. She and Jarvis worked together until just before the First World War."

"She met someone and married again," Malcolm said, "but lost him during World War I. She went dark after that, disappearing for almost twenty years. Not even Jarvis knew where she was."

"By the time she surfaced again," Gavin said, "just as Hitler was rising to power, she'd married a fourth time, but that husband was killed during the Night of the Long Knives in 1934. She was so distraught, nobody saw her again for almost fifteen years. By then World War II was over, the Soviets had moved into East Berlin, and Germany was an economic wreck."

"It didn't take much convincing for the Council to woo her back into the fold," Malcolm said. "They paired her up with Jarvis again, and like the previous times they worked together, they flirted with the idea of a romantic relationship, but nothing ever came of it."

"She married a fifth time in the late sixties, but that husband was killed a few years later by a bomb set off by the Red Army Faction, a German terrorist group." Gavin paused for a moment and looked at Elsbeth. "She has not married a sixth time. And she *is* tortured by the deaths of all her husbands."

"She married humans," Malcolm said. "Not Council members or descendants of Council members. She's always longed for a normal life. She hates going on missions, but she does it now to keep her sanity."

"What do you mean?" Elsbeth asked.

"She believes God has punished her for marrying outside her Elioudian ancestry," Gavin said. "She mostly blames herself for the deaths of her husbands. Had she not married regular humans, she thinks, they would all have died natural deaths. The only way to rid herself of the guilt is to battle the beasts that torment humanity. She's a reluctant warrior."

They rode in silence after that, the great underground forest whizzing by at almost forty miles per hour. Elsbeth knew going forward that she would look at Endora in a new light. She couldn't imagine losing a single loved one to a violent death, much less five husbands. Endora's parents were gone; she had no siblings, no children. Just work—a job bringing violence against other living creatures. It was no wonder she wasn't a bright light in a dark room.

"Is anyone having doubts about heading to Abel?" Steven asked. "Should we have spent more time at the switching terminal asking around?"

"I'm having doubts," Malcolm said. "Looking at the map, seems like they would've taken them to Seth. It's right by the entrance to the Territories."

"Yeah, you said that," Gavin said. "And it makes sense. But I still think the High Council would have to approve sending an escort team to the surface. A telephone system would've come in handy. Or email. Even a telegraph. Instead, we have to travel 150 miles just to find out if we guessed right."

"Will Sage wait for us?" Elsbeth asked. "Does anyone here think he'll go on without us?"

"I told him to go if he got a chance," Steven said. "He'll resist it, but I made him promise. It will depend on the Elioudians, I think."

"He'll wait if he knows what's good for him," Gavin said. "He knows the power of our gifts."

"I think if he sees a chance to get Nick out, he'll take it," Malcolm said. "He knows we can take care of ourselves."

Elsbeth didn't give her opinion. She just wrapped her arms against her chest and hoped that whatever decision Sage made, it would be the right one. She just wanted him safe.

Nick looked at each of them. They were serious. Their faces showed it. He asked Kaja if she'd seen the same thing, and she just nodded. He took a deep breath and looked at his brother. "Right before you knocked me down and started yelling, I imagined that very monster rising up out of that rubble. Four heads. Fire out of their mouths. The whole thing. But I didn't see it because it wasn't real. It was a flash of imagination. That's all. I was scaring myself."

Hieronymus took a half step forward. "You are certain that is the beast you imagined?"

"Yeah," Nick said.

"At the very moment Sage knocked you down to protect you?"

"A second before that. Yeah."

Hieronymus turned and looked toward the rubble of the collapsed building. Then he looked at Sage. "You are familiar with angelic gifts?"

"I know about all of them." Sage almost said something else but stopped. He looked at Ronan and started to ask, but then his eyes went wide and he jerked his head toward Nick. "Illusion."

"What?" Yeah, Nick thought, they'd seen an illusion.

"The gift of Illusion," Sage said excitedly. "The ability to alter or deceive the perceptions of others. That's what just happened." He turned toward Hieronymus. "It was Vale's blood, wasn't it? That's why you told Nick to let you know if he started feeling any different."

"I suspected that such a thing might occur, yes," Hieronymus said.

"Does it mean he was already angelic-human?" Sage asked. "And Vale's blood accelerated the timetable for his gift?"

"I suspected that to be so." Hieronymus looked at Kaja. "Did I not mention that such a thing might happen?"

"You did, sir," Kaja said. She looked at Nick and smiled. "Now there are two other children like me. I am pleased."

Ronan stepped over to Nick and cuffed him on the shoulder. Nick put his hands on each side of his head, not believing what was happening. If he had seen the four-headed giant, maybe he would understand more. "You thought I was angelic-human?" he asked Hieronymus.

"You have the same mother and father," he said. "The same blood as your brother. You also are a descendent of Seth. And Vale. I would not have understood had you *not* been angelic-human."

"Will this happen all the time?" Nick asked. "Making people see things? I mean, I didn't even try for it to happen. I didn't mean to scare all of you."

"Some gifts happen immediately," Ronan said. "And you can use them to their full advantage as soon as they manifest. Some take years of training to control and perfect. I don't know much about Illusion, don't know any Council member who has it." He laughed just a little. "But I guess you're gonna have to start being careful about what's churning around inside that head of yours."

Sage grabbed him in a bear hug and squeezed him hard. "Oh, happy day, brother. Oh, happy day. I knew this would happen at some point. I just knew it."

"Let him try again," Hieronymus said. The scout stepped over and placed a hand on Nick's shoulder. "Can you try it again? We must determine how reliable it is before we proceed."

"I . . . I don't know," Nick said. He felt better after getting such a warm reaction from Sage, but he didn't know if he could produce the gift on demand. "I'm not sure." They stared at him, clearly hopeful. His stomach felt like a flock of butterflies had just been released.

"Concentrate," Kaja said. "What were you thinking about when you had the image?"

Nick tried remembering. "Well, I was thinking about all the bones. About this whole area being the sight of a huge massacre. I had a fleeting thought about us getting caught out in the open. Then I thought about a four-headed, flame-shooting giant rising out of one of the smashed buildings and roasting us alive."

"Well, imagine it again," Sage said.

"I'm trying, but I'm nervous."

"Just relax, Nick," Kaja said. "You do not understand the importance of your gift to our journey."

"What do you mean?" He had no idea how his gift would affect their trip, but clearly the rest of them did—the way they were all nodding and quietly agreeing with her.

"It's about the combination of gifts," Sage said. "Used in unison. A part of a planned assault. Do you understand?"

Nick blew out a breath. "Not really. But if you say so."

Hieronymus squeezed his shoulder again and stepped away. He looked around and stepped behind Nick, then he motioned for the others to follow suit. "We will stand quietly behind you. Try again. But should you fail, do not worry; you will learn to control it in due time."

As Sage and Kaja disappeared behind him, Nick looked at the desolate landscape they'd just traveled through, back toward the shaft leading down to Tartarus. He knew the importance of their survival—well, of Sage's survival—but still didn't understand the whole use-the-gifts-in-unison thing Sage talked about. His hands suddenly felt sweaty. He swiped his forehead and tried picturing the big, four-headed giant again, but he couldn't see it in his mind's eye.

"You're doing it, Nick," Sage whispered. "Not the giant like before, but minotaurs." Then his voice got serious. "In fact, an entire herd of them."

Nick spun around. "Where? I didn't think that! That image never entered my brain at all!"

They all heard a loud grunt at the same time. Nick saw them on the far side of the destroyed village. They were huge, nearly seven feet tall. They walked upright like men but had faces that were scrunched and wrinkled and black. Huge horns protruded out of the sides of their heads and curved upwards almost two feet. *Perfect for ripping somebody's guts out.* Dark hair flowed down to their waists, and they each carried a club. They were solid muscle and looked as strong as the bull they'd come from. Nick counted about twenty but couldn't be sure. "That's what hurt me before," he said, his voice shaky. "After sliding down the hole. Getting stabbed by the horn made me sick. I almost died." He moved behind Ronan.

"Kaja, move right," Hieronymus said quietly. "Slowly. I will go left. Sage, stay with Nick. Ronan, come with me."

"With all due respect, sir," Sage said, "I will not do that. Kaja will stay with Nick, and I will make sure she never has to bloody her sword." In the next instant Sage was gone, teleported away.

"He really has a bad habit of doing that," Ronan said. "One of these days . . ."

"There," Kaja said. She pointed far to the right. "Sage battles."

Nick followed her line of sight and saw Sage just in time to watch him pull his sword out of the stomach of one of the minotaurs. The beast screamed, and all the others looked that way.

Before the beast could fall forward, Sage swung his sword and lopped off the arm holding the club.

What happened next was something Nick never thought he'd be able to see: the spirit of the dead beast—the demon Hannah had spoken of—rising from the carcass of the monster. Ronan told him that as soon as an angelic gift manifested within him, he'd be able to see the spirit world. And now he could. It got halfway out before Sage stabbed it in the heart and made it disappear into a cloud of dark mist.

"He killed the Watcher's demon," Kaja said. "Did you instruct him to do so?" she asked Hieronymus.

"Hannah did," Nick said. "Yesterday."

Just before four minotaurs crashed down on Sage, he disappeared. Sage had told Amelia that Fighting Arts allowed him to fight in superhuman speed, but Nick hadn't believed him. He'd seen Sage practice sword fighting hundreds of times, but clearly, he'd been dumbing it down so as not to reveal his angelic gift.

Now Sage teleported and struck so fast that as soon as one beast screamed and the rest began heading that way, he was gone and striking another. It took less than a minute for full panic to rise within the ranks of the minotaurs. By the end of that minute, at least half were dead or dying, and the other half were scrambling from one place to another, trying to avoid being the next victim.

Five made it out, fleeing at full speed away from Sage and his deadly sword. Sage stood still and watched them go and then turned toward Nick and raised his sword in victory. Nick smiled and raised a clenched fist in return.

Ronan smiled. "Sage told me stories of his battles last summer at Mammon's prison, but I never dreamed he'd advanced so far."

Kaja looked at Hieronymus. "Have you ever seen such a display?" she asked him, her voice full of awe and wonder.

"I have seen great Elioudian warriors," Hieronymus said. "But to battle a herd of bull-men singlehandedly and send them fleeing like children is something I could never have imagined." Hieronymus sheathed his own sword. "His craft of using his sword is unmatched for someone his age. Even without teleporting, he would be a formidable opponent for our best warriors."

Pride swelled so high within Nick that he felt like bursting. What he had just witnessed his brother do was beyond words. He was Superman, the Flash, Batman, and Thor all wrapped up in one package. Yet he didn't have a big head about any of it.

Sage took his time walking back over to them. He checked each of the minotaurs he'd slain to ensure they were dead and stabbed one of them to make sure.

His brother's face was all serious by the time he got back. He looked hard at Hieronymus. "I don't know if it was a good idea letting any of them run off, but I didn't want us to get separated. I'm afraid word of our presence here will spread quickly. It could cause trouble ahead."

"Perhaps," Hieronymus said. "But perhaps the word spread will be one of fear, one of avoidance. It might well make our journey easier."

"You are amazing," Kaja said to Sage. "You showed no fear."

Sage smiled at her. "This blade is amazing. Ancient Elioudians made it. It even cleans itself." He turned to Nick. "Well, I guess you've seen me in action now. It'll give us something to talk about. Remind me to tell you the *entire* story of the gargoyles. Now *that* was crazy!"

Nick threw his arms around him and hugged him as hard as he could. Sage started laughing, and then they both fell to the ground in a heap.

"You were amazing, Sage," Nick said, after they got to their feet. "I wish I could trade my gift for Teleporting."

"Yeah, well, don't be so sure about that. You haven't had time to think about your gift yet. Believe me, you have no idea what you'll be able to do with it."

Nick shrugged. "Whatever."

"I think Sage is right," Ronan said. "You're not grasping it all just yet. Don't worry, you will."

"We must go," Hieronymus said. "The journey is long and treacherous. They know we are here now, so we must be even more alert."

They walked in silence through the destroyed village. Nick saw the dead minotaurs up close as he passed. They were huge and ugly and smelled like a mixture of skunk and wet dog. One of them was missing a head. Nick looked at Sage in wonderment. He hadn't been affected by the slaughter at all. It was like he'd stepped on a roach and nothing more.

Sage walked slightly ahead of the rest of them, passing the stone buildings with caution. The last two buildings ahead looked like bunkhouses of some sort—small and narrow but towering at least sixty feet in the air. The street ran between the structures, and all of them were forced to step through scattered rocks the size of basketballs.

"Wait," Hieronymus whispered, the urgency in his voice unmistakable.

Sage stopped and looked back. Hieronymus pointed to the building on the left. "I heard a noise," he said quietly. "Up high."

They all looked but saw nothing. Nick heard both Elioudians draw their swords. Sage already had his out. Ronan stood on the left, ready with his bar.

Going around the buildings on either side would be nearly impossible. Most of the debris from the village had been stacked in a kind of crude wall—like the residents thousands of years ago had fortified their city against attack. Walking through these structures, down the center of this very narrow street, was the only way through.

A loud bang from the building on the left removed all doubt about something being in there. Nick stepped a little closer to Sage but clear of being hit if he swung his sword. A scream, low and rumbling but growing in pitch and volume, came from the roof of the building.

"Ylva," Kaja said. She looked at Hieronymus. "Are they not only in the Wastelands?"

"Some are here," he said. "I have seen a few."

"What is it?" Sage asked.

But nobody had to answer, because the ylva changed its scream into a full roar and stepped into plain view on the rooftop of the building.

"A wolf man with wings," Nick whispered under his breath. *Like Sage read about in that old book.*

Eight feet tall, its arms hung almost to its knees, and its stringy, tangled hair fell past its waist. The head didn't look exactly like a wolf's, but it was close enough for Nick to know what it was. Giant, leathery wings jutted from its back, spanning at least ten feet across. The beast had lean, rippling muscles. It flexed its three-inch claws as though loosening them for battle. The beast roared again, and a second came into view beside it. Then a third.

Nick glanced at Sage. His face wasn't as relaxed as a few seconds before. In fact, his face looked just as panic stricken as Nick felt. Ronan edged a little closer to them.

All three beasts attacked at once. But it wasn't any of those three that grabbed Sage by the throat and lifted him screaming high into the sky; it was the one that sprang quietly from the other building—the one nobody saw coming.

17

A claw clamped Sage's throat and cut off his scream. Pain speared the side of his neck. Blood sprayed into the gaping mouth of the beast as it lowered its jaws toward his face. Just as he felt its hot breath, he teleported away and landed awkwardly. His right knee collapsed, and he crashed against the stone wall. His vision blurred as blood pumped out onto the ground in front of him. Carotid artery. He wouldn't last long if he didn't get help. Minutes.

The beast screamed, flipped over in the air, found him, headed back, and streaked through the sky. Sage struggled to his feet and got his sword ready. He saw Nick cowering against the other building, Ronan beside him, with Hieronymus and Kaja in front, working their swords against the other three beasts with skill developed by centuries of battle.

"Sage!" Ronan screamed. "Protect Nick," he shouted to Hieronymus. He pushed between the two Elioudians, swung his bar at the nearest beast, and made contact, blowing it backward several feet.

The one in the air tucked it wings, opened both claws and jaws, and headed for Sage's chest. He needed to time his move perfectly because he wouldn't have the strength to do it a second time. Sage placed the tip of his sword on the ground, his arms out in front of him. After a quick breath, he tightened his grasp on the handle and waited, his bloody hands making it hard to grip.

"Move, Sage!" Ronan shouted. "Move now!"

But he didn't move. He waited. And waited. Then struck. The beast hit Sage with both claws just as Sage thrust his sword forward. Ten claws sunk into Sage's chest as the force of the blow toppled him backward. He landed on his back, the full weight of the beast rolling over the top of him. The sword had done its job. The point of the blade burst out the middle of its back, and Sage felt the beast go limp. It sped past him, twisting, its wings crossing underneath, before slamming up against the stone building.

Sage staggered to his feet. The wound on his neck barely pumped anything now. He heard two screeches behind him and looked. Hieronymus and Kaja had each downed a beast, and the third was flying off.

"Kill the escaping demons," Hieronymus shouted.

The handle of Sage's sword was moving to the rhythm of the beast's labored breathing. He yanked it out and was barely able to hold it steady as he waited for the demon to escape its dying host. Then he fell over, everything fading in and out.

"Sage!" Nick shouted. "He's dying, Hieronymus! Help him!" Sage's head slammed against the stone wall, and he saw stars.

"Push it into his neck," Hieronymus shouted. "Hard . . . hold it . . . tie it . . . there. Yes. Ronan, take care of Nick . . . Kaja knows the way back . . . can't wait . . . too much blood loss . . . bleeding stopped . . . healing but needs blood . . . Nick, you will be fine . . . Kaja, you know what to do. I will take him. Return quickly."

Jerking . . . pressure . . . darkness . . . pain . . . wind against his face. Sage felt hot breath against his face, hard pants, strong arms, soft words of hope. Then darkness overtook him.

"They are not here," the old Elioudian told Steven and the rest of Sage's rescue team. "The High Council traveled to the village of Seth to meet with them."

Elsbeth's heart dropped at the news. They'd arrived in Abel the night before, late. Their train cars had stopped outside a gate at the city wall. The guards standing post had refused to let them in before morning, so they'd pitched their sleeping bags in a darkened alcove fifty yards from the bright lights of the gate.

Elsbeth had joined Steven at the gate again the next morning, where he pled his case for entrance to a different set of guards. It had taken nearly an hour, but they'd finally been escorted into the city under heavy watch.

Inside the gate, Elsbeth would have believed she'd stepped into a heavenly city. While the streets weren't paved with gold, there were enough golden flecks that they sparkled. Streetlights consisted of diamond globes mounted on short granite posts spaced every few yards along sidewalks encrusted with rubies and emeralds. The buildings were white stone, inlaid with silver.

The seven of them walked in shocked silence at the beauty of the capital city. She couldn't imagine how many decades it had taken to build, and it was obvious the Elioudians were unafraid to use the natural resources they'd discovered in Tartarus—or did not value them in the same manner.

It wasn't a big city, maybe a ten-block square, and they didn't see that many Elioudians. Those they did see were extremely old. It made her wonder if the elderly came here to die, their reward for living a long life of manual labor.

The building in the center wasn't white like every other; it was a mixture of bronze, copper, gold, and silver, with massive support columns and an expansive front porch. The bronze-wrapped front doors stood open, and they'd been escorted to benches in the main entry hall. Once seated, they waited another half hour before a very old Elioudian hobbled in the front door and gave them the news.

"Are you certain?" Steven asked the Elioudian, who'd introduced himself as Timothy.

"I am secretary to the High Council. I recorded the details myself." Timothy pointed toward a blank spot on one of the benches and sat down. "Please, be seated."

After they all sat, Timothy continued. "A messenger arrived reporting that a boy named Sage, gifted with abilities prophesized by one of the originals of our race, was demanding escort to the surface. Because of the nature of the request, all the members of the

Council traveled to meet him. I expect their return in a day or two. Although oftentimes when Council members travel as far as Seth, they also visit the other cities in Tartarus."

"Would the Council approve providing an escort to the surface?" Steven asked.

"Certainly. The Prophecy of Seth details the importance of Sage to the defeat of the Seven. The Council understands those battles will take place on the surface. Sage is a descendent of the Elioudian people. He is one of us. The High Council would never take action that would reduce the odds of defeating the Seven." Timothy stood and pointed to a doorway on the other side of the entry hall. "Would you care for some refreshments before you begin your journey to Seth?"

All of them stood. "I'm famished," David said. "Could eat three dead horses. Kato, how about you?"

"A meal would be nice," Kato said.

"I can arrange that," Timothy said.

They were in railcars heading out of Abel an hour later, full stomachs, well rested, but in for a 450-mile trip at barely more than thirty miles an hour. Because it was already midmorning, they wouldn't make it any earlier than the middle of the night. The problem was the railcars. They'd discovered riding from the switching station to Abel—a mere 150 miles—that they were forced to stop every hour or so to stretch their legs. David was especially hurt by the cramped confines of the cars. So, the reality was that it would be midday tomorrow before they got there, assuming they didn't stop along the way and pitch their sleeping bags just inside a tree line along the track.

Elsbeth was as frustrated as everyone else about the slow pace of the trip, but at least they'd learned that Sage and Nick made it safely to Seth. The group seemed more relaxed now, and all of them believed they'd catch up with them there.

They arrived at the switching station seven hours after leaving Abel, twice as slow as Elsbeth had originally calculated. It was evening now, and she didn't think any of them had another three hundred miles in them. David insisted they eat a big dinner, spend the night there, and leave after breakfast. Nobody argued. And although Elsbeth was anxious to find Sage and Nick, she also understood that it probably wouldn't make any difference if they arrived eight hours later than she'd originally thought.

Elsbeth was just about to bed down for the night when Endora approached her. "May I speak with you privately?"

"Yes, certainly," Elsbeth said. She kept her voice steady. Over the past twenty-four hours Endora hadn't said much to anyone, and Elsbeth wondered if something was wrong.

The seven of them were in a far corner of the huge switching station, away from anything and everything. There were few Elioudian workers that late in the evening, so Endora and Elsbeth didn't have to go far to be totally alone.

"I must ask a personal question," Endora said, her slight German accent seemingly more noticeable than normal. "You must not take offense to my prying."

"OK. What is it?" Elsbeth stepped back a half step, putting a little more distance from Endora's intensity.

"Are you and Sage involved romantically? For that is the rumor among those within the Council." Endora pushed a strand of jet-black hair off her forehead.

Elsbeth sighed. "I know. We're close," she admitted. "But we're friends. That's all."

"Yet you have emotions that might grow into romantic feelings? Do you see your future in such a manner?"

Elsbeth looked away. "Anything is possible," she said. "Why are you asking me about this?"

"Because emotions cloud actions," Endora said. "They thicken your mind, dull your responsiveness. They can get you killed. They can get Sage killed."

Elsbeth didn't say anything immediately. This was a different verse of the same song that Horace sang. Endora thought Elsbeth might be a liability on this mission. Endora had probably forgotten more about fighting than Elsbeth had ever known. Was her approaching Elsbeth now part of her being *tortured*? Elsbeth didn't know, but she wasn't about to snap at her just because she was concerned about the team. "Thank you for sharing such an important piece of wisdom. I can assure you, when the time comes, my clear-eyed vision will be evident. I care for Sage and would never do anything to cause him harm."

Endora took a deep breath and nodded. "Fair enough. Consider the matter closed. Thank you for not being offended." She smiled and walked away.

Elsbeth wondered how many of the others harbored the same suspicion—that she was a liability to the team, either because without her Persuasion she would be no good in combat or because her closeness to Sage could impair her judgment. There was no way to know. She did know one thing, though: she had a lot of proving to do. Only David had seen her in action. She was no wilting flower. She just hoped she survived long enough in the Territories to show them.

Sage woke up wearing nothing but a pair of athletic shorts. A single lamp glowed in one corner. He lifted his head off the pillow and looked at his body. A tube ran from his right arm into the left arm of a man lying next to him.

Vale. The old man smiled. "You will never be the same, young Sage," he said softly. "Nor I."

"Where am I? How did I get here?" Sage blinked away the blurriness of sleep and felt a slight bump on his neck.

"It is still puffy," a voice said from the far side of the room. "But the wound is nearly healed." Hieronymus stepped up next to the bed and touched the puncture wounds in Sage's chest. "Only two of the original ten claw marks are visible now."

"You owe him your life," Vale said.

"Where's Nick?" Sage said, panic rising.

"Safe," Hieronymus said. "Ronan and Kaja got him safely back last night. He is asleep."

"How long have I been here?" He felt a surging throughout his body and looked at the tube running into his arm. A blood transfusion. Vale's blood. *Holy smoke!*

"A full day," Hieronymus said. "You have been asleep the entire time."

"I have never seen anyone so close to death yet survive," Vale said. "God is with you."

Sage looked at Vale and wondered how much of his blood he'd given. "You've been giving me blood for an entire day?"

Vale laughed, but it was weak and sounded full of pain. "I only just arrived. I had made it to the switching station on the way back to Abel when a messenger overtook me and asked me to return."

"We did not think you were going to make it," Hieronymus said. "You were walking the edge of death, barely surviving the blood loss. Your wounds had healed by the time I got you back, but we needed blood from someone within your bloodline."

"And though there are many within Tartarus in your bloodline," Vale said slowly, "I am nearing the end of my time. Just two days ago I told you the reason I believed I had lived longer than any other was to meet you before my death." He held up his left arm and touched the tube. "Now I understand the true reason."

Sage looked at his chest. The final two puncture marks were gone now. "How much blood have you given me?"

"Enough to make me very sleepy," Vale said, his words getting sloppy. "I have been here for almost an hour, and your body has drunk heavily from mine. You have healed quickly."

Sage felt his body growing stronger by the second. He felt his neck again; the puffiness was gone. He didn't hurt anywhere. Then he had a thought and looked at Hieronymus. "The beast that attacked me—I was waiting for it to die so I could kill its spirit. I don't remember if I did."

"Kaja killed it," he said. "You passed out before it died."

"How's Nick?" Sage asked. "Did you tell him I was going to be OK?"

"I did. He was scared, naturally, but he is sleeping peacefully now."

"Hieronymus told me of his gift," Vale said, his words now so slurred Sage could barely understand him. "You must encourage him to exercise it, for it might be key to making it back to Topsi . . ." And then he was gone. His jaw dropped open, his eyes rolled back into his head, and his frail body sunk against the bed.

Sage watched the old man's spirit exit his body and hover over the bed. An angel. Not unlike what Leah looked like. Three sets of wings like an Arch, a glittering breastplate, a sword, flowing hair that swirled around his head like a halo.

Sage knew his Elioudian history. When the angels made the deal with the original High Council six thousand years ago that a group of Elioudians would be gifted with special abilities and sent to the surface to battle their evil cousins, one thing all of them would have was the ability to see the entirety of the spiritual realm. Regular Elioudians, like Hieronymus, who now rushed around and yanked the needle from Sage's arm, did not have that full ability. The scout could see the dark spirits exiting the beasts in the Territories but couldn't see Vale's spirit hovering above the bed, watching his every move, a huge smile on its face.

Instead, Hieronymus was beside himself. "We have waited too long," he said, sticking two fingers under Vale's jaw to check for a pulse. He closed his eyes, as though willing Vale's heart to beat.

Sage climbed off the bed and stood reverently as Vale's spirit watched Hieronymus frantically check for signs of life. "He's gone."

"He insisted on giving you his blood," Hieronymus said. "No one could dissuade him. He was prepared for the sacrifice."

"But why give me so much?" Sage asked the spirit. "Surely I didn't need *that* much." He felt strong enough to run through a wall. Vale's spirit didn't answer. Like the Archs, it remained silent.

Hieronymus carefully pulled the needle from Vale's arm and straightened his frail body on the bed. After a silent prayer, he took a blanket from a bedside table and completely covered him. "He always hoped that his existence would somehow impact the future of the world." He looked gently at Sage. "And now it has. Do not let his life-giving gift go to waste."

Sage had no words. He simply stood there and considered the unbelievable sacrifice Vale had so willingly given. Then the old man's spirit rose into the air and disappeared through the ceiling with an expression of joy so radiant Sage's heart swelled and his eyes filled.

"Your clothes are on the chair over in the corner," Hieronymus said. He put a hand solidly on his shoulder. "Do not cry. Vale has gone home." He nodded and smiled. "Put them on, and I will take you to Nick. After I inform others of Vale's passing and make arrangements, we must go."

Sage wiped his eyes. He felt it would be disrespectful to leave before Vale's funeral—assuming they had funerals in Tartarus—but Hieronymus was right: to wait around for that would only decrease their odds of surviving the trip through the Territories. And if Sage didn't survive, Vale's death would have been for nothing.

Ronan walked in just after Sage finished dressing. He hugged him hard and inspected him closely from head to feet. "Hieronymus said you're feeling better than normal. True?"

"Absolutely true." He looked at Vale. "He gave his life for me."

"Everyone in the Council will give their life for you," Ronan said. "Get used to it."

A worm of guilt squirmed in Sage's gut. He should have seen the beast before it grabbed him. He should have been more careful. Vale should be alive right now. The thought of others dying for him turned his stomach. "Well, I'm not letting anybody else sacrifice themselves for me. Not happening."

"You mean after the rescue team gets back to the surface?" Ronan gripped his shoulder. "We sacrifice for each other. That's the point. We all work toward the same goal. Death is part of it. You saw it last summer. You've seen it today. You'll see it in the future. Embrace the fact that death is part of life. Vale gave his willingly, and you'll be stronger for it." He looked at Sage's grief-stricken face, and his eyes softened. "OK, I'm off my preaching pedestal." He smiled. "Now, go wake Nick."

When Sage found Nick, his brother almost knocked him over with a fierce hug. "You're OK? Really?"

"Amazing," Sage said. "Actually, better than normal." He told him about Vale and the blood transfusion. "We'll be heading out soon. You need to get ready."

The look in Nick's eyes, the terror, cut Sage deep. To be honest, Sage didn't feel too great about leaving so soon, either, but they had to get through before the Rephaim celebration ended.

"Where's Kaja?" Sage asked.

"I don't know. She said she wouldn't be far." Nick finished tying his shoes and grabbed his backpack.

Sage noticed his own backpack sitting next to Nick's. He pushed it onto his back. "Where's my sword?"

"Kaja has it." Nick's words shook.

"We'll be fine, Nick. I promise." Sage threw an arm around him. "Hieronymus said to meet him out by the lake. Let's go."

Sage led Nick and Ronan through a maze of pathways until they stepped into a clearing not far from the lake. Word must have spread they were back, because across the lake, up near Amelia's front door, were dozens of humans sitting on steps, watching.

"I saw Amelia when I got here yesterday," Nick said. "Kaja, Ronan, and I had just returned, and Amelia ran up and asked how you were."

"So, they saw Hieronymus carry me in?" Sage asked.

Nick shrugged. "Probably. You were unconscious when he carried you back. You wouldn't believe how fast he ran. I'm not kidding, Sage, he carried you in his arms and took off like a rocket. I bet he ran forty miles an hour."

"Are you serious?" Sage pulled his backpack off and sat down on a bench. Nick and Ronan joined him.

"Maybe faster," Nick said, his eyes wide. "I've never seen anything like that."

"It's true," Ronan said.

"Look," Sage said. He pointed toward the gate at the top of the cavern. Elioudians were streaming in by the dozens.

"Is that about Vale dying?" Nick asked.

"Probably," Ronan said. "He was the leader of their people."

The growing crowd of Elioudians entered the gate in groups of three and four. "What will happen to him?" Nick asked. "Do they have cemeteries here? Do they cremate?"

"I don't know," Sage said. "But his body is only a shell now. His soul is home. That's the main thing." He noticed more humans coming out of their homes, their attention diverted between the crowds streaming through the gate and Sage, Nick, and Ronan. "What would you say to the humans if you could say one thing?" he asked Nick. "Just one thing?" He looked at his brother, who now stared silently across the lake. For a long time, Nick just looked at them, his jaw flexing, his fingers intertwined. Sage glanced at Ronan, who nodded as though reading Sage's mind.

"I'd tell them what it's like on the surface now," Nick said finally. "I'd want to know if I were them."

"Yeah, I can see that," Sage said. "I was thinking the same thing."

"I *know* I'd want to know," Ronan said. "Can you imagine the number of questions you'd have if you'd been stuck down here for decades?"

"Do you think they're scared of us?" Nick asked.

"Scared how?" Sage asked.

"I don't know. Scared like if they talk to us, it'll make them homesick again. Amelia said it took her twenty years to get over being homesick."

"Maybe." Sage thought about it. "What if I go ask them?"

Nick frowned. "We were told to stay away from them."

"Yeah, true. But maybe they want an update. You would. And Ronan. Me." Sage looked around and didn't see Hieronymus anywhere. He'd probably gotten caught up in dealing with Vale's body. It might be a few minutes before he got back.

"Amelia didn't want an update," Ronan said. "She didn't ask one question. Maybe the only reason we're not supposed to talk to them is because she doesn't want to know."

"Could be," Sage said. "She's the only one who told us to stay away. I don't think the Elioudians care." He looked at Nick. "Think I should do it?"

Nick smiled a little and shrugged. "If you want."

"I'm gonna teleport," Sage said. "They'll all see that I'm not a normal human. You two staying here?"

Nick thought about it. "I'll stay here for a little while." He looked at Ronan. "What do you think?"

"I don't mind staying here, Nick," Ronan said. "If you'd like to wander over there in a few minutes to listen, I'll go with you."

Sage stood, looked for exactly the right spot in the center of the crowd, and didn't even have the thought fully formed before he was standing in front of them. Several flinched backward and gasped. A few appeared to be wearing remnants of the clothes they'd had when they'd dropped into Tartarus, as though desperately clinging to a past they'd never see again.

"Hello," Sage said loudly. He saw Amelia sitting on the steps just outside her front door, surrounded by a group of four men and two women. Sage was glad she couldn't shoot lasers out of her eyes. They were blazing with fury.

"Amelia asked my brother and me, and our friend Ronan, to stay away from all of you. I guess if I were in her position, to do what's best for the whole, I might've made the same request." He paused and folded his hands together in front of him. "But then I thought about what I'd be feeling if I'd dropped into this place. Let me ask you: Who was the last one to arrive? How long ago was it?"

Nobody answered. They just sat there, quiet as a tomb, as docile as kittens, most with expressions of mild irritation. Then Sage noticed one man glancing around, his eyes moving quickly from one person to another but always glancing up at Amelia before taking quick looks at Sage. He wore a beard and moustache and hair to his shoulders. His eyeglasses were round and foggy and hung crooked on his nose.

"My name is Sage Alexander. I am of Elioudian descent. I'm different, which you obviously know, given how I just appeared in front of you. I think by now Amelia has told all of you what our story is." He glanced at the bearded man, who was nodding slightly. "Amelia tried talking us out of going back to the surface. She thought we'd be killed. Well, she was almost right. I got attacked by a wolf man with wings, and we weren't even a half day into the journey. If not for what I am, I'd be dead. There's no possible way for any of you to go back."

He looked closely at several of the faces and thought he saw relief. Amelia seemed more relaxed, probably because she now knew that he hadn't shown up to try and convince them to leave.

"We're about to leave again, but I wanted to give you a chance to ask questions about the state of the world up top. It's why I asked about which of you was the last to arrive. I'd want to know how things have advanced if I'd been down here for eighty years."

The bearded man nearly shouted his question. "I'm Henry Hudson," he said, his British accent still heavy after a century. "Tell me the state of England, of the Crown."

"I've answered that a hundred times," Amelia said.

Hudson turned toward her. "You are the newest here, Amelia, but it's been eighty years. I think I'd like to know something of my homeland since that time." Back to Sage. "Have there been wars?"

And that opened the floodgates. Sage told them of World War II, Korea, Vietnam, and the terrible conflicts in the Middle East. He told them of technological advances, of trips to the moon and space probes. He talked about the fall of the Soviet Union and of Germany's role in the killing of six million Jews.

After almost an hour, Nick and Ronan walked up and sat down, and by that time Sage was fielding more questions than he could keep up with, most of which he could answer. Even Amelia took part, asking questions about the advancement of airplanes and jets and the use of aircraft in the wars. Sage told her about drones, flown remotely by pilots sitting in easy chairs a half a world away, with computers and camera-system data transmitted via satellite. But he also spoke of famine, genocide, and ethnic cleansing. Of conflicts still raging between people who have hated each other for thousands of years.

After two hours, every human in Tartarus—all seventy-seven—had gathered together and asked at least one question, and not one of them wore a scowl or gave him the evil eye. They laughed, some cried, but all were amazed at the state of the world since falling out of it.

Hieronymus broke up the party. The scout arrived and stood quietly until Sage finally acknowledged his presence. "Is it time to go?"

"I am sorry, but yes. It is time. Please meet me at the gate."

Sage watched him walk off, then turned to Nick and Ronan. "You ready?"

"Not really," Nick said.

"I agree," Ronan said.

"I know what you mean." Sage turned to the group. "I'm glad you let me give you some updates. Eventually you'll see a group show up, maybe any day now. They'll be here to rescue us. They're like us, Elioudians who look human but have special gifts. Welcome them. They are much older and can probably answer some stuff I wasn't able to." He smiled. "You never know, I might see all of you again someday."

Sage waved at them and walked away, heading up the stairs to the top rim of the village, Nick and Ronan behind him.

"Sage," Amelia said, after they were at the top. "Wait up."

She was alone, and her face was radiant. "Thank you. I was wrong for keeping everyone away from you. I was just scared."

"It was Nick's idea to give them a lesson in current events," Sage said, clamping a hand on his brother's shoulder. "And I'm glad you got answers about the advancement of airplanes."

Amelia stepped forward and hugged all three of them, tears now sliding down her cheeks. "I wanted that more than you could know, but I thought it would make me crazy with envy, not being able to see everything. Now I know it is better knowing than wondering. Thank you again, and good luck on your journey."

"I have a question," Nick said.

"What?" Amelia asked.

"Would you want your family to know you're alive? When we get back? Should we look them up and tell them?"

Sage hadn't thought to ask. *Wow, big question.*

Amelia considered. "Would some idiot billionaire explorer come try and find us if the world knew we were here?" she asked. "Because that's the last thing Tartarus needs."

"I think that would happen," Ronan said. "And we think the six remaining Princes are all billionaires. I think they'd come and lead a group of monsters to your doorstep."

"I think so, too." She looked at Nick. "Don't breathe a word of our existence. Things are fine just like they are. Maybe one day we'll be able to make it up to the surface, but we don't want the surface coming down to us."

They all nodded and hugged again. Amelia walked off but turned back. "The information you shared will give new life to our group. For the next twenty years they'll be talking nonstop about what you told them. Thanks again." She turned and practically skipped down the steps.

Sage looked at Nick and gave him a light punch on the arm. "Great idea about the updates, Nick. It was perfect."

They started up again when Nick grabbed Sage's arm. "Look." He pointed to the bottom of the bowl. A line stretched from the house where Vale had died all the way around the far end of the lake and disappeared inside the great white library.

"They're passing Vale's body from person to person," Nick whispered.

Sage saw an oblong shape wrapped in white cloth being passed hand to hand over the heads of the Elioudians. Each person in line waited, both hands in the air, for the body to make its way toward them.

"Nobody's saying anything," Nick whispered. "Look at the humans."

Sage glanced over and saw them standing perfectly still, hands raised straight in the air, heads raised toward heaven.

"What does it mean?" Nick asked.

"I don't know," Sage said. He saw Hieronymus waiting for them at the top. "We've gotta go. I'd love to hang around, but we really have to go."

Nick swallowed hard, his bottom lip quivering. "OK."

"Don't worry, brother," Sage said. "Things will be different this time. The blood of Seth runs strong through my body. And I can't begin to describe the differences I'm feeling already."

18

Two hours later they were back at the great stone wall about to turn right toward the gate. The feeling he'd had before of some ancient and powerful beast far in the distance nearly overwhelmed Sage now. "Hieronymus," he said, his voice shaky. "Please wait."

"What is it, Sage?" Ronan asked. "Do you sense something, like last time?"

Sage's vision darkened along the edges and blocked everything except a crystal-clear picture in front of him. Like before, the Sensing signal was fifteen degrees off the wall. A feeling of dread rolled over him with the force of a hurricane and drove him to his knees.

Worship Rameel, young Sage. I can be your god. Release me!

No. Araqiel is the god to worship. I am of the earth. Ruler of all. Come, see the power I can give you!

Your strength comes from me, Azazel, the most magnificent of the conquerors. Release me, and all will bow to you.

Lahash. That is the name you must worship. Eve blames me for her temptation, but power is what she sought. Come, Sage, come now!

Samyaza yet lives. Unshackle us. Allow us to transform you into your true destiny.

"Nooo!" Sage screamed, as he pressed his hands against his head. "Nooo!" He turned and found Hieronymus standing next to him. "I will teleport to the other side of the wall, near the door. Meet me there!"

"Sage, wait!"

But he went away, appearing just outside the steel door, tears streaming down his face. He stumbled and fell but drew his sword in case a beast lurked nearby. He could barely draw a breath. Rolling over onto his side, he pulled his knees to his chest and breathed, careful not to go too fast. After several beats, the demonic voices in his head disappeared.

He'd seen them. Just a flash. Two hundred of the most beautiful creatures in all creation. Huge, towering above a lake of boiling sulfur, each shackled with angelic chains so brilliant it hurt his eyes to look. They looked like gods, all of them: glorious, perfectly spellbinding. And he knew who and what they were.

The Watchers. The fallen angels from heaven. The corrupters of mankind. The fathers of all the evil offspring spawned before the flood. Shackled in the Wastelands, deep inside the most dangerous part of Tartarus. The area of the Wastelands Hieronymus said remained mostly unexplored.

Sage shivered, overwhelmed by a sudden urge to go back, to listen again to the barrage of messages transmitted directly into his head. And they knew him. By name. They called to him. Tempting, luring, bribing, but full of fear. Sage startled at the realization. *He'd sensed fear from them.*

He stood, rubbed his cheeks dry, and looked ahead of him. He suddenly felt more confident than ever before. If the Watchers feared him, their offspring should be quaking in their boots.

What has Vale's blood done to me? It had magnified his gift of Sensing by untold measures. He'd felt the Watcher's presence before, but from that to hearing voices, to seeing visions? He couldn't calculate the differences in himself.

A thought crept into his head about destiny and preordained events. He would never have sensed the Watchers without Vale's blood. He wouldn't have Vale's blood had he not been attacked. He'd never have been attacked if he wasn't in Tartarus, and he wouldn't be in Tartarus if he and Nick hadn't gone with their grandpa while he hunted for an entrance into the Dark spiritual realm. They almost hadn't gone. If not for his parents' cruise, he and Nick wouldn't have gone with their grandpa at all.

Destiny? Maybe. Preordained events? Possibly. Part of a six-thousand-year-old prophecy that was going to get fulfilled one way or another no matter who did what? The most likely explanation. A bigger force was at work. He was convinced of that now. Vale, the son of the prophet Seth, had lived longer than any Elioudian in history for one reason: to bestow upon Sage the blood of Seth. Because Sage had no chance to fulfill his destiny without it. Powerful stuff. Chills marched up both arms at the awesomeness of it.

Several minutes later he heard the locks being thrown on the steel door, and a second later Kaja stormed through, sword drawn, frantic. "I'm here," Sage said, as he stepped out of the shadow of the wall.

She breathed and closed her eyes, then sheathed her sword. "Hieronymus is *not* happy," she whispered. "We are supposed to stay together at *all* times."

Nick came through next, found Sage, and threw himself against him. "What happened? Why'd you leave? Are you OK?"

"I'm fine now." Sage hugged him and stepped away, squaring his shoulders for Hieronymus's arrival.

Ronan stepped into view and just shook his head. "You've got a bad habit of doing that."

The scout came through the door a few seconds later, turned, and locked the door. Then he looked at Sage, irritation hard on his face. Sage wasn't going to give him a chance to talk. "I saw the Watchers."

"Wha—"

"They are shackled in the deepest part of the unexplored Wastelands." Sage stepped forward and pointed. "That area needs to be off limits. Even to scouts. Forbidden entry. When you get back, you've gotta tell the Council."

"The Watchers?" Nick asked. "The fallen angels? Like, the ones kicked out of heaven?"

"The ones that created all the evil monsters," Sage said. "The reason the earth was flooded was to get rid of their corrupted human-hybrid abominations."

Hieronymus looked at Kaja. "It is as Vale suspected."

"What's that mean?" Sage asked.

"Before Vale gave you blood, I told him of your reaction when we got to the wall the first time. That your gift of Sensing spoke of something exceedingly evil and ancient. He knew immediately that the direction your Sensing indicated led to the deepest and most dangerous part of the Wastelands. The Elioudians have always believed that the Watchers were somewhere within Tartarus. There is a reason that part of the Wastelands has rarely been explored."

"No scout has ever returned," Kaja said. "Ever."

"So, now we know," Hieronymus said.

"They called to me," Sage said. "By name. I saw them. At least two hundred, chained to a wall of a huge cavern, a pit of burning sulfur in the center. There are steps, a staircase made from the skulls of a million creatures. The angelic chains are so bright and pure with God's glory they would blind you if you looked for more than a few seconds."

Kaja approached Sage and put a hand on his shoulder. Sage realized then that he had tears streaming down his face. He smiled and wiped them away. Nick gave him a hug. Ronan squeezed his shoulder. Sage looked at Hieronymus. "When you get back, the High Council needs to make that part of the Wastelands off limits."

"I will ensure of it," Hieronymus said. "Now, we must go. Time runs short."

They approached the stone village as before, but this time Hieronymus stopped them well before they could be seen by any creature lurking there. Nick couldn't see anything. His heart hammered inside his chest, and he edged closer to Ronan.

"Sage," Hieronymus said, "I want you to teleport near the spot where we first saw the minotaurs. I suspect their corpses are being fed upon, and I do not want us walking into something we cannot control."

Sage nodded. "I'll be back in a few minutes."

"Be careful," Nick whispered just as he left. He knew his brother was completely well, but the attack had happened so fast, it worried him to see him strike out by himself.

Sage appeared behind a pile of stones. Nick saw him lift his head and look around, then look back and give an all-clear sign. Nick couldn't see any of the minotaurs Sage had killed, and further on, near the buildings where Sage was attacked, those bodies had also disappeared.

Sage teleported to the roof of one of the buildings, looked around, and then teleported back to Hieronymus. "Nothing," he said. "All the bodies are gone."

"What's it mean?" Nick asked.

"It means a pack of other beasts have breakfast, lunch, and dinner for the next several weeks," Kaja said. "But it also causes some alarm."

"She is correct," Hieronymus said. "Our presence is no longer a secret. We must be exceedingly careful." He stood. "Come. We must get through the stone village before something comes back to pick up our trail."

They walked quietly through a dimly lit cavern for more than an hour. The ground was mostly dirt, but enough huge rocks protruded from it to make them constantly worried about an ambush.

"Did you remember to leave a trail?" Sage asked the scout. "So our rescue team can follow?"

"I am doing so," Kaja said. She pointed to a bag looped over her shoulder.

Nick hadn't noticed it before. "What are you using?"

"Kernels of corn," she said. "They should be able to track five sets of footprints, but if they have trouble, they will see the yellow spots of corn easily enough."

"They have no smell," Hieronymus said. "And they are spread far enough apart not to notice unless you know to look."

On they went, the Emim territory strangely absent of any threat. After another hour Hieronymus suddenly stopped, held up a hand, and dropped to one knee. The rest of them followed suit. "Do you hear that?" Hieronymus whispered.

"Yes," whispered Kaja. "Sounds of a battle."

"A slaughter," Hieronymus said. "The grunt of minotaurs and the screeching of ahools."

"What's that?" Nick asked.

"They look like a giant bats," Sage said. "Ruthless bloodsuckers. Can drain all the blood from a human body in less than a minute. They hunt in packs."

"What do they look like?" Nick asked.

Kaja answered. "They have big, black eyes; large claws on their forearms; and small bodies."

"They look like mixtures between bats and demons," Ronan added. "Incredible flying ability. A wingspan of almost ten feet."

"They swarm with a single purpose," Hieronymus said, to conclude the horrific description of what waited ahead. "We believe their minds are connected in some way. They react defensively and attack your weakness at the same time. Some of the scars I bear are from the claws of ahools."

"Maybe they have engaged the remnants of the pack of minotaurs Sage faced yesterday," Kaja whispered. "For the ahools would hesitate to challenge a group as large as what we encountered then."

Nick couldn't see anything ahead, but the sounds of battle were now clear. Hieronymus sent Kaja out front as an advance scout. She darted off and disappeared a couple of minutes later behind a large rock formation. Once back, she whispered her report. "No creatures have died, but all are heavily beaten and bleeding from the attack. They have each gone separate ways. It is clear now if we hurry."

"It is clear all the way to the bridge?" Hieronymus asked.

"Yes. The minotaurs ran past the bridge. The ahools flew left, heading toward the river."

"Then we will hurry," Hieronymus said.

Beyond the large outcropping of rock Kaja had passed earlier was a rope bridge crossing a deep chasm. It looked old and half-rotten. Nick looked down and saw nothing but jagged edges disappearing into darkness below. "Is it safe?" he asked Hieronymus.

"It was the last time I came through here." Hieronymus walked over and gave the rope a solid tug. "It feels fine."

"When did you come through here last?" Nick asked. He'd heard Hieronymus say earlier that he hadn't been this way in ten years. The rope could have dry rotted since then.

"How about I go first," Sage said. He teleported across and waved from the other side. "See, no problem."

"That's really not that funny," Nick mumbled to himself.

"I will go," Kaja said. She started slowly but picked up speed once it was clear the rope was strong enough to hold her. It took her a couple of minutes to travel the seventy-five feet.

Ronan stepped forward without comment and hurried across. He looked back at Nick and waved him over. "It's safe."

"I will wait here," Hieronymus said to Nick. "You go next."

The bridge was eight ropes tied together, woven in a way that provided a nice walking platform and handrails on each side. It shook and vibrated the moment he stepped onto it, but it felt solid.

"Don't look down," Sage said. "Just focus on me, and you'll be fine."

He couldn't help but look down. Even with what little light from above made it that far, some of the rocks looked razor sharp. The closer he got to the middle, the more the bridge swayed. He stopped for a moment to let the bridge settle. Kaja and Ronan hadn't had nearly this much trouble.

"Just look at me, Nick," Sage said. "Take one gentle step after another."

Nick took another step when a screech pierced the sky from his left.

"Squat down, Nick!" Hieronymus shouted. "Now!"

Nick looked left and saw a winged creature screaming toward him, claws out, vampire teeth bared. He ducked and felt it swoosh by, missing him by inches.

"Ahool," Hieronymus yelled. "Nick, get off that bridge!"

The beast swung around and attacked again. Its body was the size of a fox, but its head, mouth, and teeth were the size of a German shepherd's. Nick ducked again, but a claw jabbed him in the back. He cried out in pain. The beast flew off again and immediately circled back around.

"Hurry, Nick," Sage shouted. "I can't help you while you're out there!"

Nick took a fast step, and his right foot slipped off the rope. He stumbled forward, and one of his hands slipped. He landed face down on the platform rope, one arm and one leg dangling off the edge. The ahool landed on one of the handrails just above Nick's body.

"No!" Sage screamed. He teleported right next to Nick's head and grabbed one of the handrails with his left hand. He swung his sword with his right. The beast flew backward in time to avoid the blow, and Sage's swing carried his momentum over the edge. Nick saw his brother fall into the darkness below.

"Sage!" Nick screamed.

"Over here," Sage said, standing next to Hieronymus. "Now get over there before it comes back."

Ronan held out his steel bar, all six feet of it, and offered it as a brace to grab hold of. Nick climbed to his feet and reached for it but only got two steps before he had to duck again.

"Hurry," Kaja said. "You're almost here."

Just a few feet to go. I can make it. The ahool shrieked and attacked. Nick ducked yet again, but one of its claws got him on the shoulder. The beast seemed to know not to attack the others. Nick was easy pickings while stuck where he was. He stayed down, rubbed his bloody shoulder, and conjured the four-headed beast again. He imagined it rising from the abyss below, spewing white-hot flames from each of its mouths, waving fists the size of small boulders, and swiping at the flying bloodsucker. He kept his eyes on the ahool, hoping the illusion would affect it.

"He did it!" Kaja shouted. "The four-headed man!"

The ahool had just begun its latest attack when Nick saw its eyes and head rise and look at something over Nick's head. Its wings shot forward, then down, then around before it went screaming away in the other direction. Nick nearly collapsed with relief.

"You did it!" Sage said, after appearing next to Kaja. "Now get over here before it brings a flock back with it."

Just a few steps more, and Nick stepped onto solid ground. Sage grabbed his brother's shoulders. "Your gift saved you when I couldn't. Do you know that? *You* did it. In the face of great danger. It was very brave, Nick. Very brave."

Nick smiled, happy to see Sage proud of him. He felt so good, in fact, that the cuts on his back and shoulder didn't even hurt that much.

Sage saw his torn shirt and turned him around. "Let me see."

Nick felt him pressing around the wounds, but it didn't hurt. "You're OK," Sage said. "Already healing nicely."

Hieronymus stepped off the rope bridge. "The illusion you created was even more terrifying than before, young Nick. You have quite the imagination. Remember how you did it. We may need it again. Come, we must leave this place. The ahools will return and bring many friends."

They fell into the same marching order as before. But this time, Nick felt that he was finally part of the team.

19

The team listened quietly as Aquila and Ephraim told them of their adventures leading Sage, Nick, and Ronan to the village of Seth. Then Hannah spoke for an hour detailing all that had transpired since their arrival. Finally, Amelia told them everything she knew, including Sage's parting gift of information and how much the other humans had needed news from the surface.

They were in the library, exhausted from the trip. It was late, past midnight according to everyone's watches. Elsbeth wanted to get going. They were only twelve hours behind them now because of Sage's injury. According to Hannah, they were on the outside edge of being able to slip through the Territories during the celebration in the Rephaim area. If they waited until everyone got a full night's sleep, they'd be even farther behind and might risk not making it out at all.

After the briefings, Steven gave the Elioudians the gifts they'd brought—the books on the history of the Council—then requested that their group be left alone. When Amelia closed the door, Steven stood and faced everyone. "We can go now or wait until morning. Thoughts?"

"My biggest concern is what Vale's blood has done to Sage," Malcolm said. "Is there any precedent for this? His blood was special as it was. Now to get blood directly from Seth's son?" He shook his head. "He might be a very different young man when we see him again."

Elsbeth swallowed hard and tried keeping her emotions in check. She'd been thinking the same thing. What would it do to his gifts? Would it accelerate his getting more than the six he already had? Would it supercharge them?

"We can debate that later," Steven said. "Right now, we have a decision to make, but it needs to be a clear majority."

"Go," Endora said, standing. "We need to go. I can assume the scout will force them to bed down for the night. We can make progress in closing the gap. If we go hard all night, Elsbeth might get within teleporting distance."

"Elsbeth will absolutely *not* teleport into an unexplored area," Steven said. "Too dangerous."

"You misunderstand me," Endora said. "She can serve as our advance scout. She can teleport in short bursts and come back to warn us of danger. Eventually, she will get close enough to make contact. She is the only one who can do so."

Steven started to protest, but Elsbeth stood and stopped him. "Endora's right. I can teleport into an area, assess the danger, and get out before anything can attack me. I can't use Persuasion, and I'm not very good with a sword. Acting as advance scout is something I can do." She looked hard at Sage's grandfather. "I can teleport in and out of an area so fast that if you blink you'll miss me. The team needs this."

Steven sighed heavily. "I just worry. You're so you—"

"Young, yes, so I've been told." She hadn't even tried to hide her frustration. She looked at everybody. "I'm doing this. That's my *one* function. Get used to it. I vote we go now." She sat down.

"I agree," Gavin said. "Go now, and make up time."

"Agreed," said Kato.

"And I," Malcom said. "We're all experienced hunters and are of Elioudian ancestry. Nick is human and won't possess the endurance we have. I think we can catch them."

"We go now," David said. He held up his steel bar. "Itching to use this again. Can't let Sage have all the fun."

"Almost getting killed is fun?" Elsbeth snapped at him. "That's crazy, even coming from you."

David held up his hands. "Whoa, back way up, Elsbeth. You know I didn't mean it like that."

"Well, you have a habit of saying stuff you immediately have to walk back. You did it in Mammon's prison, and now you're doing it here." She took a deep breath to calm herself. Probably fatigue, but maybe not. David was just too comfortable with killing for her taste, and who knew what Sage, Nick, and Ronan were facing out there? What they would all face in the next few hours?

Kato reached over and gripped Elsbeth's shoulder. "You just need some rest," he said gently. "David didn't mean anything by it."

Elsbeth cringed that she'd sounded more like Endora than herself. "I'm sorry I snapped at you, David. I know you meant no harm."

"Already forgotten," David said. "You know how I feel about Sage."

"Let's just drop it," Steven said. "I agree with everyone else. We've been riding for two days, and I'm ready to work up a sweat. Assignments. Elsbeth has hers. She'll stay in front with Kato. Hannah said Hieronymus would leave us a trail, but I trust Kato's skills enough to track them regardless." He pointed at David. "You're with Elsbeth and Kato. Need your strength in the front. Endora, we need your Voice at the rear to protect our backside. Gavin, you're her hard cover. She can't protect herself when she's engaged with Voice. Malcom, you and I will dispose of whoever needs it. Malcolm, I'd really like to see you make it back to the surface without having to lay hands on anyone. Absorption is too close quarters for my liking."

"And mine," Malcolm said.

"But if he must use it, I've got him covered," Gavin said. "Like always."

"Then let's get rolling," Steven said. "Hannah said one of the Elioudian guards will lead us into Hell."

Thirty minutes later they stood at the entrance of the swamp, staring at a small pile of yellow corn kernels.

"So, we look for corn," David said after a laugh. "Very nice. Elsbeth, your eyes should see that clearly enough. Are we ready, then?"

A knot of anxiety sat heavily in Elsbeth's gut. This was it. They were a formidable team, but Sage had almost been killed not even a half day into the trip. She took a quick glance at everyone's face and saw nothing but confidence or determination. No fear. Not even a hint of the apprehension she felt.

"Let's get this show on the road," Malcolm said. He looked at Kato. "Can't wait to see what you've got."

Kato grinned. "You'll see soon enough."

The escort led them quietly to the steel door in the stone wall, through nearly an hour of horrible landscape not much different than what they'd seen in the Wastelands. Once they passed through the door, the camera rotation they'd worked out earlier would be implemented so that large sections of the Territories would be recorded. They'd taken hours of video of Tartarus, so the Council would be happy with that. Assuming they made it back.

As they drew closer to the entry point into Hell, the entire mood of the team changed. Grit replaced frowns, smiles died, eyes narrowed, and Steven recited what each of them were probably thinking.

"'Yea, though I walk through the valley of the shadow of death, I will fear no evil: for Thou art with me.'" Sage's grandfather grabbed Elsbeth's shoulder and gave it a squeeze, and she was comforted.

"We are entering the crops area," Hieronymus said. "When our people occupied this territory, it looked much like the agricultural areas we have in Tartarus now." He waved a hand over the great fields before them.

The grow lights were still in place, Nick saw, and the irrigation system, but the crops, a mixture of numerous different vegetables, grew wild in the fields. It didn't look as though anyone had tended to them in centuries. They had traveled for nearly two hours now, cutting through a short cave not far from the rope bridge, and hadn't seen any creatures.

"Do the grow lights and irrigation systems run automatically?" Nick asked.

"Yes," Hieronymus said. "Long ago our scientists invented grow bulbs that never expire. We built a system that requires no intervention to operate. The systems were too massive to remove when we abandoned these Territories, so we left them. All the evil creatures needed to do was plant and harvest, but you can see they have chosen not to."

Hieronymus explained that the largest Emim village was on the far side of these fields. They couldn't get back to Topside without going straight through the middle of it. "We will lie down here," he said. "In the middle of the overgrowth. We will rest and wait until later to approach the village. Most of the beasts should be away attending the Celebration of Godhood."

Hieronymus and Kaja found spots several feet away from Sage, Nick, and Ronan. As soon as Nick got flat on his back, fatigue overwhelmed him. He hadn't realized how tired he was.

Sage flopped down beside him. "Wanna hear something funny?"

Nick had already begun drifting off to sleep. "Sure. What?"

"That four-headed monster you created to scare off the ahool didn't have any legs." Sage laughed quietly. "Didn't even have a stomach. It was a monster only from the chest up."

"Really?" Nick lifted his head and looked at him. "No legs?"

"I'm thinking you mainly focused on the fire-breathing heads and didn't bother creating an entire monster inside your head." Sage nudged him in the side. "Interesting, don't you think?"

"I don't know. Why do you think so?"

"I've studied all of the angelic gifts," Sage said. "Illusion is one of the few there isn't a lot of information about. It's interesting, because if the goal is to create an illusion that you desperately need others to believe, then the image you create inside your head must be detailed enough to make it seem real to them."

"And a four-headed monster with nothing below the chest doesn't look real enough," Nick said. "OK, I get that. At least it scared off the ahool."

"Oh, yeah, it did the trick," Sage said. "But I'm thinking you need to be careful about how you build the image inside your mind."

Nick thought about that as he drifted off to sleep.

"Wake up!" Sage whispered. He gave Nick an urgent shake. "We need to move. Now. But be quiet. No sound. At all."

Nick couldn't have been asleep for more than five minutes. "What is it?"

"Emim scouts from the village," Sage said. "Hieronymus sent Kaja out to scope things out. She just reported back."

Nick climbed to his feet. Sage had his sword drawn. Ronan was beside him, steel bar ready. Hieronymus and Kaja were several feet in front of them, squatted down behind a thick stand of corn stalks. Nick snuck over beside Kaja. "What is it?"

"Chimeras," she whispered. "A pack."

Nick had no idea what those were. Seemed like he'd read about them once when studying Greek mythology, but he couldn't picture them.

"You hear them?" Kaja asked, pointing right and left.

He heard nothing at all. He cocked his head and held his breath. Still nothing. It was amazing how much better the Elioudians could hear. Good thing they were the scouts and not him.

Then a noise broke through, and seconds later a lot of noises. Heavy breathing. Grunts. Hissing. Feet crunching through the overgrown crops. Kaja looked at him and put a finger to her lips.

"I tell you," a deep voice drifted toward them, "they are near." The voice sounded like a truck grinding down a gravel road. "Be careful of the boy who disappears."

"I smell Elioudian blood," said a different voice. "Straight ahead."

The rustling through the vegetation grew louder. Nick didn't know how many there were, but it sounded like an entire herd. He closed his eyes and imagined a huge creature of enormous strength, twenty-five feet tall and twelve hundred pounds, wielding a giant sword, with a face that would stop a clock. He imagined it rising from the field far from where they now hid and bellowing a challenge to fight to the death. *"I seek revenge for the loss of my father! Come, show me your courage! Attempt to slay me, now that your village is nearly empty.*"

"Who is that?" the gravelly voice asked.

"A Nephilim dares trespass into our territory?" said another.

"Death to him!" shouted a third.

There was a sudden rush of movement in the vegetation directly in front of them as the group of chimeras rushed toward the illusion. Nick glanced that way but couldn't see anything.

"You must hold your illusion until the pack is out of our path," Hieronymus said into Nick's ear. Then to Sage he said, "Teleport forward, beyond the last disturbance in the crops. Kaja, project great fear toward the fleeing chimeras."

Ronan knelt next to Nick and put a hand on his shoulder. "You're doing great," he said. "Just keep it up."

It was all Nick could do to keep the image active in his mind with everything going on. He focused on the image of his giant, swinging his sword mightily, swooshing it this way and that, stomping his feet and roaring like a lion. *"I can smell your fear, you putrid creatures! Come, let us battle to the death, for I, Rumpelstiltskin, the greatest of all Nephilim warriors, cannot be defeated!"*

Nick wished he could see the image he was creating but knew he couldn't. He had to trust that it was as powerful to everyone else as it was within his mind. He concentrated on the giant's entire body this time; he couldn't afford to have half of the legs disappearing just as the chimeras arrived.

"We cannot not defeat such a beast," a distant voice rang out.

"We will be slaughtered," said another.

"Retreat," shouted a third.

"Your projection of fear is working, Kaja," Hieronymus said quietly. "You must concentrate now to turn their fear into great terror. Nick, have your giant crash through the field toward their village. Now, we must move. Hurry, while they are on the run."

Hieronymus grabbed both Nick and Kaja by the arms and practically pulled them through the overgrown crops. Ronan ran ahead of them, steel bar at port arms, ready for battle. "Both of you need to focus on your gifts," Hieronymus reminded them as they ran. "These beasts will not battle such a monster with terror in their hearts."

They moved quietly toward the village as Nick's giant headed the same direction. After another minute Sage appeared in front of them. "There's nothing between here and the village," he said. "But there's a least a hundred different creatures milling around on the street. Chimeras, werewolves, minotaurs, and a bunch of other creatures I've never seen before. They've seen Nick's giant, and they've armed themselves. They're ready to fight."

"Kaja," Hieronymus said, "as soon as we are in sight of the village, refocus your terror directly into the mob in the street. Nick, we need another giant, maybe two more. Have them appear directly behind us. Quickly. Make them even bigger if you can."

Nick turned around to look behind them, suddenly struck with an idea. In his mind's eye four giants appeared in the distance. They were half again as big as the other one, which in his head was still swinging his mighty sword and stomping toward the village. The four new ones wore mighty armor, had swords in both hands, and moved as a well-coordinated team. They roared and shouted and created all kinds of havoc.

Hieronymus dragged Nick and Kaja to the edge of a clearing. Directly ahead, less than a hundred yards, was an ancient village with buildings barely habitable. A mob of armed creatures stood on the edge of town watching a single giant approach from their left and four giants approach from their front.

"Horror, Kaja," Hieronymus said quietly. "Give them the most horrifying feeling of dread and terror that you can imagine. Now!"

Careful to keep his mind totally focused on the movements of his small army of giants, Nick watched as Kaja projected the abject terror that Hieronymus wanted. Her face twisted into a mask of horror, her eyes wide, tears flowing. A choking sound squeaked from her lips as she threw her hands to her face. Veins bulged in her neck just before she threw her head back and screamed a sound that sent a knife of fear to Nick's heart.

"Turn away from her, Nick," Hieronymus said, jerking his gaze away from Kaja. "March those four giants into the village."

Nick imagined it as the creatures in the village fled for their lives. His mouth got suddenly dry, and he didn't know how much longer he could keep this up.

"We must hurry," Hieronymus said.

"Make them see us as chimeras, Nick," Sage said. "Make them think we are running for our lives."

"What's a chimera look like?" Nick asked. "I've never seen one before."

"There," Sage said, pointing over to the right. "That lion-snake-goat creature."

"OK." Nick pictured all of it. Five chimeras running full speed out of the fields toward the village, with four giants at least forty feet tall chasing them, screaming and swinging long swords. The chimeras ran as fast as they could, but the giants were never quite able to catch them. The ground shook with thunderous blasts as the giant's feet pounded the ground in pursuit. The fifth giant, half the size but still a mighty warrior, bore down upon the village with homicidal intent, boasting about being the greatest warrior that ever lived.

The primary street through the village was clear by the time Nick and the others hit it, sprinting at full speed. Nick could see creatures hiding and watching as they ran past. They gave Nick and the others little notice, focusing almost all their attention on the giants. There was shouting and chaos, but most of the beasts simply hid quietly, probably hoping the giants would ignore them so long as they had the five runners within their sights.

It took them less than two minutes to make it to the far side of the village. As soon as Kaja got past the crowd, she had to turn around and run backward the rest of the way to project her terror upon them.

"Have the giants stop in the street," Hieronymus told Nick. "We are nearly safe. Just hold the image another minute."

They climbed a large hill overlooking the village and stopped at the entrance to a cave. Nick saw the scene below, the creatures still hiding and trying to escape. A group of beasts sprinted around the center of town and escaped into the fields.

"You can stop now, Kaja," Hieronymus said. "Their fear will linger for several minutes, and we are already well out of sight."

The old scout placed a hand on Nick's shoulder. "And you can also release them, young Nick. Never have I seen such a gift as yours. Is there any enemy you and your brother cannot defeat with such gifts?"

Nick cleared his mind and relaxed. He looked at Sage, who now stood beside him.

"Gone," Sage said, pointing to the village. "In the blink of an eye. Look. None of them know what just happened."

The creatures cautiously came out from behind their hiding places. They searched in every direction to figure out where the giants had gone.

"Quickly, into the cave," Hieronymus said. "Before one of them looks up here."

"You are amazing, Nick," Sage said. "Total and unquantifiable. You have the greatest of all angelic gifts, in my opinion. Well, the most fun, for sure. And you know what makes it work so well?"

"What?"

"The fact you are one twisted puppy between the ears." Sage laughed and punched Nick in the arm. "Who on this earth has a deranged mind wacky enough to create such authentic giants at the drop of a hat?" Nick shrugged and smiled. "And *Rumpelstiltskin?*" Sage laughed out loud. "You named your giant *Rumpelstiltskin?*"

"It was the first name that popped into my head." Nick started laughing. "I almost named it Sage, because I gave him the ugliest face I could come up with."

Sage pushed him forward and shook his head. "Wait until Grandpa hears about this. He's not gonna believe it!"

Ronan grabbed both boys in a huge hug. "I'm proud of both of you. And you're right, Sage. Your grandpa won't believe this story."

The cave was nothing more than a short passageway that led to a steep path upwards. Hieronymus explained that the Rephaim territory was at the top of the hill. They climbed in the same order—Hieronymus in front, Sage in the rear, and Kaja, Nick, and Ronan in the middle.

"Do you feel the emotions you project, Kaja?" Nick asked. "I saw your face back there, and it looked horrible."

She glanced back at them as they climbed and gave him a little smile. "I do. I lose myself within the emotion, building it to a tipping point and then shooting it forward over an area."

"Do they feel just as you feel?" Nick hadn't been close enough to see any of the creatures up close, but he had seen them run away.

"The closer I am to my target, the stronger the emotion affects them," Kaja said. "I had never done what I did back there, trying to affect an entire village."

"How do you keep from becoming emotional yourself?" Nick asked.

"I block out an entire part of my brain," she said. "I shield it from the projection. I don't fully understand it, but I have perfected it over the past century."

At the top of the path, Hieronymus pointed to a steep cliff. "The cliff serves as a natural barrier between the Emim and Rephaim Territories. We will climb for several hours to get to the top. Once there, we will rest for the night."

"Well," Sage said. "I can understand now how a regular human would never have made it this far. If not for our gifts, we'd all be dead."

Nick couldn't argue with that. He just wished that all five of them could teleport to the top. Looking at the cliff in front of them, their biggest challenge might have just begun.

20

They were directly in the center of a destroyed Emim village, the first group of structures since entering the Territories. Elsbeth had followed the trail without any issues. They paused before entering the village, resting from the climb up the shaft. Endora and Kato expressed hesitation about the two tall buildings on the far side.

"It's a death funnel," Endora said. "The perfect place for an ambush."

"It's where Sage was attacked," Steven said. "I'm sure of it."

They couldn't go around, and all of them knew it. That part of the chamber wasn't very wide, and somebody had stacked debris so high they risked breaking a leg climbing over. It appeared to Elsbeth like a great stone wall had collapsed into a jagged flytrap. So, they'd go straight down the middle, spread out like a military special forces unit.

Almost to the center, Elsbeth looked up and wondered if she should teleport to the top of one of the buildings for a better look.

She saw the tip of a black, leathery wing. "Contact," she shouted. "There. The building on the left."

Then chaos reigned.

Winged werewolves exploded from the tops and sides of both buildings, screeching and clawing the air with a ferocity Elsbeth found shocking. She turned when more beasts came over the jagged wall from both sides, flanking their entire group. Twenty, at least, Elsbeth thought; maybe twenty-five.

"Let's get it on!" David shouted. "Long live the queen!" He swung his bar with such force that the closest werewolves backed away. Endora belted her gift of Voice directly at the oncoming wave, and several hit the ground, stunned into complete immobility. Gavin and Malcolm went to work on them. Those too far to be affected by Voice came more cautiously, unsure of what had just happened.

At the top of the building on the left, Elsbeth saw the leader, a monster half again as big as those attacking. It waved its arms as it shrieked commands at the others. Elsbeth drew her sword and took a deep breath. She was in the best position to engage it. She cocked her sword, teleported behind the beast, and slashed down the center of its back. The blow nearly lopped off its left wing. It roared and spun around, but she had already teleported out, landing on the back of one of the stunned werewolves on the ground. She plunged her sword down into its back and was nearly thrown off when the beast jerked and bucked.

As Elsbeth pulled her sword free, she looked up and saw the leader screaming in pain, trying to attend to its wound. She teleported back to the top and again landed on its blind side. She thrust her sword into its back, pulled it out, and disappeared again. The leader stumbled and fell to its knees, screaming a wail that caused many of the attacking beasts to pause and look up.

David raced toward her and hit a beast she hadn't seen. The bar crushed its chest and knocked it several feet away. Elsbeth rushed forward and stabbed it in the heart. "Thank you," she shouted to David.

Kato and Gavin moved at such superhuman speed, their swords mere blurs of motion, that she stood mesmerized by them. What werewolves weren't dead by now were stunned into immobility by Endora's Voice.

Back at the top, the leader was trying to escape. Elsbeth teleported up and saw it disappear into a hole in the roof, a trail of dark blood following. *No way* would she go in after it. She didn't have the skill set for close-quarter combat inside a building she'd never seen before. Kato and Gavin could handle that.

She looked out onto the battlefield and counted twenty-two dead werewolves with four to go. Those four were on their backs, stunned, eyes wide with fear. David stood over them with a crazy look on his face. Endora, no longer needing Voice, killed all four by cutting off their heads. As each beast died, Kato vanquished the Dark spirit that exited its body.

Then it was over. Almost.

"I wounded the leader," Elsbeth shouted down. "I cut off one of its wings and stabbed it in the back. It's in this building, but I'm not going in to get it."

Kato and Gavin stepped forward. "We'll go," Kato said. "Stay up there, Elsbeth, in case it tries to escape that way."

"OK." She positioned herself near the hole.

"We'll cover the other exits," Steven said. "David and Endora, get on opposite sides of the building. Endora, stun it from outside before Kato and Gavin go in." A minute later Kato shouted that it was dead.

Elsbeth teleported to the ground as Kato and Gavin came out of the building. They all gathered around. "Did we get all the spirits?" Steven asked.

"I didn't see any get away," Elsbeth said. "But that doesn't mean none did."

"I can't be sure," Endora said. "The lighting isn't the best down here."

"Can't know for sure," David said. "Nothing we can do about it now."

"Any injuries?" Steven asked.

"Just need some water before we head out," Gavin said. "Feeling a little parched."

"Good idea. Everybody take five to hydrate and gather your packs," Steven said. "We don't need to hang around here long. The smell of blood is strong. It'll attract others."

Elsbeth took a close look at one of the beasts and shivered. Nothing like it had been chronicled within the *Encyclopedia of Dark Creatures* at the Tomb of Ancient Documents. She activated her helmet camera and shot some good footage of the battle scene. Then she pulled out a small digital camera and took some close-ups.

Kato approached just as she finished. "That's the Elsbeth I remember from last summer. Full disclosure, I wasn't sure what to expect without your Persuasion, but you lived up to your standards.

Great job." He gave her a high-five and walked off. Elsbeth smiled and saw Endora watching. The woman winked, gave her a thumbs-up, and mouthed, "Good job," before turning away.

After hydrating, Elsbeth picked up the trail of corn easily enough. They walked in the same formation as before, except this time she was especially alert for movement and sounds up ahead. She didn't know if the smell of death would draw other creatures, but she wasn't about to be caught unaware a second time.

The climb took them four hours. Nick didn't know how far up it was, but Sage estimated at least five thousand feet. Maybe they were halfway to the surface by now, Nick thought, but probably not. He didn't bother asking, because it really made no difference. They would get there when they got there. The focus was survival. Nothing more.

They slept under a rock overhang that kept them hidden in a deep shadow. Like the Emim area below, the Rephaim territory was full of abandoned, unattended fields and decaying houses. From where they camped, they could see almost a half mile of desolation and neglect.

What probably amazed Nick the most was the fact that the electricity and water still worked after the Elioudians had abandoned the Territories in favor of their new world. Why couldn't humans figure out a way to build stuff that never stopped working? Were Elioudian engineers centuries ahead of their counterparts on the surface? That whole thing about making themselves known to the world once the Seven Princes of Hell were gone might be a good thing. Nick hadn't seen a single sign of conflict or hatred or any of the deadly sins that ravaged his world. Maybe having the Elioudians come up for a while was exactly the thing humanity needed.

After everyone slept and ate breakfast, Nick had a question for Hieronymus. "Have you seen any Rephaim when you scouted this territory?"

"Yes," the scout said, as he packed up the remains of his meal. "Almost every time."

"How many are there?" Ronan asked.

"No one knows for certain," Hieronymus said.

"What do they look like?" Nick asked.

"Probably much the same as the Seven," Sage said. "They are great winged beasts, like Dark Angels. They look a little like Elioudians, physically. The shape of their heads, their muscularity. Mammon had golden skin. Belphegor's offspring, the one who shoved you down the hole, had skin with a bluish tint."

Hieronymus adjusted the pack on his back. "They sometimes look like that, Sage. Other times they do not. It is not for me to say what you will see."

"What's that mean?" Ronan asked.

"Before I first scouted the Rephaim territory," Hieronymus said, "I paid a visit to an ancient Elioudian named Cobar. He was on his deathbed and insisted I see him before I began my journey. He spent many years watching the Rephaim from within the shadows of their territory. Cobar documented their nature and recorded a great number of disturbing powers they developed through sorcery."

"Like what?" Nick asked. "Do they have angelic gifts, like Sage?"

"And like you," Sage reminded him.

Nick didn't consider himself in the same stratosphere as his brother. "OK, like me, too."

"While it is true that both the Elioudians and Rephaim descended from the Watchers, I refuse to consider the powers they possess as gifts." Hieronymus frowned as he thought about how to proceed. "They use their powers for destruction. For control. To rule over others. The six remaining on Topside have created havoc within humanity. Those remaining here use their powers to defeat the Nephilim and escape to Topside."

"What did Cobar see?" Nick asked. "What kind of powers do the Rephaim have?"

"The most disturbing thing is the ability to change appearance, including their body structure," Hieronymus said. "They can generate acid through touch or spray. Some can exhale fire through their mouths. Cobar documented them merging two creatures into a completely new and stronger monster."

Nick looked at Kaja. Her full attention was on the older scout and his horrifying information.

"They can see in total darkness," Hieronymus continued. "I have seen many scale walls of rock and hang from the ceiling. Cobar swore with his dying breath that the Rephaim could possess and control the body of another. His research documented examples of them possessing the mighty Nephilim."

"One can suddenly look like Nick?" Sage asked. "Is that what you're saying?"

Hieronymus nodded, grim faced. "Indeed."

And then Nick realized what Sage was talking about. *One could change to look like me, get close to Sage, and kill him.* "But how?"

Hieronymus looked at Sage. "You have seen the Seven. Can you answer Nick's question?"

Sage shrugged. "I think it's because their bodies aren't fully biological like ours. They have a spiritual component." He glanced at Nick and then looked at Hieronymus. "Only someone with angelic blood could enter Mammon's prison to rescue the Council members. Likewise, their angelic blood allows them to morph into a different shape. It's the same principle as the angelic gift of Transformation."

"I believe you are correct," Hieronymus said. He looked at them and stepped out from under the rock overhang. "It is of utmost importance that the Rephaim not see any of us, for if they do, they might succeed in having us slaughter ourselves. Come, we have far to travel."

Elsbeth stopped at the rope bridge and looked back. "Think it will hold?"

Steven gave it a solid tug, then pointed across the chasm. "Teleport over, Elsbeth, and see if the corn trail continues on the other side."

She did, and it did. "All clear. It heads off to the left."

It took them a couple of minutes to cross. After skirting the edge of the chasm for more than three miles, the landscape opened to huge fields of scattered corn plants. The path where Sage and Nick and the two scouts had passed through was evident.

They hadn't been in the field for ten minutes when Sage's grandfather stopped and dropped to his knees. "Down, everybody."

Elsbeth didn't hesitate. She dropped on both knees and looked back. The rest of the team had followed his instruction without hesitation.

Steven was examining several footprints with the tips of his fingers, eyes closed, his body quiet and still. Nobody said anything as they watched him use Pathfinding. "Dark beasts," he whispered after several beats. "Recent. Within the past several hours. A pack. Hunting." He looked at Kato and Gavin. "Bloodlust. Whatever it was is out to slaughter its prey." He edged forward and touched several broken stalks of corn. "Sage, Nick, Ronan, and the Elioudian scouts."

Elsbeth wished Steven had recruited a Council member gifted with Sensing. They could really use one right now.

"Time to use our com units," Endora said. "We need to get Elsbeth on high ground."

"Endora's right," Kato said. "We can't see twenty feet in front of us in this field. And there's no guarantee we'll hear an attack before it happens."

"And they'll probably smell us before we smell them," Malcolm added, looking up and searching in all directions. He pointed to a rock a couple hundred yards in front of them. "There, near the top of the cavern. Perfect vantage point."

Elsbeth saw it immediately. He was right. It was near the very top of the cavern, above the lighting system, which would allow her to hide in the shadows.

"The little lass should be able to guide us from there," David said. "Jolly good catch, Malcolm. Elsbeth, reminds me of when we set the trap for Mammon. You scouted it out, we all killed him later."

"Let's do it," Steven said. "Headsets, voice activated." It took them a couple of minutes to get everything set up. "I want Elsbeth to be the only one talking unless it's absolutely necessary," Steven continued. "Elsbeth, we expect you to guide us and keep us out of trouble." He looked at everyone else. "Do whatever she says. No questioning, no arguing, no back talk. She's going to keep us alive down here. Elsbeth, from up there you should be able to see Sage's group's path through the field. At the point where you need to change positions, tell us to stop. We'll squat and wait until you're ready again." Steven put a hand on her shoulder. "Ready?"

"Yes."

"Then get in position." He smiled at her, and it gave her strength.

She teleported up to the rock and found it larger than she'd expected. Flat on one side, the rock outcropping disappeared into the side of the cavern almost ten feet. She scooted into the shadows, set her backpack next to her, and grabbed her binoculars. She surveyed the field below and almost shouted out in horror.

The team sat huddled together in a field a mile long and a half-mile wide. A herd of beasts she couldn't identify had them surrounded and were methodically closing the perimeter. She fought to keep her voice steady. "You are totally surrounded. I don't know what they are yet. The closest is directly behind you, following our trail, a hundred yards back. More to the front and on both sides."

Somebody double-clicked the radio for acknowledgment.

She looked for a route that would allow them to slip through, but there wasn't one. "Give me a second to evaluate. They're so low against the ground I'm having trouble seeing what they are."

Double click.

Whatever they were, with each step they took, several stalks of corn collapsed under their weight. Frantic, she did a quick count and estimated at least fifty, though there were probably more. The closer they got, the tighter their circle became. She focused her glasses on the one nearest her and saw glimpses of brown and black fur. Four legs. Shaggy. Probably the size of a Great Dane, but much thicker and heavier. She got on the radio and described them. When the beasts in the rear were within fifty yards of the group, they stopped and waited until the rest closed the circle.

"They're communicating somehow," Elsbeth whispered into the radio. "Can you hear or smell them?"

A single click. *No.*

How would the group in the back know to stop and wait? Can they possibly see through the foliage? Do they see heat signatures? Do they have a collective mind, like a hive of bees? Then she thought of something and searched for another high spot, for someone doing exactly what she was doing.

Alternating her attention between the field and the hundreds of hidden shadow spots on the cavern walls, she finally found it: a set of glowing red eyes almost directly behind the group, just above where all of them had entered the field.

"I found their leader," Elsbeth said. "I think it's directing them telepathically. It's the only way they'd know where to go."

Down on the field, the circle grew tighter. The noose was forty yards now in all directions, with no more than five yards separating the creatures from one another. The team had formed its own circle, backs together, weapons out, perfectly still. It only took her a second to come up with a plan.

"Listen to me," she said. "I've got to sever the mental link, but you've got to cause some chaos before I do. Can somebody do that? Cause some disruption?"

Double click.

"OK. On my command. Get ready." She glanced at her team. The beasts were nearly on top of them now. They would attack any second.

Elsbeth focused her binoculars on the glowing eyes. It was too dark and far away to see much of anything else. She lowered the glasses and set them at her feet, keeping her eyes on the spot where she needed to go. She drew her sword.

"OK," she said into the radio. "Distract away."

A second later Endora's Voice blasted through the canyon with such force and clarity it nearly took Elsbeth's breath away. She teleported to the glowing red eyes and found a monster she'd once seen a drawing of in the *Encyclopedia of Dark Creatures*. An alphyn, a stocky tiger with tufts of wild fur, a lion's mane, dragon talons on its forelegs, a knotted tail, and a long, thin tongue that slid in and out of a mouth large enough to take off one of Elsbeth's arms.

She landed on a ledge barely big enough for the beast, let alone her. She jammed her sword into its back just as a chorus of mighty roars and yelps sounded from the canyon below. Her blow took the beast by surprise. She'd hit it within a second of materializing beside it, and it arched its back and tried standing on its rear legs. She yanked the sword out and swung it sideways at one of its back legs. The blow didn't sever the leg, but she heard and felt bone break.

"Attack!" Elsbeth shouted into her headset.

The alphyn tilted to one side and swung one of its front paws at her. Its five-inch talons missed her face by a hair. She teleported to the other side of the ledge and drove her sword into its right shoulder. It screamed, spun around, and knocked her off the ledge. She was halfway to the floor of the canyon before she regained her senses and teleported back to the ledge, this time at the rear, next to the wall. The beast was looking over the ledge when she swung her sword at its crippled leg and severed it completely.

Again, the beast spun, but much slower than before. Elsbeth jabbed the sword into its left side, pulled it out, and teleported to a small ledge fifteen feet away. She glanced down at her team but could only see a flurry of corn stalks. Over the dozens of growls and roars and barks of the beasts, she heard David's shouts of victory, Endora's Voice, yells of warning, and cheers of success.

Then she heard the alphyn leader trying to escape. She turned back and saw it thirty yards down the edge of the wall, barely able to walk upright, leaving a trail of thick red blood. The path leading to the floor of the cavern was uneven and crisscrossed through and around several large boulders. She waited until it got to a wide spot halfway down before making her move.

Her ambush spot was dark, in the full shadow of a flat rock jutting out over the trail. By the time the alphyn reached it, it was staggering from blood loss and dragging what was left of its hindquarters. From her spot on the high ledge, she squatted and positioned the handle of her sword near her feet, then teleported underneath the flat rock just as the beast entered the shadow. The moment she felt solid ground beneath her, she plunged the sword up through the bottom jaw of the monster, the tip exiting out the top of its head.

The beast collapsed onto its side, unable to open its mouth to attack. Elsbeth saw the light fade from its eyes as she pulled the sword out. It took nearly two minutes to die, but just as the beast drew a last breath, its spirit began rising from the middle of its back. First the wings, then two elbows, then the top of its head. She sliced its head in half just before the Dark angel's eyes contacted hers. Then it exploded into a puff of green mist and disappeared.

Elsbeth teleported back to her ledge high above the field to see the state of her team's battle. She almost laughed out loud when she saw nearly half the beasts fleeing. At least twenty were strewn about, dead. Steven looked up to the ledge and raised his sword. "Come on down, Elsbeth. We need to recoup and head out before anything else shows up."

After she gathered her binoculars and backpack, she arrived in the middle of a slaughterhouse. Everyone had already wiped their swords clean, which reminded Elsbeth that she needed to. She walked over to the nearest alphyn and scrubbed her sword against its fur.

"I doubt you fully realize what killing the leader did for us," Malcolm told Elsbeth.

"What?"

David walked up and slapped her on the back. Then Gavin, Steven, Kato, and Endora gathered around her.

"I am not sure what you did, but whatever it was, it changed their entire battle plan," Endora said.

"Really?" Elsbeth's face heated with embarrassment.

"One moment they were organized," Endora said. "Eyes confident, working as one large attack unit. The next—total fear."

"You took their courage," Gavin said.

"Their grit," David said.

"Their determination," Kato said. "Your attack cut the strings of the puppet master. Bravo." He gave her a little bow and smiled. "And only *you* could have accomplished that feat."

"How'd you know?" Steven asked. "That they were being controlled?"

"It seemed the only possibility. When I saw the group in the back stop and wait for the rest of the circle to tighten, I knew they were somehow connected mentally, and not by something at ground level." She shrugged. "If it weren't for the red eyes, I would never have found it."

"Your actions have removed all of my lingering doubt," Endora said. "I am ashamed to admit I was wrong to believe that you would not bring value to our team. We might have all been killed without your Teleportation and quick battle instincts."

"Thank you." Elsbeth felt tears building behind her eyes. *Endora said that. Endora!* It surprised Elsbeth how much she cared about what Endora thought of her. Maybe it was because the woman had overcome so much in her life, maybe it was her natural leadership traits, or maybe she just sought the approval of a strong, independent woman. She didn't know, but Endora had turned out to be a much different woman than Elsbeth had believed her to be, and her approval pleased Elsbeth more than she had ever imagined it would. Sage was *really* going to like her, especially given how she'd volunteered for this mission for no other reason than to help a fellow Council member in need. Endora didn't really know Sage, she'd never met Nick, and she wasn't friends with Elsbeth. She wanted to help because it was the right thing to do. Noble. Sacrificial. Honorable. Yes, Endora was someone Elsbeth could aspire to be.

"We've got to get moving," Steven said. "Elsbeth, front and center. See if you can find any kernels of corn for us to follow."

21

The Rephaim territory, being closer to the surface, wasn't as rocky as where the Emim dwelled. Nick still saw boulders the size of semi trucks, but they were spread out, scattered across the fields like giant anthills.

Hieronymus said they were many miles from the village of Cain, named after the murderous first son of Adam, which served as the capital of the territory. It was one of two villages he'd ever found occupied by Rephaim and where the Celebration of Godhood was being held. By now, he told them, it would be crawling with hundreds of creatures. So, they were going the long way around, through Ham, which was small by comparison.

Sage teleported ahead to scout areas but never traveled far. Kaja flanked the group on the right side, her sword always in her hand and her eyes in constant search mode. Hieronymus walked silently, his height allowing him to see farther than Kaja. And Ronan escorted Nick, who played around with Illusion, running images of fantastical creatures through his head.

Nick wished he could see the images and wondered if anyone would be able to see them when he got back home. Everyone and everything down here had angel blood. Was that the key to seeing them? He didn't know yet, and Sage hadn't said. If the gifts were bestowed primarily to battle evil angelic beings, it would make sense that only those with angel blood could see them.

They'd walked for almost six hours when Sage appeared directly in front of Hieronymus and held out a hand like a traffic cop. "Something is about two hundred yards in front of us." He went away, and Nick saw him appear in front of Kaja, who had drifted a full hundred yards to their right. She immediately headed their way.

After all were together again, Sage knelt on one knee and motioned for the others to follow suit. "There's a darkness ahead. Looks like a solid wall, but it's not. I've seen it before."

"What is it?" Nick asked.

"Shadow Manipulation," Hieronymus said. "Rephaim can access a dimension of dark energy and employ it to their own use. It can be a formidable weapon."

"Mammon used it to block cell doorways of the prison I entered to free Council members," Sage said. Then his face showed a sudden realization. "That means we can't go any further!"

"Why?" Hieronymus asked.

"In the prison, once you entered the doorway, you couldn't leave again. You were trapped. It was like a force field. Like running into a brick wall. Only by Memory Sharing and creating a portal into the past was I able to get the Council members out." Sage pointed ahead. "I don't see a way around what's up there. It stretches as wide as the canyon. I checked both ends."

They fell silent. "You didn't see this when you scouted here before?" Kaja asked Hieronymus after a beat.

"No. It appears they have created a defense barrier." The old scout rubbed his chin.

"It could be a death trap if we enter," Sage said.

"We can't just stop here," Ronan said. "Not after coming this far. And we're not going back."

Nick saw fear on Sage's face and wondered if he was reliving some of the nightmare he'd experienced in the prison. Nick had already decided that whatever made Sage nervous made him doubly nervous.

"I could go and scout it," Kaja offered.

"You mean enter it?" Sage asked.

"Yes." She squared her shoulders and stared into the distance for several moments. "I am small and agile. I can survive a simple exploration."

"I have been entrusted with your safety," Hieronymus said. "After listening to Sage, your stepping through that veil isn't something I am willing to allow."

So, they all fell silent and just looked at one another. Then Nick thought of something. "Sage, when you were *inside* the prison cell, what did you see when you looked back out? From inside to outside?" He had an idea, but Sage's answer would determine if it was worth anything.

"I could see where I'd just been standing," Sage said. "It was like a two-way mirror."

"So, if the Rephaim are standing just inside and looking out, they will see us walk right up on them?" Nick asked.

"If it's like in the prison, yes. Why?"

"Because I have an idea." They all waited for him to continue. "A diversion and an illusion."

As soon as they were within sight of the Great Wall, as Nick thought of it, they got into position. Sage teleported to the far left, behind an outcropping of rocks. Kaja snuck around to the far right and lay prone inside a shallow depression in the earth. About eighty yards separated the two. Hieronymus sat next to Nick and served as his eyes and ears. They were both hidden behind a boulder directly between Sage and Kaja yet twice as far from the barrier. Ronan protected Hieronymus and Nick, his steel bar ready for action.

Nick sat on the ground, legs crossed, and faced away from the Great Wall. His eyes were closed. He let his mind wander, flitting through thoughts of home and school and his mom and dad's cruise—anything, so long as he didn't dwell on any one thing too closely, especially gaming. He'd spent so many hours playing games and killing monsters and zombies and aliens that he didn't want any of them to suddenly appear as an illusion and distract everybody.

"They are in position," Hieronymus told him quietly. "If you are correct about your assumption of the Rephaim posting an observer, then your idea should provide an interesting reaction. You may begin when ready."

Nick closed his eyes and remembered a time when he'd been playing soccer with Sage in the green area in front of their house. They'd been playing for an hour, full speed, until Nick couldn't run another step. He'd collapsed onto his back and looked straight at the sun. It was a cool day, but the sun had shone bright and powerful, the heat quickly drying his sweaty face.

He focused on that sun now, imagined it hanging just below the roof of the great cavern in the dimly illuminated underworld. He imagined how bright the huge ball of light would be, how it would turn the territory into a wonderland of different colors, exposing shades and hues that couldn't be seen otherwise.

"Incredible," Hieronymus whispered to him.

Hieronymus had instructed Sage and Kaja to ignore the illusion, to keep their attention on the black veil and nothing else. "What are the others doing?" Nick asked, his eyes still closed as he focused on keeping the image as strong as possible.

"They have glanced at it a couple of times but are maintaining discipline," Hieronymus said. "You must be prepared to hold the image for a long time. One of the Rephaim will be required to walk close enough to the power of your suggestion to see the light."

"I know," Nick said. He'd gone to relieve himself right before he sat down. He could wait for hours if necessary.

———◄———

It took almost an hour. Nick was just starting to get weary when Hieronymus announced movement from the Great Wall. "A Rephaim has just stepped forward," he whispered to Nick. "It is staring at your great ball of fire with fascination. Another now comes."

Nick focused harder, imagining the sun a little bigger and dropping a little lower. He needed to be careful, though, not to go overboard. The last thing he wanted to do was screw it all up before it really got started.

"A third has come to look," Hieronymus said.

Sage suddenly appeared next to them. "The black wall is fading," he whispered. "It's hard to tell from here, but it is. As soon as the second one came out, I noticed it. After the third, I knew for sure."

"Perhaps the wall is a combined effort and requires the full concentration of all of them," Hieronymus said. "Look, two more have joined them to lay witness. I, too, can see the veil fading."

"Later," Sage said. He disappeared.

"I'll give them more to look at," Nick said. "Hold on to your britches."

"My what?" Hieronymus said.

He imagined the sun splitting in two, separating like the greatest fireworks show in history. It rumbled and twisted and gurgled boiling fire and shot bolts of molten lava in every direction. It came apart like a slow-motion car crash, just a few inches at a time.

"Many more have joined the group," Hieronymus said. "At least ten. The veil is nearly transparent."

"What do they look like?" Nick asked, still sitting with his back to the boulder, his eyes closed tightly.

"They are as Sage described. Great winged beasts, each of a different color, large eyes, and powerful bodies." Hieronymus paused.

"They look similar to the Elioudian people. Sage was not incorrect about that."

Nick pictured one, remembering the detail of Sage's descriptions. That gave him another idea. As the sun split in half, Nick imagined it slowly revealing a giant Rephaim, thirty feet tall, as black as the darkest midnight, two sets of mighty wings stretching forty feet across, its muscular body so thick and powerful that to even look upon it would send a wave of fear through the bravest warrior.

Sage appeared beside Nick a second time. "Nick, you are a genius. Keep it up. Hieronymus, I'm going to visit Kaja. What emotion should she project?"

"Like last time," he said. "Great fear."

"No!" Nick said suddenly. He fought to keep the image developing in his mind's eye as he spoke. "I need them to feel respect. Awe. Complete and utter compliance. Tell her that as soon as she hears it speak, send out waves of idol worship. I want them to worship it like it's their god. Oh, and Sage, what's the name of that Prince that had me shoved down here?"

"Belphegor," Sage said. "Oh, man, I know what you're thinking!" He squeezed Nick's arm. "Genius. You are a *genius*." And then he was gone.

Nick separated the suns. The great Rephaim waved his hands toward his audience before spreading them wide. He flapped his wings slowly and hovered a few feet off the ground. The fireballs popped and sizzled and cast great light over the area.

My name is Pinocchio, sent by Prince Belphegor, ruler of millions on Topside, the illusion said inside Nick's head, his voice presumably booming throughout the cavern. *He requires the presence of all fellow Rephaim.* His eyes shot a blast of fire toward the ground. *OBEY,* the voice thundered. *Come forth by the command of Prince Belphegor!*

"Sage is speaking to Kaja," Hieronymus whispered to Nick. "She has placed her sword on the ground and is using both of her hands to project the desired emotion."

"This is unbelievable," Ronan mumbled under his breath, which made Nick smile.

Bow before the Prince's messenger, or die where you stand!

"The wall is gone," Hieronymus said. "I can see many Rephaim coming this way. Soon the crowd will be more than two dozen. I am surprised they are not at the celebration in Cain. A few in the front have dropped to their knees."

Down on your knees! Nick's illusion shouted. *And prepare to leave this place!*

"More are dropping to their knees," Hieronymus said. "They are confused. Some look scared. Tell them the Gate of Jerome has been breached and soon they will join the Seven on the surface."

The Gate of Jerome has been breached! Soon you will join Belphegor on the surface. Rejoice! Your time to rule has come!

Nick heard a roar of cheering erupt from the crowd. He kept his eyes closed and his mind drilled into the scene playing in his imagination. He had the giant beast raise both hands high in the air and flap its wings. "Are they all together now, or are more coming?" he asked.

"I see no others coming," the old scout answered. "I did not believe this many would skip the celebration."

The Gate of Jerome is breached! the great Rephaim shouted again. *But time grows short. We must go now! Rule with the Seven!* Nick kept the two fireballs burning as he moved the beast backward, across the fields Nick and the others had just crossed. "Tell me if they follow," he whispered, sweat now running strong under both armpits. *Time wastes,* Pinocchio said, moving faster now. *We must not miss this chance!*

"They are moving," Hieronymus said. "All of them. Some running, some flying. Soon they will all be flying. They are nearly past Sage and Kaja's position. Kaja still projects her emotion upon them. They will be out of her range in another few seconds."

Nick turned the beast around and had it begin walking away from the crowd, leading them across the great fields. "How fast can the Rephaim fly?" he asked while turning the beasts' head and shooting fire out of its eyes.

"I do not know," Hieronymus said. "Just keep the image strong."

Nick knew they were well hidden, but even still, he tried making himself smaller. He heard the crowd getting closer, and he didn't like the idea of airborne creatures.

Pinocchio roared a mighty blast, and several in the crowd mimicked him. *The Gate of Jerome has been breached!*

"Turn the image to the left," Hieronymus said. "Now. The ancient gate is that direction."

He had the beast look back at the crowd and wave both hands. Both fireballs began following the crowd, lighting their way. Nick heard flapping wings and demonic voices as they passed. He fought off a flash of fear and focused only on the image inside his head.

After he turned Pinocchio to the left and went a short distance, he had it rise high into the air, its wings keeping it afloat with effortless ease. *Head to the Gate*, it shouted to the crowd. *Hurry. The breach will soon close.* The crowd shouted, and the last of them passed where he, Ronan, and Hieronymus sat hiding.

"I will let you know when we must move," Hieronymus said. "Hold the image. Hold the image."

You will rule the weak humans for the rest of eternity!

"Just a few seconds more," Hieronymus said. "They are nearly out of sight."

"Have Sage and Kaja left yet?" Nick asked. "That was the plan."

"Yes. They have been gone for a short time. Get ready, young Nick. Try and hold the image after we are moving."

"OK." Nick drilled his mind ever deeper into the image, sweat now pouring in rivulets out of his hair. *Rejoice!* his imaginary friend shouted to the crowd, *Rejoice!*

"Run, Ronan," Hieronymus said. "Now. I will catch you. Go."

Nick heard Ronan stomp off through the vegetation. Ronan had told the Elioudian scout that he'd need a head start once the sprinting began. Now he had one. A minute later, Hieronymus yanked Nick from beside the rock and threw him over his shoulder like a sack of potatoes. "Hold on tight," the scout said quietly.

Nick felt a strong wind against the back of his sweaty shirt. He kept his eyes clamped shut while he tried focusing on the image in his head. He lifted his head and let the wind blow through his hair. It felt like Hieronymus was running thirty miles an hour. Finally, unable to keep the image any longer, he opened his eyes.

They raced through a landscape much different than what they'd seen so far. Nick twisted his head around and looked forward. A village of stone buildings and thousands of caged animals encircled a lake. The smell of animal waste nearly made him gag. Way ahead, he saw Kaja sprinting full speed. Sage simply teleported ahead, waited until she arrived, and teleported ahead again. Ronan was running hard, but Hieronymus was gaining fast.

Hieronymus's speed was unimaginable. His powerful legs churned like steel pistons, eating up ground like a cheetah. Now Nick understood how he'd been able to get Sage back to the village of Seth so fast after his injury. "Grab my neck hard," Hieronymus told Nick. "We are traveling too slowly."

What! Nick wrapped his arms around his thick neck and held on. Soon the Elioudian passed forty miles per hour, then surely beyond what the fastest cheetah could run. They passed Ronan, who lowered his head, looked at Nick, and ran like his hair was on fire.

Because of how Hieronymus was carrying him, Nick could only see the village as they passed through. It was much too large for only two dozen Rephaim. Yet he knew they must have voracious appetites because he saw thousands of caged animals of all shapes and sizes. Hundreds of cows and horses and goats, dozens of small dinosaurs like he'd seen in pictures at school, and an entire section of tiny cages holding birds of all types. On the far side of the lake near the water, Nick saw an area that looked like a barbeque pit. A fire raged even now and had three full-size cows skewered and roasting over the flames.

In another minute, they were out of the village. Hieronymus caught Kaja. Her instructions from the old scout had been clear:

once she started running, she wasn't to stop until they reached the cliff face on the far side. Nick looked for Sage but only saw glimpses of him as he leapfrogged forward. Looking back, Ronan was only halfway through the village.

They reached the cliff face separating the Rephaim and Nephilim Territories just a few minutes later. Sage was waiting there, leaning against a rock. Hieronymus swung Nick off his shoulder and set him on the ground next to his brother. Kaja stopped and knelt on one knee to catch her breath.

Hieronymus didn't even appear winded. He simply adjusted his huge pack so it fit more squarely on his back and looked up at the cliff. After studying it for several moments, he looked at the rest of them. "We have been fortunate with the Emim and Rephaim. We did not have to fight to pass through their Territories. That might not be possible with the Nephilim. As soon as you are rested, we must begin our climb. For the Rephaim will smell our passage through their village and hunt us. It will not take long for them to get here."

It took Ronan a few minutes to join them. By the time he did, Kaja had already started her climb. Ronan looked up and shook his head. "You've *gotta* be kidding me."

———†———

The team crouched behind a row of boulders, overlooking the Emim village where hundreds of creatures of all shapes and sizes made getting through an absolute impossibility. They'd been there for an hour, discussing their options. They couldn't go around the village. The cavern narrowed at this point and didn't widen again until after they passed through. Elsbeth had teleported ahead and found corn kernels on the far side, proving that Sage's group had made it.

"I just don't understand how they got through," Gavin said for a fourth time, breaking a lengthy silence.

"I'm telling you, again, that Sage must have used Teleportation to draw them out," Elsbeth said. She pushed the frustration out of her tone and tried convincing them of a point she'd been hammering at for the past thirty minutes. "Look around. There are dozens of places to hide on this side. I think he teleported over to the edge of the village, ran away, got a few of them to give chase, maybe killed a couple, then used teleportation to draw everyone out. And while they were chasing him, the others slipped through. I can do the same thing."

"And I'm telling you it's too dangerous," Steven said yet again.

"You can't fight like Sage," Kato said. "I can tell you that first-hand. We don't know how fast some of those creatures are. If you are caught, sword skills alone will not keep you alive."

"Then how do we get through?" Elsbeth said.

"I thought all the creatures were supposed to be at the Godhood celebration," Gavin said. "Guess it's not such a big deal after all."

"Maybe the Elioudians just had dated information," Malcolm said.

"Or maybe we missed the window and they've returned already," Steven said. "Regardless, if we don't figure something out, eventually we'll be discovered."

David, who hadn't said much over the last hour—unusual for him—finally gave his opinion. "I agree with Elsbeth. We need to use her as bait."

"Can Elsbeth teleport faster than gargoyles and midnight riders can fly?" Endora asked.

"Yes. For sure. But it doesn't matter," David said. "We dodged one gargoyle a minute ago. They will find us if we sit here and do nothing."

"But we do not know if all the beasts will give chase," Endora said. "We should wait until they bed for the night."

And it begins again, Elsbeth thought. They were about to rehash the same points they'd just spent fifteen minutes arguing about.

"Enough!" Elsbeth hissed. "*I* will decide." She looked hard at Steven. "*I will decide!* Like I said before, I suggest all of you go separately after I've led most of the creatures out of the village. I think you can get lost in the confusion, but that's your choice. Maybe two groups of three is better. Since I've already got a spot picked out on the far side of the village, and since I can teleport up to thirty miles at a time, it doesn't matter how far I go or how long I'm gone. Just get through, and I'll see you over there." She adjusted her headset radio. "These things have a range of two miles, so I'll try not to go too far." She shed her backpack and dropped it at her feet. "Somebody carry my pack and let me know when everybody is across." And she teleported out.

She didn't go far. She landed in an alcove high above the group to watch their reaction to her decision. It wasn't good, judging by the violent hand motions exhibited by Endora and Steven, but it only took them a few beats to get their game plan together. They broke into two groups, with Endora in one and David in the other. Kato and Gavin also split up, leaving Malcolm and Steven to complete the two teams. Good plan.

Endora's group went far left, circling around to the edge of the cavern and stopping behind a boulder. David's group went in the opposite direction, also stopping as far to the right as they could go. That left the middle wide open—a quarter mile of open space that she hoped wouldn't end up as her killing ground.

"Are both teams ready?" Elsbeth whispered into her radio. "When I hear two sets of double clicks, I'll get this show started."

She got the clicks immediately. Rubbing her sweaty palms on her jeans, she gripped the sword hard in her right hand and studied the village through her binoculars. She couldn't see all of it because it wound around to the left, out of sight, but directly in the center were the remains of some sort of monument: a large statue snapped in half. Around the base of the monument was a dried-up fountain some fifty feet across, mostly filled with debris from the top of the statue. Stone benches, most broken, were scattered around the wall of the fountain. None of the beasts were in proximity to the monument. That is where she would make her appearance. She needed to get all the creatures to follow her, not just a few. She racked her brain about how to do it until she realized there was no way to know until she saw how they reacted to her sudden appearance.

"OK, about to give them a surprise," she whispered. "Do not leave your hiding places until I tell you to. It might take several trips inside the village to get all of them angry enough to come after me. If you jump out too early, you'll distract them, and the plan will never work. Do you understand? Sit tight until you hear from me. Once I tell you to go, I won't come back into the village."

Two sets of double clicks answered her. As she folded her binoculars and stuffed them into her back pocket, she thought about what she knew of the history of the three evil races. Could she use some of that to enrage them? Maybe. She was about to find out. She hit record on her helmet camera and teleported into the village.

22

The monument was bigger up close than Elsbeth anticipated. The part of the statue still standing was nearly ten feet tall and three feet thick. The base rose more than fifteen feet into the air and was plenty big enough for her to stand and move around.

Sword in hand and nearly gagging from the smell of excrement, rotting food, and unwashed bodies, she watched the beasts moving around below. Her heart raced as she took stock of creatures not documented anywhere within the Tomb of Ancient Documents.

It was a lumbering half man–half ape that noticed her first. The Bigfoot lookalike sniffed the air as he passed near the base of the old fountain wall and stopped. He followed his nose and eventually looked up and bellowed a grunt that must have been a universal warning, for all the monsters stopped and turned toward her.

She slowly raised her sword and shouted, "Death to you all! May your bodies burn in pools of flaming sulfur." Most of the creatures wore a look of puzzlement, but some understood her words immediately and edged closer. "The Seven fall! The first, slain by the boy of prophecy." She glanced behind her after several grunts sounded from there. "You are next." She pumped her sword in the air.

"And how will you do that, human?" one of the minotaurs asked. "Your race is puny and weak and . . ."

Most of the creatures turned toward the minotaur, which was what Elsbeth had hoped for. She teleported in front of it and shoved her sword up into its throat. As soon as she pulled it out, she teleported back to her spot and raised her dripping blade into the air. The entire process took five seconds. The beast toppled over, not yet dead but not far from it. The creatures around it fell back and gave it plenty of space.

"I speak not to your earthly bodies," Elsbeth said, "but to the spirits using you as hosts." She pointed her sword at the dying minotaur. "Observe what happens when one of your companions dies."

The minotaur was nearly gone, hands at his throat, gasping. Elsbeth teleported over, stabbed the beast in the center of the chest, and a second later vanquished its spirit into a puff of green smoke.

Back at the broken statue, elevated above them all, she raised her sword again. "I speak to you, old Dark ones, descendants of the Watchers, defilers of mankind. We will not rest until all of you are destroyed." She appeared next to one of the Bigfoot lookalikes and thrust her sword into its side. "None will escape our wrath," she shouted.

They attacked all at once.

She felt a swipe along her back from the nearest Bigfoot just before teleporting over to the front gate. "We will prevail," she shouted. She stabbed the nearest creature, something so twisted and ugly she had no idea what it was.

A roar that took her breath away arose from the village as everything headed her way. Instead of going out the gate, she teleported back into the center, swinging her blade with everything she had, cutting and slicing and stabbing her way toward the rear. Then she left again, back to the front, confusing those that responded to the center.

"Kill her," several monsters shouted at once. "She is of the Council."

She moved to the top of a roof, where a gargoyle sat watching, and lopped off its head. The body fell over with a wet thump. She killed its spirit and turned toward two other gargoyles on the same roof. Startled, they screeched and flew away.

"Up there!" came a deep-throated roar from below.

Again, she raised her sword. "The Council lives!"

Like heat-seeking rockets, several flying beasts erupted from the ground toward her. Dozens of others gathered around the base of the building, shouting for her death.

Elsbeth picked out a spot on the outer edge of the crowd and waited until the last possible moment before disappearing. She stabbed another minotaur before landing back at her spot near the broken statue.

"One by one I will slay you," Elsbeth shouted. She raised her sword high. "You have no power over me. I am of Elioudian blood, redeemed by the Almighty and hardened for battle."

The entire herd of beasts turned on her, howling, growling, snapping, and shouting curses. They surged toward her, some with speed not seen anywhere on the surface. She teleported back to the main gate and ran toward the great fields.

"I'm heading your way," she transmitted into her headset. "Make sure most of them are out before you go." She glanced back, unsure if all of them were coming, but it appeared most were. She caught a flash of something out of the corner of her eye.

"Elsbeth, jump forward!" Steven shouted. "Now!" She did it without hesitation, appearing a hundred yards ahead. "You're clear. Gargoyle almost got you. Pay better attention."

Elsbeth looked back. The air was filled with more beasts than she knew had been in the village. On the ground, it appeared the entire place had emptied out. "Come on, come on," she whispered.

Only after the airborne creatures got within a few yards did she teleport away. She never went too far ahead because she wanted those on the ground to believe they would eventually catch her.

"Almost all out," Steven transmitted. "Just another minute."

Elsbeth sprinted, shouted, sprinted some more, then teleported. The screeching of the gargoyles felt like spikes in her skull, but she stayed ahead of them. After another minute, with the village now a half mile behind her, Steven told her they were moving.

Time to confuse them. Elsbeth glanced back and saw a herd of centaurs wielding huge, spiked clubs. They closed the gap, so she decided to slow them down. She teleported onto the back of the leader, jammed her sword into its neck, and then repeated the attack on three of the others. She appeared far ahead of the herd and turned to watch. The lead centaur collapsed, which caused a pileup of creatures behind it.

The monsters began shouting and cursing at each other; then Endora's Voice echoed through the canyon, and Elsbeth knew her team hadn't gotten through unchallenged. Elsbeth's pursuers stopped chasing and turned their heads toward the village. Then, as though telepathically called, every beast turned and headed back.

The team was at the far edge, nearly to the other side, when Elsbeth appeared at the main entrance. A dozen beasts lay slaughtered in the bloodiest of fashions. She appeared next to Gavin just as he vanquished the last Dark spirit.

"They're coming back," Elsbeth shouted. "Right now! As soon as they heard Endora's Voice, they started back. We've gotta go."

They sprinted through the far side of the village, each looking back as they went. Elsbeth was by far the slowest runner and quickly dropped back. She teleported to the front when she got too far behind.

"How far back are they?" Gavin asked as soon as Elsbeth appeared in front of him.

"At least a half mile, but the centaurs have tremendous speed. It won't take them long to catch us."

They rounded a turn, still following the trail of corn kernels Kaja had left. A screech sounded behind them. The gargoyles were getting close. Again, she lost ground. Gavin, Malcolm, and Kato were unbelievably fast, but Steven and Endora kept pace well. David was a different story. He lumbered behind, but his stamina kept him within shouting distance. Elsbeth glanced behind her but didn't yet see anything approaching from the air.

"Elsbeth," Steven shouted, "come up here!" She appeared between Steven and Endora, and they slowed just enough so they could talk to her. "Find a hiding spot for us up ahead," Steven said. "And then get forward of that spot and give us intel about when to launch an ambush. If only a few have broken from the pack and are close, we'll attack and dispatch them before moving on."

"What about the gargoyles and flying wolf men?" she asked. "And the midnight raiders? Those are the ones we need to worry about most."

"I can direct my Voice and drop them from the sky," Endora said. "But you must tell me exactly when."

"Go, Elsbeth. Get ahead of us, and find us a spot," Steven said. "Make it quick. A man as old as me can only sprint so far."

She teleported ahead and saw a place immediately. They were approaching a rock wall with a literal graveyard of truck-sized boulders at its base. She radioed the group and told them exactly where to position themselves. A minute later they were there. Endora took the most forward position. The beasts would reach her first, and as soon as they passed, she would sing. The other five would attack from their positions of cover and finish them off. Elsbeth hid a hundred yards closer to the approaching hoard than Endora's hiding place.

The gargoyles came first, flying in a V formation with three on each side of the leader. They weren't flying fast, but they were low and searching hard. Seconds later, Elsbeth heard the approach of distant hooves.

Endora's Voice blasted the canyon as soon as the gargoyles flew past her. Four of the seven crash-landed several yards forward. It took Kato and Gavin little time to dispatch them. Endora sent out another blast, and the remaining three hit the ground.

"To the wall," Elsbeth commanded into her radio headpiece. "Start climbing." The sound of the herd grew louder, but she couldn't see anything yet.

Steven and Malcolm reached the wall a few seconds later, with Endora and David right behind. Kato and Gavin arrived next, then turned to face the oncoming threat.

"Endora," Steven transmitted. "Stun them as we climb."

The six Council warriors were nearly a hundred yards up before Elsbeth saw the centaurs coming, clubs in each hand. Their speed had separated them from the rest of the beasts. She counted nine, galloping in a formation that left none of them exposed to surprise attacks. They all stopped suddenly and stared at the bodies of the seven gargoyles. The centaurs had heads as big as basketballs, with foreheads protruding over their eyebrows like disfigured monkeys. Their pointed ears stuck out of wiry hair that fell to the middle of their backs.

"What kind of warriors can defeat the flyers with such precision and speed?" one of them asked, looking at the others with an expression full of fear.

"They fell from the sky," said another.

The largest centaur closely inspected the wounds of the dead gargoyles. "These blows are of the histories," he said. "The ancients speak of warriors wielding blades forged from the blood of the redeemed." He pointed to the body nearest his feet. "See the burned flesh surrounding the wound to his heart? And there, where the blade severed his spine." He looked at the others. "This is the work of angels. The blood of Light. Yet in human form. Warriors from the Angelic Response Council. As the girl in the village claimed."

"That is but legend," said another. "Childhood stories meant to discourage us from waging yet another battle at the gate." He scowled. "If the Magog do not kill you, the stories say, the Council will slay you should you make it through the Gate. They rule Topside, they say. You will surely die, they say. Lies! All lies!"

"Then what of the disappearing girl?" said the first who'd spoken. "And the voice we heard just a few minutes ago. A voice that made us stumble even from a great distance. These Council members are said to have gifts from their god."

"We will kill them," snapped the skeptic. "They are few."

Elsbeth looked at the wall. The team was at least two hundred yards up and climbing fast. They would soon be out of sight.

"There," one of the centaurs shouted, pointing his club high up the wall.

"We cannot follow," said another.

"Not into the Rephaim territory," said a third.

"More flyers coming," Elsbeth whispered from her hiding place. Flying wolf men. "Climb faster."

She got a double click on her headset. They'd climbed several more yards and were nearly out of sight.

"Up there," a centaur shouted to the first wolf man who arrived.

The beast and seven others landed among the bodies of the gargoyles. The slaughter appeared to take the fight out of them.

"Do not be troubled," the lead centaur said. "They are defenseless as they climb."

"Where is the girl who disappears?" the first wolf man asked. "We must make her ours."

"Get the others, and the girl will come," the centaur shouted. "Pull them down, and she will come." He turned and led the charge toward the wall.

"They're coming," Elsbeth whispered into her radio. "And Endora, get ready; it's the werewolves with wings. The monsters that attacked us earlier. The ones that almost killed Sage."

Elsbeth turned up the volume of her radio just as Steven said, "Everybody, slow down. Surround Endora. Make a tight circle. Her Voice is our shield."

"I will wait until they are nearly upon us," Endora said, breathing hard. "No beast can withstand a close encounter."

Elsbeth couldn't see anything on the wall now. She considered joining them but decided she could do that later. She needed to discourage the beasts from following them any further, and she knew just how to do it.

As soon as Endora's Voice ruptured the silence, Elsbeth teleported behind a rock at the base of the wall. The centaurs staggered around in drunken circles, hands clasped to their ears, clubs on the ground.

The first flying beast landed on top of one of the centaurs, stunned into immobility, face frozen in a silent scream. It didn't move at all, even when the hooves of another centaur stepped on its face. The rest of the flyers landed seconds later, no more capable of battle than the broken statue in their village. Endora stopped singing, and the canyon grew silent.

"We're climbing, Elsbeth," Steven said. "That should discourage any more from following. Come on up."

"In a minute," Elsbeth whispered.

Once the centaurs had mostly recovered, but before the flyers could do much more than move their arms and legs, Elsbeth appeared on top of a big rock in front of them and raised her sword.

"Beware, Emim abominations," she said in her most fierce tone. "None can stand against us. Listen to your histories. We are but a fraction of the power of the Angelic Response Council." She pointed her sword at the centaur who'd been such a skeptic. "Should you dare follow us farther, your dying thought will be the realization that none of your childhood stories were lies." She paused and made eye contact with several. "A blade of righteousness scorches the flesh of the unclean and vanquishes the Dark spirit within. That is our destiny. That is your curse." A growing noise from the direction of the village announced the approach of the rest of the monsters. "The hand of the Almighty is still in control," she finished. "Follow us. And die."

She disappeared behind a large boulder and quietly sheathed her sword. With her binoculars, she saw faint shadows moving high on the wall. There were deeper shades of black that had no shape or form. She couldn't teleport onto the side of a sheer wall, and she couldn't see well enough to pick a landing spot.

"Steven," she whispered into her radio. "Find a ledge large enough for me, and light it up with a flashlight. I've got my binos on you."

A few seconds later she saw a faint spot, focused on it, and went away.

For at least half the climb, Sage made fun of Nick for naming his giant Rephaim *Pinocchio*. Kaja said she didn't understand why Sage thought it was so funny. Even after he explained the story about the boy who began as a toy and whose nose grew longer each time he lied, she still didn't see the humor.

"See, he wasn't a real boy," Sage told Kaja. "He wanted nothing more than to be a real boy. That's the reason he agreed to go to Toyland, where all you do is play all day. But then he grew donkey ears because children who do nothing but play all day turn into donkeys."

"But Nick's illusion did not grow donkey ears," Kaja said. "And its nose did not grow long after it told the lie about the Gate of Jerome being breached." She looked at Nick. "I do not see what is so funny."

"What's so funny is that Nick has turned into Geppetto," Sage said. "He's become a great and powerful puppet master."

"What is a puppet?" Kaja asked.

Nick tuned them out as they climbed the steps leading up into the Nephilim territory. As high as the other cliff had been, this one was at least three times that height. They rested often, primarily so Nick and Sage could sit down, but they finally made it. Hieronymus cautioned them to remain quiet just before leading them to a small cave that only Sage, Nick, and Kaja could squeeze into. "Sleep," he told the three of them. "I will return some hours from now to wake you. And eat. You will need your nourishment. Ronan will guard this entrance."

Nick didn't bother asking where the old scout was going, because he was too tired to care. Sage and Kaja started whispering,

Ronan sat with his broad back blocking the entrance, and Nick wondered if the rescue team had ever made it to Tartarus. He thought about asking Sage's opinion but was asleep before the question was fully formed in his head.

Sleep didn't seem to last long. Sage woke him by squeezing one of his ankles. "Wake up, little bro. Time to eat."

Eyes blurry, Nick could barely make out Kaja as she packed up the remains of a meal. Sage had also eaten and crawled over to the opening. "I went exploring a little," he told Nick. "After begging Ronan for ten minutes to let me pass. This place is way different than the other two Territories."

"Different how?" Nick asked.

"It's the land of the giants. Everything is bigger here. I found a hut. One door, no windows. Just a single room. The door was at least forty feet tall. I saw a footprint that I could lay my whole body inside of."

Kaja finished packing her bag and set it at her feet. "I have heard many stories of the Nephilim's existence but have not yet seen them. They are building their numbers for their day of release."

"What do you mean?" Nick asked.

"The Nephilim Resurgence," she said. "They believe that one day the gate to the surface will be opened again, and they will rule humans once more. Fear not; Hieronymus has a plan to get you through the gate without opening it for the Nephilim. Nick, you must eat. He will return soon and expect to leave immediately."

The old scout came back more than an hour later. Nick and Sage had resorted to teaching Kaja to play rock-scissors-paper just to have something to do. Sage squeezed out through the hole first, Nick and Kaja a few seconds later. Ronan looked like he could use a nap.

"The Nephilim are unaware of our presence," Hieronymus said, once they were standing around him. "I was afraid that an Emim or Rephaim might have ventured into this territory to warn them, but I have seen no evidence of that." He squatted down and drew several lines in the dirt. "We will travel through an abandoned mine shaft. The shafts are too small for the Nephilim to enter, and they will put us much closer to our destination." He paused. "The shafts are filled with creatures also eager to avoid the Nephilim."

"What kind of creatures?" Nick asked.

"I cannot know for certain what we might face." Hieronymus gave Nick a comforting nod and looked at the others. "The gate leading to Topside is guarded at all times. Since the Rephaim attack many centuries ago, they guard the exit as though their very existence depends upon it. It will be no easy task getting through."

"How will we?" Nick asked. "Kaja said you have a plan."

"Yes, Nick, I have something in mind, but that is for later." He stood and brushed the dirt lines away with his foot. "We have a long journey. Let us not dwell any longer. Kaja, continue marking our passage."

She held up her bag of corn kernels. "I have not forgotten."

The Nephilim territory *was* the land of giants. Everything Nick saw was supersized. It was the most bizarre feeling, knowing that the race roaming around within this strange land could squash him like a bug, literally.

Unlike the other Territories, the Nephilim lived off the land like farmers. Although they passed pockets of abandoned properties, the fields were tended, animals were penned and well maintained, and there was a variety of produce. In that respect, they were not unlike the Elioudians; they used their resources wisely.

The group kept to the shadows. They didn't speak to one another, they took caution with each step, and they waited until every sign of Nephilim presence moved away before proceeding further.

Nick caught a glimpse of one giant from across a field of corn. Hieronymus raised his hand in a stopping motion and dropped to one knee. The others followed suit. From behind Kaja, he saw movement in the distant horizon. The giant towered above the crops but was so far away Nick couldn't make out any detail. It appeared that it lifted its head and sniffed the air, but he wasn't sure about that. They sat silently for several minutes. When the beast moved away, Hieronymus stood and motioned them forward.

It was like that for hours on end. They stopped and started dozens of times, hiding and waiting and listening, keeping to the shadows, ever on the lookout. Nick saw many signs of Nephilim having recently been in the area, but no other sightings. Hieronymus was a master of sneaking the group right through the heart of their territory.

Pointing toward a large group of boulders, the old scout led them over there and dropped into a deep hole. They all jumped in after him, clearly thankful for the opportunity to rest. "We will eat now," Hieronymus whispered quietly.

Only after they had finished did anyone else speak. "You know this area well," Kaja said.

"Like Cobar before me, I lived within this territory more than fifty years, and not once did the Nephilim detect my presence. I have seen every rock and tunnel, every field and lake, and have explored every mine shaft. I know the location of every house and barn, have seen all the spots they set their animal traps, and have swam every swamp. I lived off their land and studied their ways. They are creatures of habit and smarter than they look."

"So, you know how to get to the Gate," Nick confirmed.

Hieronymus nodded. "Do not worry about the Gate."

"How much farther?" Sage asked.

"A day's journey through the mine shafts, and a few hours after that." He took a deep breath and nodded. "By this time tomorrow we will be there."

"Why haven't you led any of the other humans to the surface?" Sage asked.

Hieronymus stared at him for several moments before answering. "We would have been slaughtered. Humans are too emotional; I can smell their fear. The beasts can smell it from an even farther distance."

"But we've been scared," Nick said. "Why haven't they smelled us?"

"It is because of your ancestry," Hieronymus said. "You are descended from Seth, through Vale. It is why Vale gave you his blood. He knew his blood would draw out the properties present within your own and enhance it. You do not smell human because you are not human."

The idea was overwhelming. Nick forced a laugh. "I'm not going to go bald and grow eyes like golf balls, am I?" he joked.

Kaja reached over and patted Nick on the knee. "You wish you looked as good as me. But no; that is not likely." She smiled at him, and Nick laughed quietly.

"Let us sleep," Hieronymus said. "We need to be rested when we enter the mine shafts. For only a minor mistake could get us all killed in there."

23

The mine shaft didn't go down into the earth; it went into a wall of rock. Just a hole in the wall with a string of lights hanging from the ceiling. Nick still marveled at the electrical system throughout this underground universe. He'd not once heard or seen evidence of power plants or electrical generators. Hieronymus said they'd been constructed in underground caverns and were powered by mighty rivers.

Nick heard Sage draw his sword behind him. Kaja drew hers in front of him. Hieronymus had drawn his before he entered the shaft. He glanced back and saw that Ronan now carried his steel bar in one hand instead of over one shoulder. His head almost touched the ceiling, and the shaft was barely wider than the length of his bar. There would be no swinging it inside these mines.

They walked for nearly an hour, and nothing happened. They'd passed numerous side tunnels that Hieronymus said led back out to the territory. They took so many turns—both left and right—that it felt like they had walked in three complete circles.

Hieronymus stopped suddenly and spun around. "Ronan, behind you!"

Ronan whipped around and got into a battle stance. Sage teleported behind Ronan and shouted, "Ronan, protect Nick!"

Shadowy beasts came from the rear. Nick saw a blur of movement and didn't know what it was until he realized it was Sage's sword. High-pitched screams filled the tunnel, and then a spray of blood hit the wall by Nick's face. Ronan turned, tackled Nick to the ground, and covered his body with his own.

"Stay down," Kaja shouted at Nick and Ronan. "Do not move!" She stepped up next to Sage and whirled her blade just as fast as he did.

Nick tried to look and saw shadows and motion, black blurs and red splashes. Animalistic screams filled the tunnel, and he covered his ears. Sage and Kaja pushed away from him, heading back the way they'd come. On his other side, Hieronymus also battled. He didn't move his sword nearly as fast as the other two, but his swings were so powerful that whatever attacked him exploded in bursts of bloody mess with every blow.

There was nothing Nick could do but wait. He had no sword, no way to fight, and nowhere to run. Illusion did him no good now, not once the battle began. He could conjure up images of ten more Elioudians wielding swords, but what good would that do once the beasts had already begun their attack? No. His gift would be used to prevent fights, not wage them.

"Stay calm," Ronan said into Nick's ear. "We'll be fine."

Nick heard stress in Ronan's voice and knew it was killing him to not help with the fight. He was Grandpa's protector, and Sage's, but the close confines of the mine shaft limited his gift of Might. Being Nick's protector was the best way for him to help right now, and both Sage and Ronan had seen that instantly.

The battle raged for several minutes before everything went quiet. He heard gurgles and moaning and dying breaths after the swords fell silent. Ronan lifted his head to look around, then climbed to his hands and knees.

"Nick, are you OK?" Sage asked from a distance.

"I'm fine," Nick answered. He swallowed his fear and stood. At his feet, and from there in both directions, were hundreds of dead bats the size of bald eagles. Most were cut in half, others decapitated, but all were violently dead.

"Are you sure you did not get bitten?" Hieronymus asked Nick. "For the toxin in their bite will paralyze you for several days."

Nick checked himself but didn't find any wounds. He would know if he'd been attacked. "I'm fine," he said. He looked at Ronan. "How about you?"

"No bites. I'm good."

"We must hurry," Hieronymus said. "Predators will smell the blood and swarm the mines." He turned and moved deeper into the tunnel without waiting for a reply.

Nick stumbled after him, careful to avoid the bats at his feet. Ronan steadied him from behind. The old scout jogged, running slowly enough to allow the rest to keep up without tiring too badly. They stopped occasionally for a quick breather, but growling noises coming from behind kept them moving.

"Big-tooth cats have our scent," Nick heard Kaja quietly tell Hieronymus after they stopped for a quick drink of water. "I can smell their approach."

"What's that?" Nick asked. "A big-tooth cat?"

"Two large fangs protrude from the top of their mouth," Kaja said. "They look much like lionesses but are bigger."

"Do you mean a saber-toothed tiger?" Sage asked.

"I do not know the beasts by that name, but they do resemble tigers." Kaja swallowed a gulp of water and wiped her mouth. "They hunt in packs and are fierce adversaries. Their scent gets stronger each minute that passes." She looked at Hieronymus. "We must prepare."

"They approach from behind," Hieronymus said. "There is a chamber ahead that is large enough to do battle." He looked at Nick. "I must carry you again. They will overtake us otherwise."

And in a flash, Nick was riding over the old scout's shoulder again, flying through the mine shaft at breakneck speeds. Kaja ran directly behind Hieronymus, then Ronan. Sage brought up the rear, apparently hanging back to gauge how close the tigers were getting and then teleporting forward to give them updates.

They arrived in a large chamber after several minutes, again making several turns in what was obviously a gigantic mineshaft system. The room was round and had more than a dozen other shafts leading out in different directions. Hieronymus put Nick in a small tunnel high off the ground and told him to stay up there. The other four spread out evenly across the chamber, weapons ready, waiting.

"I have battled these cats more than a dozen times within this room," Hieronymus said. "They are cautious and work together well. Do not be fooled by their first move, and do not underestimate the speed of their front paws."

Nick's small chamber required him to watch from a prone position. It looked like a natural indentation in the earth and was only six feet deep. He scooted back far enough so that only his face could be seen from below.

Ronan stood far enough away from the others to swing his bar. He appeared eager to make up for his lack of involvement a few minutes before. Kaja and Hieronymus also wore determined looks, clearly ready for what was about to happen. Sage didn't look like that at all. He stood with his sword dangling in one hand while he scratched his right armpit with the other. He wore a goofy grin and winked at Nick when they made eye contact.

He lives for this stuff, Nick realized at that moment. *He cherishes his role as a warrior for the Angelic Response Council.* His display of confidence almost unnerved Nick. He knew his brother didn't back down from much, but what Nick had seen over the past few days was beyond anything he could have ever imagined. Sage not only had angel blood running through his veins, he had ice water.

"They come," Kaja whispered, raising her sword into battle position.

Sage gripped his sword tightly in both hands. Hieronymus stepped to the left and placed himself directly into the path of the tigers as they stepped out of the tunnel. Ronan, set off to one side, was in a great ambush position.

The first tiger stepped slowly into the chamber. The top of its shoulders was almost four feet high; its head towered nearly six feet off the ground. The saber teeth protruded from the top of its mouth, stopping just below its bottom jaw.

The beast studied each of the warriors and then looked up at Nick, who scooted backward into his cubby. It moved to the left and made room for a second to enter. The first grunted, and the second went to the right. A third entered, then a fourth and a fifth.

Hieronymus's eyes followed each of the beasts. Kaja shifted her position slightly, moving left toward Hieronymus and leaving Ronan by himself to the far right. Sage was in the middle.

"Only five?" Sage asked. "Is that all you've got?" Then a sixth tiger entered. A seventh. "OK, I guess not."

Ronan shifted to the right even farther, fully isolating himself from the others. "Hieronymus, do you want me to start this?"

"Kill the first beast that entered," the scout said. "He is the leader."

In that instant, Ronan stepped forward and swung his bar at the first tiger's head. The sound of crushing bone echoed in the small chamber just as the beast stiffened and toppled over, dead before it hit the ground. Sage didn't waste any time. He teleported to the tiger closest to Kaja and drove his sword up through its head. He disappeared as soon as his blade was free.

The tigers panicked. Two of them charged Hieronymus at the same time, crashing into one another and allowing Hieronymus to step to the side and swing a strong blow across the back of the neck of the one closest to him. Its head went flying.

Kaja stepped over the body of the one Sage had killed and hopped toward a tiger that had turned toward Ronan. Her blade moved so fast that Nick couldn't see it. All he saw was a tiger there that had a head one second and then was falling sideways without a head the next.

Three tigers were left. One jumped into the nearest tunnel and fled, leaving two. They both backed slowly toward the mine shaft they'd come out of. Ronan rushed forward and crushed the head of one; the other bolted.

The entire battle had lasted less than a minute, and not one of the four victors looked shaken. Kaja had been in these types of fights for over a hundred years, Hieronymus many times that. Ronan, too. Nick had expected *them* to react as though this were an everyday occurrence. Sage, though, was only fifteen. How could he face death with such cool demeanor? Nick was beginning to understand Sage's value to the Angelic Response Council. It was a sight to behold.

"I don't understand," Elsbeth said as she looked toward a wall of solid black. "The trail of corn stops there, but so does everything else."

They'd followed Kaja's path without difficulty and had been able to avoid several varieties of wandering beasts. Now, ahead of them a hundred yards and stretching as wide as they could see in each direction was a veil of blackness that seemed familiar.

Then it hit her. "Mammon's prison," she whispered. She looked at Steven. "You wrote the report last summer from Sage's trip into the prison. That's what we saw blocking the doorway of a couple of the cells. And the dungeon of souls."

"Shadow manipulation," Steven said.

"It's a spider web." Kato said.

"What do you mean?" Malcolm asked.

"If we pass through this wall, we'll be trapped. That's what we found at the prison. Sage knows that." Kato looked at Elsbeth. "Would he allow the others to enter?"

"They went in," Elsbeth said. "The trail shows that." They just looked at each other. She didn't know if they were simply at a loss for words or out of ideas.

Malcolm finally spoke. "It's high time I carry my weight. Dad, you've studied the Rephaim more than the rest of us. Are there any other creatures in there besides them?"

"Doubtful," Steven said. "Except for the Celebration of Godhood, according to the Elioudian historian I spoke to before we left Seth, the Emim stay out of the Rephaim territory. As do the Nephilim. Since the Rephaim are the only ones who can put Shadow Manipulation into practice, we can assume a Rephaim village hides behind the veil."

"I'll draw one out," Malcolm said.

"For what purpose?" Gavin asked.

"To absorb its powers. Then to question it." Malcolm looked hard at his brother. "Then to kill it."

"What in the queen's name would that do?" David asked. "Foolish to get into hand-to-hand combat with a beast. Even I wouldn't do that unless I had to."

"It would give us some intel," Malcolm said. "Which is more than we have now."

"What if an entire herd of them come out?" Endora asked. "Remember, these are the beasts that turned into the Princes of Hell. Can you absorb a beast so powerful?"

Malcolm shrugged. "Guess I'll find out."

"He can," Gavin said. "Make no mistake."

The boulder they were standing behind gave them the cover they needed, but it wouldn't block their voices from carrying through the canyon. Steven motioned for all of them to whisper.

"In the prison, we could see through the blackness if we got close enough," Elsbeth said. "I suggest I go to the far edge to look in. I'll radio back to the others what I see." She looked at Malcolm. "If one of them rips you apart before you absorb its powers and strength, the rest will come out to see what's going on. Then we'll all be in trouble."

"I can walk to the front and sing a little song," Endora said. "Then, Elsbeth, you approach the wall between us and peer through. If the coast is clear, we step through and pass through the village."

Steven pointed at Endora and nodded. "I like that. Except you get closer together. Maybe fifteen or twenty yards. You can escort us through the village and out the other side."

"Assuming we can get out the other side," Kato said.

"If Endora stuns them," David said, "maybe the veil will fall."

"What other choice do we have?" Gavin asked. "It's not like we're gonna sneak through there. We can't go around. Let's just do this."

"Remember, we're not engaging unless one of them somehow fights through Endora's Voice," Steven said. "So, like Gavin said, let's do this."

They got into formation—Endora on the outside, everybody else in the middle—and approached the veil at a slow pace. If anything came out, they'd stun it and keep moving. They didn't plan on breaking formation at all. *Strength in numbers*, Elsbeth thought, shrouded in the protection of angelic gifts.

"Form up. Straight line," Steven said, just a few feet from the wall. "We all step through together. As soon as we're through, Endora steps slightly forward and gets ready." He looked up and down the line. "Ready? Go."

They went from a desolate and abandoned cavern as barren as the moon to a scene filled with a rank and putrid collection of animal stalls overflowing with livestock that was as loud as a rock concert. A wide path cut through the center of a village of neglected stone buildings. The smell of excrement and urine, mixed with sulfur and burning and rotting flesh, brought tears to Elsbeth's eyes. Fires burned in huge pits, roasting animals and dripping fat into the flames. The stone streets reeked with dried blood from centuries of slaughter. Thousands of animals and hybrid humans were locked in cages of various sizes covering hundreds of yards on each side of the village. The humans screamed and cried and reached out to them, babbling words Elsbeth couldn't possibly understand. Victims of experiments, they suffered from deformities found in the most horrid nightmares. Elsbeth nearly retched and turned away.

"No Rephaim," Gavin said. "Anybody see any?"

Elsbeth saw no sign of them, yet some had to be there to generate the veil. "They're hiding," she said. "Have to be, or there wouldn't be a wall." But was that true? The veils had been in place inside Mammon's prison without a Rephaim present, so maybe she was wrong about that.

"Let's pick up the pace," Kato said. "I want to get to the top of that cliff as soon as possible."

Elsbeth looked in the far distance and saw a cliff rising hundreds of feet into the air. Even from here she could see a path up the side. She stared at that distant point—anything to avoid looking at the ghastly humans begging to be released.

"Agreed," Steven said. "Pick up the pace."

They began at a slow jog but were practically running by the time they made it to the base of the cliff. David slung his bar over his back and went first. Steven went next, then Malcolm and Gavin. Kato followed right behind Endora while Elsbeth stayed on the ground looking back toward the village. She would teleport up once everyone reached the top.

Where are the Rephaim? A bigger question was: How had Sage's group made it through?

Maybe the Rephaim hadn't yet returned from the Celebration of Godhood. Hannah had told them it was held in the largest Rephaim village, not this one. That's why Sage's had scout insisted they leave when they did.

She waited at the foot of the cliff as the group above her climbed. They kept in radio contact during the ascent, and she eventually found a hiding place in case the Rephaim appeared in the village.

She wondered what her father was doing, how worried he must be. She thought he would have given nearly anything to make this trip, especially right at this moment, standing at the edge of a Rephaim village. His gift of Transformation had allowed him to spend nearly every moment of his life impersonating the beasts, infiltrating groups, desperate to discover the human identities the

Seven currently operated under. The sad reality was that his gift didn't really help the team down here. She'd gotten a ton of camera footage, and that would have to be good enough.

"We're at the top," Steven finally announced. "Just pick out spots as you see them, and come on up. No hurry, we're catching our breath."

Elsbeth looked up and saw a flat spot ahead. She teleported up and immediately found another about the same distance away. Before making her third leap, she looked down on the village for a wider view. She would never forget this place, but she still wanted her camera to capture what was here. From this distance, she couldn't see the pits filled with rotting flesh or the animals hanging from hooks, their guts piled on the ground beneath them, or desperate eyes peering out from within the cages, but the images would clearly show the depravity of the captors and foreshadow the future of humanity should the remaining Princes of Hell succeed in conquering earth.

She found the rest of the group kneeling in a circle at the top and truly felt sorry for them. The climb must have been exhausting, especially given that they hadn't yet stopped to sleep. She said nothing as she walked past them and found the trail of Kaja's corn kernels.

"We press on," Steven said. "The kids will rest. Nick will rest. We can overtake them. I'm sure of it."

"You'll kill us all before you're through," Kato said, smiling. "But in the meantime? Just torture."

They were off, same formation, same sense of urgency, same pace. They had to be getting close to Sage's group. Their frantic pace was unlike anything she'd ever done. Before leaving, she'd walked back to the edge of the cliff and looked down just to confirm they weren't being followed.

"No Emim in sight?" David asked Elsbeth after they'd been walking for a minute. "Nothing following us?"

"I didn't see anything," Elsbeth said. "But I've still got a funny feeling about it."

"You and me both," Gavin said. "Can say this, though—we're up here, and they're down there. And a lot of those creatures can't climb."

"They *have* to know where we're going," Malcolm said. "They know the Territories better than any scout, no matter how good he is. I don't think they'll follow us directly if they know another way."

"We were talking on the climb up, Elsbeth," Steven said. "We think the Rephaim might be between us and Sage's group. It's the only explanation we could come up with."

"We don't even know how they got through," Elsbeth said.

"Kaja's trail went right through the middle," Endora said.

"But were they seen?" Elsbeth asked. "We don't know that."

"We'll assume the Rephaim are ahead of us," Steven said. "It's the tactically sound assumption. Which means they could lay an ambush for us. So, heads up, everybody. And if anyone needs a break, let me know. Otherwise, let's keep the noise down. Don't want to make it too easy for them." And that was the end of it. They pressed on, now in the Nephilim territory.

24

Brother.

Sloth finished his golf swing and watched the ball slice to the right and disappear into the trees. Some in his group chuckled, but it was in good taste, not an insulting or demeaning laugh. He was the last in the group to tee off, so they all headed out toward their respective balls. Sloth's ball was far from all the others, so he had a few moments to focus on his brother's message. He motioned to his armed guards to give him some distance. They nodded and fell back, eyes searching the surroundings for potential threats, unaware that the most pressing danger wasn't within a thousand miles of here.

Yes, Gadrell. I await your account.

The angel boy and those attempting to join him have passed into the Nephilim territory. Soon, brother, the Gate will be open. We will be prepared.

What of deaths? How many yet live?

All, Belphegor. I observed them myself. They are uninjured and powerful. The trailing group is close to overtaking the angel boy and the man with Strength. The scout for the Pure Ones is a formidable opponent in his own right. In total, not an invincible force, but killing them will be no easy task. My disciples and I have positioned ourselves properly. We await the opening of the Gate.

Sloth saw his golf ball and slowed his pace. *You must time it perfectly, Gadrell. The Gate, once opened, will remain so for just a short period. Should only one escape the pits, ensure that it is you.*

Certainly, brother. Certainly. You will be in position yourself?

I will be in position, Gadrell. Remain diligent; freedom draws near. Peace be to you.

And to you, Belphegor.

Sloth would rather have had another complete the last portion of this mission for him. It was too important, however. His brother's life was at stake; control of the other Princes was at stake; the domination of humanity was at stake. He could not entrust the final step to someone else.

Once completed, he would kill Lucifer and install himself as leader of the Princes. Belphegor and Gadrell would rule together. It was well known within the Rephaim world that had Gadrell escaped during the Battle of the Gate, *he* would have ruled—with Belphegor at his side—and not Lucifer. The Prince of Pride also knew that truth. It was why Lucifer had betrayed Gadrell and prevented his escape and why he had turned the other Princes against Sloth from the beginning. Lucifer saw Sloth for the threat he could have been.

Had Sloth revealed any of this mission to the other Princes, Lucifer would have been told and stopped it immediately. No;

Lucifer would discover the brilliance of Sloth's plan to kill the angel boy just before Sloth and Gadrell struck him down.

—†—

Steven's Pathfinding came in handy when they located a hidden cove where Sage and Nick had spent the night prior to entering a series of mineshafts. They'd left behind enough food trash for two meals. Endora was convinced the group had picked up at least six or seven hours on them. The scale of the battle with the bats took Elsbeth's breath away. Blood splattered the walls and ceiling of the shafts, with some of the beasts looking as though they'd been blasted with a shotgun.

"I can't imagine what Nick must be thinking," Steven said, his face lined with stress.

"Don't let any of this bat blood get on your skin," Endora said. "It's toxic. Jarvis and I encountered these in a cave in Siberia about a century ago. Jarvis got scratched and was sick for several weeks."

"Twenty-pound bats," Elsbeth said, looking at Endora. "Were there this many in Siberia?"

"Ha! Hardly. Jarvis and I alone would hardly have survived an assault such as this. But they look the same." Endora's gaze wandered off for a moment. "It makes me wonder if somehow there is a way to the surface through natural vents too small for bigger beasts to use."

"Doesn't help us any," Kato said. "But I guess it's possible." He looked at Steven. "I'll lead the way. Gavin, pick up the rear."

They fell into a steady rhythm. Elsbeth soon lost her sense of direction as they switched and turned at such a steady rate, feeling dizzy after just a few minutes.

"More death and destruction," Kato announced. He stopped and stared into a chamber Elsbeth couldn't yet see. "With every massacre scene we find, my respect for Sage increases." Kato looked at the group. "Just don't tell any zookeepers up top what they killed." He stepped to the side so the others could see.

Elsbeth pushed her way past David and looked in. Saber-toothed tigers! She saw marks on their coats where someone on Sage's team had wiped their blades clean. The two scouts, since Sage's sword sizzled itself clean. She looked at Kato and shook her head.

"I see Ronan's bar at work in here," David said. "Impressive for an old bloke like him. When we get out of this place, I'll share some of my new swings with him. Think he would like that, Elsbeth?"

"After he soaks your head to shrink it down to size," Kato said, smiling. "Maybe spending time with that old bloke will teach *you* a few things."

"Like what?" David said, his eyes wide in astonishment.

Elsbeth couldn't tell if David was truly confused or just acting indignant. He was such a kidder most of the time that it really blurred the lines.

"Well," Kato said. "Let me name a few. Humility, courteousness, hair style, choice of wardrobe. Maybe a bottle of cologne." He laughed. "Am I lying, Elsbeth?"

"No comment," she said.

"Enough," Steven said. "We need to get moving."

"This is impressive work," Malcolm said. "Old-fashioned warfare." He bent over and felt the forehead of the nearest tiger. "Not cold yet." He looked at Steven. "They might not be too far ahead of us."

"Then let's get moving," Kato said. "Elsbeth, help me find the trail, but we're keeping the same formation."

Elsbeth found it a few feet down one of the tunnels leading from the large chamber, and they were off again. They'd been going for days without a break, and she didn't know how much longer she could last. Like Endora, Elsbeth believed they were getting very close to catching up with Sage's group. Regardless, she knew her team needed some rest. She just didn't want to be the first to admit it.

"How long do you expect we'll have to wait?" Sage asked Hieronymus. They'd been hunkered down inside a small cave for almost two hours while a parade of Nephilim giants traveled slowly down a road Hieronymus said they needed to cross.

These giants were a mixture of creatures straight out of fairytales and Greek mythology. Among them were cyclops—more than a dozen, all of which were twenty-five feet tall and had faces so ugly Sage had to turn away. Their single eyes were larger than grapefruits and constantly moving, as though searching for danger.

The ogres weren't quite as big, but their fur made them appear stockier than they really were. They had pointed ears, jowls hanging almost to their chests, and drooping eyes that appeared ready for sleep—but claws that looked ready to attack. Then there were the trolls, grouped together in a pack, strutting down the road, their hands nearly reaching their knees. They wore nothing but loincloths, but even from his hiding place Sage recognized the arrogant expression he'd found so frightening the summer before when he'd battled one and nearly been killed. The trolls made him shrink back just a little.

Hieronymus told Sage that he'd studied the Nephilim enough to know how much each of the Nephilim tribes hated one another. The most territorial of the angelic-blooded evil beasts, he'd said. Just as one pack would pass and Sage thought it was safe to cross the road, they'd see another group coming. There were more Nephilim—by far—in the Territories than the other two races. It was why the Emim and Rephaim so rarely wandered into their territory.

Hieronymus didn't know how long they'd have to wait. Nick had fallen asleep a while ago, and Kaja had been dozing for the past thirty minutes. Ronan was also catching some shut-eye. Sage wasn't sleepy at all.

"So, you've seen a troll," Hieronymus asked Sage. He whispered low enough not to wake the others.

"Last summer," Sage whispered back. "It wasn't a fun experience."

"Some say the Nephilim have more blood from the Watchers than all but the Elioudians," Hieronymus said.

"Why?"

"Because of their size. Legend says the Watchers were enormous. Are enormous. Like the Magog, the giants that guard the

Gate." The scout looked at Sage. "In your vision of the Watchers, does the legend speak truth?"

Sage watched a group of goliaths rumble past below him, as though hardly able to walk upright. He closed his eyes to bring up the vision of the Watchers chained near the fiery pit. "It was more than a vision. They knew I was there." He paused as he tried getting his head around it. "Vale's blood enhanced my gift of Sensing to the point of telepathic connection. At least with them. As soon as I saw them, they stopped struggling against their bindings and looked at me." He shivered at the memory. "As far as their size—huge."

It was hard not to focus on their beauty, he thought but didn't say. A radiance of gold, silver, and bronze had seemed to explode from their skin, which, despite the strange color, was unblemished and stretched tightly against bodies of pure perfection. Their silver hair, long and flowing, fell over shoulders as solid as steel. But it was their eyes that had grabbed Sage's attention most of all. Each had deep pools of liquid blackness that had seemed to penetrate his soul. In the few seconds of his vision, in that moment of eye contact, he'd felt laid bare, examined—almost violated. They knew him now. And he, them. His face went cold at the realization that the Watchers had probed him. They'd left something behind. A knowing. An awareness. A searing of his soul.

"Sage," Hieronymus said. "Did you hear me?"

"What?" Sage looked at him. "I'm sorry. What?"

"What did their chains look like? The Watchers. How were they bound?" Hieronymus frowned. "Are you feeling ill?"

Sage swallowed and tried clearing his head. "No, I'm OK. Um, well, it's funny because as powerful as they are, the chains binding them are small. I mean, small compared to what you'd think they would need. Have you seen angelic chains?"

"I have not."

"Well, it's one of the angelic gifts. A friend of mine, Klaus Cohen, makes them. They have an orange glow. They eat the flesh of evil angelic beasts." He pointed to the never-ending parade of giants below them. "We used one on the troll I fought. And Mammon. I'd be dead without them. Anyway, the chains binding the Watchers look like those. A brighter orange, but not much bigger."

"They are bound by the Almighty," the old scout said. "He with unlimited power needs not much to bind one of his own creations."

"I guess that's true." The chains burned flesh; he'd seen that during his battles. But from what he'd "seen," the chains also seemed to drain strength. Interesting.

"How many different species of giants live down here?" Sage ask after several moments of silence. "How many total giants?"

"It is unknown," Hieronymus said. "I would estimate at least two dozen different clans and a population of several hundred. Maybe a thousand."

"We've probably seen three hundred today," Sage said. "It's unbelievable. Imagine if they ever got to the surface. Wow. Talk about chaos."

"And yet with all their numbers, they do not challenge the Magog. Soon, when we get to the Gate, you will understand why."

Sage knew of the Magog from his lessons about the Battle at the Gate. Despite the legendary danger surrounding them, he was looking forward to laying eyes on them.

"Once the rest of these beasts pass, we should have no trouble reaching the gate," Hieronymus said. "Get some rest."

———

Hieronymus led them through the rest of the Nephilim territory without encountering any other danger. It took several hours to get to the final launching point, but they made it. Most of the journey was uphill and on the edges of the territory. They skirted villages, crawled through gaps in rock formations, stayed in the deepest shadows, and hid more times than Nick could count, while giants passed within spitting distance. They talked little, slept little, and ate little. By the time they reached the mouth of the tunnel that Hieronymus said would take them to the gate, Nick felt energized. Time to go home.

"The Gate leading to Topside must be opened from both sides," Hieronymus told the group. "The entrance on the other side exists within a spiritual realm."

They were huddled in the center of a truck-sized group of boulders. They'd taken a path into the center by squeezing underneath a flat rock resting just two feet above the ground. They rested, ate, repacked their things, and were ready to take the final leg of their journey.

"So how can we get the Magog to open this side?" Nick asked.

"The Nephilim Divine," Kaja said to Hieronymus. "Is that your plan?"

The old scout nodded and looked at Nick. "I will answer your question in time, young Nick, but I must explain the history. The

Nephilim believe that earth was stolen from them. That God never meant for it to be dominated and ruled by the weak human race. Because they survived the great deluge, the Magog think they are destined to rule the surface again. A horde of Nephilim escaped to Topside after the great deluge, before the Archangels could seal the gate. Anak was their leader. Just before leaving, Anak told them that his spirit would one day return and lead them back to the surface. The Nephilim Divine, is what they call it."

"Can I teleport to the other side of the Gate?" Sage asked.

"Yes, for you it would be the easiest way out," Hieronymus said. "When the High Council saw your gift, they knew you had a chance to make it."

"Can I open the gate?" Sage asked.

"No, but you can convince the Archangels guarding it to open it for you." Hieronymus thought for a moment before continuing. "The Prophecy of Seth spoke of your battle against the Seven." He pointed at Nick. "Do you not agree that Nick will become one of your greatest allies in that battle?"

Sage smiled at his brother. "I absolutely agree with that."

"As do I," Ronan said. "What I've seen this week has convinced me of Nick's importance."

"I believe the Archangels guarding the gate will also agree." Hieronymus looked at Kaja. "You are fully versed in the details of the Nephilim Divine?"

"Yes," she said. "I know all there is to know."

"Then you have much information to share with Nick. For of all the illusions he will ever create in his lifetime, his image of Anak will determine whether he lives to create any others."

The rescue team took a short nap, their first real sleep in nearly a week. Then they were off again. They followed the trail left by Kaja, and each time they came upon a resting spot used by Sage and his guides, Elsbeth got more excited. They had closed the gap in a major way. More than once, Sage's grandfather touched items left by his grandsons, and the images were so strong they brought tears to his eyes.

They had just left a covered sleeping area and were passing through a long stretch of open cavern when Kato spoke the words Elsbeth least wanted to hear. "We're being followed," he said. "But don't stop or turn around. Just know that I'm right."

"So, I *was* right," Gavin said.

"You were," Kato said.

They'd had a tense disagreement about it earlier. Kato, bringing up the rear the day before, hadn't seen any signs. But Gavin, who'd been the rear guard before that, had mentioned it several times. He couldn't give specific details; he just knew. Hunter's instinct, he'd called it. Which really set Kato off, since he'd been known as the Council's best hunter for the last four hundred years.

"I'll take my apologies in the form of gold bullion when we get back to London," Gavin said.

"Like you need any more of that," Malcolm said. "You already own enough to back the currency of a small country."

"A penny saved and all that jazz," Gavin said.

"What's following?" Endora asked. "You can count your piggy bank when you get home."

"I don't know what's following," Kato said. "I've seen shadows and dark spots and flashes of light when something passes in front of the ceiling lights. Multiple subjects."

"Should we pick up our pace?" Elsbeth asked. She had no idea of the correct tactics in a situation like this. "Should I teleport back and see what it is?"

"I say press forward," David said. "The blokes have been following us for days. Since they haven't attacked, why provoke them?"

"And it's not like they don't know where we're headed," Gavin said. "It's all about the Great Granite Gate. If they think we can get out, they'll attack then."

"Not that we actually *can* get out," Malcolm said.

"Stop being negative," Endora said. She looked at Gavin and Malcolm both. "Steven, you need to reel in your boys. For the last two days, all we've heard is how we might not get through the gate."

"Well, Endora," Gavin said, "just keeping our expectations in check."

"The Archangels will open it," Endora said. "We battle the evil ones. We are the only ones who do that. They opened it for our ancestors, they will open it for us. How many times must I say it?"

"But will the Magog open it from this side?" Malcolm asked.

"This entire conversation gives me tired-head," Gavin said. He glanced at Elsbeth and winked.

"Yeah, let's drop it," Kato said. "So, we lead all these beasts to the gate. Maybe we can open the gate while the Magog engage them."

They walked in silence for a while, each glancing back every so often. The constant uphill grade was starting to wear Elsbeth out. The gate had to be getting close.

"It might be time to send Elsbeth forward to see if she can catch them," Steven said. "Any objections?"

"Are you sure you can keep track of distance?" Endora asked Elsbeth. "It will be important if you find them."

"Not a problem," Elsbeth said. "Simple addition." She looked forward and saw nothing but empty caverns. The lighting in this part of the Territories was decent, and it appeared they had passed through the most populated part of the Nephilim area already.

"Godspeed, Elsbeth," Gavin said. "Go find those nephews of mine."

"And mine," Malcolm added.

She gave all of them a quick hug, focused on a distant rock a quarter mile ahead, and went there. Looking back, her team was moving again, both Kato and Gavin bringing up the rear, protecting their backside. David and Endora led the way, the Boy with Might with his steel bar propped on one shoulder. Then she looked forward, found Kaja's never-ending trail of corn kernels, and then skipped through space another quarter mile. She'd catch them in no time. She just hoped she wouldn't crush Sage's neck when she threw herself into his arms.

25

Several hours later, once Nick had memorized the information about Anak and repeated back to Hieronymus exactly what he was supposed to do, their party embarked on the home stretch of their escape to Topside. They climbed out of the rock formation, and Hieronymus led them to a natural doorway that opened to a large chamber. He pointed to a wide opening on the far side, and they headed that way.

The Great Granite Gate sat at the end of a two-mile tunnel wide enough to taxi a jetliner through. With a wide, tall, and smooth floor and ceiling, the passageway inclined at more than a 10 percent grade. Bones littered the floor, the skeletons of hundreds of long-dead warriors.

"This is the original tunnel my ancestors dug to escape the great deluge," Hieronymus said. "The Gate ahead is the original granite inundation gate. On the other side is a spiritual realm of unknown origin. Or so legend says."

"So, they herded all those animals through a spiritual realm before the flood?" Nick asked. "How'd that work?"

"The entrance was put into a spiritual realm *after* the flood," Hieronymus said. "According to our histories, God can expand and contract His realm as needed. After the Battle at the Gate, part of sealing it from the surface was to remove it from the human realm."

"I'm a little confused by that," Ronan said. "What kind of spiritual realm is it? It can't be Godspace. Surely. And I can't imagine Archangels residing in part of the Dark realm. So, what is it?" He looked at Sage. "Is there a third type of spiritual realm? Did Leah ever mention such a thing?"

"No." Sage looked at Hieronymus. "Is there a spiritual realm both angels and Dark beasts can occupy at the same time?"

"Legend describes it as an unknown entity. It is possible our director of historical studies could answer your question. We know little of what lies on the other side of the gate." Hieronymus fell silent as they continued through a maze of giant skeletons.

Sage glanced at Nick, who smiled. "We're almost home," Sage whispered to his younger brother. "So close I can almost taste it."

"I spent many years watching how often the Nephilim used this passageway," Hieronymus said. "I spent decades spying and listening to the stories they passed on to their children. They consider this entire tunnel a holy place, haunted by the spirits of their dead ancestors." He waved at the bones still lying undisturbed. "Except for the guards keeping watch at the gate, I've seen no Nephilim trespass upon this sacred ground."

"These bones should be dust by now," Ronan said. "If they're thousands of years old."

"Their bones have a strength you do not understand," Hieronymus said.

"As do ours," Kaja interjected.

"True," Hieronymus agreed. "The Magog live underneath this very passage and bring supplies to the guards at the gate using a side tunnel that leads to a small village we used to call Adam, for it was the first village established in our new homeland. We have a new Adam now, but they still refer to the original village by that name."

During the nearly hour-long uphill walk to the Gate, Hieronymus explained that two guards were always present at the Gate, but only one would be awake and paying attention. The guarding of the Gate was a position of honor for the Magog. They trained for many years to build strength and endurance, operating under the assumption that the Rephaim could appear and attack at any time. The guards served one-hundred-year cycles and typically did three cycles in a lifetime.

Once they arrived, Nick saw what Hieronymus had earlier described. On the left side of the wall stood a structure with three walls and no door, windows, or roof; it was simply a place for the sleeping giant. The bottoms of two truck-sized feet hung off the end of a crude bed.

On the right was an enormous wooden chair. In the direct center of the wall was a keyhole at least five feet tall and two feet wide. The guard standing post, absent at the moment, would be wearing the key around his neck. Only after the key was inserted and turned could the Archangels on the other side open the gate.

Hieronymus had them hide behind the battered skull of a dead giant. He pointed to the far right, beyond the chair. "See the cave opening there? It leads down a set of stairs to old Adam. The guard is either making a food run or using the necessary closet." He looked at Nick. "Once he comes back, you must begin your illusion. Are you ready?"

"I'm ready."

"Good. Then we will wait for the guard's return."

———

Elsbeth stopped at a natural opening that led to a tunnel wide enough for a fleet of trucks. Though dimly lit, it illuminated a grade she was glad she didn't have to climb. She teleported forward another quarter mile and marveled at the number of skeletons littering the ground.

Her heart quickened. She'd read about the Battle at the Gate numerous times and knew how close she was. This tunnel was part of the battleground. She teleported to the most distant spot she could see, and then she saw it: the Gate. Half a mile away. The tunnel lights ended against a solid slab of stone. She didn't see Sage's group, but she knew they were up there somewhere. She went another quarter mile. Then a hundred yards. She saw them hiding inside the skull of a giant, so she teleported directly inside.

"Elsbeth!" Sage almost shouted. He grabbed her into a bear hug just as Kaja drew her sword.

"No, Kaja," Nick said. "It's Elsbeth. She came to rescue us."

Elsbeth burst into tears as Sage gripped her in a fierce hug. "I knew you'd come," he whispered, his voice breaking. "I knew it!" He squeezed her again, and she felt tears smear against her cheek. Nick patted her on the back and tried getting into the middle of the hug.

She didn't know how long they stood there, but Sage eventually pulled away and looked at her. His eyes were swimming, and he wiped them before speaking. "How many came with you?"

"Six others."

"Did Grandpa come?" Nick asked.

She tousled his hair. "What do you think? Of course." She broke out of Sage's grip and hugged Nick long and hard. She smiled at Ronan. "I'm so glad all of you are safe."

"So, you can teleport like Sage," Nick said. "Wish I could do that."

She looked at Sage and raised her eyebrows. "Yeah, he knows," Sage said. "Which is a good thing, because how else would he understand his own gift?"

Elsbeth's jaw dropped. "What? The Elioudians we spoke to back at Seth didn't mention that."

"He's angelic-human," Sage said, as he smiled at his brother. "But I'm not telling you what it is. You'll just have to see it to believe it." He turned. "Meet our guides, Hieronymus and Kaja, the real heroes of this trip."

Elsbeth stepped forward and gave both hard hugs. "Kaja, I can't believe you continued leaving a trail with everything you've been through."

Kaja's bashful smile made her appear younger than she had just a moment before when she had been about to draw her sword.

"Sage wouldn't let me forget. He must have reminded me five hundred times. He knew you would come."

"Who else is here?" Sage asked. "Where are they?"

She rattled off the names. "They're about three miles back. We're being followed. No doubt about it."

Hieronymus looked around the edge of the skull toward the tunnel leading to old Adam. Then he looked at the gate and spoke to Sage. "The gate will only be open for a short time. Seconds. After the giant comes out of that tunnel, we'll need to wait until the rest of your rescue team arrives before we make our move." To Elsbeth. "Can you go back and have them hurry?"

"I'll go with her," Sage said. He drew his sword and held out a hand for Elsbeth. "You take lead."

Elsbeth said, "Ready? We'll go in two-hundred-yard increments to make sure we end up in the same place each time. First, that giant arm bone sticking out of the ground. The one leaning at a forty-five degree angle. See it?"

He nodded, and they went away. After several more jumps, they finally appeared fifty feet ahead of the team. It took a moment for their presence to register, but once it did, the group swarmed Sage. Elsbeth stood aside while Steven nearly tackled his grandson, tears streaming. Sage threw his arms around him. Then the group took turns slapping him on the back, shaking his hand, and tousling his hair.

"We need to go," Elsbeth said. "Now."

"How fast can you run?" Sage asked, looking at them all.

"Probably not as fast as the beasts following us," Kato said. "But fast enough."

"Hieronymus doesn't think they'll attack until the gate opens," Sage said. "I agree. If they've been following you as far as Elsbeth thinks, they won't reveal themselves now. Still, we need to get moving."

"Steven," Endora said. "Set the pace."

"No problem," Steven said. "Elsbeth, lead the way. Sage, watch our backside, and let us know what's going on."

"Got it," Sage said. "Now go. And hurry!"

Elsbeth went ahead, skipping forward in chunks while the team made their run. They slowed considerably when they hit the tunnel leading to the gate. She tried keeping an eye on Sage, but she didn't see him at all. He'd disappeared as soon as the group headed out and hadn't reported back for a check-in.

Twenty-five minutes later, and fifty yards from the giant skull where Nick and Ronan waited, Elsbeth appeared in front of Steven and stopped the group. "Take cover behind that pile of bones," she said. "Let me talk to Hieronymus before we approach."

"OK," Steven said. He bent over, gasped for breath, and practically staggered to the hiding place. The others followed.

Before Elsbeth could go, Sage appeared next to her. "We've got major trouble coming. Major trouble."

"What?" Endora asked.

"Several Rephaim," Sage said. "Hundreds of Emim beasts. Two miles back but coming fast."

David and Kato looked at each other and shook their heads. "I like my bar," David said. "But I'm not going to kid myself. We're in trouble, mates."

"I've gotta tell Hieronymus," Sage said. "We've gotta get that gate open. Now! Be right back."

Sage disappeared. Elsbeth motioned toward the pile of bones. "We need to hide."

The team had just hidden themselves when Sage appeared next to his grandfather. "Hieronymus wants all of you to stay where you are," he whispered loudly enough for everyone to hear. "He said when the beasts arrive, a horde of Magog will race up the tunnel and slaughter them all. So just stay here and watch. But . . . as soon as the gate opens, regardless of what's going on, sprint as hard as you can. For now, be quiet." He put a hand on his grandfather's shoulder. "Watch Nick in action, Grandpa. You *absolutely* will not believe it!" Steven frowned and started to say something, but Sage just smiled and disappeared.

"Nick has a gift?" Steven asked Elsbeth. "Is that what he just said?"

"It is," Elsbeth said. "He broke the news to me right after I arrived but wouldn't tell me what it is. I guess we'll find out together."

Just a few minutes after Sage teleported back into the skull, Nick heard the giant: his footfalls on the stairs heading up, heavy breathing, an occasional grunt. Then he smelled it—an overwhelming outhouse-like odor. When the beast stepped from the cave, Nick's heart nearly stopped. The monster was a hundred feet tall with a head the size of a Cadillac. Hair hung to the middle of his back; a tangled mess of greasy strands covered his shoulders. His curly black body hair was long enough to braid, but it was his face that sent a shiver of fear to Nick's gut. It wasn't so much sunken—the flat nose, the wide eyes, the chin that highlighted his underbite—it looked more like he'd been run over by a tractor and been left with a face as flat as a dinner plate. Wide scars ran across his forehead and down his cheeks, burn marks ravaged the skin around his eyes, and dozens of large moles with strands of hair growing out of them dotted his chin and neck.

"His name is Doric," Hieronymus whispered into Nick's ear. "Son of Heda, brother of Boran. Those scars are a product of Boran's rage. He is in his second guard cycle."

Nick stared at the giant as he thundered over to his chair and sat down. The air seemed to vibrate as the beast breathed in and out.

"How do you know all that?" Sage asked.

Hieronymus cocked his head and gave Sage a puzzled look. "We know all of the Magog guards and many from the other Nephilim races. Learning them was one of my primary tasks while exploring the Territories. 'Know thine enemy, saith the Lord.'"

"Never heard of *that* verse," Sage said under his breath.

"Doric hates his brother," Hieronymus told Nick. "He despises his father for allowing Boran to abuse him. He wishes Boran dead so that he will get the birthright." He grabbed Nick's arm and squeezed. "Can you weave all of that information into what you know of Anak?"

Nick had to think about it, but he thought he could. "Yeah, I think I've got it."

Hieronymus looked at Sage. "You must get to the center of the gate before teleporting. The Archangels hover just on the other said. They should open the gate for you. You must make sure you teleport only after Doric turns the key."

Ronan clamped a hand on Sage's shoulder. "You've got this."

"I do," Sage said. "No doubt."

"Then it is time to proceed. Nick, take as much time as you need, but remember that other beasts are on their way." Hieronymus maneuvered to the left and crawled through an eye socket into the giant skull, where he joined Sage and Kaja. Ronan climbed in after him.

Nick was alone outside the skull, listening to the giant's heavy breathing. He knew the rescue team was hidden somewhere in a pile of bones behind them, but he couldn't see them from where he sat. He took several cleansing breaths, reviewing all the information he would need to fool the giant. They had planned carefully—step building upon step.

They were fifty yards from the wall, far enough to throw their hiding place into deep shadows. Nick felt safe where he was and would only crawl into the skull if the giant decided to step onto what the Magog considered to be sacred ground. After a period of mental calisthenics, he finally felt ready. He leaned back against the skull and closed his eyes. "I'm about to start. Phase one. A voice from the past."

Doric.

The disembodied voice would echo through the chamber softly, bouncing off the walls and reverberating in and around the bones. Nick wished he could hear what it sounded like.

Doric.

The giant grunted, a surprised utterance much louder than the voice that called his name.

Doric, son of Heda, brother of Boran, your faithfulness has awakened my spirit. Nick raised the volume by three clicks on his imaginary amplifier.

"Who goes there?" A thunderous roar blasted from the wall.

Doric, son of Heda, brother of Boran, your faithfulness has awakened my spirit! Nick heard two stomps and felt the ground vibrate beneath him.

"Who goes there?" Doric shouted again, his voice a little closer than before. "Is it Rephaim wizardry?"

I have finally returned. The time is now. Your destiny can at last be fulfilled.

"Identify yourself," the giant shouted. "Show yourself."

I am Anak, leader of the Nephilim Expedition. Your faithfulness has been pure.

The stomping stopped. Nick heard a gasp. "The Divine," the giant mumbled under his breath.

Nick imagined swirling winds growing from within the Magog skeleton nearest the wall. It was halfway between the skull where they all sat hiding and the shack where the other giant lay sleeping. The funnel grew steadily, rising higher and higher toward the ceiling while gaining in width and strength.

From the remains of my fallen brethren, I return to seek those whose faithfulness has proven true.

When the funnel reached a hundred feet in the air, Nick imagined a face forming, lips moving as the disembodied voice found a home.

You, Doric, son of Heda, whose birthright rests within the beating heart of another, are the one I seek.

"It is not possible," Doric said. His voice rattled with uncertainty.

We ruled the humans once, young Doric, and will rule them yet again.

Nick formed Anak's face fully with the swirling winds of the funnel: broad forehead, high cheekbones, wide and powerful jawline, tight, narrow lips, and penetrating, commanding eyes.

"Boran does not believe," Doric said, hate spewing at the mention of his brother's name. "Yet he lords his birthright over me. Only believers deserve the honor of a birthright."

I, Anak, fathered many sons, but none as powerful as you. My spirit has waited these many centuries to reveal itself. The time has come to use the key.

The ground vibrated as Doric began pacing. "I will die to protect the key," he said.

As your faithfulness commands!

The rest of Anak's body formed within the swirling winds. Taller and wider than Doric, it wore the classic outfit of a Greek god—beautiful reds, deep blues, and magnificent greens. Nick added a breastplate and forearm and shin guards, giving the giant the look of a royal centurion. As his body formed fully, the dust from the whirlwind fell away, leaving only Anak's visage for Doric to focus on.

Tell me of the Moab Commandment, young Doric.

"It is our most revered commandment," Doric said. "Never to leave my lips."

Do you fear this to be Rephaim wizardry?

"We are cautioned to consider such things." The giant's voice held less certainty than before. "You are Nephilim," Doric said. "Should I repeat for you what you should know already?"

The most closely kept commandment within the annals of Nephilim history should not be repeated except within the presence of like others. You have again demonstrated your worthiness of the birthright. Yes, I know the commandment: deceived by blood, destroyed by faith. Led by the Divine we rise again from death, entrusted because of our faithfulness. You have shown that faithfulness, Doric, and it is time to use the key.

"You speak the hallowed words of the Magog priests," Doric said, "but the Rephaim wizards have tricked us before."

You have heard of the Fallen Guard, Doric? Nick smiled as he heard the great giant draw in a sharp breath.

"You rose from within his very bones," Doric said.

What do your leaders say of his death?

"That he fell victim to Rephaim sorcery."

He fell victim to his unwillingness to grasp his own birthright. The Nephilim Divine speaks of three attempts by Anak to again lead his people back to the surface. Do you not know the details of the Divine?

"Every guard knows of the Divine," Doric said with a hint of indignation. "It is part of our most basic training."

The Fallen Guard was my first attempt. You are the second. Should you fail your test of faithfulness, I will next rise from within YOUR bones. Hieronymus had told Nick that the Elioudians believed that the Fallen Guard died from a sudden medical condition but that the Magog believed it to be the evil work of the Rephaim.

"The sorcery of the Rephaim—"

Would the Rephaim have left the key around the neck of the Fallen Guard, young Doric? Like you, Tron did not believe the very eyes within his head. So, he fell, and I waited until I again found someone worthy of a birthright. Nick wiped a bead of sweat off his brow. He felt relaxed, the image of Anak held strong within his mind. The information Hieronymus had given him was proving invaluable.

"What will happen if I unlock the gate?" Doric asked. "It cannot be opened from this side."

The first crack in the dam! His heart suddenly racing, Nick took several breaths to calm himself. *After my escape, the Elioudians sent a group to the surface to battle us, the Rephaim, and the Emim. They called this group the Angelic Response Council. Their activities are recorded within the annals of our history.*

"We have all been trained to watch for Elioudian wickedness," Doric grumbled.

We have a spy within the Angelic Response Council who has the ear of the Archangels standing guard on the other side of the gate. It is a boy, a false prophet, a spirit who takes human form and can appear upon my command.

"You control a spirit?" Doric asked. "I have heard nothing in my training about this."

Your doubt sounds eerily like that of the Fallen Guard. Yet here I stand within his decaying bones.

Doric stammered. "I . . . I do not question the spirit of the great Anak, yet you are but a spirit. The Archangels will not be fooled by the spirit of a mere child."

Then I will summon him here to draw your blood.

"Go, Sage," Nick heard Hieronymus whisper. "Give him a taste of your sword. Command his appearance, Nick."

Present yourself before me, Hercules, and show this doubter the power of Anak! The voice of Anak boomed within Nick's imagination.

"Who is this?" Doric asked. "You bear a sword . . . Ah! You have stabbed me!" The ground vibrated when the giant stomped his foot. "Again, you cut me!" Another vibration rocked the ground.

Enough, Hercules. Wait near the keyhole until I give your next command.

"What is this trickery?" Doric raged. "Your human boy stabbed a guard of the gate!"

I give you one chance to turn the key, young Doric, before you fall dead where you stand and I am forced to wait to find another so worthy of a birthright!

"You are sure I will receive a birthright if the gate opens and I leave this place?" Doric's voice sounded cautious but full of hope.

You will rule armies and be a giver of birthrights. Time runs short. The boy spy is already being missed within the human world. Turn the key so I can send him to fool the Archangels. Once the gate is open, the Nephilim will again rule the humans, and prophecy will be fulfilled.

"I did not like being stabbed, human scum. When I sit at my throne on Topside, I will remember your arrogance."

Nick heard footsteps pounding toward the middle of the gate. He practically held his breath in anticipation.

"He has taken the key from around his neck," Kaja whispered to Nick from inside the skull. "He is sliding it into the hole. He is turning the key. Now, Nick, command Sage to go. Doric has made three complete revolutions of the key."

Go, Hercules, convince the Archangels to open the gate. Young Doric, step well back, for the fire of the Archangels will roast you where you stand. Only I have the power to extinguish their flames from Heaven!

"Prepare, young Nick," Hieronymus said. "Like before, you must keep the image strong while I carry you."

26

Elsbeth and the rest of the team sat spellbound at what had transpired in front of them. She heard Endora gasp, watched as tears slid down Steven's face. Gavin and Malcolm gave each other quiet high fives as soon as they witnessed the whirlwind of dust transformation.

"The gift of Illusion," Kato whispered beside her, never taking his eyes off the drama.

David almost laughed out loud when Nick called Sage Hercules, forcing Elsbeth to shush him. Only she kept watch behind them, desperate to find any sign of the beasts who would attack as soon as the gate cracked open. She didn't see anything, although it didn't mean they weren't there.

"He's turning the key," Malcom whispered. "Get ready."

"As soon as Sage disappears, get ready to sprint," Steven said. "As soon as that gate moves, move!"

The giant's footsteps grew closer, but Nick sat quietly with his eyes closed, giving all his focus to keeping the image of Anak strong and powerful. He didn't really fear being discovered, because he knew Doric's attention was fully on the gate, but he still needed to back the giant up more. Or send him away.

Go into the depths, and bring assistance, Doric. I will destroy the Archangels that guard the gate, but they will summon help. You will need all the might of the Magog to leave this place.

"But I want to watch—"

Go! Quickly! The gate will open within moments!

After a frustrated sigh, Doric moved toward the tunnel leading to old Adam. With each step he took, the better Nick felt.

A sudden grinding sound filled the chamber. The floor vibrated. Nick opened his eyes. The entire chamber began glowing from the red flames of the Archangels' heavenly swords.

"The gate opens," Kaja whispered. "Doric has not yet descended into the tunnel."

"And we will not waste time," Hieronymus said. He climbed through an eye socket and peeled the pack off his back. He bent over Nick and looked him straight in the eyes. "You are Nick the Brave. Never have I met any such as you and your brother. You are the hope for the Angelic Response Council. I pray that we will one day meet again."

Nick choked up, and he knew the image of Anak was gone.

Gavin and Malcolm exploded from their hiding place first, with Endora and Kato on their heels. Steven and David were only moments behind. Elsbeth knew she could teleport straight through the gate, so she watched behind them.

Seconds later the entire tunnel came alive with Emim beasts and monsters as they also burst from hiding places within the bones of the long-dead Magog giants. Hundreds of beasts, streaming up the tunnel in a frenzy, nearly froze her in place. Then she saw the Rephaim—at least a dozen—flying low above the crowd, black wings spread, eyes glowing red, pointing and motioning and barking commands in a language she didn't understand. One was noticeably larger than the others. It flew in the center, claws out, clutching a sword in one hand.

Elsbeth spun around and looked at the giant. He was their only hope, but he didn't even realize he was about to be attacked because he was so focused on the gate. She looked at his partner, the one sleeping through all the commotion. She took a deep breath and teleported away as the leading edge of the horde got within a few hundred yards.

She appeared on the chest of the sleeping giant, drew her sword, and jammed it straight into his chest. His eyes jerked opened, and his hand came up and slapped his chest. By then Elsbeth was already next to his right ear.

"You're being attacked!" she screamed. "Get up. Doric needs you!"

"What is this!" Doric roared as he spun toward the herd of beasts stampeding toward him.

"Ring the bell," shouted the other giant. He rose from his bed and grabbed his sword. "The battle begins anew! Ring the bell!"

Elsbeth didn't wait to see what that meant. She teleported to the slowly opening gate as Hieronymus yanked Nick onto his shoulder, burst into the open, and raced full speed toward her, Kaja and Ronan at his side. Behind them, still well ahead of the beasts storming toward the gate, was Elsbeth's team. Seconds later they all slithered through into a scorched landscape that stretched for miles. Even worse than the Dark realm surrounding Mammon's prison the summer before, the sky was the color of drying blood, a tapestry of mottled reds and blacks that shifted and merged within itself like some alien, flesh-eating bacteria. The sulfur-tinged air was hot and sticky, with soft winds coming from everywhere at once.

Elsbeth looked back into the chamber. The sleeping giant shouted again. "Ring the bell, Doric! We will be slaughtered." He jumped forward and swung his sword in a low arc, catching three minotaurs midchest, cutting them in half. Then two gargoyles attacked the giant's eyes, and a third slammed into his jugular vein with the force of a missile.

Doric saw the attack and ran over, grabbed the gargoyle off his partner's neck, and crushed it in his fist. An instant later he ripped the other two in half. "Therdum, we must close the gate," Doric said. "I will ring the bell!"

But Doric would have no chance to ring the bell. He fell under the weight of a hundred beasts. Therdum staggered toward Doric and swung his sword in a blur of motion. Each swing cut down several beasts, but dozens more avoided his blows and attacked. A few seconds later, he was down also.

The gate was nearly three feet wide now and getting larger. If it got much bigger, it would take a while to close. Dozens of beasts could escape. The Archangels, bigger than any angels Elsbeth had ever seen, stood straight and tall and floated several feet off the ground. Their flaming swords shot fire at a round four-foot indentation in the middle of the gate. A wheel with arcane writing and a symbol of the Alpha and Omega—the beginning and the end—turned slowly as the heat of the flames somehow activated its rotation. At the moment the Alpha and Omega symbols seemed a macabre joke to Elsbeth: the beasts residing inside the Gate had nearly destroyed humanity at the beginning and would do so again at the end.

"Stop!" Sage shouted to one of the Archangels. "We're all out! Close the gate!" He pointed at black smudges in the distant sky. "Close the gate! Hurry!" The gate stopped opening at four feet, but it didn't close.

"The Magog have to close it," Hieronymus said as he put Nick down. He looked to the sky and his eyes went wide. "Rephaim."

"Probably Belphegor," Sage said, "since he set this entire thing into motion. Elsbeth, take a stand! Use Persuasion to hold them off! Everybody else, get ready."

She clenched her teeth, raised a palm toward heaven, and let the power flow into her. "Use me," she whispered, "for there is power in Your name." Light that she couldn't see at first but that solidified as it grew in intensity punched through the red sky and rained down into her upraised palm. A current of purity circulated within the marrow of her bones, pushed up and out, and built strength as it traveled along her nerve centers. Just before a ray of purity exploded out of her other palm, aimed at the approaching horde of Rephaim, a solidness gripped her—a peace so complete and all-encompassing that her fear of the approaching beasts meant nothing. She let loose with a beam of light that missed the huge Rephaim in the center but knocked others around him from the sky. The largest beast redirected his path toward them, which would give Elsbeth's team some time.

"We must prevent the beasts from escaping," Hieronymus said.

"We need a giant to close the gate," Kaja said.

Elsbeth glanced back at her team. They were in a defensive position against the approaching Rephaim, but they also had to worry about the beasts approaching the gate from inside. She shot another blast of light into the sky, and the Rephaim scattered even more. The largest of the beasts, Belphegor, turned away but didn't go far.

"Endora and I will protect the open gate," David said. He raised his bar for battle. "Endora, are you ready?"

"Sage, you must ring the Magog bell," Hieronymus said. "It will bring more giants from below. Topside cannot survive if these beasts escape. Only the Magog can defeat so many."

"Got some smaller giants coming!" Gavin shouted.

Elsbeth saw an entire herd of smaller giants—cyclops, trolls, and ogres—sprinting toward them, armed with clubs or swords. Endora elbowed David out of her way, positioned herself in the opening, and gave the herd a sample of Voice. Dozens of beasts skidded to a stop and grabbed their ears. Several fell over onto their sides, stunned into immovable statues.

"Sage, go," Hieronymus said. "The bell is above the passageway leading to old Adam. If you can't get to it, you'll have to teleport into the village below and alert them. These beasts will overpower your friends."

"Nick," Kaja said. "Can you create an illusion of a Magog? Can you draw some of the beasts away from the gate?"

Nick's eyes, wide and terrified, were full of tears, but he nodded. "I think I can."

"Steven," Elsbeth said. "Take him to a place where he can concentrate." She glanced back at Belphegor and shot another blast toward him, but he skittered away, unharmed. "Everybody, the battle is about to begin. Let's do this."

Sage teleported into the fray, landing on top of the chair Doric had been sitting on when they arrived an hour ago. Both giants were down now, and the army of Rephaim and Emim creatures were huddled well away from the few that lay stunned on the ground near the gate, victims of Endora's Voice.

Brother Gadrell.

Yes, Belphegor.

I am nearly there. The girl with Light prevents my approach. You must free yourself, kill the girl, and join me outside the gate.

Sage froze. What was this? Where had that come from? He shook his head and looked around. The chaos around him revealed no answers. Had he imagined it? Nick? No, impossible. His brother was busy conjuring up something else. He shrugged it off and looked up. Nearly fifty feet above him, hanging at the end of a thick rope, was a bell twice the size of the Liberty Bell.

I cannot get close to the gate, Belphegor. The Singer's stunning voice thwarts all, but I am safe. My disciples protect me.

Beware of the angel boy, Gadrell. He is somewhere within the cavern.

Sage hesitated again. This was real. A conversation between the Prince of Sloth and one of the Rephaim within the chamber. He visually searched the cavern again. Deep in the shadows, away from the direction of Endora's Voice, he saw a line of smaller Rephaim lined up in front of one nearly twice their size and identical to Belphegor. Gadrell, brother to Belphegor? Was that possible? How was Sage intercepting their telepathic communication?

Vale's blood. Mammon had telepathically influenced Sage last summer, and he'd been saved only after Elsbeth blasted Sage with Persuasion, so he knew telepathic communication was the Rephaim race's primary means of communication. This was different. His enhanced gift was intercepting messages *not* meant for or aimed toward him.

Kill the singer, Gadrell. You must escape while the gate remains open. I will arrive soon and join the fight.

Shouting from below drew Sage's attention. He saw several creatures pointing at him. Two wolf men screeched and launched themselves into the air. Sage drew his sword and waited until the last possible moment. He felt supercharged. Confident. Indestructible. Fearless.

"Come on," he shouted. "Give me your best shot."

The beasts opened their claws and jaws and screeched a war cry that echoed through the cavern. Just as the first claw hit Sage's chest, he shoved his sword forward and teleported away, landing on top of the bell above his head. He'd left his sword behind, the point sticking out the middle of the monster's back. It fell to the ground, a scream dying in its throat. The other beast pulled up, confused about where Sage had gone. Endora's Voice suddenly grew louder as she stepped back into the cavern.

"No, Endora!" Sage shouted. "Get back outside! They're going to kill you!"

She didn't listen. She inched forward and belted her stunning gift like a foghorn, driving the beasts farther from the gate. The other winged wolf man attacking Sage tried to escape, but it screamed and stiffened, dropped, and bounced against Doric's chair, landing in a heap next to the dead one.

"Get your sword and ring the bell," Endora shouted between verses of song. "Hurry, I can't keep them away much longer."

Sage teleported to the ground, pulled his sword free, and went back up, placing his feet solidly on each side of the bell. He swung his sword as hard as he could, then hit it again and again.

Hurry, Gadrell. The gate will soon close. I cannot defeat Lucifer without you.

Soon, brother, we will strike the Singer down.

"Get out, Endora," Sage shouted between rings. "They're about to attack you!"

A roar sounded from behind the horde of beasts, near one of the largest skeletal remains. It rose in volume until it nearly drowned out Endora's Voice. A great monster formed from within the rocks of a cavern wall and began struggling against its stone imprisonment, fighting and pushing and grunting as though finally freed after thousands of years. Thirty feet tall with spindly legs, ten arms with giant pincers, and an oblong, curved head, it had gallons of mucus dripping from its snout and slimly oil covering its bright-purple skin. It belted a growl as loud as the foghorn of a ship and showed multiple rows of razor-sharp teeth.

Nick. His warped imagination was at play again, delaying things until the Magog arrived. Sage smiled as every monster in the chamber turned toward it. Most pushed away from the illusion, including those nearest the gate who weren't already stunned by Voice. But the cyclops and trolls attacked, wielding their clubs in a flurry of blows. When their weapons met nothing but air, the momentum of their swings toppled them forward. Waves of confusion rippled through the witnessing beasts.

"Sage, hurry," shouted Gavin from outside the gate. "Elsbeth's trying, but the Rephaim out here are getting closer."

Sage rang the bell over and over, and the sound roiled through the cavern in waves. He glanced at the gate and saw a glow from the fiery swords of the Archangels. Endora still sang, while David waited at the threshold of the gate, ready to beat any beast that somehow made it through. Nick's imaginary monster was being ignored now. The beasts turned away once the attacking trolls shouted something in a guttural language Sage didn't understand.

"We need you out here, Sage!" Elsbeth shouted, her voice small through the gate.

Yet still he rang the bell. He put every bit of strength into his swings and wondered if the Magog would ever hear it. When the ground began shaking with the thunder of footsteps climbing the stairs, when the roars of indignation came from deep within the ground, he knew help was coming. Nearly every head in the chamber turned toward the side passage.

"Let's go, mate," David shouted as Endora paused for breath again. "You got those wankers' attention. Time to mosey along. Now."

"Meet you outside," Sage shouted back.

Endora backed toward the open gate, aiming her gift in all directions, her neck straining from the effort, her face red and angry and determined. Sage glanced at the Rephaim Belphegor called Gadrell, still protected by the row of smaller Rephaim. The beast lifted his nonsword hand, roared, and threw a spear Sage didn't notice until it was too late. It hit Endora center chest and threw her back against the gate. The sick sound of the spearhead against her flesh seemed louder than humanly possible. She rolled over, bloody steel protruding from her back. Her stunning gift fell silent. The crowd of beasts charged the gate.

Elsbeth screamed. "Noooo!" She ran to the gate opening, her face a mask of horror and rage. She raised a hand toward heaven, shouted something Sage couldn't hear, and let forth a blast of blinding Persuasion that ripped through the crowd of oncoming beasts like a futuristic ray gun. "Help me. David! Help me! Get Endora!"

Although nearly two dozen beasts fell from Elsbeth's blast of purity, dozens more rolled toward her in a wave of destruction. Sage saw Gadrell pushing forward, grabbing smaller beasts and shoving them into his path to protect himself from the killing light.

The Magog were storming up from their underground city, but they didn't sound close enough to stop Gadrell from getting out. Sage couldn't let that happen. The beast appeared every bit as powerful as the Princes Topside. Gadrell rose to the ceiling of the chamber and headed toward the gate. Elsbeth again hit the oncoming wave with her light, but she wasn't looking up. Gadrell was seconds from escaping.

Sage teleported onto Gadrell's back and plunged his sword into the base of his right wing. The beast screamed and spun, raking his sword behind him. He caught Sage in his left shoulder. Sage started to fall but repositioned himself just as Gadrell spun again. The beast stopped in midair, feet from the gate but high off the ground, and Sage struck with his sword again. Gadrell spun a third time, this time twisting and curving his upper body into a spring and launching himself toward the floor. Sage bounced against the beast's back and nearly fell off, yet he stabbed out with his sword and caught a piece of Gadrell's face, tearing a gash from his ear across his cheek and ending at his mouth. The wound spurted blood as he screamed and raged.

Sage heard his name being shouted from below, but the noise of the cavern overwhelmed the rest. Again, Gadrell spun and twisted, jerked and rotated, trying to throw Sage off. They were still at least fifty feet from the floor, and Sage caught a glimpse of Elsbeth aiming her upraised palm in his direction. Sage nearly got another stab in but missed when Gadrell shot high into the air. A blast of Persuasion missed until Gadrell flew directly into its beam, taking a shot in the side of his head. The light of purity enveloped Gadrell's face and the blood gushing from the wound, some of which splashed into Sage's eyes, nose, and mouth. He swallowed some before he realized what he'd done. Nearly gagging, he tried spitting it out, but he felt his throat burn as the blood slid deeper into his body.

A second blast of light hit Gadrell in the chest and threw him toward the gate. He tumbled out of control. Just as the beast crashed into the edge of the open door and spun out into the spiritual realm, Sage teleported away. He landed back on the bell. He spit and stuck a finger down his throat to try and make himself vomit, but nothing would come up. The taste of Gadrell's blood, infused with Elsbeth's Persuasion, made him lightheaded. More than that, the inside of his head tingled like a virus had attacked his brain.

"Behind you, Elsbeth!" David roared.

Sage looked at the doorway. Elsbeth spun around and shot light high into the air. "Sage," she shouted. "Get out here!"

He teleported next to Endora's body and tried dragging her toward the gate, but he didn't get a chance. David grabbed him around the waist, ripped him away from her, and threw him several feet outside. Seconds later, beasts fell upon Endora in a flurry of claws and fangs. Her body was violently yanked into the cavern and disappeared in a mist of blood and gore.

Now outside the gate, David turned and pushed his bar sideways across the opening, waist high. "I'll hold them in! Elsbeth, hit them with some light!"

She spun back toward the horde of beasts and raised her palm toward heaven. The blinding light exploded into the snarling monsters with a brilliance that forced Sage to turn his head away. The collective screams of the beasts nearly overpowered the roar of the first Magog coming from the bottom of the stairwell.

Sage joined Gavin, Kato, Ronan, Malcolm, Hieronymus, and Kaja, protecting Elsbeth and David's backside. He glanced over to the side, where Grandpa, sword in hand, protected Nick, who cowered behind him. Their group was caught between the beasts trying to escape the Gate and Belphegor and his offspring. The Prince of Sloth had more than twenty beasts with him, over twice the number Mammon had brought with him last summer to defeat Sage and his smaller team. The offspring, much smaller than the Prince of Sloth, hovered like missile-armed helicopter drones, waiting for just the right moment to attack, while Belphegor tended to Gadrell, who lay on the ground at his brother's feet, his face ravaged by Sage's wound and the effects of Persuasion upon it.

An explosion of rage blasted from within the cavern. "What is this! You attack our Gate!"

"Magog," David shouted back to the rest. "One . . . no, two . . . three of them. Four. And another. Those are some huge fighters. Would love to have *their* strength."

"We are attacked!" one of the giants boomed.

Some of the beasts turned and headed toward the giants, but some edged closer to the open gate. "They're coming again!" David said, readying his bar. "Get ready!"

Three of the Magog, each armed with clubs the size of small trees, began swinging them in a wild frenzy. The Emim creatures didn't run and hide like Sage thought they might. They attacked.

"Watch out!" David said, as he pulled Elsbeth away from the doorway. "Get back, everybody!"

A stampede of beasts, chased by one of the Magog, nearly trampled Sage and his team. They all hit the ground as more than three dozen creatures made it through before a Magog stepped in front of the gate and swung his club back and forth along the ground, crushing every beast in its path. The Magog didn't stop everything from escaping. Several winged creatures flew to the highest part of the gate and made it out.

"Elsbeth, up there!" Sage shouted.

She hit a gargoyle with Persuasion before it got twenty feet out the door, but several others escaped in opposite directions. Winged wolf men got out, at least four ahools, and three of the same breed of a creature Sage had never seen before. None of them stopped to join Belphegor's battle. Within seconds they had disappeared in the distant sky in all directions. He saw two cyclops—a male and female—a half-dozen chimeras, some minotaurs, a small group of Belphei, a few youst—even bigger than the one Ronan had killed within minutes of his and Sage's arrival in the Wastelands—and several novence, the small goblins that had tried to snatch Nick from the minotaurs. The entire herd fled away from the gate, leaving Belphegor and his offspring alone to defeat Sage and his team. They sought the freedom they had long been denied, unwilling to risk death for the Prince of Sloth.

A resounding thud from behind startled Sage. The Great Granite Gate had finally been closed, blocking out the furious battle raging inside. Too late.

Kill the boy, Belphegor. I am unable to fight. Fire rages through my body. We cannot rule with him hunting us.

Sage climbed to his feet. Belphegor comforted his brother, stroking his head, whispering quietly, lost to everything around him. *They have no idea that I can intercept their thoughts*, Sage realized. *Can I use that to my advantage?*

I am afraid, Gadrell. The boy . . . he is nothing like we have seen.

You must be strong, brother. Be fearless, or your disciples will abandon you. Sons or not, Belphegor, they will gain strength from your courage.

Sage started to react to Belphegor's admission, but he knew he could not. Vale's blood had given him this advantage. To waste it now would be inexcusable. He hardened his face and made eye contact with several of Sloth's sons. Maybe it was Sage's imagination, but they seemed to sense Sloth's fear.

"Spread out," Sage shouted, as he pointed his sword at Belphegor's offspring. "Sloth will be the first to die. The rest of them will be next." He wished he had Endora, but she was gone. He glanced at the rest of the team as they lined up in a row in front of Nick and Grandpa. Elsbeth stepped next to Sage, tears flowing from eyes narrowed in rage. She stood with her feet apart, hands ready, glaring at the beasts in front of her with an expression Sage had never seen before. He knew Elsbeth hadn't known Endora well, yet she seemed the most determined to exact revenge.

It is time, Gadrell. I fight for you and for Lucifer's deceit. Move behind us. We will protect you.

As Gadrell crawled away, his face ravaged from Sage's sword strike and his body weakened from Elsbeth's Persuasion, he appeared too frail to go far. Belphegor rose slowly into his full height, his wings spread wide, blue skin glistening. His legion of evil progeny stood silent, staring at Sage and his team, swords ready, seemingly waiting for permission to begin.

"What are they doing?" Elsbeth whispered to him.

He's terrified, Sage knew but didn't say. He remembered Vale's words when speaking about Mammon being hit with Elsbeth's Persuasion: *All of them were affected by the purifying light. Weakened. They will begin to bicker, to distrust one another, each suspecting conspiracies and plots to overthrow the others. If you destroy a second in the same manner, using Persuasion as a weapon against them, they will weaken further.*

"Not sure," Sage whispered back. "Team, don't look into Sloth's eyes. I made that mistake last summer."

As soon as Sage spoke, one of the Rephaim with Belphegor stepped up and spoke quietly into his ear. Sage recognized him—it was the same beast that had pushed Nick down into the Dark realm. Behind them, Sage saw Gadrell dragging his body away using his arms, too weak, apparently, even to crawl. Sage ignored him; a Rephaim affected with Persuasion was the least of his worries.

Belphegor drew a sword. "Soon, my sons, soon." He voice was a mixture of distant thunder and a gravel truck dumping a load. He pointed his sword at Sage. "Let us avoid the shed of blood. You come with me, and the rest will leave unharmed."

"The same offer Nearatook made on your behalf," Sage said. "For what purpose?"

"Sage, you can't be serious," Grandpa said.

Elsbeth glared at him, her hands still raised. She didn't have to say anything for Sage to understand her message.

"Make sure your camera is recording," Sage whispered to her. To the Prince of Sloth, he said, "For what purpose would you have me leave with you?" He stepped out in front of his team.

"To kill you, of course," Belphegor said. "I will drain your blood and secure it inside my laboratories. It must have many useful properties. I offer a painless death."

During his battle with Mammon last summer, Sage had discovered that Rephaim could spit acid. He knew they could manipulate shadows and transform into human form. He glanced at the faces of Sloth's sons and found all of them wearing Sloth's expression. He also noticed their eyes were glazed over.

Had he summoned them by force? Was Sloth controlling them? Did they share his fear of Sage? He did a quick assessment. Sloth had nearly a dozen offspring lined up on each side of him. Sage's own team, less than half the size, stood opposite. David and Ronan were bookends, with Gavin and Kato next to them. Hieronymus and Elsbeth stood on each side of Sage in the center, with Malcolm and Kaja on each side of them. Grandpa guarded Nick in the back. Sage knew that Nick would be Grandpa's primary responsibility. He would fight, but only if a beast got close enough to harm Nick.

If Sloth and his sons were telepathically connected, the Prince needed to be the first to fall. "I will consider your offer," Sage said. "But I offer you a trade as well."

The Prince laughed. "Do you?"

"Show me now what form you currently possess in the human realm. Transform, and speak his name. Do so, and I will go with you after my friends have been allowed to leave." The others began to protest, but Sage turned and gave them a withering look. "Quiet!" Back to Sloth. "If you refuse, I will know that you had no intention of allowing my friends to live."

"You seek to destroy the Seven by—"

"The *Six!*" Sage shouted. "I killed Mammon. Consider that as you decide my offer."

Slay him now, Belphegor. Your fear radiates off you. Your sons need leadership. They stand ready, confused by all the talking.

We are twins, Gadrell, of one mind. My sons cannot sense my hesitation. Secure yourself, for soon I will strike.

Sage saw Gadrell in the distance. Although still primarily using his elbows, his legs were starting to work, and he was picking up a little speed. His wings had unfolded, and Sage wondered if he was about to attempt a full escape. Couldn't worry about him right now; he would eventually die from the two hits of Persuasion. Sage turned his head toward Elsbeth, and she glanced over at him. "When I signal, hit Sloth center chest," he whispered. She nodded.

Sloth took a deep breath before speaking again. "You seek to destroy our empire."

"As you seek to destroy us," Sage said. "But imagine the power you would wield with the other five by having me as your trophy. Decide carefully. For one thing is certain: you will not survive this battle, should it come to that."

High above them all, the two Archangels, flaming swords washing the scene in flickering light, remained motionless. Sage glanced up at them, and they didn't even appear to notice what was transpiring below them. Sage had found them in that exact position when he teleported out to get them to open the gate.

"You have no chance of survival today," Sage said, pointing his sword at Sloth. "Terror grips you. It weakens your resolve, it confuses your sons. Did you see Mammon's destruction? Was he not a more powerful beast than you? Decide, Sloth. Indeed, let us avoid the bloodshed. Reveal your human self. Allow my people to walk away. Then I will go with you."

Knowing the current human identity of the Prince would make tracking the remaining five easier for the Council. Sage knew there was a flaw in his trade offer and suspected Sloth would see it.

He did. "If you are so certain of victory, why sacrifice yourself?"

"Because there are no guarantees in battle," Sage said, ready with his answer. "Some of my people might be hurt or killed. My offer prevents that." He gripped his sword and felt the buzzing within his bones that signaled his gift of Teleportation. "Yes, you risk the existence of the other Five, but your power would be unmatched among them." He pointed to Gadrell, now on his feet, staggering away. "And the one who just escaped the gate will live. The two of you might even overthrow Lucifer. Decide now, but know this: if we battle today, you will be the first to fall."

Elsbeth stepped forward and aimed a palm at Belphegor's chest. Sage saw a flash of fear move behind the Rephaim's eyes. "You cannot move fast enough to avoid Elsbeth's Persuasion," he said. "Decide now, or die."

Sloth closed his eyes and cocked his head. Then his lips began moving as though in whispered conversation with someone living inside his head. *Run, Gadrell. Protect yourself. Should I die today, take your rightful place within our world.*

Yes, brother.

Sage leaned his head toward Elsbeth and whispered. "Hit him. Now!"

The brilliance of Elsbeth's purifying light caused Sage to squint his eyes. As soon as the beam exploded into the center of Sloth's chest, Sage teleported next to the beast and swung his sword with a blow that rattled his own shoulders. Sage's blade hit Sloth's non-sword arm, and it sank deep. Belphegor screamed, spun, and spit acid toward Sage, swinging his sword faster than Sage could move out of the way. The acid caught Sage on the left side of his face, just as Sloth's sword hit Sage's sword at an angle, slid up the steel, and sliced a gouge from his elbow to his armpit. Sage nearly dropped his sword but teleported away before toppling over.

The acid crawled into his left eye, splashed onto his neck and shoulder, and burned away a chunk of his hair. Panic rose in his throat. He dropped his sword, ripped his shirt off, and frantically wiped at the tarry substance before it ate flesh down to bone.

The sounds of battle exploded all at once. David shouted, Kato belted a war cry, Ronan yelled something Sage couldn't understand, and beasts roared. Sage's face was on fire. His skin sizzled and smoked; his mouth and nose filled with an oily, toxic residue that drove him to his knees. Swaths of bloody skin stuck to his shirt every time he wiped his face.

A flash of motion from his right caught his eye. "Sage, watch out!" somebody shouted.

He instinctively grabbed his sword and teleported away, not sure where he would appear. He ended up a few feet in front of the raging Sloth, just as Elsbeth hit him with another blast of Persuasion, this one in the side, just below his left armpit. The Prince fell back, and all the other beasts paused at the same time. Belphegor's telepathic connection with his sons had broken.

Sage staggered away, his skin still burning but already much less so. The blood of Seth. He was healing at a supersonic rate. As the burning diminished, tingling replaced it. A blow from behind knocked him forward. He landed on his elbows, spun over onto his back, and screamed when his bare skin contacted the ground. One of Sloth's offspring, a claw dripping with Sage's blood, dove toward him. Sage raised his sword and impaled the monster.

David shouted and laughed as he swung his steel bar. Ronan battled in silence. Kato's, Gavin's, and Kaja's swords were blurs of steel and slinging blood. Hieronymus's powerful blows sounded like small thunderclaps. A beast screamed a dying howl when Malcolm latched himself upon its back and clamped his hands on the side of its head, draining the beast of its strength. Elsbeth turned her Persuasion to two offspring, both trying to flee, and cut them down with blasts to the back.

Belphegor attacked as Sage climbed to his feet. The Prince swung his sword across his body. Sage tried teleporting but knew he wouldn't make it. He raised his sword for a block, but Kato knocked him backwards and took the blow himself.

And died because of it. Belphegor's powerful blow glanced off Kato's rising sword, ricocheted upward, and caught Kato under his left jaw. The steel traveled through his head and exited just above his right ear.

Sage screamed his friend's name as he collapsed backward, dead before his body hit the ground.

David stepped forward and swung his bar into Belphegor's backswing. The Boy with Might torqued his body, rotated his shoulders, and flexed his wrists with the flat, waist-high blow. Sage saw nothing but a gray blur until the steel slammed into Belphegor's right ribcage. Ribs broke with a sound like a gunshot.

The Prince doubled over. David stepped into his own backswing, spun, and circled the bar around for another shot, barely breaking his momentum. The Prince leaped into the air and landed in front of David after his bar met nothing but air. Belphegor's empty claw raked David from collarbone to stomach and opened four gaping wounds across his chest. David tried spinning away, but the Prince punched out with his sword and stabbed him in the thigh. David fell and rolled onto his back, maneuvered his bar, and blocked Belphegor's crushing downward sword swing.

Sage heard shouts and clashes of steel, grunts and screams. Elsbeth shouted something to Gavin. Malcolm, Ronan, and Hieronymus were somewhere off to his left. "Project great terror!" Hieronymus yelled at Kaja. "Everything you have!"

Sage teleported next to David just as Sloth's sword clanked away from David's bar. The Prince spit acid at Sage again, but he ducked and teleported behind the beast. Sloth crouched as though about to launch himself into the sky, but Sage sank his blade into the base of his right wing. The Prince screamed and spun and swung his blade over Sage's head. David leaped to his feet and punched Belphegor in the chest with the end of his bar. He fell back, his left wing jutting outward to break his fall. His right wing hung loose, crippled by Sage's strike.

David's war cry rose above the clamber of battle as his home-run swing connected with Belphegor's ribcage on the other side. The beast rolled over and collapsed onto his back, and his weakened wing crumbled. Sage connected with a solid blow on the base of his left wing, then teleported to his other side just as David's bar came from a downtown overhead swing. The steel crashed into

Belphegor's left shoulder, but the beast jabbed his sword out and caught David in his other thigh.

"Hit him, mate," David shouted to Sage as he stumbled back.

The Prince of Sloth was already climbing to his feet. Sage ducked low when he saw a blast of Persuasion light up the landscape from his left. "Into the fiery pits you go," Elsbeth shouted. The blast hit Belphegor at the base of his only working wing. It spun the beast around, directly into the path of Sage's knee-high sword swing. His blade sunk a couple of inches into the Prince's right calf. The beast stumbled.

Hieronymus came out of nowhere and grabbed Belphegor's dangling right wing. He ripped it up, then down, then sideways. The flesh tore and jerked and sprayed jets of red blood against the Elioudian's white skin. Belphegor roared and pulled away, but Hieronymus yanked him back.

"Watch out, mate," David shouted. His bar came in low and fast, its aim true and brutal. It hit the Prince's left knee with the crack of snapping timber. The Prince stumbled from David's blow but didn't fall. The beast howled, swung his sword without any power, and missed David's head by several inches. With one final yank, Hieronymus wrenched the right wing away and tossed it aside.

The next beam of Persuasion hit Belphegor's left wing a second time. It amazed Sage that Elsbeth could hit with such accuracy. She hit him again, and the Prince's eyes started showing pinpricks of light. The same thing had happened with Prince Mammon the summer before; Persuasion's purifying light rippled through the Prince's body before exploding out of his eyes.

The end was near, but Belphegor still had fight in him. He launched himself at Sage, his sword somehow more accurate and powerful. Sage blocked the blow, and it rattled his arms and shoulders and knocked him back. The beast advanced, ignoring David and Hieronymus, intent on killing Sage. He spit acid, which Sage dodged, then jumped as high as his broken knee would allow, landed behind Sage, and swung his blade. Sage leaned forward and felt the wind of the steel pass within inches of the back of his neck.

The sounds of battle seemed less now. Grandpa shouted commands at Gavin and Malcolm. Ronan grunted with each blow he delivered. Elsbeth shot blasts of Persuasion at other beasts. Kaja was somewhere outside the fray, projecting her gift into the environment.

David's bar and Hieronymus's sword hit Belphegor at the same time. Hieronymus nearly severed Sloth's left wing, and the Prince's sword bent when he raised it to block David's strike. The beast screamed as more white light exploded from his black eyes. *How can he see anything?* Smoke began drifting from his wounds.

"It's happening," Elsbeth shouted to Sage as she ran up. "The Persuasion is cooking him from inside out." She hit him again, in the chest, and knocked him back beyond the reach of David's bar, which passed within inches of the Prince's head.

That might have been a kill shot. Sage rushed forward as David lost his footing when his bar swung all the way around. Hieronymus attacked the left wing, first with another sword strike, then when he grabbed it and began tearing it off. Belphegor tried spinning around, but Sage hit him above the knee on his good leg.

The mighty beast fell. David hit Sloth's sword hand, and the damaged blade skittered away. Hieronymus heaved, planted his foot on Sloth's shoulder, and tore the wing away. The sound of ripping flesh and Sloth's screech of pain and rage were music to Sage's ears.

"Do you need help, Sage?" Gavin asked as he ran up.

"Just take care of everything else," Sage said.

"All dead," Gavin said.

Pure white light streamed from Belphegor's eyes. Hieronymus swung his sword so fast and with such power that Sage didn't even know he'd done it until Belphegor's sword hand went flying. Gavin took his other hand off right before David crushed his one good knee.

The Prince of Sloth, frothing at the mouth, tried speaking but failed. As his eyes radiated rays of white, as the Persuasion crept slowly across his body, sizzling skin like a spreading virus, Sage stepped over Belphegor's body and thrust his sword down.

It is finished, Gadrell. Rule as you should have all along. Sloth died with Sage's sword piercing his heart.

Rest in peace, brother. I am free and will rule as we planned.

"Gadrell," Sage whispered. He pulled his sword free and looked at the last place he'd seen Sloth's twin. Gone. "Anyone see where Gadrell went?" he asked the others.

"Who?" Elsbeth asked.

"Belphegor's twin," Sage said. "The Rephaim that escaped through the gate. He crawled off that way."

"How do you know his name, mate? David asked.

Sage looked in every direction, but he didn't see Gadrell anywhere. There was no telling how far he could have gone by now.

Once his sword had sizzled itself clean, he sheathed it and found everyone staring at him.

"How do you know that beast's name?" Ronan asked.

He shook his head, fatigue washing over him. "I'll explain it later, OK?" He turned and saw Grandpa holding Nick's hand. His brother had sweat covering his face, but he was alive, wide eyed, and appeared well.

"Look at the bloke's face," David said. He pointed to the fallen Prince. They all formed a circle and watched its face morph into dozens of different human identities. "What's that, then?" David asked. "What in the queen's name is going on?" For well over a minute Sloth's face melted from one human image to another.

"I'm recording," Elsbeth said. She aimed her helmet camera at the dying Prince and stood perfectly still. "The Council will want to see this."

"The human identities it possessed over the centuries," Steven said. "It's the only thing it could be. We're seeing who he's been." He looked at Sage. "Did this happen when Mammon died?"

"Maybe." Sage shrugged. "David was beating Mammon's head so hard with Samson's jawbone that's about all I saw."

"And I was a little too crazy to notice," David said.

"So, will the last one be who he was most recently?" Elsbeth asked.

"Good point," Sage said. If so, it would be different for the Council this time. They'd be able to begin their research on the human identity of one of the Princes immediately, which might lead to the other Five.

Sage stared, shocked, at the last human face that appeared. In fact, they all stood silently for several moments, speechless.

"Well, that will be interesting," Grandpa said.

"Yeah," Gavin said, "I'd say that's pretty accurate."

"I can't believe it," Elsbeth whispered. She grabbed Sage's hand and squeezed.

"I've always said American politicians were barmy," David said.

"But this takes the cake," Malcolm said. "How will they explain it? I mean really. How?"

"Holy smoke!" Nick said under his breath.

"I second that," Ronan said.

"I'd say Council investigators have their work cut out for them," Elsbeth said. "Glad I'm not part of *that* team."

For several long moments, they just stared. Then Sage broke the silence. "What about Kato?" He walked over to his friend's body. The top half of his head was gone. Sage knelt next to him and said a quiet prayer. "He saved my life. It should have been me lying there." He wiped his eyes, took one of Kato's hands, and looked at Grandpa. "We can't just leave him here."

"I'll carry him home, mate," David said. "We'll wrap him up. I can handle the load." He put a hand on Sage's shoulder and squeezed. "He was a hero until the end."

Elsbeth knelt beside Sage and took hold of Kato's other hand, tears flowing. "He was getting married, Sage." Sobs shook her shoulders as she cried. "Her name is Savannah. Kato was *so* happy." She looked at Sage. "He wanted us to meet her. To attend their wedding. He said you would really like her, Sage. He was so, so happy."

Sage grabbed one of Elsbeth's hands and squeezed. The enormity of all the sacrifice pressed against him. First Vale, then Endora and Kato. Maybe it was the stress, fatigue, the sudden wash of relief that he'd survived, or Elsbeth's raw emotion, but he pulled her into a quick hug. He released her after a moment, embarrassed to meet her eyes.

Elsbeth stood and looked at Grandpa. "We have to find Savannah, to tell her. Who can do that?"

"I will make sure it's done, Elsbeth," Grandpa said. "Don't worry about that. The Council will handle it properly."

"And Jarvis?" Sage asked. "Will the Council notify him about Endora?"

"Certainly." Grandpa gripped Sage's shoulder. "Death is part of this, Sage. That fact doesn't make it easier, but we must press forward, regardless."

"Endora was a hero," Elsbeth said. "She saved our group at every turn. We *never* would have made it without her."

"No truer statement has ever been spoken," Grandpa said. "They both gave their lives for the rest of us."

The group fell silent, several heads bowed. Sage barely noticed the scorched landscape, churning red sky, and sulfur-tinged wind. The Archangels hadn't moved, although their eyes seemed to be in constant search mode. He wondered why they hadn't helped. He knew he'd probably never know the answer.

"What about getting back?" Nick said, breaking the silence. "Grandpa, can you lead us out of here?"

"It's what I do," Grandpa said. "Pathfinding from within a spiritual realm is all about the colors."

"What's that mean?" Nick asked Sage.

"A portal into the spiritual realm gives off certain colors. They're nearly impossible to find from our side because there's so much color everywhere and they tend to blend in with the environment. But from this side, he will see them from far away."

It took David nearly an hour to get Kato's body secured for transport. They put him in the sleeping bag from Kato's own backpack, then tied his body tightly with some climbing rope. Next, David fashioned a harness from rope and carabiners and slung Kato across his shoulders.

Sage sat quietly and watched the others gather their belongings while his own body finished healing. It would be a while before his hair grew back, but the acid scars on his face and neck were healing nicely. The pain was gone. Even Grandpa mentioned how quickly his body was regenerating.

There were twenty-three dead beasts scattered around a battlefield no larger than a basketball court. The fighting had been brutal and violent, and everyone except Elsbeth, Grandpa, Nick, and Kaja was banged up. Although Sage hadn't seen it, everyone else said that Kaja's projections of terror had caused the beasts to hesitate during critical points of the battle. The hour spent gathering their things and preparing Kato's body for transport had given all of them time to heal.

After everyone was lined up and ready to go, Grandpa asked the Archangels if they would burn the dead bodies. They didn't respond, and Sage figured they probably wouldn't. Grandpa led the group away, Sage following David at the back of the line, with Hieronymus and Kaja beside him.

"What about Kaja and Hieronymus?" Nick asked Sage. "How do they get back? They can't live in our world. And they can't get back through the gate."

"I was about to ask the same thing, young Nick," Hieronymus said. "I suspect we will simply travel to the very hole you fell into."

"Oh, yeah, didn't think of that." Nick grinned and shook his head.

"But what of Belphegor?" Hieronymus asked Sage. "Who was he? What is so important? Why did everyone stare so long at his last human face?"

"I'll explain it as we walk," Sage said. "But here's the deal. Where we come from, high-powered politicians don't just disappear out of thin air without people noticing. Especially when it's the president of the United States."

27

Two days later, they ended up in the same cave where it all began. Sage came through first, squeezing into a dark chamber that, from the human realm, looked to be a shadowy crevice ending in a dead end. It was one they hadn't explored and the probable escape route of the Rephaim that had shoved Nick down the hole.

Nick came out next, then Elsbeth and the rest of the group. When his grandpa came out last, he turned back and looked at the opening for several seconds before turning to Sage. "We didn't come to this part of the cave, did we?"

"No. But Nick and I got close. On the second day here. You spent the afternoon in the jungle that day, and we almost got to this point before turning back."

They'd passed multiple entrances into the human world before finally finding this one. Sage had stepped through all of them while the rest of the team waited. As soon as he discovered he'd stepped into the human realm at the wrong location, he'd gone back to join the others.

Hieronymus had been wrong about the spiritual realm outside the Great Granite Gate being of unknown origin. It was the Dark realm. Just like outside of Mammon's prison. Just like the part of the Wastelands they'd dropped into. Clearly, Belphegor had had a pathway between this part of the Dark realm and his section of the underworld. Which meant the Council now had a way to get into Tartarus without going through the Granite Gate.

The complex geography involved in traveling from one realm to another made Sage's head hurt. It made him fully understand now why his grandpa's job was so important. The Council was mapping entrances to and from both spiritual realms to allow for quick continent jumping. During the two-day journey they'd had before finding the cave, Sage had stepped into a snowy mountain region; a swampy area; a desert; another cave, but one with deep, red rock behind a raging waterfall surrounded by bathing gorillas; the bottom of an ice-cold lake; and a deep forest with armed guards patrolling and cameras hanging from trees, probably Camp David.

His grandpa had told him once that spiritual realms were vast and complex universes that reminded him of a house of mirrors. With so few Pathfinders in the Council, when an entrance was discovered, it took years to map it out in a manner that kept it secret from the human population. The Council couldn't afford to have its members disappearing into the side of a hill or vanishing in the middle of a street in front of a regular human. When you added in the folding dimensions that somehow allowed someone to travel across the globe in a fraction of the time, it was enough to drive a person crazy.

They heard voices the closer they got to the mouth of the cave. Nick led the way, moving way too fast for David, who was careful not to bump Kato's body against the rock walls. When they broke into the sunlight and the heat, Sage took a deep breath and raised his face to the sun—the hot but glorious sun. The noisy campsite, now almost resembling an armed compound, fell completely silent. Nearly two-dozen tents crowded around the original three that Sage, Ronan, and Grandpa had pitched. People Sage had never seen before stood completely still, staring at the group that exited the cave. It wasn't Sage's sudden appearance that held everyone's attention. It was Hieronymus and Kaja.

Elsbeth took charge. She grabbed the Elioudians' hands and led them toward the tents. "Professor," she said, as she pushed her way through the crowd. "Professor!"

Sage saw her disappear into Grandpa's tent and knew he wouldn't see the two scouts for a long time. Hieronymus had agreed to stay and answer as many questions as the professor might have, and Sage thought they might number in the thousands.

Theo stepped out of Sage and Nick's tent, and Sage ran over and nearly knocked him down giving him a hug. Sage saw tears on the old man's face, but he didn't say anything about them.

"Gave us scare," Theo said after a moment.

"Two Princes down, five to go," Sage said. He told him about Kato and Endora, briefly described how they died, both sacrificing themselves so that the others might survive. Then he told him of Prince Belphegor's last human identity. "The Council won't have any problem finding stuff out about him."

"So that explain it. World crazy about missing president. No one know how he disappear. Last seen in Camp David." Theo stepped back and gave Sage a long look. A frown creased his forehead, then the blood drained from his face.

"What?" Sage asked.

"You are different," Theo said. "Vision radiate off you." He grabbed Sage's hand and pulled him toward the tent. "Must sit down. Get grandfather. Ronan. Gavin and Malcolm. Hurry. I wait."

It took a couple of minutes for Sage to get everyone rounded up. He shouted at Elsbeth, who'd just exited out of the professor's tent, and told her to come, too. Once they were all inside, Theo motioned to Sage. "Zip tent."

They all stood around Theo, whose face had drained of color. Sage looked at Elsbeth and shrugged. She frowned and mouthed, "What's going on?" Sage shook his head.

"What is it, Theo?" Grandpa asked.

"The moment I touch Sage, powerful vision." Theo wiped his forehead, and Sage noticed his quivering hand. "Powerful."

"About what?" Sage's stomach did a flip.

"Your death," Theo said. "And Philip."

"Who's Philip?" Elsbeth asked.

"Grandpa's son from his second wife," Sage said. "Born in the early 1800s. Malcolm and Gavin's half brother. I've never met him."

"What's his gift?" she asked.

"Possession," Sage said. "He has three vampires as bodyguards."

"Unfriendly vampires," Malcolm said.

"The loon of the family," Gavin spat. "Certifiable. A complete sack of nuts."

"Easy, Gavin," Grandpa said. "What about Philip, Theo? What's going on?"

"I have explained visions in past," Theo said. "You know how they work."

Sage knew. Sporadic. Incomplete. Subject to alteration from events not yet known. But this was Theo, the most accurate in Sight in Council history. He would take anything he said with a dose of heavy probability.

"I know triggering event of vision," Theo said. "You must find him. Soon."

"We haven't seen that quack in ninety years," Gavin said. "He's in the wind. Why's he so important now?"

"He kill Ronan, then Sage." Theo wiped a shaky hand across his forehead. "Must find him. All you have millions of dollars. Use it. Find him. Before he find boy. Hurry."

Sage looked at Ronan. The big man crossed his arms and frowned, then glanced at Grandpa. Grandpa's face paled.

Sage stepped forward and knelt at Theo's knee. "Tell me. What's Philip going to do? What boy?"

Theo took several deep breaths and shook his head. "I cannot."

"Then why did you mention it at all?" Sage asked.

"If I tell more, knowledge affect actions, which alter free will decisions. If Philip find boy first, possess him, take power, he will destroy Council." Tears slipped out of Theo's eyes. He stared at the ground for several moments, then looked at Gavin. "You find him. Somewhere in mountains. Berkshires. Use money. Find brother. Save Ronan and Sage."

EPILOGUE

After camp broke, after Hieronymus and Kaja dropped back into the earth, after David and Ronan attacked the passage leading to the chamber with the hole and caused a cave-in, and after the hike through the jungle back to Grandpa's truck, Sage slept during most of the ride home. So did Nick.

The professor had conducted hours of video interviews with the Elioudian scouts, then downloaded the hundreds of hours of video from the rescue team's helmet cameras. Two helicopters had come in and taken everything away, including Kato's body. Sage wasn't sure when he would see everyone again, but he hoped it would be a while. He was tired and cranky and nervous about Theo's warning. Gavin, before leaving the jungle, had promised Grandpa that he and Malcolm would begin their search for Philip immediately and would let him know if they found him. Grandpa figured they would learn about this mysterious boy when it was meant to be. He was right, and Sage decided he wasn't going to dwell on it.

All four of them slept most of the first day after getting back. On the second day, Sage went to the barber and got his head shaved. After staring in the mirror for most of an hour afterwards, he decided he liked it OK. There was no evidence of Sloth's acid attack, at least. He texted a picture to Elsbeth, and she replied with five lines of LOLs and funny emojis.

On day three, the day his mom and dad were due back home, Sage and Nick cleaned the house from top to bottom. They dressed in decent clothes, then invited Grandpa and Ronan over to wait for their arrival. Ronan again brought up the topic he had mentioned just before he and Sage descended into the underworld to rescue Nick. They'd discussed it some in the truck ride home from the jungle, but Sage hadn't really commented much. It was Grandpa's decision and something that needed to be done. Who was he to argue?

"Sage has to move," Ronan told them now. "To a different town. Maybe a different state. The Princes know who he is. More than that, we need to tell Kevin and Jenna. Everything. It's time."

Sage looked at Nick, who probably didn't understand the entire ramifications of all of that but was certainly the most qualified to predict how Mom and Dad would react to the news that their entire family was a key component in the battle between good and evil. He'd gone through it himself two weeks ago.

"Ronan's right," Nick said. "We should tell them. Family meeting. All of us. I have stuff to say, even though I'm the youngest."

"You've earned the right to say whatever you want," Ronan said. "Really, moving won't be that big of a deal. Your grandpa owns four houses especially purchased for this very contingency. He has six other places that could also work."

"Wow, Grandpa," Nick said. "Just how rich are you?"

"Rich enough. A man can accumulate a lot of stuff in 750 years. Money will never be a problem." Grandpa looked at Ronan. "You've got a few nice places yourself."

"True." He paused. "The biggest challenge will be talking Kevin into selling his business. And this house. His roots are deep here."

"Maybe," Grandpa said. "But after hearing about Sage's activities these past two summers and how Nick is part of it now, it won't take them long to get on board."

"Time to break out your box of evidence?" Ronan asked.

"Yep." Grandpa held up a thumb drive. "Although, honestly, a box filled with old pictures of me from a hundred years ago showing how I haven't really aged and old 8 mm film from the 1930s won't be nearly as convincing as this video. It's why I had the professor burn me several scenes onto it. Five minutes of Kevin and Jenna watching clips of Tartarus, the Elioudians, the Wastelands, and snippets of the Territories will do the trick. I just wonder how long it will take them to get over the shock."

Sage wondered the same thing. This would be no easy meeting, but time was a thing now. The Princes knew who he was. Mom's and Dad's lives were in danger as a result. No, the meeting wouldn't be a pleasant thing, but love and protection were the core message, and who could argue with that?

They all heard Dad's car pull into the driveway at the same time, because all of them glanced at the door, then looked at each other. Nick jumped from his chair and charged out the door. Sage followed, with Grandpa and Ronan on his heels.

Nick had Mom in a hard embrace by the time Sage hit the porch. "Hey, Dad," he said, as Dad closed his car door. Sage gave him a hug. "What's the rest of the world look like?"

His eyes widened when he saw Sage's bald head, but he just frowned, smiled, and didn't comment on it. "We saw some places you just wouldn't believe, Sage. The Greek Isles. Fantastic. I love Greek culture and history. I was talking to your mom about getting you and Nick out of Oklahoma so you can both see some exotic places. Think you'd like that?"

Sage grinned. "I'm always in favor of safe, exotic places, Dad. For sure. And yeah, those Greeks, especially their mythology. That's some interesting history. You know, about where they got the idea about all that stuff." He walked around and gave Mom a hug.

"Sage! Your hair! Where is it?" She rubbed his scalp and frowned. "All that beautiful brown hair! What in the world would possess you to shave it off?" She looked at Grandpa. "Did you put him up to this?"

Grandpa grinned. "That's a story to tell, Jenna. For sure."

"Ronan," Sage's dad said. "Have you been following the story about the president? Missing? Just like that? It was the talk of the cruise for the last few days. Nonstop coverage. Biggest global story of our lifetimes. How does the president of the United States just go missing?"

"Yeah," Ronan said, "we heard about that while on our trip. Crazy thing, I'll tell you."

Sage, Nick, and Ronan carried all the suitcases in and took them straight into his parent's bedroom. Mom commented about how nice the house looked and gave both her boys hugs when she found out they'd cleaned it without prompting. Grandpa insisted that they all sit in the living room because he wanted to have a family meeting. It took a couple of minutes to get everybody situated like Grandpa wanted, but he finally did.

Sage was on the recliner facing Mom and Dad, who were beside each other on the sofa. Nick was in a chair opposite Sage. Ronan stood along the wall near the front door, and Grandpa had the floor, near his open laptop, with the thumb drive in his hand. As Sage looked at his family, Kato and Endora flashed in his mind. He thought about how such powerful warriors had been struck down, despite centuries of battling some of the worst beasts on earth. Should Dark beasts attack Sage's family . . . he couldn't even finish the thought.

His mom looked at him and smiled, pointing to his hair and mouthing, "Baldy," before smiling wider and making hand signs of *I love it*. Sage would die protecting her. And Dad and Nick. This would be hard. Breaking this awful news to them. The move. But not as hard as mourning their deaths. Sage signed *I love you* back to his mom and turned his attention to Grandpa.

"So, family meeting," Dad said. "Haven't had one of these in a while. What's going on?"

"We have a story to tell you and Jenna," Grandpa said. "And it's going to take a while. I guess I should start with my childhood. Maybe the year I was born. The year of our Lord 1268."

CONCEPTS AND CHARACTERS

THE ALEXANDER FAMILY

Sage Alexander: The warrior featured in the ancient Prophecy of Seth. Sage Alexander is fiercely loyal to his family, willing to do anything to protect them. A loner as a child, with a passion for sword fighting and other hand-to-hand combat weapons, he slowly grows in confidence, skills, and leadership traits. He will eventually receive all angelic gifts and is destined to become the most powerful warrior in the history of the Angelic Response Council.

Steven Alexander: Sage's grandfather. Angelic-human with the gift of Pathfinding. Retired, he travels the world to hunt for entrances to the Dark realm. He is a master of disguise, a necessary skill for those who live for centuries. He has three angelic-human sons from marriages in previous centuries.

Kevin Alexander: Sage's father. Human. He carries the angelic-human gene, but angelic gifts skipped him. Released from the influence of the Prince of Greed, his new outlook on life motivates Sage to continue to destroy the remaining Princes of Hell.

Jenna Alexander: Sage's mother. Human. She also carries angelic-human genes, but angelic gifts have lain dormant in her bloodline for five generations. Her angelic bloodlines are nearly as pure as Steven Alexander's side of the family, a necessity for the Prophecy of Seth to come true via Sage's birth.

Nick Alexander: Sage's younger brother. A fun-loving, confident boy with a love of online gaming, Nick has a vivid imagination but heretofore has been excluded from the world of the Angelic Response Council and their spiritual war.

Malcolm Alexander: Sage's uncle and the oldest son of Steven Alexander. Angelic-human gifted with Absorption. Nearly five hundred years old, he is a battle-tested warrior capable of absorbing the powers of the evil races and rendering them useless. He partners with his younger brother, Gavin.

Gavin Alexander: Sage's uncle and the younger brother of Malcolm. Angelic-human gifted with Fighting Arts, Gavin is an opinionated Elvis fan, particularly fond of his witty nephew Nick Alexander.

THE ANGELIC RESPONSE COUNCIL

Leah: Sage's Guardian Angel and his primary trainer during the first fifteen years of his life. A constant influence, even though she has been reassigned to guard someone else.

Elsbeth Brown: Rescued from time by Sage, Elsbeth is angelic-human, gifted with Persuasion and Teleportation, a terrifying combination in the eyes of the Dark Beasts. Unique among the Angelic Response Council due to having two gifts, she is fiercely independent and Sage's most loyal companion.

Ronan Barrister: Gifted with Might, Ronan is Steven Alexander's bodyguard and confidant. He's known Sage since his birth and serves as a mentor to the boy. His choice of weapon is a two-hundred-pound steel bar he carries in a holster in the center of his back.

Theophylaktos Alastair: Angelic-human with the gift of Sight. More than a thousand years old, Theo volunteered for assignment in Sage's hometown for the specific purpose of befriending Sage and providing him with friendship and guidance as he matures into the leader and warrior he needs to become.

Kato Hunter: Angelic-human gifted with Angelic Fighting Arts. Rescued from time by Sage, his village and family died off while he was imprisoned in Mammon's collection site. His loyalty to Sage is unquestioned. Trained in the Fighting Arts by Beowulf, a warrior of ancient legend, he delivered to Sage Beowulf's legendary, self-cleaning sword.

David Brock: Gifted with Might, British, and rescued from time by Sage, David's over-the-top boasting rubs on Elsbeth's last nerve. Yet he and Sage have a strong mutual respect, and his brutal, half-crazed fighting style is welcomed on every mission.

Endora Morgan: Angelic-human gifted with Voice. Endora is a troubled soul with a less-than-complimentary reputation on the Angelic Response Council. Nevertheless, she is a strong and capable fighter that proves an inspiration to those who truly come to know her.

Horace Brahms: Council professor of history gifted with Animation, Horace Brahms is an expert on Tartarus and the three Territories of Hell. Although he is too old now for field operations, Horace is always prepared to share his knowledge of the underworld with other members of the Council.

ELIOUDIANS

Achim: Keeper of prophetic writings. Member of the High Council within Tartarus.

Aquila and Ephraim: Residents of Tartarus, these men occasionally patrol the Wastelands outside of Tartarus.

Elah: Senior academic fellow in the village of Seth. Holds a seat on the Assembly of Histories.

Hannah: Director of historical studies. Hannah is able to provide historical context on the Elioudian race and information on the dangers of the Territories to Topsiders.

Hieronymus: An out-scout. The only guide who knows the path from the village of Seth to the surface via the territories of the Nephilim, Emim, and Rephaim. Hieronymus is a tremendous warrior and leader.

Issur: Senior brethren of the Convention of Exploration.

Kaja: An out-scout in training. The only Elioudian gifted with angelic abilities, young Kaja regularly works with Hieronymus. Her gift of Projection is often useful in surviving the dangers of the Territories.

Maarav: Overseer of exploration. Member of the High Council within Tartarus.

Vale: Angelic liaison. Leader of High Council within Tartarus. Vale is the son of Seth, the ancient Elioudian prophet and Sage's great-grandfather many times removed.

REPHAIM

Aamon: Prince of Wrath.

Asmodeus: Prince of Lust.

Beelzebub: Prince of Gluttony.

Belphegor: The Prince of Sloth. The least respected of the Seven Princes of Hell, twin brother to Gadrell, who remains trapped in the underworld. Sloth believes Lucifer was instrumental in trapping his brother, and even above his designs upon Sage Alexander, his goal is to release Gadrell so together they can exact revenge upon Lucifer and rule the Princes of Hell.

Gadrell: The Prince of Sloth's twin brother. The most powerful of the twins, Gadrell would have ruled in Lucifer's place had Lucifer not betrayed him and ensured his continued imprisonment within the underworld.

Sathanus: Prince of Envy.

Lucifer: Prince of Pride.

Mammon: Prince of Greed. Killed by Sage and his team of rescued warriors, Mammon's influence had begun transforming Sage's father into a beast. That attack on Sage's family cost Mammon his life.

Zagan: One of the lineage of Belphegor, Zagan can be in constant telepathic communication with his father.

REPHAIM POWERS

Acid Generation: The ability to generate acid through touch or spray (e.g. acid spit, acid blood, etc.)

Cloaking: The ability to mask one's origin within the body of a human.

Flying: The Rephaim's powers of flight rival those of the angels.

Merging: Ability to temporarily merge two or more beings into a single being, which results in a completely new and stronger being.

Night Vision: Seeing in total darkness.

Possession: Ability to take control and inhabit the body of an individual.

Shadow Manipulation: The ability to create or manipulate darkness, often by mentally accessing a dimension of dark energy and manipulating it.

Shape Shifting: Ability to change appearance or body structure.

Summoning: Ability to summon beings for assistance—specifically, Dark beasts and their creations.

Wall Crawling: Ability to adhere to solid surfaces, including walls and ceilings.

THE ANGELIC-HUMAN RACES

Elioud: The angelic-human race that most closely resembles the angels of light. Their blood is 75 percent angelic and has been washed clean by their repentance. They repented of their evil ways and created the underground prior to the Great Flood that destroyed mankind and most of the evil offspring of the Watchers. The Elioudians fought the three evil races prior to the Great Flood and lost thousands. They are the primary occupants of Tartarus and have sealed Tartarus from the Territories of the other evil races. The maximum lifespan of the Elioudian race is three thousand years, yet few reach that advanced age. They are a peaceful people and live in a society that honors everything good and pure. Six hundred years after the flood, and immediately after the Battle at the Gate, the Elioudians gave birth to two hundred children that looked human. These special two hundred were gifted with supernatural powers. A hundred years after these children were born, they were sent to the surface of the earth as the Angelic Response Council. They were to live among the humans and seek out those from the evil races that escaped from the underground.

Emim: Larger than normal humans, they specialized in corrupting the flesh of the animal kingdom by creating hybrids and creatures that are bred to terrorize humans. The early Greeks took note of these atrocities and created a library of mythological monsters patterned after them. The goals of the Emim are immortality and indestructibility. They can pass to and from the spiritual realm. With modern technology now at their fingertips, Emim alchemists and scientists feel they can cripple the human race and bend it to their will. Many Emim creatures still live within their designated territory underground, above Tartarus. Those creatures have tried for centuries to escape to the surface but are unable to defeat the Magog guarding the exit.

Nephilim: Giants and various species of giants, such as trolls, ogres, cyclops, Sasquatch, Goliath of Gath, Gog and Magog, and titans. The Nephilim possess no powers other than enormous strength and size. Prior to the Great Flood, they ruled over man in brutal fashion and were the most physically powerful beings on earth. They were idolized by the early Greeks, who created an entire mythology about them and their offspring. Their ranks thinned to near extinction, but they are making a comeback on modern-day earth. Like the other evil races, they can survive in the spiritual world and freely pass between realms. Most of their various species live within the spiritual world and make targeted attacks against humans with the express intent of luring members of the Angelic Response Council into battle. The largest Nephilim, the Magog, still live underground in the territory above Tartarus, where they guard the only exit out of the underworld.

Rephaim: The evil race that most closely resembles the demonic fallen angels, the Watchers. They are clearly the most powerful of the evil angelic-human races and the biggest threat to rule earth. They collect the unclean spirits of those they kill and, through sorcery and witchcraft, can transform from their natural demonic state into the identity of the captured soul. Some are great magicians, capable of casting spells. Their ability to change appearance makes it difficult to find them within the human population.

The Seven Princes of Hell are Rephaim, linked together through a telepathic connection. A measure of their power comes from their telepathic unity. Each has a territory within the Dark realm and can manipulate shadowy dark matter, spit acid when in their natural form, and fly nearly as well as an Archangel. Through the centuries, the Seven have gained great wealth and power on earth, positioning themselves as humans to rule or undermine society. Each has assumed different identities over the past six thousand years, transferring their accumulated wealth from one identity to another. All are multibillionaires. Their one weakness is they are so few in number. While the Seven can procreate, their offspring are weak in comparison. Their offspring are sterile, significantly smaller, live no more than two hundred years, and do not possess the ability to live full-time within the Dark realm. Their offspring can, however, transform into human appearance and utilize sorcery and witchcraft. For the past one hundred years the Seven have strived to create more of their race by combining medical science and sorcery. The Seven escaped the underground six thousand years ago at the Battle at the Gate. Approximately two hundred other Rephaim still exist in their designated territory underground above Tartarus. Each of the Seven has a distinct appearance in their natural form. The only one who has not attempted to extend his lineage is Lucifer, the Prince of Pride, who rules the Seven.

ANGELIC RESPONSE COUNCIL ANGELIC GIFTS

All angelic-humans are born with a healing factor—a certain regeneration of the flesh that results in the slowing of aging and immunity to illnesses and other defects. This superhuman longevity could be considered a gift in and of itself, but since all angelic-humans possess it, it is not considered as such. Many of the angelic gifts are only effective against other beings possessing angelic blood.

Note: The term "Dark beast" refers to the offspring of the Watchers, the original fallen angels who created children with human women. Specifically, the term refers to the Emim, Rephaim, and Nephilim, all their offspring, and the creatures they created.

Physical Gifts:

Absorption: The ability to absorb and deplete another's powers or skills, rendering one's opponent absent of anything. However, the absorbing Council member cannot use these powers or skills; they simply dissipate once absorbed.

Angelic Chains: The ability to forge chains that can bind Dark beasts and their offspring and creations. The chains are forged using certain raw materials mixed with the blood of the one bearing this gift.

Animation: The ability to bring certain inanimate objects to life for brief periods of time. This is a line-of-sight gift—the Council member must be in close physical proximity to the object and have total focus on the task the object is commanded to perform.

Bell Making: The ability to forge bells that stun Dark beasts and their offspring and creations. The bells are forged using certain raw materials mixed with the blood of the one bearing this gift.

Elemental Transmutation: The ability to alter chemical elements, changing them from one substance to another by rearranging the atomic structure. This gift does not apply to biological organisms. These Council members are often paired with Bell and Chain makers, but not always. They are also alchemists, producing potions and poisons that can kill Dark beasts' offspring and creations.

Fighting Arts: These Council members are gifted with superhuman speed in sword, knife, or hand-to-hand combat. They also see their opponent's movements in slow motion, making it extremely difficult for an opponent to land a blow. They are capable of using a wide variety of hand-wielded weapons.

Might: Near superhuman physical strength. The strength of Nephilim giants. The most famous Council member with the gift of Might was Samson from the Old Testament. Council members with Might have fighting skills that are brutal and unrefined but devastating due to the power behind each blow. Like Samson, they have long hair, through which their strength flows.

Mimicry: The ability to take on the abilities of certain animals.

Teleportation: The physical ability to move from one place to another without occupying the space in between. Teleportation occurs in the present. Teleportation into the past cannot occur except when used with Memory Sharing from within the spiritual realm.

Transformation: The ability to transform appearance to resemble a Rephaim. The Council member gifted with Transformation is not a shapeshifter that can resemble anything. This gift is very narrow—they can resemble only one of the Seven Rephaim Princes.

Voice: The ability to generate vocal sounds of higher amplitude than a normal human, tuned to the exact frequency of Dark beasts and their offspring and creations. The frequency stuns them into immobility, making them easier to deal with.

Mental Gifts:

Clarity: The ability to see the manifestations of the Seven Deadly Sins on the human body in those humans who have fully succumbed to one or more of the sins. Those gifted with Clarity see physical transformations take place—and those transformations match the physical characteristics of the corresponding Prince of Hell.

Echolocation: The ability to determine the location of Dark beasts by use of reflected sound waves. A type of built-in sonar that's specifically tuned to angelic blood.

Illusion: The ability to alter or deceive the perceptions of others possessing angelic blood.

Pathfinding: The ability to track an individual or object via supernatural means using enhanced senses and a superior intelligence quotient. This tracking can move from the human world into the spiritual realm. Council members gifted with Pathfinding are the hunters, the Council detectives, those assigned to find Dark beast locations of importance to the Council. They can touch an item and receive snippets of images from the past. The images vary in intensity and type. Some are mere impressions, some are simply names or pieces of personalities, and some are actual replays of events. Pathfinders can see entrances into Godspace, the realm where Dark angels cannot exist. The entrances appear as a breach in the atmosphere—different colors or a shimmer.

Persuasion: The ability to channel purifying light through one hand and project it directly into a Dark beast through the other hand. This gift is the rarest and most powerful of all and historically has only ever been given to one member of the Angelic Response Council at a time. Dark beasts fear this gift the most because of its ability to flip them from Dark to Light.

Possession: Direct Possession is the ability to take control of and inhabit the body of Dark beasts, their offspring, or their creations. Very dangerous and risky to use—some Council members have used this and never returned to their own bodies, leaving behind an empty shell devoid of consciousness. Their souls are believed to be lost to the other side, exposing all their knowledge of Council operations and personnel for possibility of discovery by Dark beasts. Indirect Possession means that, once inside the mind of one

Dark beast, they can link with a second Dark beast but not control them. Indirect Possession allows those with this gift only to explore the mind of a third being, not to control it.

Projection: The ability to project overwhelming emotions—both good and bad—into the surrounding environment.

Memory Sharing: The ability, through touch, to enter the memory of another angelic-blooded being while that being is in a subconscious state. The person in the subconscious state must remain that way for the memory sharer to remain connected. Sage Alexander is currently the only Council member possessing this gift. Once Sage is in a memory, he can only observe, with no physical or verbal interaction occurring. Memory Sharing can be used in conjunction with Teleportation to travel into the past memory of another, but this is only possible within the spiritual realm, where time does not exist in the same manner as it does in the human realm. The spiritual realm serves as a sort of time portal for Sage to travel into the past through another's memories. If the Memory Share connection is broken (the subconscious subject wakes up or dies) while Sage is in the past, he will immediately Teleport back into the present to the spiritual realm location where the Memory Share connection was made.

Sensing: The ability to sense or recognize Dark beasts, their offspring, and their creations, as well the ability to see, smell, taste, feel, and/or hear more than a normal human.

Sight: The ability to perceive the future—a type of precognition, but with limits. The exact order of things is not known, especially to the young. This ability grows with age, meaning the most valuable Council members with this gift are the extremely elderly. The eldest are generally kept hidden in utmost secrecy because of their high value. They are revered by all within the Council. Those gifted with Sight often see multiple possibilities of the same event, but they cannot see the extremely small details that might influence the outcome of an event. Those with Sight must rely on faith that God's overall plan will prevail.

Summoning: The ability to summon living, breathing organisms for assistance. Whether the Council member summons humans or animals, this gift kicks in only they have switched into fight-or-flight mode.

THE MONSTERS

Ahool: Most closely described as a giant bat—a bloodsucker. Big, dark eyes; large claws on its forearms; a fox-sized body covered in gray fur. Its face is a mixture between a bat and a classic demon. Wingspan of ten feet. Ahools hunt in packs and are kept as a defensive tool against nighttime attacks at the castles of at least three princes.

Alphyn: A stocky tiger with tufts of wild fur, a lion's mane, dragon talons on its forelegs, a knotted tail, a long, thin tongue, and a large mouth.

Belphei: A humanoid creature, eight feet tall, with broad shoulders, short wings, claws, a bald head, tall, pointy ears, and multi-colored skin that appears as thick as elephant hide. Created during Belphegor's experiments on captured humans.

Centaur: Powerful and muscular, half man, half horse. With heads as big as basketballs, their foreheads protrude over their eyebrows like disfigured monkeys. They have pointed ears that stick out of long, wiry hair.

Chimera: A monstrous, fire-breathing hybrid creature composed of a lion, a snake, and a goat. A creation of the Emim race.

Cyclops: One-eyed giants of immense size and strength.

Gargoyle: A flying monster created by the Emim race. They live in family units and are very protective of one another. They feed on human flesh and are vicious and powerful.

Midnight Raider: A beast with a lion's body and the head of a pointy-eared gorilla. It has black wings sprouting from its back and a sleek tail with two large spikes on the end.

Minotaur: A creature with the head of a bull and the body of a man. A violent creature of incredible strength. One of the many creations of the Emim race.

Novence: A four-foot-tall, goblin-type creature. Hairless, with pure-white skin, pointed ears, teeth like a deformed werewolf's, and feet big enough for a man twice its size. Created during Belphegor's experiments on captured humans.

Yeren: An ape-like creature with deep red hair. A meat eater, cunning, it hunts in packs and has off-the-charts athletic ability and the strength of ten men.

Youst: A twelve-foot humanoid man with four horns, wings, and white fur. Specifically created during Belphegor's experiments on captured humans.

Ylva: Flying wolf men. Eight feet tall, with arms almost to their knees, stringy, rippling muscles, and heads that resemble wolves. Big, leathery wings spanning at least ten feet.

The Watchers: The fallen angels. The fathers of all Dark beasts. A gold, silver, and bronze radiance explodes from their unblemished skin, stretched tightly over bodies of pure perfection. Their silver hair, long and flowing, falls over shoulders as solid as steel. Their eyes are pools of liquid blackness that penetrate the soul.

ABOUT THE AUTHOR

Steve Copling has spent more than thirty-five years in law enforcement and corporate security. Over the years, he has worked in field training, crime prevention, SWAT, criminal investigations, narcotics, and internal affairs. He has also held multiple supervisory positions at sergeant, lieutenant, and captain ranks. He currently serves as deputy chief in the Plano, Texas, police department.

Copling's career as an author began as a favor to his sister, who happened to be writing a screenplay about a murder. Because her background didn't include police work or investigations, she asked him to take a look at it. He immediately recognized that her fictional suspect would have gotten caught within five minutes in the real world. He agreed to write the story for his sister as a manuscript that she could later convert into a screenplay.

Even though that first manuscript never saw the light of day, Copling was hooked. He went on to write two crime novels, *The Listener* and *The Shooting Season*. His professional background and knowledge of police procedurals inform his writing, and he often draws from his experiences when writing crime fiction. However, unlike most crime writers in today's marketplace, his writing is free of profanity. Appealing to a wide audience, Copling's books are clean enough for teenage fans of police narratives yet still intriguing enough to captivate suspense readers of any age. He is working on a third crime novel, titled *The Noise Before Defeat*.

The Sage Alexander series is his first foray into young adult fantasy and will ultimately comprise seven books based on the seven deadly sins. It was born out of an endearing request from his grandson Sage, who asked Copling to write him a book for Christmas. His ultimate goal with this series is simply to write stories that Sage and his brother, Nikhil, will love reading.

Copling has three sons and five grandchildren. He and his wife of forty years live in Plano, Texas.

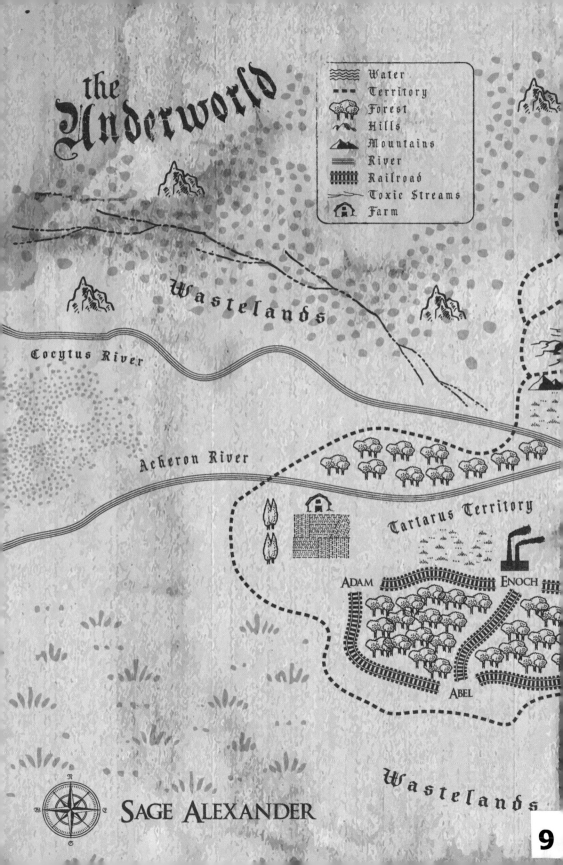